Ruth Hamilton was bo... ... ...
her life in Lancashire. ...
With Love From Ma M... ...
London's Girls, Spinning Jenny, The September Starlings, A Crooked Mile, Paradise Lane, The Bells of Scotland Road, The Dream Sellers, The Corner House, Miss Honoria West and *Mulligan's Yard,* are all published by Corgi Books and she is a national bestseller. She has written a six-part television series and over forty children's programmes for independent television. Ruth Hamilton now lives in Liverpool with her family.

For more information on Ruth Hamilton and her books, see her website at:
www.Ruth-Hamilton.co.uk

BILLY LONDON'S GIRLS

Ruth Hamilton

CORGI BOOKS

BILLY LONDON'S GIRLS
A CORGI BOOK : 0 552 13895 7

First publication in Great Britain

PRINTING HISTORY
Corgi edition published 1992

5 7 9 10 8 6

Set in 10/11pt Plantin
by County Typesetters, Margate, Kent.

Corgi Books are published by Transworld Publishers,
61–63 Uxbridge Road, London W5 5SA,
a division of The Random House Group Ltd,
in Australia by Random House Australia (Pty) Ltd,
20 Alfred Street, Milsons Point, Sydney, NSW 2061, Australia,
in New Zealand by Random House New Zealand Ltd,
18 Poland Road, Glenfield, Auckland 10, New Zealand
and in South Africa by Random House (Pty) Ltd,
Endulini, 5a Jubilee Road, Parktown 2193, South Africa.

The Random House Group Limited supports The Forest Stewardship
Council (FSC®), the leading international forest certification organisation.
Our books carrying the FSC label are printed on FSC® certified paper.
FSC is the only forest certification scheme endorsed by the leading
environmental organisations, including Greenpeace. Our
paper procurement policy can be found at
www.randomhouse.co.uk/environment

Printed and bound in Great Britain by Clays Ltd, St Ives PLC

Thanks to:

Eddie Evans
(Dr) Sonia Goldrein
Sylvia Hughes
(Dr) Richard Leech
Diane Pearson
Margaret Smerdon
(Dr) Tony Smerdon
David Thornber
Michael Thornber
Margaret Vincent

3 September, 1939

A bird sang. It perched on top of a lamp post and sent its carefree anthem to the heavens as Chamberlain's weak monotone marked this as no ordinary Sunday. The Prime Minister's voice echoed and died away, leaving in its wake a feeling of unreality, as if those who had heard it had been listening to a play on the Home Service. There were only two wirelesses at this end of Noble Street. Windows and doors were thrown open to allow the sombre news to spread and, as the bulletin ended, the whole area was still and quiet except for the brave starling.

The woman stopped running and fixed her gaze on the bird. A warm sun glinted on his oily plumage, making him exotic, rare and colourful. Part of her mind studied him and wondered at his beauty, but the urge to escape was still undeniable. On legs that threatened to buckle, she made her way to the main road and turned left for the town. Behind her, the starling began a fair imitation of a blackbird. They were like that, starlings. They could be anything they wanted to be, go anywhere they wanted to go.

She stumbled into the recessed doorway of Benson's Butchers, flattening herself against a corner where cool ceramic tile met wooden frame. War. There was going to be another war. Somewhere at the back of her mind, she felt concern for her countrymen. But a state of war implied that there had been peace, and she had not enjoyed it, could not remember freedom from fear.

I am feeling sorry for myself, that's all. That bird will fly off in a minute, I wish I could. At least the girls were out this time, I hope they enjoy their picnic. The flashing round Dr

9

Harrison's chimney looks loose, I must tell him when I see him, it might let the rain in.

When she stepped out into the sun, the bird – or one very like him – was pecking avidly at some titbit squashed between tramlines. If a tram came, if danger threatened, he would no doubt take wing again. She touched her injured shoulder. Tomorrow, it would be as black and blue as the feathers on her busy friend, her friend who could soar and swoop and taste freedom between iron tracks.

An unexpected smile flickered at the corners of her mouth as she remembered Dad's pigeons. Bluey and Firecrest and Chu-Chin-Chow, the latter so named because her father had insisted that this prize bird had been bred in China. He'd been a warrior, her dad, a mountainous man with a total disregard for the law of the land and for those who attempted to enforce it. His face had been made raw in childhood by the fierce winds of Western Ireland, while the fight-flattened nose had seemed to spread and grow redder with every pint of stout, and there had been many such pints. Yet although his hands had resembled a pair of shovels, they had been tender at times. Calloused fingers stroking home a stray feather, touching the face of his only daughter with love and pride. 'None shall hurt ye, me darlin', not while I live.' Pearls, those words had been, precious jewels sliding in warm Irish brogue from between blackened and broken stumps of teeth.

No Dad now. She had stood with him hour after hour in the back yard waiting for the pigeons to return from France or Belgium or Holland. Yes, she had stared into many a sky like this one. An old sock had hung on top of the lavatory shed to indicate wind direction, and Dad had always carried a battered stopwatch to time the arrivals from foreign parts. She had missed her father before, but not as achingly as she did today. It was all getting too much. She was reaching the end of her rope, and there was a war coming . . .

Chamberlain has given up at last. He always had about as much chance as King Canute any road. Borders will start closing now. Only birds will cross between countries. This starling has more freedom than all the people in England. France will go down. Stuck in an awkward place, is poor France, forever pig in the middle. I wonder if he's asleep yet? He usually falls asleep after . . . after the Sunday beating. It's always worse on Sundays. Bad enough the rest of the week, but there's not much to occupy him on a Sunday.

Her eyes filled with tears. She didn't know where she'd gone wrong, but her very existence seemed to annoy the man she had married, the father of her children. Should she run to one of her brothers, tell them about her plight? No, they would only take his side. They weren't beyond lifting the strap to their own wives at times. After all, keeping a woman in line was reckoned to be part and parcel of a man's mission in life. Should she walk to Queens Park and meet her picnicking daughters? Better not. They would realize what had gone on, it would be just another worry for them.

A gang of tattered lads in knee-length trousers and torn shirts whooped past, each brandishing a stick or a toy gun.

'Fight, fight, fight for dear old England,
We are sure to win the war,
For we'll get a salmon tin,
And we'll put old Adolf in,
And he'll never see his mammy any more,' screamed the motley group.

The starling balanced now on an overhead cable, wings ruffled, beak wide as he squawked like an angry parrot. The war had begun. Typically, it showed in the children first. Two men scuttled along with small suitcases. One was Chippy Heyes, the local master carpenter, and he was accompanied by a senior apprentice, a lad who had almost served his time. It was plain from their snatched conversation that they had already been called in to create gas-proof centres in public buildings.

Dear God in heaven, this is really happening. It's not just a bloke in London talking on the wireless, it's here in Bolton, and in Manchester, Liverpool . . . everywhere. That Zeppelin dropped twenty-one bombs on Bolton in 1916, there were about thirteen killed in Kirk Street. It was in September too, and this is September. Will they come today, while my girls are out at the park? No, they'll not be lined up ready yet, the bombing planes. They happen thought Chamberlain would back down at the last minute, he seems such a daft beggar. This arm feels like it's been pulled out of its socket, I hope I can work tomorrow. I'll sit in church for a bit. Praying never did any harm, did it?

The church of Saints Peter and Paul was a cool, calm place. Here, she had worshipped for as long as she could remember, with Mam and Dad, both dead now, with her brothers who no longer practised their faith, with school friends, neighbours and workmates from her mill days. It was her refuge, her final hiding place. She sat at the back, buttocks perched on the edge of the pew, elbows resting on the wooden shelf in front of her, head in hands. He would not come here. He had never been here, except on the day of his marriage.

The girls have just left school, haven't they? And there's been all this talk about call-ups at eighteen, I wonder if the bother will go on for four years? Happen they'll get exempted anyway, with them working in food shops. There'll be rations, and there's a lot of houses round here, a lot of folk to feed. I can't stand it. I can't stand a war as well as everything else. Something is going to snap inside me. It's like I'm on the edge of a cliff waiting for somebody to give me a shove. He's pushed me this far, I reckon he can finish me. Unless I do for him first, and it's not in me. Mrs Shipton's funny, she keeps telling me to grease the stairs or put calamine lotion in his soup. That's awful, is that. I shouldn't be thinking these thoughts, specially in church.

The priest stood still and silent in the gloomy doorway that connected church and vestry. A terrible hatred bubbled in the region of his stomach, so he swallowed hard against the acrid taste. He would not vomit. Twice this morning he had received the Blessed Sacrament, and he didn't want to spit the Son of God on to the flags. Loathing and holiness were not good bedfellows, and his disobedient gut simmered like some Shakespearian witches' cauldron. The woman had been beaten again. He could tell that from the way she was sitting so unevenly, as if she depended on one arm.

He stepped back into deeper shadow. If she wanted to talk, she would come and find him. Sometimes she needed an intermediary, but often she spoke directly to her Maker. A good woman, she was, no lack of prayer in her. If only her husband would step under a tram, leave her and the girls in peace . . . He blinked rapidly. There should be no space in his heart for such destructive hopes. Better to pray now for the state of the world, for the enlightenment of the German people who had so foolishly allowed themselves to fall under the spell of an anti-Christ.

She eased her bruised body back until she was upright, hands plucking at the front of her bottle-green coat, the coat she'd worn to mass this morning. She should leave him. She should take the girls and find a couple of rooms in somebody's house, go for a mill job, put her daughters to train for weaving or spinning. It was a straight enough choice – they could have hell at home or hell in their working lives. But wasn't there an old saying about putting up with the devil you know? And one of the girls might be fit for mill work, but the other certainly wasn't, hadn't been completely steady on her pins since that fall down the stairs ten or more years ago. Shop work wasn't easy, but at least you didn't come home at the end of the day with headaches, ringing in the ears, and with your clothes sticking in the stiff, salt residue of a day's sweat.

He'd find us anyway, find us and drag us back. Even if we moved to Bury or Blackburn, it would only be a matter of time. We couldn't take the shame of it, any of us. Oh God, he's so tight-fisted, and so nasty when he's had a drink. All he cares about is making money, and he doesn't want money for us, for his family. He wants money for money's sake. We're the cheapest labour he could get, me and the girls. Aye, he'd find us all right.

After a hurried prayer that was little more than an afterthought, the small woman left the pew, genuflected, and went out into the street. Groups of men were gathering on corners to discuss the outbreak of war, while their wives stood in doorways gazing at the sky as if they expected instant and immediate bombardment. She walked slowly into the town centre, not stopping until she reached the Town Hall steps. Here she sat and stared at the monument, her mind empty of thought, her heart devoid of feeling. The great clock above her head celebrated the time with each quarter, but she did not hear it.

Then it arrived in Bolton, the awful noise that would fill the years to come, the screaming, wailing siren that warned of enemy aircraft. Her brain crashed into gear immediately. Where were her daughters, would they find shelter? Should she stay here, should she run home? There were proper shelters where she lived, places specially built to protect the residents of Deane and Daubhill, two densely-populated areas that squatted side by side, ugly warrens into which thousands of shabby houses had been crammed. It was safer there. She didn't know why it was safer, but it was. So many people, people she knew, folk who would help and protect each other.

And so, as the siren died away, her decision made itself. She would stay till the end of the war. Not with him, she wasn't really staying with him. She was merely hanging on to familiar things, familiar people. She'd been born and raised in Deane and Daubhill, knew the streets as well as she knew the backs of her own hands. And the Shiptons, the Tattersalls, the Shaws – these folk were part of her pattern, they were woven into the cloth of her life. It was not the right time for a fresh start.

She trudged home to stand alongside her neighbours as they faced a long period of tense silence. Month followed empty month while the people of Britain fed their hopes on newsreel propaganda, hid their fears behind a blanket

14

of routine and normality. When the real war eventually came, the woman worked, prayed, put up her blackouts, took the beatings, protected her daughters, prayed again. The Second World War was two years old when she finally acquired the weaponry with which she might defend herself.

By that time, her name had been Ellen Langden for over sixteen years.

CHAPTER ONE

December, 1941

The streets of Bolton were silent and dark, every house blacked out, every door firmly closed against potential chaos. On this, the 826th day of the Second World War, the British were supposed to feel a sudden burst of confidence, a boosting of morale, a lifting of spirit. America was in it. America was in it right up to her neck, for, on the previous day, Pearl Harbor in Hawaii had been bombed by the Japanese.

But life continued just as it had for the past 825 days. At ten o'clock in the evening, all was still. Many people were in the shelters; those who preferred to remain at home sat huddled in corners and stairwells, or lay on blankets spread beneath sturdy kitchen tables. Those with cellars crept below ground to spend a restless night on canvas fold-away cots, while a few rare brave souls showed their defiance of the Luftwaffe by remaining in their beds.

The man best known as Billy London was in none of these places. He stood, as usual, behind a counter in the larger of his two shops, fingers numb with cold as he counted the day's takings. A mirthless grin stretched itself across his narrow features. Four pounds, four shillings and elevenpence. Not bad going for a little general store in the middle of a war. The Co-op down the road probably hadn't taken as much, but then the Co-op had socialist principles. Billy himself had used to hold such ill-based maxims, way back in his youth when he'd been a dogsbody in the East End. But only a true businessman had a chance of surviving world-wide conflict. And Billy had recognized some years ago that his strength lay in the making and storing of money. He was an out and out capitalist, and he carried his status like a flag. When it came to business, William Langden was in a class of his own.

He sat back on his stool and gazed round at the shelves. The place was dimly lit by two flickering gaslights and a stub of candle on the mahogany counter, but the man could have laid his hand on anything in the shop even if he'd been blindfolded. This was his Aladdin's cave, the showcase for his achievement. Not that all the stock was visible, oh no, he kept the better and rarer stuff in the back and stacked away in the upper storeys of the six houses he owned. In those six houses lived families he trusted, folk who, for a peppercorn rent, occupied the lower floors and kept a watch on Mr London's assets, stuff he had started salting away as long ago as 1938. He hadn't needed a crystal ball. Anyone with a grain of sense might have seen this war coming, yet even Chamberlain had been fooled. Not Billy London, though. As the Bolton folk often said, Billy London had his head screwed on the right way.

So by the time war had been declared in 1939, he had collected enough stock for half a dozen shops, and people came from miles around to register their ration books with him. The more they came and bought, the more ration points he accumulated, and he was able to replace much of what he sold. The black market side of the business was reserved, of course, for special and trusted customers, folk who could manage to pay over the odds for things he had carefully stockpiled. The missus didn't approve of this seamy side of trade, though she did not air her views. She'd never have dared to open her mouth on the subject, not in his presence, but she showed her aversion by simply failing to sell from underneath the counter. To counteract her stupidity, Billy moved about between the two shops so that his illicit dealings were fairly and evenly shared between the residents of Deane and Daubhill.

The Derby Street shop served the people of Daubhill. It

had three counters, which formed three sides of a square, while the fourth side contained a door and a large display window. The counter opposite the door was for groceries, the others were occupied by newspapers, sweets and tobacco on one side of the shop, then alcohol and general ironmongery on the other. He was thriving. And the *Daily Express* told him that he would continue to thrive.

He glanced at the front page.

PRESIDENT ROOSEVELT TONIGHT REPLIED TO JAPAN'S UNDECLARED WAR ON THE UNITED STATES BY DECREEING MOBILIZATION AND ORDERING THE ARMY AND THE NAVY TO PUT INTO OPERATION PLANS ALREADY PREPARED TO MEET JAPANESE ATTACK.

He was acting as Commander-in-Chief of the American armed forces. Tomorrow, a hastily convened session of Senate and Representatives will hear a message from the President asking for an immediate declaration of war against Japan.

Billy's grim smile grew even broader. With the Yanks and the Japanese involved, the war could go on for years yet. And during those years, a clever man might become a rich man. He licked his dry lips, as if tasting the advent of true success. There were no notices about credit up on the walls of the London Stores. Billy believed in credit. Credit meant he could charge interest or take an item of value in lieu.

His smile faded until the features of his face had rearranged themselves into their habitual non-expressive mode. Had it been in his nature to be contented, then the man everyone knew as Billy London would have been a happy one. He had a decent, if somewhat modest home, two daughters who had helped in the shop ever since becoming tall enough to reach a shelf, a compliant and docile wife, and more money than most.

But Billy was essentially morose and miserly. Had Charles Dickens been around to look for a model for his Scrooge, he would have found an ideal candidate here on Derby Street in Bolton, Lancashire. This was a slight figure, thin almost to the point of emaciation, hands as delicate as any girl's, neck stringy and stretched across a pronounced Adam's apple. His eyes were a cold and colourless grey, while a large nose overshadowed a mouth like a slit in brown paper. His skin was dark, always tan, even in winter.

Billy London was not like other shopkeepers. No snowy white apron would ever envelop his slender form; nor was he given to wearing a brown button-through overall. His clothes were always the same, always impeccable. Dark trousers, polished shoes, a waistcoat, a good jacket and, to top it all, a black bowler hat. Few people had ever seen Mr London's hair. Some wondered whether he might be bald, because beyond the odd tipping of the brim, he never moved his hat. It was even rumoured that he slept in his bowler, for those who had seen him answering the door of his home in Noble Street had noticed that the hat was on his head, even at the oddest of hours.

Nobody liked him. For a start, there was the way he treated his wife and kiddies. He snapped at them, barked like an angry greyhound, and there were tales of noises and screams coming from his house on Saturday nights when he'd been at his wholesale whisky, and on Sunday afternoons when, as legend had it, he usually found an excuse to beat his little wife. Then there was his manner, sort of smarmy yet superior all at once. It was as if he considered himself to be in a higher bracket than everybody else, as if coming from London gave him an edge on ordinary northern folk. Yet you could tell he wasn't really up to much, because posh Londoners talked like King George and Winston Churchill and the man who read the news on the wireless.

It was his East End accent that had christened him 'Billy London', because his real name was Langden. If anyone asked his name, he said 'Langden', and when questioned about where he came from, he said 'Landan', so the people of Bolton simply corrupted both to 'Lundun'. He was Mr London from London, yet he was married to Mrs Langden. Everyone gave his wife her real name because she was a Bolton lass and 'talked proper', so she got her due while he got his. Few would ever have dared to call him Billy, not to his face. He was Mr London and he accepted this title with equanimity. Indeed, he had cashed in on it, because 'The London Stores' was a good name for a shop up north; it gave it a kind of metropolitan status, as if his business was a cut above the rest in the area.

The war had indeed proved a bonus for Billy. And he considered this to be his right, for hadn't he been gassed last time round, and hadn't he lost most of his stomach? Wasn't he reduced to living on bread and milk, porridge and thin stews, and didn't he need the scotch to help him digest his meagre meals? So he was only getting what life owed him.

'Are you there, Mrs Langden?' The voice was that of a child, a whispering child who apparently thought that the sound of her voice would bring the German planes over the houses again. 'Mrs Langden?'

He stepped round the counter, strode across the floor and opened the door. 'What are you doing out at this hour? And no, Mrs Langden isn't here. She's closing the shop on Deane Road tonight. Come in before the warden catches us showing a light.'

The pathetic girl hesitated. She was into her teens, yet she looked like an undernourished ten-year-old. 'I wanted the missus . . .'

'I bet you did. That wife of mine will have me in the poor house. And what's your mother doing sending you out in the middle of a blackout? Shouldn't you be down the shelter, or in your bed?' He had learned, over the years, how to simulate concern for their welfare. Even the smallest child would grow in time, and another adult would mean another customer. But he had better watch this one – it looked as if she might be on the scrounge.

The child shook her head sadly. 'Me mam doesn't know I'm out. Only me dad's dead, see. They brought a telegram today and me mam's gone all quiet. There isn't no food in the house. I thought Mrs Langden would . . .'

He dragged her into the shop and slammed home the door. 'You thought she'd give you something. And you know I won't. Is that it?'

She nodded mutely.

'Have you brought anything at all? A ring, a bit of silver?'

'No. We haven't got no silver. And I couldn't ask me mam to give me her wedding ring, 'cos she's not talking and she doesn't listen. I think she can't hear me, Mr London. It's like she's gone deaf all of a sudden.'

He stared at her. In spite of the December cold, she wore a skimpy off-white dress, an awful garment made from the inferior cotton that was being spun in the mills specifically for shrouds. With a sigh of impatience, he drew the hunter from his waistcoat pocket. 'It's ten past ten. Time you were inside, young lady. And it's no use begging off of me, I'm not a rich man. People think I'm made of money, but I'm struggling the same as everybody else.'

A tear rolled down her cheek. It was funny, the way he spoke. When he said 'young lady', it came out as 'yang lidy'. Her dad had used to call her that, but he'd said it in familiar flat Bolton tones. 'I'll . . . I'll go home, then,' she said listlessly.

'Hold your horses.' His eyebrows shot upward as if the sound of his own voice had surprised him. Yes, he was surprised. Was he going a bit soft in the head? After all, the Tattersalls weren't the best customers. And little Linda here wasn't a particularly endearing sight with her ragged dress and runny nose. 'I'll see what I can find,' he muttered. Then, in a stronger tone he said, 'And don't you tell anybody, see? I can't have them thinking I'm a soft touch. They'll all be in here with their sob stories if they find out I've given you something. Understand? And anyway,' he grunted. 'I'm not giving you this for nothing. We'll sort something out, you and me, a way for you to pay me back.'

She nodded and flattened herself against the door. With sad round eyes she watched as he filled a few sheets of newspaper with stale buns, a quarter of butter, some ends of bacon and a bit of tea screwed up in tissue. He coughed. 'Wet the buns,' he ordered brusquely. 'Wet 'em and stick 'em in the oven for ten minutes, come up a treat, they will. Or you could have them toasted. Does your mam like Hovis, Linda?'

'Turog,' she managed.

'That's it, I remember now. Here's a fresh Turog for her. Now. Cross your heart and hope to die if you ever tell what I just done for you. And it's only a loan, don't forget.'

She wet her finger and went through the motions.

He cleared his throat again. 'Tell her . . . once she starts listening again . . . tell her I'm sorry about the old man.' He had to say things like that. It was all part of being a shopkeeper. It stuck in his craw at times, but he had to go through the motions of being interested.

'He was . . .' She swallowed painfully. 'He was only thirty-four, Mr London. He was younger than me mam . . .'

'And how old are you?'

'Nearly thirteen.'

He looked her up and down. 'You know my other shop? The one on Deane Road? Well, I could do with a girl there, somebody to sweep up and mop the floors. My daughters are old enough to do the real serving now, they've got proper approved jobs. What do you say? Seven o'clock till school time, then after school till six. Ninepence a day, I'll give you.'

She nodded vigorously. 'Ta, mister.'

'It's not charity!' He was almost yelling now. 'It's an honest job, one I'll pay you for. But before I pay you, I'll take the price of what you've been given tonight. I don't want none of you thinking my shops are charitable institutions. Only don't forget to tell everybody that Mr London helped you out in your hour of need, gave you a job. Not a hand-out, mind, a job. Now, take your food and go home.'

She fled gratefully into the blackness outside.

Billy London sank on to his stool and shook his head slowly. Fancy that! Fancy him giving stuff away. He could scarcely believe what he had just done. Never in his life had he been guilty of a charitable act. Why start now? Even the stale buns would have fetched a penny or two in the morning. And tea – he'd given away precious tea and a fresh brown loaf. Well, it had only been a small loaf, hadn't it? And he would get it all back in labour – he would make sure of that.

He blew out the candle, turned off the gas, then left the shop by the front door, carefully locking up his property with three separate keys.

He was partway down Noble Street when he heard the drone, two or three stray German bombers flying low in the inky sky. Still, they never dropped much here, did they? Whereas the poor old East End was half-flattened by now, razed to the ground night after night according to the papers. He had people there, didn't he? People he'd better not think about . . .

A high-pitched sound reached his ears, a strange noise that was a mixture of scream and whistle. It was a bomb! The bleeders were dropping bombs near his home, his shops, his livelihood! His body was suddenly hurled into a doorway as a massive explosion shook the earth; he could feel the tremor in the building against which he was leaning. Orange flames darted high in the air, leaping and dancing about over the roofs at the back of Deane Road. Billy was not a fanciful chap, but he suddenly thought how strangely joyful the fire was, how odd it seemed that something pretty could be so destructive.

Then he began to sweat, awful beads of icy cold water that quickly covered his shaking body. No, it couldn't be.

He'd never had shell shock, had he? There'd been just about everything else, from a bullet in the gut to a chestful of gas, but he'd never gone to pieces in 1918, so why now? Why was his head full of weird pictures? Oh God, this wasn't happening, couldn't be happening! He couldn't see! He was blind, blind! No, he wasn't. He was in a trench. Beneath his feet he could feel the corpse of some poor Tommy who'd already copped it. But he had to stand on the body, otherwise he would sink into that sea of mud. Horses were screaming somewhere across the field, horses with their bellies ripped out and their legs shot to bits. A fool of an officer was yelling 'fire at will' and some daft sod was asking 'which one of the buggers is Will?'

'Mr London? Come in out of the road.'

His throat was dry. 'I can't. Peterson's dead. Get his tin, see if there's any tobacco left in it.'

'Mr London? There's been a bomb further down. You'll have to come in our house till the all-clear goes off. Are you all right? Mam? It's Mr London, he's gone all funny. Mam, listen to me . . .'

He could hear them, but he couldn't see them. That was the trouble with the Krauts, you never bloody saw them till they were on top of you. Thousands of them, there was, bleeding thousands of them only yards away across no man's land. He wanted to run out and shout obscenities at them, but he had to stay where he was on top of the dead soldier. Anyway, he shouldn't be here at all, should he? He was in charge of stores, a nice cushy little number – what the hell was he doing in a trench?

'Mam – I can't get Mr London to move. He keeps saying funny things about Krauts and fire at will. Mam, can you come and get him in?'

Yes, there was a few of them who'd had cushy little numbers, but it was every man for himself now. They'd all been brought into the fighting, all the desk wallahs and training sergeants, all the clerks and medics and storesmen. There was no escape. Everybody was dying. There was blood all over the place, blood and bodies and parts of bodies . . .

Someone was shaking his arm. He turned to look at the corporal next to him, and a puzzled expression came over his face. Where was he? It was dark, very dark. In the dim doorway stood Mrs Tattersall with little Linda in that skimpy white frock. 'What happened?' he asked quietly.

'A bomb,' said the grief-stricken woman. 'They killed my Harry, now they're trying to get me kids as well.'

He moved his feet. There was no dead soldier underneath his shoes. And yes, they were shoes, proper shoes, not worn-out and ill-fitting army boots. 'A bomb, you say? Gawd, for a minute then I thought I was . . . somewhere else. I'd better get home.'

'It's all right, Mr London,' said Linda. 'They got the back of Deane Road. It won't be your house. Come in and have a cup of tea.'

Mrs Tattersall stared vacantly ahead. It was obvious that she had retreated back into the shock from which the explosion had temporarily released her.

He backed away and touched the brim of his hat. Yes, he knew about shock. It could do some funny things to a person, could shock. 'Mrs Tattersall?'

'Eh?' She stared at him as if he were a stranger.

'I sent some bits with your girl. Get yourself a bacon sandwich.'

'You what?'

'I'm sorry about your husband. Get inside, try to stay warm.' Yes, it was necessary to go through the motions even now. Better to pretend concern, because concern showed in the takings.

The sweat was beginning to dry, but he still shook like a leaf. It was as if he had just been on a journey in some impossible time machine, a machine that had transported him back some twenty-three years. But he was all right. Yes, he was going to be all right. This was 1941, the year of the bombing war. No horses, no cavalrymen, no trenches, not for him. The war was in the sky this time, leaving every civilian open to its tactics. He thanked God that he had left London, though. Here, a bomb was a

26

rarity, a topic for conversation. In the East End, such devices were an everyday occurrence, a matter of fact and a fact of life.

The thin, starved-looking girl touched his arm tentatively. 'Ta for the stuff, Mr London. I'm going to try and get Mam down the shelter now. Will there be any more bombs? Will there?'

'I doubt it. There's not much worth bombing round here.' He studied the pinched features, wondering whether the girl would be strong enough to hump bags of potatoes. 'And don't forget, you're working for me now, right?' He was feeling better, almost normal by this time. 'I'll be off, then.'

Linda half closed the door and watched him walk away. If her dad hadn't died, and if there hadn't been a bomb, she would have been giggling, because she always laughed when Mr London said 'be awf wiv yer'. He was funny, was Mr London, he couldn't say 'off' properly. She sighed, closed the door, then set about the business of preparing her mother for the shelter. It was like dressing a stiff china doll, all spiky fingers and unbending arms. 'Mam! Come on, put your coat on.'

'Eh? Where's Harry? Has he had his tea? I bet he's up the Albert playing darts and sinking pints. Where are we going? Stop pulling at me, will you? What's the rush, and where's your brother?'

The youngster bit back her tears. 'Our Tony's in the shelter. And that's where we're making for. We have to go in the shelter, same as everybody else.'

'What for?' The eyes were wide, like those of a small child.

'To hide from the bombs.'

'What bombs? Why is there no fire? Didn't I get two hundredweight put under the stairs? That oven'll be cold. I've done tatie pie too for our suppers . . .'

Linda, who was stronger than she looked, pulled on a tattered cardigan before dragging her dazed mother out of the house and into the communal shelter in the back

27

street. The building was full, as always, and as soon as they were inside, Linda and her mother bumped into Mrs Langden who was standing in the doorway. 'Have you seen him? Have you seen my husband?' asked Mrs Langden. It was plain from her twisting hands that she was in a state of agitation. 'We've got to find him before anything happens.'

Cissie Tattersall began to giggle uncontrollably.

'Sorry,' explained Linda, who was still fighting the tears of bereavement and shock. 'Me dad's dead and me mam's took it bad. I can't get through to her at all. She's been like this since they fetched the telegram.'

'Oh. I'm sorry. I'm very sorry, Mrs Tattersall.'

'And we've seen Mr London,' Linda went on. 'He was on his way through to Deane Road, likely looking to see if the other shop's all right.'

'Dear Lord!' Mrs Langden pulled a shawl over her coat. 'They'll get him.'

'No, they won't, Mrs Langden. He said there wouldn't be no more bombs. I asked him, and he said there wouldn't be owt else tonight.'

'It's not bombs I'm worried over. It's . . . it's summat else altogether.'

Linda pushed her mother on to a bench, then turned to face the other woman. 'Don't go out, Mrs Langden. There's fires out there, fires and dead bodies. You can't do nothing. Stop in here where you'll be safe.' Gently, she eased the shopkeeper's wife into a corner next to a warden. 'Stay there,' she admonished with a maturity that denied her age. 'There's none of us going out till the all-clear. We have to stop here, it's the rule.'

Mrs Langden began to rock back and forth. 'They'll get him,' she said so quietly that Linda could scarcely hear over the buzz of chatter in the crowded area. 'They'll go over him good and proper. Gone too far, he has. Too far this time . . .' Yes, and he had taken her with him. She was over the edge of the cliff, falling, falling . . . With her head in her hands, she wept. Her daughters would be here

28

in a minute, so she had better get the weeping over and done with.

Billy walked quickly down Noble Street, passed his own home without pausing to check on the safety of his family, glanced across at his six intact houses, then almost trotted round the corner on to Deane Road. The fire fighters were wetting some of the buildings in case the fire behind might spread, but his shop was safely out of range of the flames. He heaved a sigh of relief and turned to go back home. There was no point in hanging around if his shop was safe.

As he passed the bottom end of a back alley, he saw dark figures outlined against leaping flames, tall men with bundles in their arms. The bundles were being laid out in rows on the cobblestones. He remembered other rows of bodies from a different war, so he simply turned his head away and marched on smartly. No way would he allow any of his memories back. He wanted to forget all of it – London, the First War – everything. The future was what mattered, prosperity was the main thing. He didn't want any repeat performances of tonight's little episode, no more flashbacks into the past. A shiver travelled the length of his straight spine. How real it had been! How near had he come to teetering on the brink of insanity? Perhaps a man could have shell shock for years without ever knowing it. No more, though. He raised his chin defiantly and strode towards his own house.

Then, just as he reached a gap between the terraces, an arm reached out and grabbed him by the throat. 'Is it him?' whispered a familiar voice. 'Shine the bloody torch, lad, we don't want to waste our time on t' wrong bloke.'

A weak light flashed in Billy's eyes. 'Aye. It's him all reet, ugly bugger, he is. I'd know that face anywhere, it looks like t'worst end of a bad accident.'

He was dragged into the narrow passage, his damaged lungs struggling for air as the hand tightened round his neck. There were three of them. Yes, she had three brothers, and they were all present and accounted for.

Though he couldn't imagine why they had lain in wait for him on this particular occasion.

The grip on his neck slackened just as he thought he was losing consciousness. 'Well?' asked Jack O'Hara, the eldest of the three. 'What's tha got to say for thissen? Has t' bloody cat got tha tongue? Or has tha sold it? You'd sell owt, you would.'

'I . . . I don't know what you mean.'

Jack laughed mirthlessly. 'Did tha hear that, our Terry? Have I got this right, our Joe? He doesn't know what he's done! He doesn't know what he's done to our sister.'

'It was nothing,' mumbled the cowering man. 'Just a bit of a row, that's all it was. I'd had a few and the girls were messing about. I told her to keep them quiet. I didn't hit her hard, honest.' This was unbelievable. Her brothers had never taken him to task before, not for keeping order in his own house.

Jack, whose accent was thicker than most, carried on doing the talking. 'This isn't about a bit of a bashing. Tha knows we wouldn't tek t' time of day or night over a clout or two. Oh no, this is summat else altogether, summat you've known about for years, Billy London. You've brought our sister down, you have. You've tret her worse than any man we've ever known. What did tha leave behind thee in London, eh? What sort of a game do you call this? Bloody criminal, it is.'

'I . . . I don't—'

'He don't know what we mean, Jack,' interrupted Terry. 'Big mister businessman doesn't know what we're on about. He could happen do with a bit o' learning.'

Joe, the youngest and biggest, stepped forward with his hooded torch. 'Trouble, that's what we mean, Billy. Big trouble. And it's followed you all the way to Bolton, caught up with you at last, it has. And so have we.'

Billy swallowed audibly. These men might be Boltonians, but they still carried their Irish father's temper, a vicious temper that had landed the senior Mr O'Hara in prison on more than one occasion. 'There ain't any trouble. I came up here in good faith for a fresh start, didn't I? There's no law to say a man can't move about in his own country.'

'Aye,' growled Jack. 'You set off up here in the middle of a depression, when every other bugger was making for London in the hope of work. Always puzzled me, did that, why a man should come to Bolton when there was no work. Still, you fetched plenty of money with you, eh? Whose bloody money was it? Where did you get that lot from, Billy-boy?'

'It was mine! I'd worked for it . . .'

'That's not what we heard. We heard plenty tonight, see. Enough to put you behind bars for a good long stretch. But the main thing is what you've done to our girl. Only girl we had in our family, and we promised our mam we'd see to her, look after her, like. And we're going to start by beating the living daylights out of you, you bad devil.'

'Where will that get you?' He tried to keep his voice steady. 'What can you gain by knocking me senseless?'

'A lot of satisfaction,' said Joe. 'You can't treat an O'Hara bad ways and get away with it, London-lad. Her's had the shock of her life today, the shock of her bloody life. How do you think she felt when she opened her door and found that mess you'd left in Bow, eh? What sort of a woman do you think she is? Our Ellen's no cheap tramp, tha knows.'

'She's . . . she's well looked after,' muttered Billy, his tone high-pitched as it emerged from a throat as dry as sandpaper. 'And so's the girls. They want for nothing, do they? Good food, nice clothes, a warm house . . .' His voice trailed away as they closed in on him.

They beat him viciously yet carefully, obviously making sure that he would be hurt but not killed. Over and over they kicked him and punched him, flinging him about until he resembled a battered rag doll. 'Tha'll never forget this day, Billy London,' whispered Jack breathlessly. 'It's Monday December the eighth 1941. Remember it. Remember it as the day thy past caught up with thee.'

It occurred to Billy that they were strong, these men who had been judged too old for war. But they were foundry workers, every one of them with muscles bulging from the wielding of hammers and the lifting of heavy crucibles. It hurt like hell. He could not remember pain like this; not even in the field hospital tent had he suffered so badly.

At last they were gone, melted noiselessly into a night where pandemonium reigned just yards away; yet the activity was not near enough for Billy London, who could not even crawl or shout for help. A cruel December ice bit into his wounds until he was a solid, frozen bundle of suffering. One arm lay crushed beneath him. He could not move it, and he knew that it was broken. He was unsure about his legs; they were so chilled and bruised that he would not have dared to attempt to stand. His mouth hung open to allow a flow of blood which congealed quickly in the freezing air, and his swollen tongue rested against cracked teeth. There was no help for him; every able-bodied man was involved in rescuing victims of the bomb.

The certainty that he was dying filled his numbing mind. It did not worry him, for death would mean a blessed release from unbearable anguish, yet he forced himself to remain conscious for as long as possible. Why had they done it? Why had her brothers attacked him? The answer hovered somewhere above his head, in a place that was just out of reach. And it didn't matter anyway. Nothing mattered now. There was only the pain . . .

He was found at about two o'clock in the morning. His rescuers, believing that he had been caught in the blast, chattered to one another about how Billy must have crawled away from the bomb site, about the fact that his good clothing had kept him alive, about how lucky he was to have been discovered at all in such a dark place. Billy London heard none of this; he had been unconscious for several hours.

They took him to the infirmary where he woke after two

days, his arm in plaster, his head heavily bandaged and most of his teeth gone for ever. A doctor leaned over him. 'Fortunate man,' he proclaimed. 'That bomb took fourteen lives – you were lucky to be blown away from it. We've set your arm and strapped your ribs. Oh, and I had to take away your teeth, so we'll get some dentures fitted when the swelling reduces.'

Billy tried to speak, but his tongue still filled his mouth.

The doctor smiled reassuringly. 'You're in shock, of course. Your wife came down and gave us your name, but she wouldn't stay. I think she realizes that you need the rest.' That wasn't what she'd said, not exactly. But it wasn't a doctor's place to tell a sick man that his wife didn't care if she never saw him again . . .

When the doctor moved on to the next bed, Billy lay staring at the ceiling. His head felt as if it were being rebuilt, as if an army of bricklayers were tapping away with trowels and buckets of cement. And he couldn't even ask for an Aspro, because his tongue was stuck to the roof of his mouth. Dear God, what had happened to him? Where was he? He tried to straighten his mind, but the hammering was too loud. Were they guns he could hear, was that the sound of cannon? No! Years had elapsed since that particular episode; this was a different era altogether! He wasn't in London any more, he wasn't at the German front, wasn't in danger. But London had come to him – wasn't that what they had said? What who had said . . . ? Her brothers, yes, her brothers. He must concentrate, must think hard. He had two shops, he was a man of substance. This wasn't his war, it wasn't!

For several more days, Billy London hovered in a place that didn't really exist, a strange place halfway between now and then, an area of nightmare and sweat and rough handling. Every time the nurses cleaned and changed him, he went through excruciating pain, but at least the pain was real, it was in the present tense. Left to himself, he relived times past, actually saw the blood, the gore, the horrors of his own life. There were times when he watched the gas coming, when he struggled for his mask, when he tasted it, smelled it, choked on thick clouds of yellow mustard.

His body healed. After a time, they fed him on gruels and soups, then a dentist came in and took impressions for false teeth. The pain in his head subsided, the bruising yellowed, his arm felt better. But he was a broken man; something inside had snapped and he couldn't get his mind in order. And, as if to underline his reduced circumstances, the teeth, when they arrived, didn't fit properly.

The nurses sat him in a chair, padded him out with pillows and cushions, made him as comfortable as possible. With his intact arm, he struggled to turn the pages of the newspaper. The United States had declared war on Italy and Germany. Forty million Americans were armed and ready to step into the European war. Hong Kong was fighting to the death with swarms of invading Japanese. He understood all that, knew all that. Yet every time he returned to his bed, he was back in that trench with the dead soldier under his boots. The shakes were terrible during the nights.

At last, the visionary young doctor diagnosed shell shock, and Billy was moved to a convalescent home in Blackpool. He knew with an unwavering certainty that he would never be the same man as he had been. He needed only to look into a mirror to see the visible changes, shrunken features, ill-fitting teeth, rounded shoulders, dark-rimmed eyes. But it was the change in his head that was the most shattering. He couldn't arrange his thoughts properly during the days because his nights were so terrifying, so haunted. And large chunks of his past were missing, as if some giant hand had taken an india-rubber and erased half of his life.

The home was right on the front, and Billy sat for hours on end looking across the water, pushing out of his mind all thoughts of the beating he had taken, all questions as to why he had been punished so viciously. Perhaps he knew the answers. Had he cared to allow them into his consciousness, the reasons might all have been there for him to analyse. But it was as if a part of him had deliberately retreated into delayed shock, as if his mind were guarding itself for a while against the inevitable. Billy's faith was not strong, but he wondered at times whether God had given him this island of silence, this time to mend until the awful truth came back to him. Because he knew somehow that the truth was indeed too awful to face . . .

They fussed over him, got him a wireless, gave him a single room with a comfortable bed, nice furnishings and the best view from the window. Other residents of the Maybank Rest Home were old men, those who had suffered so badly in the Great War that they had been rendered incapable of leading a normal life. And Billy suddenly realized that he, too, was old. Not in body, because fifty-one was no age at all, but he was aged in spirit, had been adult ever since he'd reached the age of reason in the orphanage back in Stepney.

No! He mustn't think of Stepney or Bow or even of Mayfair. Names of places, that was all they were. Names of places, yet he could remember none of the people who had occupied his life in London. He'd made a clean break, a fresh start, a damned good life for himself. Where was that life now? Where were his daughters, where was his wife? 'A good little body' everyone called her, but she'd never been near to apologize about what her three older brothers had done to him. 'The trouble has followed you from London.' He shivered as he heard those words echoing in his brain, the last words he remembered from that night, the ominous message that had dripped slowly from a flat Lancashire tongue. Yes, they did speak slowly, these people, sometimes giving the impression that they were almost retarded, yet he knew how quick they could be. Quick to temper, fast with a fist, forthcoming with a killing reply whenever he lost his patience in the shops.

The shops. What was he going to do about them? How

was he going to get home, and what sort of reception would he get if he did ever reach Noble Street? Because he was convinced now that his wife was 'in it', that the so-called good little body had set her brothers against him. Why? Could he face the why? No! No, not yet . . .

Gradually, the dreams began to change. In his sleep, he became a boy again, an East End orphan who was pushed from pillar to post, from one distant relative to another. It was as if he had to go through his whole life in dreams, and he often woke crying and shaking, only to fall back into the same dream as soon as his eyes closed again.

There was a house with a lot of children in it and a woman called Aunt Annie. Some of the children were hers, some weren't. Billy wasn't hers and Billy was her least favourite. He spent many a day locked in a cupboard under the stairs because he hadn't behaved himself. There were three bedrooms upstairs, and every child was allowed a shelf for his or her things. Billy's shelf was always empty. On the landing there was a chest that often had a new baby sleeping in its bottom drawer. Where or why Aunt Annie got these babies he had never managed to work out, for she was a singularly unmotherly soul with no time or love for children. Perhaps she had got paid for having them?

There were no gas brackets upstairs. Instead, there were small paraffin lamps with glass globes that were usually broken, so wicks were often exposed, their naked flames burning smokily into the bedrooms. Of course, there had been a fire in which Aunt Annie and most of the children had perished, but young Billy had been rescued just in time from his prison under the stairs.

'Mr Langden?' Someone was shaking his shoulder. Thank God it was morning! He pushed himself into a sitting position. 'Is the arm all right now?' asked the visitor.

'Not bad. Still aches a bit. I think they took the plaster off a bit early. Who are you?' The man wore an ordinary navy blue suit, so Billy reckoned that this was no doctor.

'My name's Carter. Dr Carter. I see you're surprised because I don't choose to wear a white coat. Don't believe in uniforms, Mr Langden. Had enough of uniforms in the RAF, used to be a medic stationed down south. I was supposed to get the poor beggars in a fit frame of mind so that they could carry on the Battle of Britain.'

Billy stared hard at him. 'Are you one of them bleeding head doctors?'

'I am. I understand you've been having trouble sleeping. This has been put down to shell shock because of the bomb in Bolton. You see, the explosion probably brought back a lot of disturbing memories. Most of the men here have disturbing memories. It's my job to listen.'

'I'm OK,' growled the patient. 'And I was nowhere near that bomb. The damage done to me was nothing to do with the war.'

'I know.' The doctor's tone was quiet.

'How do you know? And how bloody much do you know?'

'More than you want to talk about, more than you're ready to discuss just yet. I had a long talk with your wife, Mr Langden. She told me what had happened. Do you wish to prosecute your brothers-in-law?'

Billy paused. 'Naw,' he said eventually. 'Wouldn't be worth it.'

The doctor walked to the window and gazed out. 'Why not?' he threw over his shoulder.

The figure in the bed sat rigidly still.

'Are you afraid of being prosecuted yourself? Are you really ill in your mind, or are you sheltering from something?'

'I . . . I don't know. The sweats in the night is awful. I sometimes dream about the war, my own war, then I go back to when I was a kid. It's as if I can't think straight any more. And I can't afford not to think straight, Doc. I've two thriving shops to see to.'

Dr Carter swivelled on his heel. 'Have you?'

'What do you mean? Course I have. One's on Derby

Street, the other's on Deane Road. She looks after one while I see to the other.'

'Will she have you back, though?'

'She's got to! They're my shops, mine! I built the businesses up before the war, bought properties, stored a load of stock . . .'

'Calm yourself. Listen. Over the next few days, you are going to talk to me. About your childhood and your life in London, about what you did before you came up here. No point in beating about the bush any longer. There are things you have to face, Mr Langden.'

'Is she . . . is she angry?'

The doctor nodded.

'Not like her to be angry. That was why I married her, because she was so easy going.'

'Perhaps she's been pushed too far?'

'Why? How? What am I supposed to have done?'

Dr Carter stroked his chin thoughtfully. 'I'm not sure about you, Mr Langden, not sure at all. To all intents and purposes, you are suffering from a trauma of some kind. Because of that, I cannot expose you to further shock until you choose to remember for yourself—'

'Remember what?'

'I don't know. I know what I've been told, but that isn't necessarily the truth. But there's something in your past, isn't there? Something rather unsavoury?'

Billy sighed. 'You're right. It's as if I don't want to know. See, until that bomb dropped and I got the beating, I'm sure I knew everything. I knew what I'd done, where I'd been, how I'd got where I was. Then when that night happened, I lost things.'

'Shell shock. You'd probably had it since '18, but it took another explosion to make it catch up with you. Did you relive in detail your time in the trenches?'

'Too bloody right, I did. Only now, I've started going over my childhood when I'm asleep. Bits keep coming back to me. Like Annie's. I remember Annie's house now, and all the kids and the fire. And the orphanage is coming back. But there's a gap, a great big gap between the last war and now. I know about now, I know about the shops and my wife and daughters. But I can't remember about London after I got back from the war.'

'So you've lost about ten years of your life?'

Billy sniffed loudly. 'I don't know. I can't remember when I came north.'

'It's still there, isn't it? Just waiting to be dug out.'

'Yes.' He paused. 'It's something bad, ain't it, Doc? Something I done that's bad.'

'Perhaps.'

'Did I . . . did I break the law?'

'Possibly. You're not ready for it yet, Mr Langden. I'll come in and see you tomorrow. Try to rest.' He made for the door.

'Doc?'

'Yes?'

'They said trouble had followed me up from London. Is that right?'

'Just rest. It'll all come back to you when you're in a fit state to manage it.'

It came back that night, long before he was ready to cope with it. The nurses found him screaming and thrashing in his bed at three o'clock in the morning. After settling him down again, they left him to sweat his way through the missing years, years that hadn't mattered until now. How easily he had left Bow; how easily he had dismissed as unimportant a chunk of his life that had been unpalatable! For ages, he had deliberately ignored it. And now, when it had finally caught up with him, some part of his brain had switched off for a while, made it difficult for him to recall the true facts.

Yes, he knew now why he had been beaten. The 'trouble from London', if it had indeed arrived in Bolton, would be sufficient to make the O'Hara brothers more than angry. He groaned silently into his pillow, because he didn't want the staff coming in again. The burning question was, where could he go from here? There would be no place for him in Noble Street, no chance of him ever running his shops again.

He licked cracked lips and reached for a glass of water. How the hell had he managed to forget all that? And had he really been stupid enough to think that the past would never cause any repercussions?

For the remainder of that night, he lay wakeful. He was a man with a history now, a history that had flooded back to him in the space of a few moments, in the twinkling of an eye. None of it was new to him; it was like picking up a book he had been reading yesterday, or perhaps more like re-reading something he had read years ago. Yes, he was a man with a past, a man without a future. They would take away his shops, his houses, his boxes of cash, his store of pledges that he had grabbed from customers who had been unable to pay in ready money. Would he spend the rest of his life here, in the Maybank Rest Home? Would he become one of the walking wounded, a man incapable of taking care of himself? Or perhaps he might end up on the streets like a tinker or a beggar.

She wouldn't have him back, not with her Catholic principles, all that bowing and scraping and Holy Marying every night. She might be a quiet little woman, but as far as her religion was concerned, she was rigid. Where could he go; what could he do? He hadn't a single penny to his name, because he'd never bothered with banks, didn't believe in them. There were hundreds of pounds stashed in the coal cellar in Noble Street. She knew where it was. Oh yes, she would have taken it by now, grabbed it and stuck it in the Post Office under her own name.

As for relatives – well – he had none. There was just one mate, old Cedric. Cedric Wilkinson had been the one from Bolton, the one he'd met in London all those years ago, the chap who'd planted the seeds of an idea in Billy's mind. Not that Cedric had known from the start about the grand plan, because Billy had kept it close to his chest, but at least Cedric had given Billy the name of a town, somewhere to aim for after the escape.

Yes, old Cedric was the only person in whom Billy had ever confided, because Cedric had realized the truth as soon as Billy had appeared in the north. And he'd kept his mouth shut all these years, so he was, at least, a dependable sort. He lived in Barrow Bridge, didn't he? Yes, it was a nice part of Bolton. Perhaps Billy could stay with him for a while, just until he got on his feet.

But how would he get on his feet? He couldn't work, not at an ordinary job. No-one would employ a man with a chest like his, not even in the middle of a war. And he didn't want to work for someone else, he had been his own master for far too long.

Cedric was a bachelor – that was one good thing. There'd be no wife to make life difficult, no woman to stop her husband from having a friend to stay for a while.

Dr Carter returned just after breakfast. 'Bad night?' he asked pleasantly.

'Terrible. I think I've remembered. I think I know why her brothers knocked me about. Trouble is, I don't know what to do next, where to go from here.'

'No family apart from your wife and children?'

'Nobody. Just a friend, someone I've not seen a lot of. He comes in the shop from time to time, but . . .'

The doctor placed himself in a chair next to Billy's bed. 'Write to him. You can't stay here for ever.'

'I don't know his address.'

'Give me his name and an idea of where he can be found. Our welfare people will try to trace him for you.'

Billy swallowed hard. 'Have I worked it out right, Doc? Have they found me, the London people?'

'Yes, I'm afraid so.'

'Did . . . er . . . did Ellen take it bad?' He didn't often say her name. Even when they had been alone together, he had seldom called her Ellen. She was just 'the wife', or ''er at 'ome', or 'the missus'. 'What's happening?' he asked, his tone becoming frantic.

The doctor shook his head slowly. 'Nothing much. All I've been told is that you opened your shops with stolen money. But I think there's a lot more to it than that, a lot that isn't being said. The London people are staying with your wife.'

'What?' Billy shouted so hard that he almost lost his lower denture. 'In my house? They're staying in my house?'

'So I understand.'

'Bleeding hell! There's no chance for me now, is there? Not if they're all in it together. And it was my money, it was. I was the one who done all the running. I was the one who done the work. It wasn't fair. I only took what was mine by rights . . .'

'Mr Langden?'

'What?'

'I think we'd better go back to the beginning, back to your life in London. The sooner you get it all off your chest, the better.'

Billy sighed impatiently. 'I was an orphan, but I managed to grow up. I had a few jobs, went to war, came back, had a few more jobs, came up here.'

'And the trouble? The trouble you're in now?'

'My business. I ain't telling you.'

'That's your prerogative. But I suggest you do some serious thinking. There's more than one life involved here. What about your children? Have you considered them?'

'They never consider me, never have.'

Dr Carter rose to leave. 'Very well. If you don't want to talk, I can't force you. But you'd better study your options very carefully before setting foot out of here. We'll find your friend. The rest is up to you.'

Left alone with his thoughts, Billy gazed unseeing through the window. He pondered long and hard about the old days, the days that had been missing since the beating. 'The rest is up to me?' he muttered beneath his breath. 'It's always been up to me.' Yes, all his life he had fought to survive, to eat, to stay in one piece.

Now, everything he had striven for was about to be taken from him. Everything. And it wasn't his fault. Well, not all of it . . .

CHAPTER TWO

Ellen and Lilian

The room was bright, though not one of the wall-mounted gas brackets was lit. It was a large roaring fire that illuminated the scene, a huge and noisy conflagration that filled the kitchen with heat and spitting sounds.

A tiny figure knelt on the rag rug in front of the leaping flames, face lined by marks of concentration as she used sharp scissors to cut a pile of items into tiny pieces. It seemed that all the bits had to be of a certain size, as if she were preparing to make yet another peg rug out of discarded clothing. But Ellen Langden's intentions were far from constructive. Although her movements seemed calm and controlled on the surface, there was something about the set of her spine and the straightness of her neck that spoke of a deep, silent anger. With slow and careful deliberation, she went about the business of reducing two of her husband's suits to strips, laying the fruits of her labour in a long straight line before the grate. From time to time, she stopped cutting and made patterns instead of lines, criss-crossing bits of jacket and waistcoat into intricate arrangements, adding a snip of tie, a shoelace, a belt buckle to the collage on the mat. When a design pleased her, a grim smile would linger at the edges of her mouth, giving her the appearance of a child at play.

His bowlers were already burning, while the dress and coat in which she had been married were, by this time, ashes in the pan beneath the fire basket. Marriage lines had been used among the newspapers to light the fire early

43

that morning, and all the photographs of her husband were now melting alongside his favourite headwear.

A terrible feeling of power was taking root in Ellen's mind, a strange sensation, one she had seldom encountered before. She was in charge. He wasn't here any more. With each handful cast into the fire, she was burning another lie, another sin, another year of her unpalatable marriage. It was foolish and she knew it, yet she could not stop herself. It was a cleaning process, as necessary as the weekly leading of the grate, the daily stoning of her step, the monthly polishing of shop shelves. But it failed to clean her soul. No matter how many of his things she burned, she would never be able to cleanse her inner self . . .

'It's hot in here,' whispered the figure in the bed beneath the window. 'I can hardly catch my breath.'

'I'm getting rid of him,' said Ellen quietly. 'I don't want nothing of him left in my house, nothing at all.' His face flashed into her mind, and she blinked against the intrusive ugliness. 'He's gone,' she reminded herself aloud. 'Gone, gone, gone.' Her head moved in time with the words.

'You'll still have his children. You can't get rid of his children.'

Ellen leaned back on her heels and glanced across at the sick woman. There had been few opportunities for talking, because this person was too ill to discuss things at length. But at long last she seemed awake and aware enough to hold a conversation. 'They're my children too,' said Ellen. 'More mine than his, always were. He'd never no time for them till they could help in the shops. After that, he just used them as servants, "bring me, fetch me, carry me" was all they heard from him. Outside school hours, they were forever in the shops. Well, he's wiped his feet on my lasses for the last time.' She stopped to draw breath, eyeing the large figure at the other side of the room. 'Are you all right?'

'No. But then I never shall be. Take my mind off the

pain, Ellen. Tell me what it's been like with him. Go on, I want to hear all about it.'

Ellen raised a surprised eyebrow. 'What? Take your mind off your pain by giving you mine? How will that help?'

'It just will, that's all. Give me something to concentrate on, something outside myself. The journey nearly finished me, but I shall rally in a while.'

A pan sizzled in the scullery, and Ellen leapt up and rushed out to look at the beef tea that was simmering on the little gas hob. She stirred the mixture thoughtfully, then tasted the scalding liquid before pouring it into an enamel mug. Tell her what life had been like? She raised her eyes to the cracked ceiling and tried to pray, but there were no words for the Lord in her head. Tell her? Her of all people? This was turning into a very queer business.

She returned with the cup and placed it on the mantelpiece while she helped the ailing woman into a sitting position. 'Drink it all,' she admonished quietly. 'It'll stick to your ribs, keep you warm for the winter.'

'I shan't see the winter out, Ellen. You know that and I know it. I'd never have come up here to torment you if there'd been any other way. But they have to have their rights. I couldn't just stay down south knowing I was going to die. My daughters have to have what's lawfully theirs.'

Ellen held the cup while the woman drank noisily. 'You'd have come sooner or later. It had to happen, I suppose. And if we're going to face facts, what about after you've gone, eh? Do I brand myself a scarlet woman and throw myself and my two girls out on the streets? Is that what I should do?'

'Not at all.' The breathing was heavy after the effort of drinking. 'Please?' She reached for Ellen's hand and held it in a grasp that seemed tight and strong for a terminally ill person. 'I told you, my name's Lilian. In my youth, my friends called me Lily. He called me Lil. Take your pick, but I'd rather you didn't use Lil. I'm sure you'll appreciate the reason for that.'

'Right, Lilian.' Ellen extracted her hand with difficulty. 'It's all been a shock to me, has this. Can you imagine how I felt when I opened that door and heard what you had to say? This is hard, very hard, but if it makes you feel any better, I'll call you Lilian.' She turned away and picked up a few more strips of cloth which she fed to the fire. 'So.' Her face remained averted from the bed. 'You want to know about my life with the man they all call Billy London? It's been hell. Happen I should call it purgatory, because there's been an end to it and there's no end to hell. He's no good. In fact, he's likely the most evil person I ever met in all me born days. What more can I tell you?'

Lilian sighed. 'Not a lot. After all, he is my husband.'

Ellen turned swiftly on her heel. 'Oh no, he isn't. There's only one form of marriage accepted in the sight of God, and that's a Catholic ceremony. Even a mixed marriage like mine is recognized. Whatever you say, that devil is my husband.'

'Not in the eyes of the law, though. As far as the courts go, Bill is my husband. Abigail and Letticia are his real children. There are certificates if you want proof.'

'And mine are bastards?' whispered Ellen. 'Is that what's down for my poor twins, to be branded as illegitimate? How am I going to face that lot out there?' She waved a hand towards the front of the house. 'Have you any idea what it's like hereabouts? Have you? A bit of gossip, and they gather like hounds round a fox.'

Lilian sniffed. 'Much the same as it is down London, I should say. There's idle talk wherever you go.'

'And how am I going to face it on my own?' asked Ellen, her voice still low. 'When your girls take over the businesses and I'm left without a penny to my name? What about Theresa and Marie? Do I just tell them I'm sorry, that there was a mistake and they've worked all them years in them shops for nowt? Is that what I'm supposed to do?'

'No! Use your brain, woman! I've not much time left, but I'll use what little I do have to get some sense into you.

Listen. You tell your neighbours that Billy and I were divorced and that he never told you about me. If he had told you, you wouldn't have married a divorced man, not with your religion. My girls think I'm divorced anyway. Look at me, Ellen! He stole my money, money that was left to me. That money would have gone to my girls, but it didn't – it went to yours.'

'They worked for it—'

'I know that. So as far as I can see, it's all equal. My girls have a right to inherit because the money was mine. Yours have rights because they've earned them. All I ask is that you look after my daughters.'

There followed a short pause. Ellen pushed a lock of hair from her heat-dampened forehead, then bent to toss the rest of the clippings on to the fire. 'Aren't they old enough to see to themselves?' she asked eventually.

Lilian pushed herself up the pillows and coughed painfully. The disease was in her lungs now, and she had not much breath left in her. 'Abigail's approaching twenty-one, not long qualified as a nurse,' she said throatily. 'Head full of boys and what to wear, but she's a good girl at heart, even though she does act hard. And it is an act, believe me. She had a lot to deal with till I sold the house and got a bit of money behind us. Even then, there wasn't much to spare, because I became unfit for work and we were living on capital. And, of course, there was her training to pay for. As for Letticia – we call her Tishy – she's a bit different. She's nineteen, but—'

'But she's not all there,' interrupted Ellen. 'I've noticed she seems to have a chair or two missing. I'm sorry, only I have to speak me mind.'

Lilian grimaced. 'Ellen, she has a severe anaemia. My poor little girl needs attention, a good doctor on hand. As for her mind, well, she's just a bit dreamy, that's all. Plays the piano, writes stories, spends a lot of time being creative.'

'There's no piano here. She'll not get chance to do much music here. What am I expected to do with her? Put her in

47

the shops? She'd never count past sixpence, poor soul. Do I send her to the mill? Ever been in a mill, missus? I couldn't send a dog in there, let alone an ailing girl. You want me to look after your girls once you're dead? Why me? Why not somebody in London? Have you nobody there who'll see them right?'

'No.'

'Oh.' Ellen stirred the embers with an iron poker. 'How did you manage, then? After he left you, like?'

Lilian fixed her eyes on the scullery door and spoke in a low voice. 'I was quite well-born, you know. My father was a tailor, but Mother came from a well-to-do family who turned her out when she became involved with a tradesman. I was their only child.' Her voice trembled slightly. 'Ellen, I was the ugliest thing on two legs. Nobody could understand how my beautiful parents got a freak like me.'

'Stop that, now,' snapped Ellen.

'I am telling the truth. So ugly, I was, that I thought I would never marry. But at least we had our own house, Mother, Father and I. It was willed to my mother by a maiden aunt who liked my father and approved of the marriage. So, when Billy walked out, we struggled for years with me working full-time, then I sold my parents' house and did a few hours' work here and there until my health failed. I am a trained nurse. So is Abigail.'

Ellen crossed the room slowly and perched on the edge of the bed. 'How did you get tied up with Billy?'

'It was after the last war,' said Lilian. 'I was nursing soldiers in Kent. He was one of them. I thought I could manage him. He seemed manageable enough, gassed, most of his stomach missing. A quiet man he was in those days. But the main thing was that he posed no threat.'

'What do you mean?'

Lilian shrugged. 'I trained in London. When I was a student, I was attacked one night by three men. They stole all my money, beat me up . . .'

'And what? Go on, you might as well tell me.'

'It wasn't the robbery that hurt. Or the beating. It was the three of them laughing at me. They stood there poking fun at me because of my appearance. They said things like "imagine waking up to a face like that every morning", and "how many mirrors has your boat race cracked?" Something died in me that night, I suppose it was hope. But I wanted children. I desperately wanted children. When Billy asked me, I knew he was my only chance of a family.'

Ellen reached out and stroked the sweating forehead. 'You poor girl,' she mumbled. 'You poor, poor girl.'

A weak laugh rumbled in Lilian's chest. 'I didn't give him a good life, Ellen. When I had my two children, he was of no further use to me. We worked in Mayfair, looked after a family there. Billy was a jack of all trades, and I looked after Miss Abigail who lived upstairs. I called my first child after her. When she died, she left me all the cash she'd won on the horses – there were drawers full of it. Billy used to put the bets on for her, so I suppose he felt he deserved the legacy just as much as I did. He disappeared with it one night and I've never seen him since.'

'Aye. That's when he came up here, I suppose. Took me in good and proper, he did.'

'I used to threaten him.' The voice from the bed was fading as sleep arrived. 'He was only a shrimp of a man. But he dragged me down, Ellen, turned me into a . . . into a . . . nasty person. I never touched him, but I used to stand there, big as a house, just looking at him. I didn't need to hit him. He knew I could have killed him with one arm fastened behind my back. But I became a shrew . . . a shrew . . .' A gentle snore told Ellen that the sedative drug had taken effect at last. She studied the face on the pillow and decided that it was indeed ugly. Kind, long-suffering, but ugly all the same. Lilian was a giant of a woman, almost six feet tall. It was obvious that she had been fat before the illness had claimed her, because the flesh hung about her in nasty yellow folds. Her hair was lank, straight and of a dull, grey-streaked dark brown, while the eyes were small, black and very deep set. What had Billy seen in such a woman? The answer was obvious and arrived immediately. She was a nurse and could therefore take care of his many maladies. And she had been a woman of property, the sort who would appeal to his terrible greed for ownership.

Ellen dragged herself back to the fire and sat staring into its orange depths. Although the room was stifling, she shivered as she thought about what the man she had called her husband had done. Coming up to Bolton, pretending he had never been married, going with her for instruction at church, buying the shops and the houses with money that wasn't his, drinking, swearing, beating her half to death.

What was she going to do now? If he didn't come back here after his convalescence, the neighbours really would begin to talk. Yes, she knew what it was like to be talked about, because her own next door neighbour was a victim of gossip. Seven children Vera Shaw had, some of whom were reputedly not her husband's. So bad had the gossip become that Ellen, taking pity on the poor woman, had started making deliveries to the back door in order to save Mrs Shaw from having to visit the shops.

Would she be the next in line for the wagging tongues? Oh, she could hear them now – 'Did you know he had another wife?' and 'Them girls of Ellen Langden's is bastards' or, worse still, 'She knew he was already married, took him for his money. Fancy her going through a church wedding with a bigamist.' Yes, it was going to be tough. Her mouth hardened into a thin straight line as she considered her options for the future. Perhaps Lilian was right, perhaps the best thing would be to pretend that there had been a divorce years ago, a divorce Ellen hadn't known about. After all, Billy was a protestant and protestants went in for divorce and suchlike.

She stood up and looked at herself in the mirror over the range, standing on tip-toe in order to achieve a sight of herself. At four feet and eleven inches, Ellen was smaller than her daughters, tiny, blonde and still quite pretty. Her hair was naturally curly, so she had no need to encase it nightly in steel curlers or tied rags. Now forty-one years of age, she retained the bearing of a younger woman, though how she had managed to remain so upright she could never understand. For years he had kept her subdued by threatening her physical safety and that of her children. He was a cruel man, a criminal. And she had been an almighty fool.

Ellen glanced at the snoring intruder. How much had Lilian done to make him so violent, so hard? When he beat Ellen, was he really hitting back at Lilian? Or was he reliving the childhood he so seldom spoke of? She stared again at the mirror. Round blue eyes gazed back at her. She was an attractive woman with hardly a line on her face; she could have married any man – certainly a better man.

The door at the bottom of the stairs opened. 'Mam?'

'Marie.' Ellen spoke in a stage whisper. 'What are you doing up at this time? Aren't you meeting the milk cart in the morning? Two churns we want for Deane Road, don't forget. And I hope you haven't woke the others.'

Marie sidled into the room. At sixteen, she was a pretty girl, with blue eyes that were brighter than her mother's, dark curly hair and a round, mischievous face. But there was none of the usual cheekiness in her expression on this occasion. 'I've been talking to Abigail,' she said. 'And I've got it all out of her. Me dad was married before. Did you know that?'

Ellen shook her head, unsure of how to reply.

'But you can't be married twice, can you? Except if your first wife dies.'

'They were . . . divorced.'

'Oh.'

'And I knew nothing about it.'

'Divorce is a sin,' pronounced Marie. 'I hate my dad. I hated him before, but now I hope he never comes home.

Abigail says she owns our shops and our houses. All these weeks they've been here and she's kept that to herself. Only now, she's gone and lost her temper and told me everything just because I touched her lipstick. She says we'll all have to leave or pay her rent once her mam's dead. Is it true?'

'I don't know.'

'But . . . but why didn't you tell us who they were? Why did you keep saying they were friends of Dad's? If they're my stepsisters . . .'

'Half-sisters.'

'Well, whatever they are, you should have told us. Our Theresa doesn't know, she's asleep. But Abigail's all cock-a-hoop with it, how she's going to get her own back on me dad for divorcing her mother and making off with the money. Will I have to go in the mill?'

'No. I don't know. Look, this lady is very seriously ill and—'

'Abigail says she's got cancer.'

'Then she probably has.'

'Abigail's a nurse.'

'Yes.'

'Abigail says—'

'Shut up with what Abigail says!' Ellen craned her neck towards her daughter. 'Abigail doesn't know her manners, I can tell you that much. And her mother is having a visit tomorrow from a lawyer. It's not up to Abigail, any of this. Mrs . . .' She waved her hand at the sleeping woman, still uncertain of what to call her. 'Mrs Langden and I will decide what's what. Us and the lawyer fellow. You can tell Abigail to keep her thoughts to herself for now. It's not up to her, any of it. Now, get up them stairs, or you'll be fit for nothing in the morning, miss.'

Marie turned to leave, then whispered over her shoulder, 'Mam, what are you going to do about Dad?'

'Eh?'

'Well, you're not really married, are you?'

Ellen gritted her teeth. 'We will be.'

Marie stopped in her tracks. 'What? You'll have him back? After he's beaten you with the brush and kicked you when he was drunk?'

'Yes.' But it would be on her own terms, oh yes . . .

'You can't.' Marie faced her mother. 'This is your chance to get rid of him.'

'No.'

'But, Mam . . .'

'Bed,' said Ellen without raising her voice. But then Ellen never raised her voice. Yet Marie noticed a new edge to her tone, a steeliness that had never been apparent before. Recognizing that her mam meant business, the girl left the room, closing the stairway door quietly in her wake.

Ellen Langden spent the whole night in the horsehair rocker, occasionally rising from fitful sleep to soothe Lilian whenever the pain became unbearable. Lilian ranted and raved each time she woke, telling Ellen about her childhood and how happy it had been, recalling how her mother had died beneath the hooves of a bolting horse, reminiscing about her father's subsequent depression. 'He was never the same again after Mother died. Senile dementia, the doctor said, though my father was a very young man. Six months he lived without Mother. I nursed him. When he was gone, I went to train at the hospital . . .'

Great tears of pity coursed down Ellen's cheeks as the story unfolded. To be born ugly was not a crime, but to be treated as ugly was criminal. 'If I could have looked like you,' said Lilian more than once. 'If I could have been normal, an ordinary size . . .'

'Stop it. God loves you.'

'I doubt it. Will you look after Tishy? Will you?'

'Yes.'

'And the lawyer will come tomorrow?'

'He will. And tomorrow's today now. It's nearly four o'clock in the morning.'

'Ellen?'

53

'What?'

'I think I've wet the bed again. I'm sorry, so very sorry.'

'That's all right. No need to apologize.'

'Put me in hospital. Get rid of me as soon as you can.'

'No, I won't. Now sit up while I change your nightie.'

'You're a good woman. Should have been a nurse.'

Ellen sighed loudly as she struggled to move the heavy woman. 'I'm not good, Lilian. Not any more. I've one or two things to say to that husband of ours, things he won't like. When I've finished with him, he won't know whether he's fish or fowl. In fact, he'll probably put that many miles between us, he'll meet me again coming the other way round the globe. I've not done with him yet, lass. In fact, I've hardly started.'

Lilian laughed tiredly. 'There's something about you, Ellen. I can see you're not the type to lose your temper, but I wouldn't like to be on the receiving end of your anger. I don't care what you do to him, as long as you look after my girls. Especially Tishy.'

Ellen sorted out the bed, put the soiled linen in the scullery to soak, then went to stand in the freezing back yard for a few moments. It was good to be alone, even for a short while. If only Lilian hadn't come! Then life could have carried on the same . . . No! Life had not been good, had it? Lilian had given Ellen a chance to get the better of him, to put him in his place and keep him there. And, after all, facts were facts. Even if Ellen had never found out, Lilian and her daughters would have existed all the same.

When morning came, Ellen riddled out the ashes, emptied the pan and stirred the fire to new life, this time using coal as fuel. Lilian smiled ruefully from the bed. 'It's not liver for dinner again, is it?'

'Eh?'

'That nearly raw liver you gave me yesterday.'

'Oh. Your Abigail says it's good for you.'

Lilian's tiny black eyes twinkled. 'It was horrible. And

so undercooked that a good veterinarian could have got it back on its feet. I hate raw meat.'

Ellen smiled. That such a sick woman could make jokes was a source of great wonder to her, as was the sudden realization that she liked Lilian. Yes, she liked Lilian a lot.

Cedric Wilkinson had remained a bachelor for one very good reason. He had, for some considerable time, been head over heels in love with the woman whose name used to be Ellen O'Hara. This unrequited passion of his had been a source of great confusion in his life, because he knew Billy London's history. He had stood by like a great spineless oaf while Billy had left one wife and taken another. For this weakness, Cedric had never forgiven himself.

Mind, he hadn't always loved Ellen. He'd only started to love her after the illegal marriage had taken place and, at first, he had thought that what he felt for Ellen was pity. After all, he had met the first wife in London, so he was bound to feel sorry for the bigamist's victims.

But his feelings for Billy's second wife grew and grew until he could scarcely contain them. In his wallet, he carried a wedding photograph folded in half so that Billy's face did not show. Whenever he was working in the Deane Road or Derby Street areas of Bolton, he would hang around the London Stores until he spotted either Billy or Ellen. If Billy was about, Cedric would know that Ellen would be at the other shop, so he would climb into his little motor van and dash off to buy whatever came into his head. For many months he could only think of asking for firewood, and his back yard shed was filled with several dozen wired bundles of cut sticks.

For a reason Cedric could not fully comprehend, he avoided Billy like the plague, hadn't seen him for years, not to talk to. Perhaps he had, without knowing it, been afraid of facing up to Billy, of telling him that bigamy was wrong and that Ellen was too good for such treatment. Yes, he felt uneasy about Billy London, sensed somehow that there was something unsavoury, even threatening, about the small shopkeeper.

Cedric was a tall man, well-built and strong, yet as gentle as the proverbial lamb. There was nothing remarkable about his face except for the fact that he blushed easily and had large green eyes with long dark lashes that swept his cheeks whenever he blinked. As is the way with most shy people, he blinked frequently, and was generally known at work as the draught-maker. 'You could sweep the floor with them eyelashes, Ced,' the girls in the office would say, smiles broadening as he blushed a deep pink right to the roots of his thinning brown hair.

Cedric was happiest on the road where, between industrial painting and maintenance jobs, he found a degree of solitude that suited his modest and rather introvert personality. Because he worked on many government projects, including hangars and munitions buildings, he was given a van and a generous petrol allowance, together with as much green paint as he could find a sensible use for.

But such benefits were suddenly a nuisance, because he found himself in a difficult position in January 1942. He was expected to drive to Blackpool, pick up Billy, escort him back to Bolton, then allow the man to live with him until further notice. As this strange request had come from a branch of the War Office, Cedric knew that he could not ignore it. And, conscientious chap that he was, he probably would not have ignored it whatever the circumstances.

He was an uneasy man. No way could he find it in himself to pick up Billy without talking to Ellen first. Talking to Ellen was not easy for Cedric. Words would form in his throat, sensible words that just wouldn't come out of his mouth in her presence. Even the weather was a subject that defied discussion when he entered the shops, which was how he had come to finish up with a shed full of firewood. 'Two bundles, please,' seemed to be the full extent of his vocabulary when he visited Deane Road or Derby Street.

So what was he going to do today, Sunday 25 January? Was he going to sit here on Noble Street for ever while the world twitched its curtains? He sighed heavily. Perhaps he should have gone to the shop yesterday when it had been open; perhaps he should have travelled straight to Blackpool without seeing Ellen. But no, he couldn't have discussed this situation in a full shop any more than he could have set off for Blackpool without fully understanding why. He would have to talk to her, really talk. The thought terrified him, made him sweat in spite of the cold. With unsteady hands, he opened the van door and stepped on to the pavement. His fingers still shook as he raised the knocker of number nine.

Theresa answered the door. She was his favourite twin simply because she looked like her mother, petite, blonde and soft-featured. She had a limp, did little Theresa, something to do with a fall when she had been a baby, but she was a beauty. He removed his flat cap and kneaded it nervously into a tight ball. 'Is your mam at home?'

'Yes, she's in the back kitchen. Do you want to come in out of the cold?'

He hesitated for a moment. 'Er . . . yes. Thanks. Yes.'

Theresa led him through the vestibule and down the narrow lobby. She was walking quite well today, thought Cedric as he shambled along behind her. 'Mam,' she called. 'It's Mr Wilkinson.'

As soon as he entered the room, Cedric recognized the woman in the bed. Before he could check himself, his jaw had dropped to allow a single word to fall several inches above Theresa's head. 'Lily!' he gasped.

Ellen turned from the range and stared hard at the man in the doorway. With her elbow, she slammed shut the oven door before placing a steaming pie on the table. 'Come in,' she said softly. 'Theresa, go in the front room with the others. I think Mr Wilkinson's got some explaining to do.'

When the door had closed behind Theresa, Cedric found that he could not take his eyes off the woman in the bed. Although she must have lost half her weight, this was without a doubt Billy's first wife. 'What's happened, lass?' he finally managed. 'What's up with you?'

'Cancer,' came the flat reply. 'And I never thought I'd see you again, Cedric. Though I did wonder how much you knew when the detective traced Billy to Bolton. Were you in on his plan?'

'Eh?' He dropped his cap, bent to retrieve it, then caught his head on a corner of the table as he straightened. 'I was in on nothing, me.'

'He always was clumsy,' sighed Lilian. 'He was the same when he stayed with us in London back in the twenties. Every time he came in from work, he fell over the furniture.'

Cedric looked from one to the other, flinching slightly as he caught Ellen's questioning stare. 'I never . . . I didn't . . . I mean . . .'

'Sit down,' said Ellen. 'And don't ask me for a bundle of firewood.'

He perched on the edge of a straight-backed chair near the table.

'Well?' Ellen leaned forward. 'Did you know about this mess, Cedric Wilkinson?'

'I did and I didn't,' he mumbled almost inaudibly.

'Eh?'

'Not till it were too late. There were nowt I could do, Ellen. Like, I knew he were a wrong one, only it weren't my business. At least, I didn't think, I mean I never . . .' His nerve deserted him, and he sank into silence, cheeks glowing with guilt and embarrassment.

'I see.' She placed herself in the chair opposite his. 'How could you let him do it, lad? How could you just stand back while he did this to me and Lilian? You knew he was already wed, didn't you? Didn't you?'

He nodded mutely.

'And you never said a word to me. Mind, you've never said much, have you?'

He forced himself to look at her. 'I couldn't . . . hurt

you. I did ask him once if he'd got one of them divorces, but he just laughed at me. And,' he gulped hard. 'The twins came so quick after you got wed – I just hoped you'd never find out. I were mixed up in me mind, lass.'

Ellen tutted her impatience. 'You big, soft, gormless lump. A word, that was all it needed. Just one word from you, and I'd never have married him. We're putting it about that he was secretly divorced, but you could have saved me a lot of pain. And Lilian too, and the four girls. Why didn't you speak up?'

'I don't know. At first, it was because of Billy. It doesn't do to get on the wrong side of him. Then, later on, after you were married . . .'

'Go on,' said Ellen. 'Spit it out.'

The clock on the mantelpiece ticked loudly while Cedric blushed more brightly than ever. His head drooped dolefully.

Lilian coughed. 'He didn't want to harm you, Ellen. He didn't want to harm you because – well – look at him. The poor man loves you. It's written all over him.'

Ellen remained motionless. 'I know all about that, thank you. For years he's been coming in the shops for no reason at all, always buying from me, forever getting stuff I'm sure he didn't need. I've watched him falling over doorsteps for long enough, I can tell you that. But if he cares about me, Lilian, why didn't he save me from all this? It makes no sense. Mind you, the day Cedric makes sense, I'll hang flags out.'

Cedric stared at the tablecloth, fixing his eyes about an inch away from the salt and pepper pots. They were talking about him as if he weren't there, as if he were a brick or two short of a load. And he wasn't, he knew he wasn't! With a supreme effort of will, he raised his large head. 'I didn't always care, Ellen. It was something that came on with the years.'

'Like arthritis,' interspersed the voice from the bed.

Cedric and Ellen stared at one another. Then suddenly, for no apparent reason, Ellen smiled at him. 'It's not your fault, lad,' she whispered. 'But you should have done something about it, shouldn't you?'

'Aye. Aye, I should. Only what do I do now?'

'What about?'

He cleared his throat. 'I'm supposed to go and pick him up from this Maybank Rest Home in Blackpool. They reckon he wants to come and live with me because you won't have him back.'

Ellen's smile remained fixed on her face. 'Oh, I'll have him back all right. You bring him here, Cedric. Let him live with both his wives, let him reap the harvest at last. Fetch him, I've nothing to be ashamed of. We've committed no crime, me and Lilian.'

He gulped loudly, his Adam's apple moving several inches up and down his throat. 'You what? Fetch him back here to Lilian and you? What about your daughters?' His tongue was suddenly loosened by the strength of his emotions. 'What'll you tell the kiddies? Nay, you can't live in a house together, all of you. What will folk think? What will the priest say? It's not right.'

Ellen folded her arms and tilted her head to one side as she studied him. 'It never was right, but it's none of our doing. I can't very well turn Lilian out the way she is. As for the neighbours and the church, they'll be able to see Billy for what he is. We're doing nowt wrong. All I'm doing is helping a dying woman. All she's doing . . .' Ellen tilted her head towards Lilian, 'is lying down and keeping as comfortable as she can. What's wrong with that? Well? Have you got an answer?'

'It's just . . . wrong,' he shouted.

'And was it right before? Was it right just because nobody knew about it?' Ellen's face was serious now. 'Hiding something doesn't make it proper, Cedric Wilkinson. Now, go and fetch him. Tell him if he doesn't come back here, he'll have no income, that'll sort him. There's no savings buried in the cellar now, because I've banked the lot, so he's worth nowt a pound. And make sure he fetches the suit he went in with, because it's the only one he has left and he's getting no more. If he wants clothes, he can pay a bob in the pound every week, same as everybody else. It's all done legal now. If he goes against what me and Lilian want, I shall get him done for bigamy.' She rose and drew herself to full height. 'I'm in charge now, Cedric. The clog's on a different foot this time. Go on. Be quick, he'll be dying to see us both.'

'Are you sure, lass?' She was so beautiful at that moment that he could have died happy just looking at her. She was good and gentle and kind, was his Ellen. Ah yes, and strong too. There was a new side to the little woman, one he hadn't seen before. 'What if he kicks up? And there again, this here welfare man told me to take him to my house.'

Lilian reached out a hand and pointed at Cedric. 'You heard what she said. Bring him here. I want to see the man who walked out on me and two children. And Ellen wants to look at him too. She wants a word with the chap that ruined her life. Go on. What are you waiting for?'

He struggled to his feet, dragging half the tablecloth with him. With his face aflame, he righted the cloth and made for the door. 'I'll see you later, then,' he said lamely.

'Just drop him at the door, Cedric,' said Ellen. 'There'll be goings-on here that won't be fit for a bachelor's ears. I'll see you when you run out of firewood, about next Christmas.'

After he had left, Ellen called the four girls into the kitchen. They stood in a line in front of the dresser, Marie and Theresa together near the scullery door, Abigail alone by the dresser mirror, Tishy lingering near the hallway. 'Your father's coming home,' announced Ellen. 'Even though he's divorced from Lilian, he is still the father of all of you. He didn't divorce his children—'

'I wish he would,' interrupted Marie. 'I wish he'd take a running jump into the cut.'

'Quiet.' Ellen's voice was not raised as she admonished her daughter. 'We have to get on as best we can. You'll be living here from now on, Abigail and Tishy. You'll be living with your father.'

Abigail sniffed. 'I'll be living in the nurses' home when I get a job. If they've got a room, that is. If they haven't, I shall make my own arrangements.' She looked down her narrow nose as if assessing everybody and finding them wanting. 'I am quite capable of managing my own life, thank you,' she finished crisply.

Everyone looked at Abigail, so she preened herself almost unconsciously, running her fingers through the dense blackness of long wavy hair. She was not a pretty girl, but it was obvious that she believed in making the best of herself. There was powder and rouge on her narrow face, while her legs were made up with tanning lotion even though she was not preparing to go out. They hadn't been out at all since arriving, yet this hardfaced girl put on full make-up every morning. Ellen didn't like her, couldn't take to her at all. She shivered as she stared at the girl, realizing what it was about her that was unattractive. Yes, that was it. She had her father's thin lips and beakish nose; she seemed to have his nastiness too.

'Your mother would like you to stay with us,' she said. 'And there's your sister to think of.'

Abigail let out a bray of laughter. 'Tishy? No need to think about her. She's in a world of her own, a law unto herself. She doesn't need me.'

Ellen turned her attention to the younger of Lilian's girls. 'Will you live with us, Tishy?'

Tishy gazed solemnly round the room, her eyes resting on each occupant in turn. She was a stunningly beautiful girl, thin to the point of transparency, with large soft blue-grey-violet eyes and hair of rich, deep auburn. 'Is Mum really going to die?' she asked.

Lilian nodded slowly.

'Gone for ever,' said Tishy to no-one in particular. 'Yes, I shall stay here if I can have a piano. There is space in the other room. May I have a piano, Mum?'

Lilian took a deep breath. 'Yes. There's money for a piano if Ellen and your father will have one in the house.'

'We'll have one.' Ellen's chin was raised defiantly as she made this sudden decision.

Marie stepped forward, her round face creased into a deep frown. 'I don't want him back,' she declared bluntly.

Ellen smiled. She was always the first with a plain statement, was Marie. Firstborn of the twins, first to walk and talk, first to scream for her own way. 'He's got to come back, he's your father.'

Marie pouted, thought for a moment, then said, 'It's a sin. Like I said before, divorce is a sin. If you have him back, you'll have to tell in confession.'

Lilian spoke up then. 'Your mother and father will get married again, Marie. It's all connected with your Catholicism, so I don't completely understand it. But once I'm dead, your mother will get her union re-sanctified. That will be the best thing for everyone.'

Marie faced her mother squarely. 'Will it? Are you going to let him carry on walking over us like he has these past years? Our Theresa's terrified of him, frightened to death, she is.'

Theresa reached out to restrain her twin, pulling her back against the huge mahogany dresser. 'Don't, Marie,' she whispered. 'I'll be all right.'

'We'll all be all right,' declared Ellen. 'Things are going to be very different around here from now on. Tishy and Abigail will be here for a start, living here as Billy's daughters. And there won't be any nonsense, not from anybody.' She stared for a long time at her younger daughter, the one who had struggled into the world ten minutes after Marie. They were twins, yet they had different birthdays, one born at five minutes to midnight, the other at five minutes past the hour. It was as if Theresa had held back all her life, right from the start, right from the day she was born. Ever the appeaser, the peacemaker, the drier of Marie's tears. Yes. It was time for them all to stand up for themselves, especially Theresa.

'We are going to have our meal now.' Ellen reached some plates from the top of the range. 'Then we shall wait for your father. When he arrives, I want you four to stay in the front room. Lilian and I have some business to discuss with him.'

'I should think so,' said Abigail. 'After all, it was our money he used to buy his shops.'

Ellen faced the girl squarely, wiping the plates with a tea towel as she spoke. 'We've worked for our share, Abigail. My girls have been dogsbodies ever since they could walk and talk, so don't be thinking you can have it all back just because you're his eldest. It will all be fair and above board, madam, so put that in your pipe and smoke it.'

Abigail opened her mouth to make a quick retort, but Lilian managed to get in first. 'Abigail, you're him all over again. Please don't be greedy. Please don't try to take from Theresa and Marie what is rightfully theirs. And look after your sister. You're a good nurse, a clever girl. How can you be so hard? How can you spend your life caring for the sick and still remain cold?' She turned to Ellen. 'She's a match for him,' she whispered under her breath. 'More than a match.'

Abigail bit hard on her lower lip, squashing the pain in her chest. She knew how she looked, she knew she was coming over as a real bitch. This was how she'd got through, by hitting back at life and all its occupants. The mother she loved was dying. Somebody should pay for all the pain, restitution should be made. She sniffed, tightened the belt of her blue frock, and stared without expression into the fire.

The girls sat at the table and ate pie and peas while Ellen fed Lilian her broth. The two women watched the group at the table, listened to the awful silence in the room, a deep and resentful quiet that was broken only by the clatter of cutlery on plates. They were so different from one another, these four girls. Marie with her round bright face, Theresa looking like a frightened rabbit searching for a hole to bolt into. And Abigail was already a bitter young woman, very much her father's daughter. Then there was poor Tishy, Tishy who was special and beautiful in a terrifyingly ethereal way.

When the girls had left the room, Ellen sat at the table and ate her own dinner. The food seemed to stick in her throat, and she had to make a conscious physical effort to push it down her dry gullet.

Lilian had dozed off again, leaving Ellen completely alone with all her terrible worries. What would it be like with all the girls living here and without Lilian to act as a buffer on the less pleasant occasions? It wasn't going to be easy. Marie had been used to ruling the roost over her twin, but now she would be forced to bow down to the very superficial superiority of Abigail. Marie already hung on the older girl's every word, and Ellen did not relish the idea of offering shelter to someone who would lead her own child astray. Then there was Tishy with her little bits of drawings and senseless poems, Tishy who sang in the middle of the night just because she felt like it. How would quiet little Theresa get the attention she deserved with such a queer soul in the house?

Ellen sighed heavily as she washed the dishes in the scullery. He was coming back; he was on his way at this very minute. Even with the London people in the house, life had been quieter and easier without him.

With cool deliberation, she raised her chin, dried her hands, then went to sit in the kitchen rocker. She worked on her fears, calmed herself by placing her faith where it belonged, in the hands of the Lord. From a nail by the fireplace, she lifted her father's rosary, a pretty chain of jet beads with a crucifix of real silver attached. Her mouth moved as she spoke her prayers inwardly. God was on her side. God, the Blessed Virgin and all the saints. Surely London had little power against such formidable troops?

Oh yes, it would be different from now on. She had his measure this time, she could manage him. What had Lilian said? 'I married him because he was manageable.' Lilian was right. Armed with the right implements, any normal soul could win hands down over a bully.

And Ellen was armed.

CHAPTER THREE

Homecoming

By the time Cedric Wilkinson reached Blackpool and found the Maybank Rest Home for Retired Servicemen, he was in as much of a temper as he was capable of generating. He cursed and swore, first under his breath, then, as he neared his target, more and more loudly until he was shouting a few choice expletives every few seconds or so. He wasn't normally given to displays of passion, even when alone, so his solitary ramblings and yellings gave rise to much blushing. Fortunately, there was little traffic on the road and few people were about to witness his very visible discomfort.

But the more he thought about the situation, the more angry and frustrated he became. He couldn't help her. He could do nothing for 'his' Ellen. The thought that his beloved should be subjected to such pain, misery and shabby treatment set his nerves on edge. And a lot of it was his fault too, so the guilt sat heavily on tense shoulders as he hunched his body over the steering wheel. He ground teeth and gears noisily and simultaneously, drove with two wheels on the pavement on several occasions, turned left when he ought to have turned right, and found himself gripping the wheel so tightly that his knuckles had turned blue with tension before he'd even reached Preston. And he needed to be quick, had to be back in Bolton before it got dark.

As a trip to Blackpool involved a journey lasting a couple of hours each way, there wasn't much time for pleasantries when he reached the convalescent home. He simply grunted a less than affable hello to the matron, picked up Billy's brown paper parcel of bits and pieces, then marched out to the van. It was only then, when they were both seated, that Cedric gave himself a chance to look at his companion. 'Bloody hell,' he said, unable to stop himself from making a comment as the engine shuddered to life. 'You look like you've been dragged through the privets feet first and with your head strapped in a bucket. What happened?'

Billy took a Woodbine from a paper packet of five and lit it slowly, enjoying the luxury of his first puff in weeks. 'I got done over,' he replied at last. 'Beaten up by three big bleeders with size thirteen boots.'

Cedric drove in silence for a while until he found his way back to the main Preston road. As ever, he needed to think what to say – it was no use opening his gob and coming out with a lot of senseless rubbish. He cleared his throat several times while he pondered. 'We're not going to my house,' he managed at last. 'Ellen says you've to go straight back home.'

'Did she now?' This rhetorical question was delivered with the air of a man who couldn't have cared less, yet Billy's anxiety was almost a tangible entity, so clearly did it show in the twisting of his hands. After throwing his cigarette end through the open window, he immediately grabbed for the packet and lit another.

'Aye.' With great effort, Cedric held the van steady. 'They're both there, her and Lily. Lily's been took bad ways, looks as though she might be on her last legs. Got a right shock when I saw her, I can tell you. It's some kind of cancer. I reckon she'll not be with us for long.'

'Not before time, bad bitch. I should have hammered her while I had the chance. Knocked hell out of me, she did. It was like being run over by a steamroller, getting thumped by that fat slob.'

This was too much for Cedric. The vehicle slewed to a crooked halt as he slammed his foot hard on the brake. And suddenly, miraculously, his tongue was loosened.

Looking straight ahead through the windscreen, the large man spat out words that expressed the contempt, the hatred and the jealousy he had felt for more than sixteen years.

Like Ellen, he did not raise his voice even in anger, yet the bitterness was plainly audible. 'Long enough I've held back, Billy London. Aye, London they call you and London you are, a wide boy from the big bad city – and a bully. A bully and a bloody coward, that's you to a T. Spivs I think they call your type.

'I never liked you, not from the start. You were a wicked bugger even in them days when you lived with poor Lily. Supposed to be grateful, was she? Because she was so big and plain? And I know she never hit you. Forced herself not to hammer you, she did, because she used to talk to me about it. "Cedric," she said, "if I start on him, I'll kill him." Lily had too much sense to clobber you. I only wish I'd done it for her. She's a good woman, is Lily, too good for your likes. And as for Ellen – why did you marry her when you were already wed? And why didn't I bloody stop you?' He paused for breath, but no answers came from his passenger.

'It's for Ellen's sake I've come, not for yours. As far as I'm bothered, they could have left you locked up in that home for the rest of your life, only she wants you back. They both want you back, so that's where you're going.'

At last Billy spoke. 'You can't take me there. It wouldn't be right.'

'Would it not?' What had Ellen said? Something about things not being made proper just by staying hidden? Oh, he would work it out in a minute. 'You're going back to Noble Street,' he pronounced. 'It's a mess of your own making, is this, and you can just bloody well get it cleaned up. It's nowt to do with me. I hope the pair of them put you in prison where you belong. They can, you know.' He nodded sagely. 'Aye, they can put you away and swallow the key if they're so minded.'

After speaking for more consecutive minutes than he

had managed in years, Cedric leaned back and closed his weary eyes. It was hard going, this conversation business, especially if you got a bit worked up about things. And he couldn't help being worked up about Ellen. But at times like this, which were fortunately few and far between, he realized why he'd never gone in much for discussions and the like. It was all giving him a headache. Why, he'd sooner paint two aircraft hangars and a munitions factory any day. Even if he was getting a bit fed up with green paint.

'Right then. What are we waiting for?' asked Billy. 'Are we going to sit here till it gets dark? And I thought you was my mate. All these years I thought you was on my side—'

'Then you thought wrong. I just kept me mouth shut, that's all. And I wish I hadn't. I wish I'd told Ellen what you were up to sixteen or seventeen years ago. Any road, I've nowt more to say to you, nowt that won't keep. I'll drop you off on Deane Road. I think you can find your own way from there.' Yes, even when drunk, this rat always found its way to its nest.

The remainder of the long journey was accomplished in terrible silence. Billy, feeling more than a little sorry for himself, sniffed a few times in the hope that Cedric would puncture the quiet with a remark or two, but nothing was forthcoming. After a while, he gave up the sniffing. The smell of paint and turpentine was not suitable for inhalation in short, sharp gasps. Not for a man who'd been severely gassed while fighting for king and country.

Dusk was beginning its rapid descent as Billy was deposited at the Deane Road end of Noble Street. He stood on the corner clutching his packages to his chest, watching with narrowed eyes as the little black van disappeared leaving a trail of grey exhaust emission in its wake. He suddenly felt terribly alone. Alone, miserable and depressed. The nursing home had kept him going somehow, had provided support, routine and company during these past weeks. It hadn't been the best place on earth, but there had been no decisions to make, no real effort required. Now, he was out in the big cold world again, lonely and friendless. He'd never needed friends, never wanted them. Till now.

On the other hand, he wasn't really alone, was he? Oh no, he was worse off than that, much worse. He was over-crowded, bursting at the seams, because they already sat there in his head, Lil and Ellen, two female spiders wait-ing to devour him the minute he stepped into their web. He could feel them waiting, could sense it in his bones. Kids too. He sighed and turned to walk towards his shop. Four girls, four more of the female persuasion sitting in the lair ready to pounce as soon as he put in an appearance.

The shop looked exactly the same as it always had, pale brown blind pulled over the window, a CLOSED sign showing on the door, adverts for Camp Coffee and Nestlé Milk fastened to the brickwork between ground and first floors. The step was stoned clean; even the boot-scraper on the right hand side of the doorway had been rubbed down and painted a bright shiny black. So she seemed to have everything in hand, then. At least she hadn't been letting the business slide. Perhaps life would go back to normal once Lil was off the scene.

He shivered, pulling the darned and patched overcoat over his vulnerable chest. It had been a good coat till that night, the night of the bomb. No. Things could never be the same again, he knew that for certain. She wouldn't take kindly to coming in second, wouldn't Ellen. Catholicism was all about cleaving and keeping to only one woman at a time. Though he had married one at a time, hadn't he? Not like some he'd read about in the papers, men who kept two separate households going for years on end. Still, she wouldn't take it well. It would be rosary beads and holy water for her, the doghouse and public condemnation for him. Why, he might even go to prison like the blokes in the newspapers.

Shaking with cold and fear, he made his way up the back of Noble Street till he reached his own yard. After making sure that no neighbour was about, he bent and put an eye to the latch hole in the back gate. Nothing. The blackout was up at the window and there wasn't the slightest sign of life. He cursed silently, straightened, and began to walk up to Derby Street. Once there, he stood outside his other shop and fished a large bundle of keys from a pocket. It would be warmer inside; perhaps he might be able to think and plan more easily once his brain and his feet had thawed out.

After struggling for several moments, he swore aloud and staggered back from the door. She had changed the locks! Not one of the keys fitted. He had no need to seek better light, no need to try again, because he knew these keys by feel, by instinct. Where could he go? Not home, not yet, not without some sustenance.

A thought struck him. She might not have changed the lock on the back gate. He scurried round the corner and found, to his immense relief, that the key to the gate still fitted. With his breathing fast and shallow, he let himself into the rear yard, pushed open the lavatory door, then wrenched open a small wooden cupboard on the wall above the tippler. It was still there. Behind the caustic soda crystals and donkey stone and chlorine bleach stood his precious bottle of malt, the one he had used to take a nip from after serving difficult customers.

He sank on to the lavatory seat, unscrewed the bottle cap and took a large mouthful. The effect was immediate and gratifying; because his body had been starved of alcohol for so many weeks, the whisky seemed to spin through his bloodstream, making him warmer, calmer and more optimistic.

An hour later, he was still sitting on the lavatory with an empty bottle drooping from loose fingers. Most of his senses seemed to have deserted him. He couldn't see, probably because it was pitch dark, was hearing little, feeling nothing, and thinking in short rapid bursts of what almost amounted to gunfire. He was pickled and he knew it. He was on a cold outside tippler in a cold back yard on a cold January night. This was because of Lil. Lil had come back to haunt him and to destroy the life he had so painstakingly built for himself.

Tears filled his eyes and nose, so he pulled a sleeve across his face. It occurred to him that if any of Billy London's customers could have seen him now, they wouldn't have believed their eyes. Billy London wiping his snotty nose on a disgustingly filthy coat. A sorry state of affairs this was. He retained just about enough intelligence to deduce that he was in what the locals would have called a right state and no mistake.

One thing was eminently clear; he needed to get out of here and into the warm. If he stayed put, he would end up with a case of double pneumonia and a few more weeks in a hospital bed. He paused for thought before standing up. Hospital might be the safest bet. No, he had better get back and face the music. Rather now, with a bellyful of whisky, than later on when a return of faculties would no doubt leave him open to all kinds of pain.

He staggered down Noble Street, head reeling, legs like jelly, right arm using house walls as guidelines. In the gaps between blocks, he stumbled along like a sleepwalker, arms outstretched as he searched for something solid to support him.

At last, he was there. The drink had done its usual job of rising to the surface, causing his skin to flush with sweat which cooled immediately to freezing point as the icy wind surrounded him. On hands and knees, he crawled up four steps to the front door, then collapsed like a heap of rags just as he arrived within inches of safety.

Some thirty minutes later, he lay flat on a vestibule floor, looking for all the world like a tramp on the brink of death from starvation. A head swam in and out of focus a few feet above him. 'Mr London? Is that you?'

He swallowed loudly and painfully. 'I think so.'

Vera Shaw stared down at her next door neighbour. He was in a proper mess, drunk as a lord and with his lovely clothes all gone to rags and pieces. There had been some queer goings-on at number nine, stuff Vera had kept her counsel about. After all, who was she to start chucking the first brick? But the house was full of secretive strangers, while this here fellow had been gone for ages, no sight or sound of him for well over a month.

'Take me in,' groaned the bundle of dirty cloth on the floor. 'Get me warm.'

'Shall I go and fetch your missus?'

'No!' He crawled along the hallway and into the back kitchen while Vera followed, her eyes staring and mouth ajar as she witnessed a vision she had never expected to see, Billy London on his hands and knees, Billy London brought down at last. 'What have I to do?' she asked when she had finally got him stretched out on the filthy food-stained sofa.

'I dunno. Jus' let me sober up.' He hiccuped, belched, then closed his eyes.

Vera stood with her back to the fire, lifting her skirt slightly to allow a little warmth to the backs of her knees. She should get Ellen; she knew she should get Ellen. Yet there was something about this situation, something that made her sense that she might turn it to her own advantage. Drunks had a habit of talking over-much once you got them going. Happen she could squeeze a bit out of him, enough to improve her case when she wanted a bit of extra tick in the London Stores. 'Are you all right?' she ventured.

He snored, snorted, then woke with a jerk. 'What? Who's that?'

'Can I get you summat? A cup of tea, happen a nice mug of cocoa? I think I've got a bit of sugar left.' She rooted aimlessly through a pile of debris on the table. 'And there's a sardine round here somewhere if I can lay me hands on it.'

Billy groaned. He was in Vera Shaw's house. Nobody ever went in Vera Shaw's house if they could help it, nobody decent. She was a slut. Seven children, she had, three fostered out and attending the Lostock Open Air

School, two in the Cottage Homes, another two farmed out with her mother somewhere near Atherton. Her husband, a dozy beggar if ever there was one, worked in the Midlands. He had a heart murmur and a certificate in first aid, so he'd volunteered for ambulance service as far away from Vera as he could get. And he couldn't be blamed for that.

'What the hell am I doing here?' asked the crumpled wreck on the sofa.

'Resting,' came the swift reply.

'Stinks,' he sniffed. 'Like a flaming ash pit in here.'

Vera didn't turn a hair. She didn't go in much for housework, wasn't one for scratching about in corners every day. In fact, she'd lost her children because she wouldn't clean the place up a bit. The Welfare had come and taken them away just because the baby had done a few bits of muck on the floor while he was between nappies and she hadn't got round to shifting it. But she didn't care about people calling her a dirty cow. All she was bothered about was folk saying she was a loose woman. She wasn't loose, just a bit on the easy-going side. 'Where've you been all this while, Mr London? Haven't seen you about since last month. It hasn't been the same without you.' She smiled, displaying an assortment of uneven and discoloured teeth.

'Hospital. Got done over by her brothers.'

'Oh, I see. What for, like?'

''Cos of Lil.'

Vera thought about this for a moment or two. Was Lil the one in the house, her stuck in bed under the back kitchen window? Or was Lil one of them two funny-talking girls she'd heard in the yard on their way to the lav? 'Who's Lil?'

He yawned loudly. 'The wife.'

Vera stared into the near distance, one hand straying upward to touch first the rows of steel curlers at the back of her head, then the four bronze-coloured metal wave-maker clips that sat two each side of her centre parting.

The wife? Wasn't Ellen his wife? A nice enough little body, Ellen, always ready to do a good turn for a neighbour. But a bit of a holy Josephine all the same, one who expected everybody to be as good as a flaming nun. Feeling very confused about who was whose wife, and wondering whose husband Billy really was, Vera knelt on the floor beside the sofa. He was groaning now, and tears of self-pity were beginning to trickle down his cheeks. Beer-tears, Vera called them.

Not drunk enough to stop talking altogether, yet sufficiently inebriated to be careless, Billy pieced together the sad tale of his life as a twice-married man. 'Down London, I married her . . . ugly, big as a house, but she had property . . .' He began to drift again, eyes rolling in dark sockets. 'I'M THE MAN!' he shouted so suddenly that Vera slipped back against the table. 'I'm the man, but she hit me.' He nodded vigorously, convincing himself that this was no fabrication. Lil's words had been sufficient attack – it didn't take much imagination to translate them into action. 'A bleeding woman hit me. Knocked me about murderous . . . just 'cos I enjoy a drink. A man's got to have a drink, see. But she didn't like it, and she let me know about it too.'

'Who did?'

'Eh?'

'Who knocked you about?'

'Lil.'

She tried again. 'Who's Lil?'

'The wife. Didn't I tell you before?'

'Oh. Her in the bed under the window? Is she your wife?'

'I think so.' His head was swimming. Drink, he had been led to believe, was supposed to improve the appearance of a woman. But the more he looked at Vera, the more hideous she became. Though she was swaying about a bit. Perhaps she would look better if she managed to stay still for two minutes together. Her face wavered and became blurred at the edges, almost as if she were under water. He shook his head until his vision cleared slightly. God, what a sight she was. Thin as a rake, dirty red hair encased in curlers, and a terrible squint in her left eye. Was this the one who got all the men? 'You're ugly,' he declared unevenly. 'In a different way from Lil. She's as fat as two pigs, you're too thin. Where's your chest? Did you never get a chest?'

Vera ignored him. If she so chose, she could show him a trick or two that would have him legless, even more legless than he was at this moment. She knew how to go about pleasing a man, and it was nothing to do with looks. 'Listen,' she said with the air of one addressing a child below the age of reason. 'If Lil's your wife, who's Ellen?'

'The wife.'

'So you've got two wives?'

''S right. Glutton for punishment. I got wife number one and wife number two.'

'How come?'

'I dunno. It just happened.'

'I see.' She reached across and lifted a greasy army coat from the floor, draping it across his legs. 'Did you get a divorce from number one?'

'Can't remember. Don't think so. See . . . what's your name?'

'Vera.'

'See, Vera, I had to escape. It was like getting out of prison. We worked for Doctor Wotsisname . . . lemme think . . . Doctor McDade. Mayfair, he lived. Dotty auntie . . . upstairs . . . left us money. Abigail. Aunt Abigail. Called the first daughter . . . I ran off with the cash. Followed Cedric home. Ran away. I had to save myself. I jus' ran and ran and—'

'Away from her. The one who hit you.'

'Yes.' Exhausted, he sagged against the rancid arm rest and fell into a fitful sleep.

Vera pondered for a long time. If this one here had been married to Lil, then the two strange girls were likely his and Lil's. Then he must have come up here, married Ellen and given her the twins. If that was the case, what the hell was Ellen Langden doing giving house room to that lot from London? Mind, she was on the saintly side, was Ellen. It would be just like her to turn the other cheek and open her door to the first wife, especially if the woman was ill. And she must be ill, because she was forever in bed.

Right, what to do now? Should she go next door and tell Ellen that Mr London had come out with it all while under the influence? No. That wouldn't do any good. It'd be like playing her ace before time, using her best card when she could hang on to it for a better purpose.

She would just bide her time, he would wake up in a bit. With any luck, he would have forgotten what had happened, then Vera might use it against him as and when required. She stood up, moved a pile of clothes off the table, then pounced on the stray sardine. Planning always made her hungry. As she chewed on the oily fish, Vera Shaw grinned to herself. She'd have her cake and eat it from now on if she played her hand close to her chest. Cake, biscuits and as many sardines as she wanted.

While Billy London snored in the kitchen of number seven, his four daughters and his two wives waited with ebbing patience in various rooms of number nine. Ellen and Lil occupied the kitchen as always. The girls, who had been relegated for several hours to the relative splendour of the front room, had begun to wander about the house as tension and boredom increased.

Tishy had discovered the cellar and was ensconced there. She liked the dark. Dark was beautiful and secretive, it allowed her to think, to imagine, to be herself or to act out in privacy whichever part suited her at a particular time.

She was currently wrestling with the idea that her mother was going to die. Death, for Tishy, was connected with starlings and stray dogs. She'd kept a pet starling for a while in London. The poor broken-winged creature had loved her, had sat on her foot whenever and wherever she

77

walked, and had depended on her for food and mothering. When he had died, there had been a lavish funeral service in the garden, involving cups of pretend tea served from a dolls' teapot, wreaths of dandelion and buttercup and some real ham sandwiches. The starling was suddenly gone for ever. That was what Lilian had said, 'He is gone for ever.' The same thing had happened to the bedraggled old mongrel they had taken in. A box, a few flowers, some singing of sad songs, a wooden cross above his grave and Mother saying again, 'Gone for ever.'

Tishy sat very still in the blackness, trying hard to imagine life without her mum. For ever was a long time, for ever never ended. She would have to live here in this house with Ellen and a man called Father, a man she couldn't remember. There'd be Marie and Theresa too, of course. She liked them. Marie was jolly and bouncy, Theresa was sweet and kind and generous with her toffee ration. Then there was Abigail, Abigail with the sharp tongue and those sharper fingers that often nipped and pinched tender parts of Tishy whenever Abigail was annoyed. She was often annoyed. Mum, that large gentle soul who had been the hub of Tishy's universe, never got angry, not with her younger daughter. The sympathy, the tenderness, the love – all these would be gone soon. Gone for ever.

The cellar door creaked open. 'Are you in here, Tishy? Tishy? Answer me.'

Tishy froze in her corner, shrinking even further into deep shadow.

'I know you're in there. Come out, or I'll lock you in with the ghost. He's a big dark man, a coal spirit, one of the miners who died digging under the ground.' Abigail's tone was sinister yet amused at the same time. 'He'll jump out and eat you.'

'Don't be silly.'

'Ah, so you are there. I thought so. Find the darkest corner and you'll find my little sister. We're supposed to be upstairs waiting for Daddy-Dear. That's what I've decided to call him because he obviously loves us so much.

He was due back hours ago. Come out, I won't hurt you.'

Tishy crept out and immediately bumped into her sister who quickly dealt her an angry blow in the ribs. 'Why don't you look where you're going?'

'How can I look when I can't see? It's too dark to see.'

Abigail hit out again, this time to the shoulder. 'Then what are you doing in a place where you can't see?' She hated herself for the way she spoke to Tishy, yet she couldn't seem to help it. The girl annoyed her thoroughly, making her angry with herself, guilty too for losing her temper with someone so vulnerable. She was a nurse and she ought to know better . . .

'Thinking.'

'About what?'

'What it will be like after Mum's gone for ever.'

Abigail dragged her sister towards the stone steps. 'It'll be bloody miserable, that's how it'll be. I want to go back to London, but we have to stay to make sure we get our share.'

'Share?'

'Of the shops.'

Tishy thought about this. 'How do you divide a shop into shares? Do you chalk lines like a hopscotch?'

'Stop being stupid. You know you're not really stupid, so don't pretend. There'll be no point in acting the fool once Mother's gone. You'll get no attention from anyone here. To divide a shop, you sell it and take your money.'

'Ah. Then I can have a piano.'

Abigail wondered for the millionth time how she came to have a strange sister like this one. 'You and your piano. Can't you think of anything else? Don't you want a nice husband and a nice house? Or to travel round the world?' Did Tishy want or need any of the normal things? Oh, if only Abigail could treat her own sister better!

'No.' The voice was low and sad. 'I just want Mum.'

'Mother's dying and that's a fact, something we can't change. I feel it too, Tishy. I don't want my mother to die.' Yes, she did feel it, though she seldom let it show.

Abigail's main aim in life was to hide her emotions. She didn't understand why, but it was somehow important that people did not know her properly. She would be strong come what may; she would never wear her heart in a position that might expose it to damage. But she must, she really must try to be kinder to Tishy.

'Have some pride,' she said now, achieving a gentler tone. 'Remember when we were children? Everybody used to taunt us about having no father. Well, I stood up to people, pretended he was dead or some sort of war hero in a special hospital. You didn't. You were Mother's echo, weren't you? "He left us, my mum has to work because he left us." That was why I used to get so angry with you, Tishy, because you had no pride. You still have none.'

'Ellen says you're hard-faced,' remarked the younger girl as she was dragged unceremoniously up the steps. 'I heard her telling Mummy. And she says you paint your face and legs like a trumpet.'

'Strumpet. The word is strumpet, and I'm hardly one of those. What else was said?'

Tishy thought for a moment or two. 'Mum says that you were never nice, you were always a bit nasty like Bill – that's our father. She said you broke my toys deliberately so that I'd have nothing to play with. You're expected to be a bad influence on Marie.'

'Am I really? We'll have to see what I can do about that, then.' They emerged into the hall. Tishy wandered off to the 'best room' at the front of the house while Abigail stamped upstairs. From the kitchen, Lilian and Ellen listened. 'If she gets too much for you, you must send her away,' sighed Lilian. 'She probably wants to go anyway. Let her find a job somewhere else, somewhere with accommodation.'

Ellen said nothing. Her dislike for the mean-faced girl was growing by the day, and Ellen didn't admire herself for it. It was bound to happen, she supposed, with six females living in such close proximity for much of the time. They hadn't dared to let Lilian's girls out, not yet, not till they'd got their story straight. And to get the story straight, they needed to have the main character on the stage. Where was he? Ellen glanced at the clock. Cedric should have been back in Bolton hours ago. Happen they'd had an accident. It would be just like Cedric to have an accident. A flicker of hope kindled briefly in her breast, and she squashed this with a quick, guilty prayer. It was wrong to want somebody dead, no matter what he'd done. And anyway, she'd rather poor Cedric was safe, big, soft, daft lad that he was.

Lilian echoed the little woman's thoughts. 'Where is he? I never knew where he was half the time when we lived in London, always out and about, supposed to be putting Miss Abigail's bets on. Of course, Doctor McDade and his wife didn't know about Miss Abigail's gambling. They kept her in an attic like something that had outlived its usefulness, but she knew the score when it came to horses. Eleven hundred pounds she left to me. "All the spare change in my room", it said in her will. I was dumbfounded when they gave it to me. I thought it would set us up for life. But he took the money and left me to struggle with two baby girls and a full-time job. So I see he hasn't changed much, never where he should be.'

Ellen shrugged her shoulders and lifted a soot-blackened kettle from the hob. A cup of tea wasn't always the answer, but it never did any harm.

Upstairs, Abigail was perched on the edge of Marie's bed. Marie and Theresa still had their usual room, while Abigail had been forced to share the marital bed with Tishy. Ellen had taken to sleeping on the sofa in the front parlour, and Lilian's bed had been specially bought for her to die in.

Abigail studied Marie closely. She was a pretty girl, the sort who didn't need paint and powder to enhance her natural charms. Abigail was, of course, rather jealous. She usually hated pretty girls, mostly because they knew they were pretty, partly because she envied such natural self-assurance. But Marie seemed to be totally unaware of her beauty, seldom looking in a mirror to arrange her dark brown curls, never appearing to care about how she looked or what she wore. 'You could make something of yourself,' pronounced Abigail. Her motives were far from altruistic; she simply sought to live up to Ellen's words. If she was expected to be a bad influence on Marie, then she had better get started, in spite of the fact that something akin to conscience was trying to hold her back. 'The boys will really go for you if you make an effort.'

Theresa, who was sorting underclothes on the next bed, said nothing at all, though her eyes kept straying towards the other two girls.

Marie snorted with laughter. 'What would I want with boys? I'm only sixteen. Anyway, I'm too busy in the shops to be bothering with lads. Since your mam came, our Theresa and me have to work both stores. Why can't you look after your mam during the days – being as you're a nurse? Why can't you let our mam come back to work?'

Dark brown eyes flashed with barely concealed impatience. 'Mother seems to like having Ellen around her. Perhaps she's punishing her for taking our father away.'

'Rubbish!' shouted Marie hotly. 'Dad was divorced from Lilian when he met our mother. And Mam didn't know he was divorced either. She'd never have married him if she'd known.'

'Why not?'

'Because it's wrong, it's a sin.'

Abigail blew out her thin cheeks and whistled softly. 'You're quite well up on sin, aren't you? Have you ever been with a boy? I'd like to bet that you haven't.'

'Course I have. There were boys in my class at school, there's boys at church. And they come into the shop and—'

'Not that, stupid. I mean making love, kissing and so on. Have you kissed a boy?'

Marie frowned thoughtfully. 'Yes, I kissed Bertie Summerfield on my fifth birthday after the party. He tasted of jelly and stank of hair oil. It was horrible. Then I kissed him again for a dare when I was about nine. I won two ounces of lemon drops for that.'

'Huh.' The other girl stretched herself out on the bed. 'So you've never been all the way?'

'All the way to where?'

'All the way to doing it.'

Marie pushed a hand through her hair. 'I told you. I did it on my fifth birthday, then—'

The girl on the bed started to laugh. 'You've no idea what I'm talking about, have you? No idea at all what goes on in the big grown-up world. Hasn't your mother told you things?'

Theresa pushed a pile of clothing into the tallboy and closed the door with a soft click. Without turning her head, she said, 'We don't talk about them things, Abigail. Not in our house. Marie and me are Catholics, so we're good girls. We don't think about boys and suchlike.'

Abigail continued to giggle throatily. 'What about babies? Do you know where they come from?'

'Yes,' replied Marie.

'From God,' answered Theresa simultaneously. 'And don't start thinking you know something we don't, because we do know about babies. Mrs Tattersall told us some of it and we heard the rest in the playground. But babies are a blessing, however they get here.'

Marie smiled at her sister. 'Tell her what you want to be, Theresa.'

'No, she wouldn't understand.'

Abigail propped herself up on an elbow and leaned towards Marie. 'What is she going to be, then?'

'A nun,' said Marie. 'My twin sister wants to go into the convent. Mam doesn't like it on account of our Theresa not having a lot of education. Only the educated nuns get the good jobs, so Theresa would be just a skivvy, like a cleaning woman.'

'Then why does she want to do it?'

'To do some good,' said Theresa. 'I want to have a useful life. And there's no need to laugh. There's nothing funny about nuns. Being a nun is just another way of serving God.'

'How dramatic,' sneered Abigail.

Marie sighed deeply. 'She's only doing it to get away from him, from me dad. She thinks she'll be safe in there as a postulant, out of his road, like. I've told her before she's only running. Mam doesn't want her to go in. If she'd been a lad, we wouldn't have minded her being a priest, only we don't want her locked up in a convent.'

Abigail rose from the bed and sidled across to Theresa. 'Little Sister Saint Theresa,' she said with a cruel edge to her voice. 'Trying to get away from life. That's never been my problem, I've always believed in meeting everything head on. It's the only way. I mean, can you imagine what it's like on men's surgical? Or, worse still, on women's medical? But at least I stay in touch by working in a hospital. Why bury your head in the sand? Are you so afraid of our father that you have to lock yourself up for ever? Why not fight back?'

'She won't,' said Marie. 'She believes in turning the other cheek. If you turn the other cheek with my dad, you're likely to end up with both sides of your face battered. He's not a nice man, not even a good one. Mind, he leaves me alone now, else he knows I'd hit him back with the nearest heavy thing I could lay my hands on. She won't, our Theresa won't. She doesn't even kill flies and cockroaches.'

Abigail stared hard at Theresa. 'You're quite nice-looking,' she said grudgingly. 'With a bit of powder and lipstick, you'd be attractive. It's very unusual to have such definite blue eyes with blonde hair. Why don't you let me make you up? Then you could come out with me and Marie?'

Theresa backed away, her slight limp suddenly more pronounced. 'We're not allowed out, not till Dad gets back.'

'But why?' screamed Abigail, whose temper was all but lost after being cooped up for weeks in this house. 'Why do you have to do as you're told all the time? We should just go out and enjoy ourselves and to hell with what our mothers say. I'd go alone, but I don't know Bolton. Can't you think for yourselves?' She suddenly hated herself again. Always acting a part, always pretending to be a know-all.

'I can,' insisted Marie. 'But we have to wait and see what Dad says about being divorced and all that. We don't know what we're going to say to the neighbours. Mam doesn't want you and Tishy talking to anybody until she's sorted it out with me dad. See, Theresa and me might have trouble at church.'

'Why?'

'If the priest finds out that Dad's divorced. They got married at our church, did Mam and Dad, so it looks as if the priest didn't know about your mam, otherwise there wouldn't have been any wedding. It's all a bit mixed up. Theresa and me weren't supposed to be born in the first place, and—'

'That's silly,' said Abigail. 'Didn't Theresa just say that babies are a blessing no matter where they come from?' It occurred to her that she liked these two, that she didn't want them in trouble. In a strange sense, she was bound to them, because they all had the same father. Yes, and what kind of a father was he going to be?

Marie nodded wisely. 'Aye, she's been saying that a lot lately. Because we don't feel proper, me and her. Dad already had a family, didn't he?'

'But they weren't married.' Theresa's voice was very quiet. 'The first marriage doesn't count because it wasn't Catholic.'

'You are so ignorant, both of you,' said Abigail now. 'So . . . bigoted. Does any of it matter? Do you care who's illegitimate and who isn't? And does this precious God of yours blame us for being born? What sort of a God is that?' Her eyes flashed dangerously as she spoke. 'What sort of God allows war and disease and famine? I'll tell you what sort, shall I? The kind that gets made up by people like you, people with stupid little lives. You need to feel that there's something at the end of it, don't you? Well, there isn't. We just close your eyes for that last time and that's the end of it. I've been there, I've seen it. I've watched people die, and there's nothing holy about it. There's no heaven, no hell, no pearly gates or infernos. There is no God. He's just a . . . a figment of imagination.'

A terrible silence filled the small room. Theresa walked to the window, checked the blackout, then turned up the gas light. Marie, unsure of how to cope with such sophisticated talk, fiddled first with her hair, then with a corner of the woven quilt.

Theresa spoke at last. 'I'll pray for you, Abigail.'

'Don't bother.'

'I'll pray that you come to know God's love. There are powers we don't understand, there are things that can't be explained. Look at Saint Bernadette. Just an ordinary girl, but she saw Our Lady. And the water at Lourdes can cure people, it—'

Abigail shook her head. 'Ellen has practically drowned my mother in Lourdes water. Has she improved? No, not a bit.'

'Happen that's because she doesn't believe.' Theresa did not raise her voice. 'You have to believe to be cured. And your mam's not a Catholic.'

'No, my mother is intelligent, so she's agnostic. That means she has an open mind. You two wouldn't know what real freedom of thought is. Mother never fed us any of this religious nonsense. Because that's all it is, another set of stupid rules used to control people. Religion and politics are very much alike. It's a case of frightening the masses into some sort of submission.'

Marie cleared her throat. 'Abigail?'

'What?'

'This freedom of thought – doesn't it mean that me and Theresa can believe in what we like?'

Abigail, who had not expected such a sensible response, allowed a few seconds to elapse before replying. 'Of course it does. But it also means that you haven't to push it down my throat, all this about Catholic is best and Catholic is married. That's just what you believe. You can't make other people believe it too, not if they don't want to.'

'I'm sorry,' said Theresa quietly.

'It's all right.' Abigail's tone softened. 'You can't help having been brainwashed from birth. My mother used to be quite a strong Christian until things started to happen, things that made her realize that no-one was sitting in the clouds looking down on her. Once she understood how damaging and misleading religion can be, she decided not to inflict it on us. So. We'll just have to agree to differ.'

A loud knocking at the front door caused all three girls to stiffen. Theresa blessed herself hurriedly while Marie ran and put her arms around the shaking girl. 'Don't worry. He won't hurt you.'

Abigail folded her arms as if to hide her nervousness. 'I won't recognize him,' she muttered. 'Tishy certainly won't. Oh, why did Mother insist on coming here? Why couldn't we have stayed in London? A lawyer could have dealt with all this. Shall we go downstairs?'

'No,' said Marie. 'Our mothers want to see him alone first. We'll just have to wait our turn.'

Theresa stared at Abigail, realizing something new, something totally unexpected. Abigail was terrified, frightened of their father, frightened of a lot of things. This was all an act, all a cover for uncertainty and insecurity. She smiled at the sad, dark girl, pitying her, understanding the brash talk, the painted face, the apparent lack of care for anyone.

With an unusual show of tenderness, Abigail placed a hand on Theresa's shoulder. 'Don't worry, now. I'm here, just remember that. If he starts anything, he'll have me to deal with.'

Billy London wasn't dealing with much at that time. He lay stretched out on the peg rug, eyes glazed, mouth moving as if to frame words that simply would not translate into recognizable language. Vera Shaw and Ellen stood over him, both panting after the exertion of carrying him into the house. Tishy hovered in the doorway, hands fidgeting with the belt of her dress.

'Go into the other room, dear,' said Lilian. 'You can see him tomorrow. Tell the other girls to go to bed in a few minutes.'

'Do I have to go to bed too?'

'Of course.'

Tishy went reluctantly from the room. That dirty, smelly man on the floor was her father. The idea of having a tramp for a father appealed to her. He would have stories to tell, songs she could learn. With a sigh of resignation, Tishy closed the door. It would all have to wait until tomorrow.

'How long has he been in your house?' asked Ellen.

Vera raised her arms in a careless gesture and smiled. 'A couple of hours. He wasn't fit for anything and didn't want to come home.'

'I'm not surprised,' said Lilian acidly.

'Oh, but he often gets in this state of a night, doesn't he?' asked Vera with feigned innocence. 'It's the drink, you see. Some of them can't hold it, can't behave after they've had a few. Sundays is the worst, though. Drinks himself into a state after his dinner, then turns rotten. I hear it through the wall. Like paper, these walls. You usually send the girls out on a Sunday, don't you, Ellen? And I've got to sit there listening to the screams. Pitiful, it is.'

'Thank you, Vera.' Ellen's tone was quiet but firm. 'We'll manage now.'

'Oh.' Vera's thin face fell. 'I could help you get him up to bed.'

'No, ta.' Bed, indeed. This fellow would be sleeping on the front room sofa for the foreseeable future. Ellen would have to make do with a chair. 'I think it would be best if you went now, Vera. We've a lot to do tonight.'

Vera smiled to herself as she left the house. Yes, they had a lot to do all right. Like sorting out who was who and what was blinking what!

Lilian studied the creature on the floor. 'Was I really married to that?' she asked. 'Look at him. A drunk, a bully, a coward and a damned fool as well. Did I ever love him?'

'Probably not.' Ellen heaved a great sigh. 'I doubt I'd have married him myself, but I was three months gone with the twins when I finally walked down the aisle. And I've been praying about that sin ever since.'

The bundle groaned and rolled sideways. 'That's right,' he muttered. 'Talk about me as if I'm already dead.'

Ellen turned on her heel and walked out to the scullery. Thirty seconds later, she returned with a bucket of very cold water. This item she emptied to the last drop over his head while he yelled and screamed obscenities at her. 'There,' said Ellen softly. 'That should wake you up.'

He sat bolt upright with his clothes steaming in the heat from the fire. Lil had been giving Ellen lessons, that would be it. She'd probably told the tale of how she used to get the better of him, how she kept him under control at every opportunity simply by acting strong. 'I'll see to you later,' he said to Ellen now.

'Will you?' she asked sweetly. 'I very much doubt it. Lilian and I will be calling the tune.'

He looked at Lil for the first time. She hadn't improved with the years, though there was less of her than there used to be. She was dying; he only needed one glance to know that. Dark yellow skin hung in folds where her several chins had been, while her eyes were surrounded by huge black circles that looked like craters in her head. 'What's the tune then, Lil?' he asked almost cockily.

'That's the drink talking,' declared Lilian. 'He's always a big boy when he's had a few too many. Tell him, Ellen. I'm too tired for talking.'

Ellen perched on the edge of the horsehair rocker. 'It's very simple,' she said. 'For the girls' sake, you have to say you were divorced from Lilian. If you don't, we'll make sure you get put in prison for bigamy. And you have to tell people that I didn't know you were divorced. When

Lilian . . .' She glanced across at the bed before continuing. 'When Lilian's gone, you and I will have to get married again just to make sure everything's legal and proper.'

'And what if I say no to all that?'

The women looked at him, each knowing that he could not refuse. Like a drowning man, he would probably grab at anything that happened to be floating past. 'Well,' said Ellen slowly. 'Lilian has given me proof of Aunt Abigail's will. It's with a solicitor. There would be no problem convincing a court that you made off with that money. Now, you are going to sign those shops over to me. I'll keep them in trust for the children. Lilian and I have talked this out, and she wants my two to have their share as well. And, of course, if you choose not to marry me when the time comes, I'll follow Lilian's instructions and you'll be out on the street without a shirt to your back.' She took a deep breath. 'No, you'll not be on the streets. You'll be nice and warm in prison, eh? As for the six houses, they can come to me and all. I'll have them outright, not tied up for the kiddies. Lilian thinks I should get some compensation for what I've been through.'

He sat dripping water, his head waving slowly from side to side as he tried to take in what was being said. Was this a nightmare induced by alcohol? Surely he must be dreaming? Ellen would never threaten blackmail, wouldn't throw water over him, would never talk to him like this. Like what, though? It was the same quiet voice, the same gentle manner. 'Who do you think you're talking to?' he asked sullenly. 'The bloody cat?'

'I'm talking to you. What you did to Lilian was rotten and what you've done to me all these years is a sin. It's not my sin, because I knew nowt about any of it. But you have to make these girls legal, all four of them. Yes, I'm talking to you, Billy Langden. And I'm telling you now, married or not, we'll never be man and wife together again.'

He staggered to unsteady feet and leaned over her chair. 'You bugger,' he spat. 'You're not trying to tell me what to do, are you? You of all people? Stupid, that's what you are. You were stupid when I met you and you've learned nothing since. I'm going, do you hear? I'm going for good.'

'Then go. Me and the girls will do all right without you. Our Marie will look after me.'

He lifted his hand to hit her, staggering back as an arm slid round his throat. For a sick woman, Lilian was still terribly strong. The sudden power had risen out of anger, an awful fury that had erupted as she watched how the bigamist treated his victim. 'Hit her,' she gasped, 'and I'll kill you. I swear on my mother's grave that I'll see you off.'

He turned to face the dreadful figure of his dying wife. 'You couldn't kill a flea,' he said, pushing away her weakening arm.

They stared at one another for several seconds, then Lilian took a deep breath, clenched her fist and dealt him a sizeable blow to the chin. He dropped like a felled sapling as Lilian stumbled back to the bed after hitting him for the first and last time in her life. 'That was for me, Bill Langden,' she breathed. 'For me, for Ellen, for the girls.' She glanced at her companion. 'But mostly for Ellen. Yes, mostly for my friend.'

CHAPTER FOUR

Coming to Terms

By six o'clock the following morning, it was plain that Lilian had only hours to live. It was as if her attempt to defend Ellen had taken every ounce of her depleted strength, and she now had nothing left to fight with, no reason to continue. And, hoping that William Langden was in no two minds about what the future held in store for him, she could perhaps leave this world with fewer regrets.

She drifted in and out of consciousness while Ellen mouthed many decades of her rosary and prayed that each lapse into coma would be the last. 'Holy Mother, take her,' she whispered after every Glory Be. 'Let her pain be over.' But Lilian lingered. Ellen found herself wondering why the woman was hanging on so tenaciously, then it came to her in a flash that Lilian was probably waiting for the girls to get out of bed. 'Shall I fetch them?' she asked as the dark eyelids flickered. 'Do you want me to go upstairs and get Abigail and Tishy?'

'Yes. Ellen?'

'Hello, I'm still here, love.'

'Don't let him hurt them. Don't let him hurt your little Theresa either. She's . . . terrified. Something's happened to her. He's . . . hurt her. Be clever. Get a . . . hold over him. The will. Tell the lawyer . . . keep copy of Aunt Abigail McDade's will. Doctor McDade is old now, but he promised . . . testify about the robbery. Threaten Bill with the bigamy charge. Keep him under, Ellen. Prison. Tell him prison. Scared of . . . being locked up.

Shops are girls'. My will . . . my own will . . . just about a hundred pounds. Use it, my money, for all four of them. My friend. My . . . good friend. So glad I met you.'

Tears poured down Ellen's face. 'It's all right, lass, don't you fret. The lawyer fellow's got that statement of intent. Aye, it's all wrote down now in black and white, everything our blinking husband did wrong. Don't worry about me and the children, Lilian. I don't want you worrying.' She sniffed loudly. 'God love you, brave soul that you are.'

'I . . . I don't . . . believe.'

'That's all right, lass. God believes in you, and that's what counts. All them years you've struggled on your own, all them years of nursing and bringing up the children, they all count as service in the eyes of the Lord. He'll not turn his back on you, Lilian. There's many a so-called good Christian that won't get to the front of the queue when it comes to Judgement Day. It's them that have lived a good clean life as'll get in first, and you're a saint if ever I saw one.'

'Get the girls. My Tishy . . . genius . . . piano. Abigail hard to understand. Try.'

'I won't let you down.' Ellen made an effort to dry her streaming eyes. After what this tortured soul had been through, the least Ellen could do was to let her go in peace. Though how she would cope with Tishy's strangeness and Abigail's apparent waywardness, she did not begin to imagine.

She went upstairs and, after setting a match to a nightlight on the mantelpiece, she roused Lilian's daughters. 'You'd better come,' she whispered. 'I'm sorry, but I think you ought to know your mother's on her last.'

Tishy jumped out of bed and ran downstairs immediately. Abigail remained where she was, bolt upright in the bed with her hair falling over her eyes. Ellen noticed, not for the first time, the hardness of the features, that determined set of the mouth. 'Aren't you coming?'

'Yes. It's Tishy she wants, though.'

'Oh.'

'It's always been Tishy for as long as I can remember. "Tishy is special" and "look after your little sister". That was all I ever seemed to hear. Give her a few minutes alone with her favourite. I'll be along shortly.'

'I'm sorry.'

'About what? I know what you think of me, Ellen. My sister has a habit of listening at doors, so I know I'm not wanted here. Your opinion has been clearly expressed. I shall just take my money and run.'

Ellen closed her mouth firmly. It wasn't up to her to tell Abigail the terms of Lilian's will and that there wasn't much cash coming – the girl likely knew already that Lilian wouldn't be leaving a large sum. And as for the shops – well – Billy Langden was still the outright owner, wasn't he? He wouldn't reign for long, because Ellen would force him to hand over control. But even so, the business would have to be kept going until Marie and Theresa had reached their majority, an event that would not happen for over four years. At that point, a sale could only be brought about if and when everybody involved came to some sort of agreement. Ellen understood Lilian's reasoning. She was no doubt anxious for Tishy to have security for the immediate future, and such security could be maintained while Ellen held the shops in trust. Perhaps Abigail was right, perhaps Lilian had made Tishy her number one priority. 'I'm sorry if I've judged you wrong. Anyway, this is not the right time for us to be wondering what we think of one another. Your mam's worse, so I thought you should come down.'

'Thank you. For looking after her, I mean. I expect you think that I should have done the nursing.'

'No, I never said that, did I?'

'I'm a nurse.'

'Aye, and she's your mother. It's not like looking after an ordinary patient when it's your mother. I do understand, Abigail.'

'Do you?' The pointed chin quivered slightly. 'Do you really?'

'Yes. You'd be surprised how much I can understand. Just try me some time. I may not be the world's brightest, but I do know about human nature. I can see you're hurting and I can see you're trying your best to hide it. That's just you, the way you are. We're all different. But I'm here if you want a shoulder to cry on.'

Abigail tossed her head, throwing the hair back from her face. 'I don't cry. I never have, even when I was young.'

Ellen stared hard at the tight-lipped girl. 'You'll cry one day, lass,' she said softly. 'And when you do, it'll be a good long howl, because you'll let out all you've kept locked inside for so long. Come on now, shape yourself. Your mam's waiting for you.'

'Is she?'

'Yes.' Ellen's tone was determined. 'You were her firstborn, and never forget that. A firstborn is always special to a woman, always important. She loves you. I know she does.'

'Yes.' The whites of her eyes shone in the gloom as if they were already filled with tears. 'My mother has been a fine woman, Ellen. Only I know what she gave to us, how hard she worked to keep us all together. The only thing she owned was her home, and she had to sell that when nursing got too much for her. Then there was my training to pay for, of course.' She drew back her shoulders. 'Is my father in the house?'

'He's asleep in the front room.'

'Right.' Abigail bounced out of the bed and pulled on a dressing gown. With sudden haste, she pushed past Ellen and ran down the stairs, turning left instead of right when she reached the bottom. Flinging open the door, she stepped into the front room, reaching immediately for a box of matches on a side table. The mantel popped as she lit it.

'What the hell?' Billy sat up, turned over and rolled on to the floor.

Abigail stared down at him. 'Hello, Daddy-Dear,' she said. 'It's been a long time.'

'Eh?'

'Just thought I'd have a look at you, make sure you're alive before I go to watch my mother die. Have you had a nice life?' Her tone was conversational, dangerously pleasant.

For answer, he lifted his blanket and held it against himself like a protective barrier.

'Because we haven't. Since you ran off, it's been decidedly difficult.'

He coughed thickly and put a hand to his aching head.

'My little sister isn't even fit for war work, she has trouble counting the fingers on both hands. I'm a nurse, I expect you didn't know that. Mother did private nursing for years after you left us. She couldn't get a job in a hospital because she had children and they wanted single women. Now she's a victim of cancer. Well? Have you nothing to say for yourself?'

'Get out,' he snapped. 'Get out of here and mind your own business. What happened between your mother and me is nothing to do with anybody.' He was getting just a bit fed up with this lot. Every time he turned round, there was a female hovering over him with a bucket of water, a raised hand, or a mouthful of invective.

Abigail's thin nostrils flared slightly. 'I was a part of it,' she said softly. 'I was the one who had to look after Tishy while Mother worked and left us with a neighbour. There was never any money, never anything to spare for clothes or decent shoes. It was only lately, with the money from her house, that Mother managed to save enough to have you traced, then a bit of cash for Tishy's second-hand piano. Finding you cost over a hundred pounds.' She looked him up and down. 'Hardly worth it, I'd say. Did you know that Tishy is extraordinarily talented? Did you know she's good enough to play on a concert stage? No. You know nothing because you chose not to know.'

'What do you expect me to say or do?' he yelled. 'Your mother led me a dog's life—'

'Did she? Ah yes, but life is the operative word here, isn't it? You've had a life, Mother hasn't.' She took a step towards him. 'My mother is a good woman. She didn't deserve what you did to her. Well, listen to me, Daddy-Dear. Lay one more finger on anybody here, on me, on Tishy, on either of your other daughters, and I'll kill you. I know all about poisons, all about where to push a knife to make sure it hits the right spot. I'll do to you what you did to my mother – I'll finish your life. Right. Do we understand one another? Has the hangover cleared, are you hearing me?' Her voice was strident now, firm yet cold.

He looked at her. There was something familiar about this one, something he'd seen in a mirror many times. Yes, she was definitely his daughter. And she was strong too. Strong, clever and furious. 'I heard you,' he answered eventually. 'Just don't get too big for your boots, that's all. It's time some of you women learned your place. Remember I'm the man in this house.'

She laughed, emitting an awful chilling sound that made goose pimples rise on his arms. 'You're not a man. You're a failure.' She turned on her heel and marched smartly from the room, closing the door firmly.

Ellen looked up as Abigail entered the kitchen. 'It's getting too much for her,' she whispered. 'Get our Marie up, tell her to fetch Doctor Harrison.'

'There's no need for that,' answered Abigail. 'I have everything I need.' While the others stood by helplessly, she filled a hypodermic with morphine, struggled to find a vein that had not yet collapsed, then injected her mother gently with the pain-killing drug. 'There you are, my love,' she whispered. 'All better now, Mother, all better now. Lie still, sweetheart, let the sleep come.'

Ellen turned abruptly and faced the sideboard. Suddenly, she could not bear to watch Abigail. There was something terribly pathetic about the girl, and Ellen, like Theresa, was beginning to realize what it was. This young woman was afraid, terrified of letting anyone near her. It was all a front, all of it. Yes, even the lipstick and the leg paint were shields against life. And although she had turned her back on the dreadful scene, Ellen could still see it in her mind – the tortured figure on the bed, the thin girl by her side, the auburn-haired adult child who hovered by the fireplace like a beautiful moth near a flame.

What was it that Vera Shaw always said? Aye, that was it, 'life's a bugger'. She was always saying that, was Ellen's next door neighbour. She was right, she really was. Where was the rhyme and reason to this episode?

Without turning her head, Ellen crept out to the back yard. They should be alone at a time like this. Death was family business, not a spectator sport. The starlings were there, as ever, hovering about in the vain hope that somebody would have enough rations to spare the odd crumb. For a few moments, she stood and stared into a leaden sky. Yes, this was the rhyme, the reason. They might not be the same starlings as yesterday's crew, but they were still starlings. That was God's plan, wasn't it? Lilian was dying, but there would still be people. That was where the hope lay, and she should not be standing in a freezing back yard questioning God.

'Do go inside where it's warm, Ellen.' It was Abigail's voice.

Ellen rubbed her eyes with a corner of her apron before swivelling on her heel to face the girl. 'I thought you'd want to be by yourselves, like. Just family.'

Abigail fixed her gaze on the wall behind Ellen's head. 'You're Tishy's family now. There's no-one else.'

'I'm yours and all, lass. Has Lilian gone?'

'No.'

Ellen stepped forward. 'Just tell me what you need. What can I do to help you, Abigail?'

'Nothing.' She pulled the dressing gown tight against her thin body, then walked down the yard, banging the lavatory door as soon as she had arrived in the one place that offered some solitude. The chill air seemed to bite right into her bones as she perched on the rough wooden seat, and she clenched her teeth to stop their chattering. Perhaps the ice would freeze her soul too, would help her to stop feeling altogether. But no, the workings of her mind continued, talking her into other times, other places . . .

It had been a nice house, the one in Bow. The cellar had been made into work rooms, and in those rooms Abigail's maternal grandparents had done their tailoring. Grandfather's table had stood beneath the window, while Grandmother's sewing basket had sat in front of the brick fireplace. Abigail and Tishy had been forbidden to move any of their dead grandparents' things. That cellar had remained a monument since the death of Abigail's grandfather. Even the sign that had announced Lilian's mother as 'Court Dressmaker' had been framed and hung in the hall. The sign was upstairs in this house now, packed with a few other little treasures in a box under a bed. Lilian Langden's life was in a box under a bed in a strange town, a town where people didn't understand, had no knowledge, no memory of Lilian. Lilian Langden's life was ebbing away in an unfamiliar kitchen while her daughter sat in a hiding place where no-one would see her grief.

She shivered and dropped her head, biting hard on her lower lip. Selling the family home had broken Mother's heart and spirit. She had been born there, had lived there alone after her parents' deaths, had been married from that house. The dismantling of the cellar must have completely finished Mother. Abigail nodded. Yes, the cancer would have been with her even then, two years ago, because otherwise she would not have relinquished her home for a tiny flat in Stepney. Just to find him, just to get up here and chase some security for her daughters!

Abigail forced herself into an upright position and rocked to and fro, a slippered foot tapping softly on the flagged floor. The main thing was to hold on, to stay in one piece. There would be a funeral to arrange, an unusual affair without hymns or prayers. The burial would be here, of course. There was no point in taking a body back to London. Anyway, the bombs had already destroyed two East End cemeteries. At least Mother would have a chance of staying buried at this end of the country.

If she concentrated hard on the practicalities, there would be no time for weeping. After Mother's funeral, she would have to find work somewhere. No-one was allowed to remain idle during a war, and she didn't want to be idle. But where would she go, what would she do about Tishy? Tishy, Tishy – it had always been Tishy, hadn't it? Yet she loved her sister. In spite of her impatience, in spite of the way she treated the silly girl, she did love her. Didn't she? After all, Tishy was a sick girl. If the London doctors' prognosis should turn out correct . . . None of it bore thinking about. She wished that she could stop thinking, stop completely.

The whitewash was peeling from the wall, and she unclenched her hands to pick absently at a few flakes of paint. Her mother was dying. The terrible pain would have abated by now, it was relatively easy to cut back the pain. But no-one could stay the hand of the grim reaper. She shook herself impatiently against this fanciful thought. Death was not a person, not a pale rider on a black horse. Death was merely a fact of life, the only fact, the sole certainty. She rose to her feet, tightening her belt once again, this time so fiercely that the corded length dug into her slender waist. She would go in now. She would be brave and she would never cry.

Ellen was waiting in the yard. The two women stared at one another for several seconds, then Abigail marched into the scullery. Ellen took a handful of crumbs and stale porridge oats from her apron pocket, scattering this meagre bounty for the birds. One cheeky starling hopped down from the wall, and she smiled at him sadly. Was he the one who had been with her since the start of the war, the September starling? Ah, she was being stupid again. But he was looking at her so cockily, as if asking, 'Is this the best you can do?'

'Sorry, lad,' she whispered. 'I can't give you anything else till you fetch me your ration book.'

Her legs felt like lead as she walked back into the house. The scene had not changed much. Abigail sat on the edge of the bed, fingers resting on her mother's wrist as she sought a pulse. Tishy had wandered to the table where she stood humming a sad tune.

Ellen placed herself at the foot of the bed. Lilian's face had begun to slacken and relax as the morphine did its work, and a thin stream of saliva oozed from a corner of her mouth. She smiled faintly at Ellen. 'Better now,' she mumbled hoarsely. 'Not hurting.'

Ellen smiled back. 'That's good.'

They gazed at Lilian, watching as her face changed. A slight smile played over the thick lips as pain receded, while the lines in her skin seemed to smooth themselves, making her younger, less careworn. 'It doesn't . . . hurt any more,' she repeated breathily. 'So glad you're . . . here. And Ellen too. Be good. That's all I ask . . . that you be good . . .' She closed her eyes and a great rush of breath poured from her mouth in a final rattle, then she was gone.

Ellen looked from Tishy to Abigail. This was a terrible moment; the only way to deal with it was to be businesslike. Yet the words would not come as she looked at their two faces. Tishy continued to hum softly, while Abigail remained a motionless mass of tense nerves. That girl would crack, Ellen was sure of it. At last she found her voice. 'It's over now, girls. Shall I see to her?'

'No.' Abigail lifted her chin. 'I'll do it, and Tishy will help. This is the last thing we'll ever do for her.' Her eyes were dry and fierce. 'You get the doctor, Ellen. We'll need a certificate. And tell Theresa and Marie what has happened so that they'll stay out of here for a while.'

'She was a grand woman, a mother to be proud of,' Ellen swallowed her sobs determinedly. 'Are you all right, Tishy?'

Tishy nodded. 'For ever's a long time, isn't it?'

'Yes. But she's gone to a better place. There's no pain where your mother is now.'

The door opened. 'Is there any tea in the pot?' Billy stared at the trio round the bed. 'Oh. Is she dead?'

Tishy glanced over her shoulder. 'You didn't love her, so you can go away. I shall speak to you later.'

He hovered in the doorway, uncertain what to do next. It looked as if his life was about to be dominated by women and he didn't like the idea. But he couldn't push his way in, not with Lil's body still cooling. 'I'll be in for my tea later, then,' he said, just for something to punctuate the silence.

Abigail spoke without taking her eyes from her mother's dead face. 'How many sugars?' she asked.

'Two.'

At last she swung round to look at him. 'Fine. Two spoons of sugar. I'll try to make sure it is only sugar.'

The door banged behind him.

'What did you mean by that?' asked Ellen. 'Are you threatening to put poison in his drinks?'

Abigail smiled grimly. 'Remember my mother's advice, Ellen. Keep him in his place, keep him worried. It will be a long time before Daddy-Dear accepts a cup of tea from me. He is a doomed man.' She sighed dramatically. 'Will you boil some water please, Ellen? I'll just give Mother a good wash.'

Tishy walked across the room and pushed her hand into Abigail's. 'I don't like him,' she said. 'That man who's supposed to be our father. At first, I thought he might be interesting, like a tramp or a gypsy. But I think he's just going to be a bore and a miserable person. Is Mum properly dead? She doesn't look dead, she looks asleep. We've only got one another now.'

Abigail pulled her hand away and forced Tishy to sit on the horsehair rocker. She didn't want Tishy, didn't want anybody. Abigail Langden intended to make her own way in the world. She wanted no help, and she certainly needed no hindrances. Mother had asked her to look after

Tishy, but that request had come too often. It was time for Abigail to break free. But could she? Would she . . . ?

With a toss of her head, she approached the bed in order to prepare the body. Angrily, she bit on her lower lip. She would not cry. Never, under any circumstances, would she cry. But the scene was misted over all the same, and Abigail had to bite her lip for many days to come.

Billy London leaned forward, eyes almost popping from his head. 'What?' he yelled at the man in the pin-stripe suit. 'The houses are mine, the shops are mine! I built the business up, put a lot of years into it. Everybody round here will tell you how I've worked from dawn till dusk, day in and day out . . .' His voice faded under the man's arrogant, unfeeling stare.

The solicitor placed his elbows on the table and tapped his fingers together thoughtfully. 'There is a great deal of documentary evidence to support the late Mrs Langden's statement. Firstly, there is Abigail McDade's will, then I have a letter from a Doctor McDade who states that you absconded with your late wife's inheritance. With this stolen money, you bought the shops. Later, with profits from the shops, you purchased seven houses. The business premises are now to be held in trust by the second Mrs Langden. On her death, they will pass to the four Misses Langden. To Mrs Ellen Langden, you will donate, by deed of gift, the domestic dwellings.'

'I'm not having this! I'm going to fight it, I shall get a lawyer of my own, somebody with a bit of common sense and decency, not a bleeding crackpot . . .'

Ellen raised her head and looked at the girls who were sitting motionless round the table. 'I think you can go now,' she told them. 'Your part of this is over.'

Abigail was the first to rise. 'I'd like to make it plain that I am very disappointed by this outcome. What am I going to do with a quarter share in two shops? I have no intention of working in a shop, no wish to stay in this part of the country. Is there no way of releasing my money?'

'Not yet,' said Ellen. 'Not till Marie and Theresa are twenty-one.'

'Will I get a share of the profits in the meantime?'

Ellen sighed. 'Profits are usually ploughed back in, Abigail. It makes sense if you think about it. When the time comes for selling, the shops will be worth more. The only people who can take money from the tills are the folk who work the shops and get wages for the hours they put in.'

The girl drew herself to full height. 'Well, this is probably the only time I shall agree with him.' She pointed to her father. 'This situation is ridiculous. Though I am pleased that he doesn't benefit in any way. Come along, Tishy.'

All four girls left the room with Abigail leading the way. The solicitor cleared his throat. 'Get a lawyer by all means, Mr Langden. I'm sure the courts will be interested to hear of your bigamy. You will also be prosecuted for theft, and possibly for fraud, if you should choose to make a case. There is no way out of this for you. Your safest bet is to pretend that you were properly divorced from the first Mrs Langden before you married for a second time.'

'Bloody hell!'

'There's more to it,' said Ellen. 'You and me have to get married again. I've told the priest the truth, and we're telling the neighbours that you were divorced. Even if you had been divorced, we would have had to remarry once Lilian died. I'm not having my girls illegitimate in the eyes of the Church. So we're getting married all over again.'

'And what if I won't do it?'

Ellen gave him a hard stare. 'Then you go. I'm in charge of this house now, Billy Langden. Them middens across the street are my responsibility too, all six of them. I say who lives here and who doesn't. I've made me mind up. Either you wed me proper or you go to prison for what you did to Lilian. It's up to you.'

'That's blackmail.' He looked frantically at the solicitor. 'You heard her, you're a witness. Isn't that blackmail?'

'No. Mrs Langden is simply stating her terms. The facts are plain. You committed at least two crimes that we know of, and Mrs Langden is prepared to clothe and house you on her terms. Furthermore, you will be protected from prosecution if you agree to such terms.'

'What about Lil's girls? They know she never got divorced from me, don't they?'

Ellen shook her head slowly. 'No. To save her pride, Lilian told her daughters that she had divorced you. She brought them up here because she knew she was dying and she wanted to get them some security. Everything is going to be taken away from you, lad. Everything you care about, any road. I know you've no interest in me or the girls, I know you can't see past making money. So, you've two choices. Either you live here under these terms, or you go to prison. I reckon you'd be there a long while too.'

The lawyer tapped his chin thoughtfully. 'Which is it to be then, Mr Langden?'

'It's prison either way, ain't it? I either get a wife as a keeper or we do it properly over at Strangeways. What's the difference?'

'The difference is that here you can go to work, have some spending money and the freedom to walk in the street. There is no freedom in a real jail, Mr Langden. I imagine that your sentence would be at least five years for the bigamy, with a few more added on because of the theft. There is also a possibility that your current wife might prosecute you for cruelty. Isn't that correct, Mrs Langden? Haven't there been some recent assaults on you?'

'And on my daughters.'

Billy jumped up, causing his chair to crash backwards into the dresser. 'I can't bloody win, can I? What about her sending her brothers to do me over, eh? What about that?'

'I never sent anybody,' said Ellen smoothly. 'And my brothers were all at home with their families the night you had your accident.'

'What?' he screamed. 'They done it! You know it was them!'

'You are at liberty to bring a separate prosecution for that,' said the solicitor. 'Proof will be difficult to find, but . . .' He shrugged and spread his arms in a careless gesture. 'It's your prerogative.'

Billy stared at the woman he had called 'the wife' for more years than he cared to remember. She sat as still as stone, no emotion registering on her face. Yet he could feel her strength, it was in the room with them like a separate living thing. 'Can you do all this to me?' he asked.

'Yes, I can,' came the simple reply.

'Why? You're supposed to be my wife . . .'

'"Supposed" is the word, isn't it? I've put up with your rages, your drunkenness and your greed for a long time, just because you were my husband. If I hadn't had any children, I'd run out in the street now and tell everybody that I'm not married to you, that Billy London was never my husband. I'd be proud of that. I could tell them all what you did, about the bigamy and everything, only I can't do it because of Marie and Theresa. It's for them, all for them. Anyway, you can please yourself. If you want to go to prison, then go. We'll manage, we'll face the world somehow. But if you're stopping here, we get to that church and make my girls proper as soon as possible.'

He had never known her to make such a long speech. And the fact that she'd said all that without anger made it more real, more ominous. A trickle of fear poured down his throat and he swallowed quickly. He was giving her power; he had no alternative but to give her power over him. She had always been such a quiet and biddable soul, but the change in her was so deep as to be almost unnoticeable on the surface. It was there, though. He could sense that beneath the cool exterior there lurked a terrible raging fire, one he would never be able to extinguish. 'All right,' he muttered. 'There's no choice.'

'Then sign here, please, Mr Langden.'

He looked down at the paper that had suddenly appeared on the table. 'What's this?'

'An admission of your part in these matters.'

'What?'

'Should you be inclined at any point to renege on this agreement, a signed confession will be extremely useful to Mrs Langden.'

As if his legs were suddenly refusing to support him, Billy leaned heavily on the dresser. His breathing became sharp and shallow, each intake sticking like glue in his throat. 'He'll have a turn now,' said Ellen mildly. 'He usually has one of his turns when he's not getting his own road. Get it signed. Once you've put your name to it, everything's over and done with. If you don't sign, I'm going for the police.'

'You rotten cow,' he gasped. 'I'll get you for this.'

'Did you hear that, Mr King?' Ellen looked at the grey-haired man next to her. 'That was a threat, wasn't it? You know, there's plenty to be said for bringing this all out in the open. It'd only be a nine days' wonder round here. It might be just as well to get him arrested and have it all done with. We'd get over it, me and the girls.'

Billy leaned forward, picked up the pen and scribbled his signature next to a pencilled cross. 'You need witnesses,' he said with difficulty. 'That's no good without two more to sign, and you can't put your names to it.'

Mr King smiled. 'This confession is merely a little extra, Mr Langden, rather like the seasoning for a main meal. We have a complete menu already. It was just that Mrs Langden wanted you to admit liability. Now, if you don't mind, I shall bid you good day.' He picked up his hat and made for the door. 'Don't bother to see me out,' he said. 'I shall find my own way.'

With his breath miraculously restored to him, Billy turned on his wife. 'You'll never manage the shops and the houses,' he spat. 'What will you do if I refuse to help you?'

She half-smiled. 'We've managed all these weeks. And if you don't work the shops, you'll soon get fed up of having nowt to do. There'll be no wages either for them that don't put their time in. You stick to Deane Road, our Marie can keep an eye on you there. I'll do Derby Street with Theresa. Linda Tattersall cleans now, I suppose you remember taking her on. Cissie Tattersall's never got over you giving her them bits of bacon and tea, so Linda thinks the sun shines out of you. Aye, you'll carry on as normal,' she said. 'If you know which side your bread's buttered.'

He stared into space, completely lost for words. There was little he could say, nothing he could do. If he gave her the thumping she deserved, he'd no doubt end up in custody within the hour. If he refused to marry her, to work, to do her bidding, he would immediately condemn himself to prison. Well, he would just have to pretend to go along with it. There were plenty of ways of skinning a cat. And this one had turned out to be a cat after all.

Abigail rather liked Doctor Harrison. He was an honest and terribly direct man with no tendency towards pulling punches. When he had visited Lilian, he had always taken Abigail on one side afterwards. 'It will be weeks rather than months', had changed to 'just days now', then finally, on the afternoon preceding the death, he had advised Abigail to measure her mother's life in hours. At thirty-five-ish, he had been young enough for war service, but he had obviously been chosen to stay behind and run his enormous practice. Abigail was glad about that, pleased to find that not all remaining doctors were geriatrics.

He sat now in his consulting room at a large desk covered in books, papers, bottles, jars and boxes. His shirt sleeves were rolled up to elbow level, a stethoscope dangled from his neck and a half-empty cup of so-called coffee was grasped in his right hand. 'Bloody chicory,' he cursed, slamming down the offending article. 'What with that and saccharine, there's hardly a taste bud left on my tongue. What can I do for you, Miss Langden?'

Abigail jerked a thumb in Tishy's direction. 'It's her,' she said flatly. 'She's not eaten since Mother died, not properly. I don't know what to do with her, and neither does Ellen. You see, I want to get back to London and my job, but I can't very well leave her in this condition.'

'Take her with you, then.'

Abigail looked up at the ceiling then back at him. 'I can't. She'd have to be left during my shifts. There's no-one to look after her, so she'll have to stay here with our father and Ellen.'

Clive Harrison cast an eye over Tishy. Thin as a rake, beautiful and transparent, she reminded him of a wood nymph, or of something that would not have looked out of place in 'A Midsummer Night's Dream'. 'You're anaemic,' he said. 'I'll give you some iron tablets.'

Tishy blinked rapidly as if she had just woken from a deep sleep. 'Pardon?'

'She's very jumpy,' explained Abigail. 'We've been going into the shelter most nights now that Mother's gone, and it's reminding her of London. The blitz frightened her halfway to death. She simply can't go back there, it's too much for her. So what am I to do?'

He raised his shoulders. 'Stay with her. Find work here, there's plenty to do in the local hospitals.'

Abigail clicked her tongue impatiently. 'There's no room in that house. Tishy and I are forced to share a bed – there's very little privacy. I can't stay there, and I have been ordered to work, you know.'

'What about Tishy? Doesn't she work?'

Abigail grinned ruefully. 'Tishy was allocated to work in the hospital kitchens, but she kept forgetting to go. Or she'd wander off in the middle of a shift. In the end, she was given permission to stay at home.'

The doctor stood up and wandered to the front of his desk, perching on its edge just inches away from the girls. 'Tishy?'

'Yes?' Soft blue-grey eyes looked up at him, and he noticed an impossible flash of violet near the centres of the irises.

'Can you read?'

'Of course I can,' she said indignantly. 'I've been reading since I was five, Mum told me. And I can write stories and poems too.'

He stroked his chin pensively. 'What's twenty-four and eighteen?'

'Numbers.'

'Can you add them together?'

'Why?'

He chuckled. 'Good question. What's two and two?'

She looked at her fingers. 'Four.'

'Good.' He reached across and patted her knee. 'A learning problem,' he said almost to himself.

'Oh, it's more than that.' Abigail's tone was quite shrill. 'She goes off at crazy tangents, can't hold a thought for two minutes together. Then she gets fixations, like this current one about food. She thinks if she doesn't eat, then she'll die and go to Mother. I've explained that death is a state and not a meeting place, but she can't seem to grasp the concept.'

'I want my piano,' said Tishy suddenly. 'I'll eat when I get my piano.'

'Ellen's doing her best to arrange that. You have to be patient.'

The doctor chuckled. 'There's one in my drawing room, just through that door. Will you eat one of my sandwiches if I let you play my piano?'

Tishy jumped up and clapped her palms together like an excited infant. 'Yes, yes, of course I will.' She ran from the room and screamed her joy when she located the longed-for instrument.

A few moments later, Clive Harrison found himself almost transfixed to the spot as he listened to Tishy's playing. As far as his untrained ear could tell, there was not a single note out of place throughout the whole Beethoven sonata. And there was a special quality to the execution, as if the girl were feeling and living the music at a depth that was hard to understand and impossible to express. 'Good God!' he exclaimed to Abigail. 'You've got

110

a rare talent in the family. This sort of thing very often happens to a truly gifted person, faculties diminished by the power of a specific ability. How long has she played like that?'

Abigail tried to count the years. 'I'm not sure. There was a woman in the street in Bow who gave Tishy free lessons. Actually, I don't think they were lessons, because Tishy isn't really capable of learning anything approaching a true discipline. But the lady didn't charge because she got so much pleasure from listening when Tishy visited. I think the skill was always there. She doesn't read music. She hears gramophone records and the occasional radio broadcast, then just picks up the tunes. No-one is quite sure how she manages it. But believe me, this is the only good thing about her. With the exception of her piano playing, everything she does is utterly infuriating. She is impossible to live with.'

'She could play for the troops. That's the sort of war work Tishy might do.'

'No!' Abigail drew breath sharply. 'Even you don't seem able to understand. She can't travel, not without people to look after her. And she couldn't go with strangers or into a war zone. She isn't normal, Doctor. She has never been normal, never could do ordinary things.' She leaned back in the chair, a look of despair and frustration occupying her dark eyes. 'What am I to do? About myself, I mean?'

Dr Harrison studied the girl in front of him. She seemed a sensible if rather tough sort, the kind of woman he admired. He suspected that she was probably a good nurse too, efficient, knowledgeable, capable. There weren't many of those about these days. Nurses who hadn't gone into military service were quickly snapped up by the general hospitals. He nodded almost imperceptibly. She might be extremely useful. He was not given to whims, but he decided to follow his instincts this time. 'I'm opening a nursing home just off Chorley Old Road. It will be mostly geriatric cases. The idea has been cleared with the authorities, provided I can get the necessary staff. How would you feel about applying for the post of matron? There's a decent flat, food, heating and lighting laid on, and a reasonable salary. This would solve your problem without moving you too far away from Tishy.'

Abigail's face didn't even flicker. 'A matron? At my age? I've been qualified for just a few months.'

'Don't see why you can't do it. It'll take a young head and a strong spine to get the place organized. There'll be about thirty patients altogether, most in shared rooms, some in singles. You'd have to hire staff, of course. Many will be untrained, so you'd have to work out some kind of educational programme. There's a lot of money round here, Miss Langden, old money. With old money there are usually aged relatives to care for. Many wealthy people prefer to offload such encumbrances. I intend to rob the rich in order to do research for the poor.'

'Oh. Why?'

He put his head on one side and studied her. There was little of the philanthropist here, he thought. She wasn't exactly a charitable type, but then she would be working at the capital end of his venture. 'I'm interested in vitamin deficiency, particularly now when children's diets are poor. Though, in fact, the children of Bolton probably eat better now than they ever did in the past, especially in view of the fact that cod liver oil and various other extracts are being distributed. Nevertheless, I fear that we might be breeding an anaemic lot just because of simple deficiencies. Your sister is a case in point, though her anaemia can't be blamed on the war. But is her illness genetic, or are we missing something that should be staring us in the face? Tishy's problem is, I think, severe.'

'Pernicious?' No expression registered on her face.

'Possibly.'

'I see.' There was a brief pause while she struggled to push her sister out of her thoughts. 'I'd have my own room?'

'Yes, as I said before, you would be fairly comfortable.'

'Uniform provided?'

'Of course.'

She rose and offered him her right hand. 'Very well. I shall apply. Unless you get a better qualified applicant, I suppose I shall be working for you soon.'

'Working with me. The chief responsibility will be yours. I shall be a mere visiting doctor, one among many.'

They shook hands. It was then, when Abigail touched him for the first time, that she realized she was attracted to him. There was nothing special about his appearance, he was just an average man of average height and moderate good looks. But, for some reason she could not quite pinpoint, she found him exciting and recognized immediately that she wanted to know him better. It had been months since her last boyfriend, and she was more than ready for a diversion. Was he married? If so, was he truly wedded to his marriage? Their eyes met. His were hazel in colour, though their main attraction lay in the intelligence that shone from them. 'I think you and I will do very well together, Miss Langden,' he said.

'Abigail. My name's Abigail.'

'Clive. I'll take you to see the house soon.'

'But I haven't even applied.'

'The job's yours,' he said without hesitation.

She stared at him levelly. 'Why?'

'Because you don't mess about, you know what you want from life. It's a ruthless quality, but very necessary when it comes to business. This will be primarily a business venture, though I shall, of course, expect patient care to be of the highest quality.'

'Naturally.'

Tishy burst in at the door then, two spots of colour glowing on her otherwise pale face, eyes ablaze with excitement. 'Can I come every day? I can find my own way now.'

He smiled broadly. 'Of course you can. Come at nine o'clock each weekday morning. We'll find you a duster and a bit of polish, you can help my housekeeper. And I'm

113

sure that your music will have the waiting patients cured before they've seen me.' The girl looked unbelievably beautiful in that moment; it was as if he had handed her the moon and stars as a gift. 'And I shall paint your portrait when I find time,' he added. 'Just a little hobby of mine.' Yes, someone should commit that bone-structure to canvas. She was perfect. It was hard to understand how an ugly little man like Billy London could have fathered such a child. Her mother had not been attractive either. Perhaps Tishy was a throwback, perhaps she favoured a distant ancestor.

He handed Abigail a box of pills. 'Give her one at meal times and make sure she eats something. Here's your sandwich,' he said to Tishy. 'Cheese and pickle, eat it up.'

'Thank you, thank you, thank you,' chanted Tishy as she made for the hallway.

'I'll see you soon, Abigail.'

'Yes.' She would see him soon. She intended to make sure of that.

When the last customer had left the Derby Street shop, Ellen turned the sign to CLOSED and began the business of counting takings and checking ration points. Theresa dusted shelves, polished weights and scales, covered the bacon, and rearranged a collapsed pile of blue sugar bags. 'Mam?' she said as their tasks neared completion.

'Hello?'

Theresa sidled over to the till. 'Don't get upset, but I'm going to ask you if I can leave home. Leave for good, I mean, go and work somewhere.'

'Eh?' Ellen's usually calm face registered shock and fear. 'We're not on about that convent again, are we? I thought you'd got over all that. You're not going in, and there's an end to it.'

The girl hung her head. 'No, I'm not going in. But I want to get away from our house.'

Ellen straightened her apron and pulled the thick cardigan tight across her chest. 'Things are all right now.

You've no need to be frightened of your dad, and no need to be ashamed over his divorce. We're married again. You know we got married yesterday. Happen he's changed for good this time.'

'It's not just him, it's Abigail and everything . . . it's so crowded.'

'But Abigail's going to work in that nursing home of Doctor Harrison's – didn't she come in and tell us this afternoon?'

Theresa's chin dropped even further. 'I don't want to live with her, but I don't want to live without her either. He's scared of her. As long as she's there, me dad's not so bad. Once she's gone, he might start up again.'

'Oh no, he won't.' Surely he wouldn't dare . . . ?

'How do you know?' The voice wavered as Theresa fought her tears. 'Either way, I want to get out. She talks about . . . things. I hate hearing her talking about there being no God and . . . other things as well. But it'll be worse once she's gone. Mam, I want you to find me a place, a live-in place where I can work. I need to feel safe.'

Ellen studied the younger of her twin daughters. She looked pale and drawn with worry. Billy's effect on her had always been noticeable; Theresa had never been endowed with Marie's natural exuberance. He was all but killing this one, making her old before her time. 'But I'd miss you, lass,' said the mother quietly.

'And I'll miss you too. But it has to be done.' The girl raised her eyes at last and looked directly at Ellen. 'I am terrified of him, more feared than I am of any bomb. I know it's a sin, but I don't love him. He is a cruel man, and I want to get away from him. I don't care if I never see him again.'

'He's not the same since his accident, love. You know how quiet he's been, hardly a word out of him.'

'I once read a book that said it's always quiet before a storm. Mam, I can't bear to be in the same room with him, even in the same house. I'd sooner move a hundred miles away, even if it meant leaving you and Marie. I know I'm a coward, but I have to go. I'm sixteen now, nearly seventeen, and I know what's best for me. You have to help me to get away. And I can work, even though I've got a limp. You know I'm a good worker, Mam. Please?'

Ellen shivered as a deep sigh escaped from the very depths of her soul. Life had changed beyond recognition since Lilian had arrived with those two girls. And now, on top of everything else, Theresa was looking for a complete change of scene. Not that Ellen blamed the child, oh no, not at all. But what if Marie did the same? What if she lost both her daughters?

She shuddered again. The thought of being virtually alone with him filled her with dread. Tishy wouldn't count, Tishy would be no use in a crisis. Would there be a crisis, though? He'd been so meek of late, going to the Deane Road shop every day, doing his job, picking up a wage like everybody else. There had been no excessive drinking, no shouting, no violence. But how long would that last? After coming back from Blackpool, he had looked like a broken man, but now he seemed to be gaining in physical energy every day. Would he revert to type?

Ellen looked at Theresa's face and knew that she could not force her to stay. It would be wrong to use any of the girls as protection, and this one was already a bag of nerves. 'All right,' she whispered. 'Give me a week or two. I'll find you somewhere to go. There's reserved occupations all over the place, and we'll need to make sure you don't get called up.' Mind, she wouldn't get conscripted, not with her bad leg.

'Thanks, Mam. I don't want to leave you with him, but—'

'I'll be fine. Look, I still remember what it's like being sixteen. I know you want a taste of life, spread your wings a bit.'

'That's not the reason.'

'I know, but I can pretend, can't I? God help me, Theresa, but I hate that man more with each day that goes by. And I went and married him all over again yesterday afternoon.'

'For our sakes.'

'Nay, don't you go blaming yourself. There's neither of you could help being born. Right. Let's pull the blinds down and get home. Marie'll be waiting for us.'

Marie knew that he had the pound note; she'd seen him palming it earlier in the afternoon, but the shop had been too busy for her to tackle him. As soon as the door was locked, she faced him, arms akimbo, face set in stubborn lines, feet planted well apart as if she were bracing herself. 'Put it back,' she ordered in as stern a tone as her high-pitched sixteen-year-old voice could achieve.

'Eh? Put what back?'

'The pound note in your pocket. It'll show up as missing any road when we come to weekend and check the books. So you might as well stick it back in the till while you've got chance.'

He folded his arms and stared at her. 'Who the bleeding hell do you think you're talking to? Nobody's ever questioned me before about money in this shop. It's mine to take, so put that in your pipe.'

She stood her ground. 'This shop is mine, not yours. Mam's in charge of the shops till we get old enough. You can't just take our money when you feel like it.'

'Can't I? Who's going to stop me?'

Marie inhaled deeply before speaking again. 'Me and Abigail, that's who. We'll stop you working here, then you'll have no wages at all. We can't afford to employ somebody as makes off with profits. You've said that often enough yourself when you thought the shops were yours.'

He took a step in her direction. 'How long have I fed and clothed you? Best of everything not good enough for you, eh?'

Even now, she continued to stand her ground. 'You've been feeding and clothing us for as long as I can remember.'

'And what thanks do I get?'

'You were doing it with Lilian's money.'

117

'Prove it!'

'And hitting us, and hitting me mam, and making our lives a misery. So put it back.'

He hesitated. 'I was only borrowing it.'

She smiled grimly. 'Oh well, that's different. Stick an IOU in the till and I'll take it out of your packet on Friday. But listen, if this money's ever short, you go. Linda Tattersall never touches the till, so that leaves just you and me, and I'm not likely to pinch stuff of me own, am I? I'm sorry, Dad, but this isn't yours any more. None of it's yours.'

'You hard little bitch!' He raised a hand as if to strike her, but she dodged away easily, quickly putting the counter between herself and him. 'Come here,' he yelled. 'I've had enough of this lot. Who put all the effort into these shops? I did. Who stockpiled for the war so that we'd have plenty to bargain with? I did. And now you're telling me what's what, are you? Well, I'll show you who's the boss round here . . .' He stopped suddenly, noticing that she had picked up the largest of the weights.

'Any nearer, and I'll clobber you one good and proper,' she said breathlessly. 'You can't frighten me, I'm not like our Theresa. And I'll tell Abigail. She won't take no nonsense from you. Come on, then. What are you waiting for?'

He took the pound from his pocket and tore it in half, throwing the pieces into the air. 'Take your money,' he snarled. 'I'll have my day with you, young lady. And with your mother and bloody Abigail. There's tricks up my sleeve you'd never dream of.' With anger darkening his thin face, he unlocked the door and walked out into the night. He would get them, all of them. There'd be no escape for anybody once he'd got some sort of plan together. Yes, they might feel safe for the moment with their shops and their houses and never mind the poor bloke who'd sweated years to set everything up for them.

But this poor bloke was thinking about having his revenge. And after the event, all his worldly goods would be returned to their rightful owner. He stopped at the corner to light a Pasha, coughing as the acrid smoke hit complaining lungs. Bloody Pashas. But he knew where to go for a proper cigarette – and a bit of comfort into the bargain. Yes, he'd made himself a nice little friend lately, somebody who was glad of a few bits of food smuggled out in his pocket from time to time. He smoothed the suit that had been specially bought for Lil's funeral, the one he had worn again at that bloody stupid wedding yesterday. Ellen and her daughters could go on believing they held all the trump cards. But the famous Billy London knew different, didn't he?

CHAPTER FIVE

Cissie and Vera

Cissie Tattersall was a tall, big-boned woman with a friendly face, ordinary blue eyes and unremarkable mousy brown hair. But although she had no outstanding features, she was somehow put together well, as if her Creator had done a fair job with poor clay. She therefore gave the impression of acceptable attraction without being beautiful. Cissie was a simple soul who had married in her teens, given birth to two live and two stillborn children in her thirties. She apparently expected little from life and, as is the way with those who expect little, she got next to nothing.

Harry Tattersall had been a miner, a coal-face worker whose wages had, at least, kept the rent paid, and had put food on the table and clothes on the backs of their children. Because he had opted to go to war, Cissie had lost him, and there would be no more wages, not even from the army. The widow's pension, when it eventually came through, was a pittance, so everyone was glad of Linda's coppers earned at the London Stores.

Cissie was further pleased when Mr London began to drop in from time to time with a bit of cheese, some spilled sugar and, occasionally, a few ounces of precious tea. It was nice to have someone who took an interest in the Tattersall family. He was known far and wide as a miserly sort, was Mr London, but Cissie chose to take him at face value. She would never forget that it was he who had sent food while she was still in shock over that telegram, that it was he who had offered to employ their Linda in the little cleaning job.

120

So, every time he came to her back door, she greeted him with a friendly smile and a proper cigarette if she'd managed to get some. He had moods, and she accepted his moods along with his gifts. Folk were all different, she reckoned, and it wasn't up to her to judge them.

He was in a bad humour tonight, so she made him a nice mug of hot tea, and dug behind the alarm clock for two Craven A she'd been saving for herself. 'Here you are, Mr London. A proper smoke instead of them Pashas.'

'Ta.'

She sat opposite him. 'How's it going, then? I hear you had to get married again after the missus found out about your divorce.'

He spat into the fire. 'It's a marriage in name only. I sleep in the front room, she sleeps in the kitchen.' He felt better for putting his cards on the table. She was a slow sort, but perhaps now she might realize what he wanted from her. 'We live separate lives,' he added meaningfully.

'Oh. Why?'

'The wedding was just for the girls. We've nothing in common, her and me.'

She coughed nervously, worrying about pushing him too far. 'And is it true what they're all saying? That Mrs Langden owns the houses and the girls got the shops?'

'Naw, she's just holding them in trust. I agreed to it, you see.' How far could he confide in this one? She seemed grateful enough, honest enough . . . 'Still, never mind. My daughters would have inherited the business anyway, wouldn't they?'

Cissie walked to the fire and stirred a pan of stew. 'She's giving all the pledges back. Bella Hewitt says she's got her husband's best suit and the watch too. Your wife never charged a penny, either. They'll all be queuing up at the pawnshop to give their stuff in for a few bob, stuff that you used to hold for them when they'd no money.'

He shrugged lightly, determined not to let his temper show. 'Nothing to do with me any more. If she wants to act stupid, I can't stop her. I can give advice, husbandly advice, but when she acts deaf . . .' He lifted his shoulders further in a gesture of helplessness.

'Is she really in charge of the shops, then?'

'Yes, till the girls come of age.'

'But what about you, Mr London?'

'What about me? I just opened the shops, that's all. I'm just the damned fool who did all the work. You know, it's a good job I met you, Mrs Tattersall. This is somewhere I can come for a bit of peace. Five women I've got at home now, all grabbing at what used to be my money. It's nice here, specially when your kids are out. I feel comfortable in your house.'

She smiled, preened herself slightly and patted her hair. 'You're very welcome, I'm sure.'

'I'm very lonely too, Mrs Tattersall.'

'Me name's Cissie. Aye, and I get spells of loneliness too. I miss my Harry, he was a good bloke. Many a night I cry myself to sleep. If it wasn't for you and your kindness, Mr London, I don't know how we'd have managed lately. It's not easy, being a widow woman.'

'You can call me Billy. Just when we're in here.'

'All right, then.' She had no intention of calling him Billy. It wouldn't seem right, calling Mr London by his first name. 'Do you want another cup of tea?'

'No.' He placed his mug on the table, walked across the room, then proceeded to show her what he did want. After a few feeble protestations she gave in, and their coupling took place in great discomfort on the rag rug in front of the fire.

Afterwards, she fastened her blouse while he watched her. 'You liked that, didn't you?' he asked, pot teeth displayed in a grin of triumph.

She glanced sideways at him. 'I didn't mind.' She kept telling herself that she didn't mind, that it didn't matter. It was just a way of paying for extra food, that was all. And she was starting work in Barlow's canteen next week, so happen she wouldn't need to pay like this again. 'Tony and Linda will be back in a minute, they've only gone to me mam's up Claughton Street. I think you'd best be off, Mr London.'

'Billy.' He smoothed what was left of his hair and replaced the new bowler. 'I'm Billy to my friends. I'd say we were friends now, wouldn't you, Cissie?'

She tasted the stew, her hand trembling as the spoon travelled to her lips. 'Aye, I suppose we are. Only what about your missus? What would she say if she knew what's just gone on here?'

He chuckled mirthlessly. 'She couldn't care less. I've told you, we only got married the second time to make the daughters legitimate in the eyes of her flaming Church. You're just what I need, Cissie. Somebody warm and welcoming.'

'Eeh, lad.' She suddenly felt a degree of pity for him. 'I can't be your fancy piece, we'd be bound to get noticed. I know you're lonely, and I know what that's like. But I can't make myself cheap, Mr London. My Harry wouldn't have liked me to get cheap.'

'I'll look after you. I'll see you're always fed, put some fruit on one side every time we get some. And I can easily fetch you that extra quarter of cheese and a few bacon ends.'

Cissie replaced the pan lid. 'You make it sound like a bit of a business arrangement, as if I'm a streetwoman.'

'No, I'm fond of you,' he said testily. 'I wouldn't have bothered if I hadn't been fond.' His tone softened. 'I'm just sorry about your husband, sad to see you left on your own to bring up two children. It must be terrible for you.'

She gathered her courage and looked him straight in the face. 'They're all saying as how you left your first wife to rear two by herself. And after the divorce, she had to struggle on with never a penny off you. They say she crawled up here on her hands and knees to make sure her lasses got their money back. So why do you feel sorry for me when you never felt sorry for her?' She took a backward step as a strange expression flickered briefly on his face.

Billy fiddled with his tie, his eyes wandering from her suddenly penetrating gaze. 'You don't know what that woman done to me, Cissie. A man can take so much and no more. She was bigger than two houses, and she used to hit me.' Strange how he was beginning to believe this lie. It was a good way to get sympathy, saying he'd been the victim of this female giant's rages.

Cissie put a hand to her open mouth. 'Ooh, did she?'

He decided that a bit of even fancier embroidery would not look out of place. 'Broke my arm once, cracked two of my ribs. It was horrible, a nightmare. A man with a bad chest doesn't need broken ribs. I had to leave her. If I hadn't gone, she would have killed me. I didn't want to leave the girls, but she was dangerous.' He inhaled sharply, remembering his real fear of Lil. She'd never needed to lift a hand. Just the sight of her standing there with a certain expression on her face had been enough to put him to flight.

She thought for a moment. 'They say you took her money.'

'Who's this "they"?'

'Everybody. Folk in the shops and in the streets and that. They've talked about nowt else for days, ever since your first wife died.' Without understanding why, she picked up a dinner plate and clutched it to her chest.

He stepped nearer to her. 'Listen, that money was mine. I earned it and she took it, never even offered me half. Anyway, this is nobody's business. Just like you and me is nobody's business. We need one another, Cissie. I'll be back to see you in a few days.' He turned abruptly and left the house through the scullery.

Cissie sank on to a chair. She wasn't the strongest of women, and she knew it. There'd always been a man in charge of her life, first Dad, then Harry. For a reason she could not understand or even question, Cissie's attitude to men had always been one of implicit obedience. So, she was probably stuck with him. He wasn't what she might have chosen, with his bony body and awful denture breath, but he was male and he was ready to take some of the responsibility from her shoulders. For that, at least, she should be grateful. Yet she was scared, and she couldn't work out why. Was it fear of being caught, fear of Ellen Langden's anger? No, it was something else, and she couldn't quite put a finger on it.

With a heartfelt sigh, Cissie Tattersall stood up and put more salt in the stew. Tony and Linda would eat well, and that was the main thing.

Billy London made his way down Back Noble Street. It had become his habit of late to enter the house by the rear door, eat his specially prepared light meal in the kitchen, then he usually went through to the front room where he was condemned to spend his nights. Ellen sometimes passed the time upstairs with the girls while he ate his tea. When he had finished eating, he often sat in silent anger listening from the isolation of the parlour while the five of them piled back into the kitchen for cocoa, a chat and a laugh. That they were laughing at him he had no doubt; his evenings were almost unbearable these days, and the whole situation was driving him mad.

It was towards such an evening that he walked after his visit with Cissie Tattersall. He was still working to find a plan, to discover some way of getting rid of all of them. How could he manage to do away with five people? It wouldn't be easy, but there must be a way round this. The night was clear and crisp, with stars dotting an ink-black sky. There had been no siren yet, so he was not in a hurry to reach home. As he passed Vera Shaw's gate, a match was struck and a familiar voice asked, 'Is that you, Mr London?'

'It is.'

As far as he could see, she seemed to be muffled up to the eyeballs in scarf and high-collared coat, and the hand that held the flickering light was apparently gloved. 'Waited a good while for you, I have. What have you been up to?'

'Pardon? Is that anything to do with you?'

'Might be.'

'How's that?'

She shuffled towards him, plainly unsure of her footing on the icy pavement. 'These here walls are very thin, Mr London. Specially if you put a glass to them. Mind you, I haven't got no glasses, but a jam jar's nearly as good. That solicitor feller got right excited over your bigamy, didn't he?'

He coughed and put a hand to his throat. 'What are you talking about?' he asked when the paroxysm had passed.

'And you told me yourself, didn't you? The night you got drunk and come in our house. Two wives, you said. Wife number one and wife number two, you said. I asked you if you'd got divorced from the first one, and you said you didn't think so. Well, now we know you didn't. Everybody's putting it about that you were divorced, supposed to save your faces, eh? Only I know you weren't. You come up here and married your Ellen while you were still wed to the other one.'

Her ashpit door was slightly ajar, so he grabbed this item for support. 'Have you told anyone else?'

'Would I go and do a thing like that, now?' It was clear from her tone of voice that she was smiling. 'No, I've not said one word. But I've been thinking about it, like. I mean, if I told the police what I've heard, you'd get yourself investigated, wouldn't you? Then you could well go to prison. I mean, it's a crime, is bigamy. Aye, you could serve years for that.'

'Lil's dead now. It don't count now that Lil's dead.'

Vera chuckled. 'Oh, it does. Her being dead makes no difference, lad. And it was her brass you ran off with in the first place. We all know that. Your Ellen doesn't care who knows that, but the police might be interested. And Ellen'd soon bother if I told the neighbours she was never even legally wed on account of you already having a wife. Bad enough for the Catholics to think she'd married a divorced man – even if she didn't realize at the time. How would it be if folk got told she'd been living over the brush all them years and that the two girls are bastards?'

'You bitch,' he spat. 'Listen who's talking. How many fathers have your lot got between them?'

'Aye, now you know what I've put up with all this while, folk talking behind me back. This would give you lot a taste of the medicine, eh? The bloody medicine I've been having to swallow. Any road, happen we can act sensible and come to a bit of an arrangement.'

'Such as?'

'Such as some extra food and a few proper cigs.'

He took a step back. 'But I'm smoking Pasha myself half the time. Do you think I'd smoke this Turkish compost if I could get hold of Woodbines or Craven A every day? As for extra food, there's none about, there's a war on in case you hadn't noticed.'

She reached out and tugged at his sleeve. 'I bet there's enough for Cissie Tattersall, though. Oh yes, you've been followed. I've been at the back of you ever since you left Deane Road, only I got fed up of standing outside her house, so I came home and waited here. I bet your fancy woman's not short of a bit of tea and sugar. And if it's company you're after, you don't need to go as far as Emblem Street to look for it.'

'You? An ugly cross-eyed cow like you?'

'Ah, so I was right, Cissie is your bit on the side. Better looking than me is she? There's more to it than looks, Mr London. Same as anything else, practice makes perfect. I don't mind giving you a good time as a swap for the odd half pound of butter. And I'll keep me gob shut about your business as long as you like. It's up to you. A few bits and pieces left inside my back gate twice a week, that would make sure I kept quiet. That's what you want, isn't it? A nice, peaceful hush?'

The siren sounded, its terrible wail drowning Billy's responses before they had formed. He pushed Vera into her back yard, his head completely filled by the sound of the air raid warning. He needed to organize his thoughts, but the shrill noise went on and on like the scream of a wounded dinosaur.

His breathing became laboured as he grew more angry and confused. Women. It was all down to women. Bloody Lil, bloody Ellen, those four girls all grabbing and scheming and grasping. They were all against him. Even Cissie Tattersall was probably in it for what she could take out.

Rage bubbled blindly to the surface. This one here was the worst of them all; she suddenly seemed to embody every damned thing that was wrong with his life. He raised his hand and used the palm to push her away from him. That was all he was doing, he told himself. He was only pushing her away. But he couldn't seem to stop lashing out at her. The second push was violent, and she slipped on the glassy flags, her head making violent contact with the lavatory wall. As the siren died away, he heard a scream, a sickening thud and the unmistakable sound of splintering bone.

With shaking fingers, he struggled to light a match. She lay like a heap of discarded clothing, crumpled and distorted next to the wall. A slow trickle of blood oozed from a nostril. She did not seem to be breathing. The match burnt his fingers, jerking him back to full awareness. He had done it now, hadn't he? He had gone and killed Vera Shaw.

The instinct for self-preservation came to the surface at last. Galvanized by fear, he slid out of the yard and in at the next gate, pausing for a few seconds to control his breathing. He must act as if nothing had happened. When he entered the kitchen, Marie looked up from her meal. 'Where've you been?'

'Cissie Tattersall's. I took her a bit of dirty sugar.'

Ellen, who was for once sitting by the fire, raised her eyes from the paper. 'Very charitable, I'm sure,' she said quietly. 'Happen there's hope for you yet.'

He removed his hat and overcoat, then reached a bowl of broth from the range shelf.

'You're shaking,' commented Marie.

'I'm shivering to death,' he replied as normally as he could manage. 'The streets are frozen over.'

After forcing the food down his reluctant throat, he went through to the front room. He needed to make sure that he followed the same routine as always, right down to the minutest detail. After a few minutes, he came back to the kitchen. 'Finished with the *Evening News*?' he asked. This request had been sticking in his craw for weeks now. Before Lil came, Ellen would never have dared to read the paper until he'd had it first. She passed it to him without comment as the four girls came downstairs ready for the shelter. At least he would have the house to himself. Had he closed Vera Shaw's back gate? Would anyone find the body tonight? No, it was pitch black out there.

When the house was empty, he sat huddled over the fire, his mind slowly clicking into gear as he began to feel the benefits of warm air on his skin and hot food in his stomach. He hadn't really killed her, wasn't truly a murderer. A murderer was somebody who set out to finish a life, not a poor bloke who gave a woman a bit of a push. He couldn't help the ice, he hadn't ordered the weather.

Feeling more than a little sorry for himself, he got up and took Ellen's medicinal brandy from the dresser. He was entitled to some comfort, after all. This had been a terrible shock to his system, and a man with a bad stomach and gassed lungs couldn't afford such shocks. He hardly gave a second thought to Vera Shaw, except to wonder when the body would be discovered. She had been a woman of no importance until she had decided to start threatening him.

The brandy filled his veins, and he started to have a feeling of self-righteousness about the whole affair. It wasn't his fault, any of it. If Lil had given him his half of the money in the first place, he probably wouldn't have pinched the lot. And if Lil hadn't come up here with those two stupid girls, he could have carried on as a free man, a man in charge. And if Ellen hadn't turned against him, he would have continued to rule the shops. And if Vera Shaw hadn't been so bleeding stupid, she would still be alive at this minute. It had been an accident anyway, and surely no-one would connect him with it. After all, he'd never had much to do with Vera Shaw, hadn't bothered with her except to serve her in the shops.

He began to feel a lot better. No point in blaming himself for what hadn't been his fault. The bombers came over and he ignored them as usual. If a bomb had a few names on it, then the ones in the shelter were just as likely as anybody else to get it. With one world war under his belt, Billy felt fairly confident about surviving a second. The planes droned their heavy way through the night in search of a sensible target. It wouldn't be here, not again. Bolton, in Billy's opinion, was a place of little significance, and the town had already received its fair share of German mistakes. Silence reigned as the Luftwaffe passed over and away to somewhere more vital. Billy yawned, stretched and dozed in the double glow of fire and brandy.

A hammering sound loud enough to disturb the dead woke him from a deep sleep. He shuddered back to consciousness and glanced at the clock. Ten to nine. There hadn't been an all-clear yet, so everybody would still be in the shelter. What was this bloody awful racket? On feet made unsteady by alcohol and recent sleep, he stumbled to the back door. 'Who's that?'

'Warden. Hurry up and open this door. I knew you were in. I know you never go down the shelter.'

Billy opened the door. 'What's the problem?'

The man stepped into the scullery. 'Bit of light showing at your neighbour's window, so I went for a look. Spark out in the back yard, she was. Come a right cropper from the look of things.'

'Oh. Who?'

'Mrs Shaw next door. We've sent her down to the infirmary in an ambulance. I thought I'd better let you know, in case you start worrying over where she is.'

'I see. Had an accident, has she?'

The warden rubbed his frozen hands together. 'Very bad, that yard of hers. Like a flaming skating rink, it is. She might have been going to the lav, but she had her coat and everything on as if she was ready for the shelter. Happen she slipped on her way out. God, it's freezing out there, I'm starved through.'

Billy tried to swallow his fear. 'Drop of brandy?'

'Not supposed to, not on duty. But being as it's so cold, I'll have a spoonful.'

They went through to the kitchen where Billy poured a hefty measure into a glass. 'How is she?' he asked carefully.

The warden drank deeply, shivering as the warm fluid hit his stomach. 'Looks like a fractured skull, might have broke her back too. They didn't like moving her, but they couldn't very well leave her where she was. One of them said her pulse was weak, and they were worried over her bleeding in her brain, summat of that sort. They've sent a wireless message down to Birmingham to try and trace her husband. Happen they're feared she won't get through the night.'

'What a shame. Did she . . . come round at all?'

'No, not a flicker out of her as far as I heard. When I first found her, I thought she was already a goner.'

Billy breathed more easily. 'Well, we'll just have to see what tomorrow brings.'

'That's right.' The warden pulled his scarf more tightly round his throat. 'I'd best get back to it, then. See you again, Mr London.'

'What? Oh yes. Cheerio.'

Alone once more, he paced the room like an animal in a cage. He was so tense that he failed to hear the all-clear sounding in the street. She wasn't dead! The bleeding woman was alive, could wake up at any minute and say he'd tried to kill her. No, she wouldn't. The warden had said she was practically a goner, surely it was only a matter of time. He must stay calm, had to look normal and ordinary. But if she did recover, he'd be done for theft,

131

bigamy and attempted murder as well! He had better pack his bags and run, make for London, see if he could lose himself there. No, that would be distinctly abnormal behaviour, the police would be on to him like a shot. What should he do?

'Having trouble sleeping?' It was Abigail's voice.

He turned to find the five of them standing in a row watching him. He hadn't even heard them come in, so engrossed had he been in his problem. 'They've just taken Vera Shaw away,' he muttered. 'She's at the infirmary.'

'Why?' asked Ellen. 'She's never had a day's illness in her life, as fit as a flea, is Vera.'

'She's been in an accident, cracked her skull in the yard.'

Abigail studied her father. There was something about him tonight, a terrible edginess that she recognized only too clearly. She hated to admit it, but she was very like her male parent. When she had a worry, or something to hide, she tended to pace the floor. What was the matter with him? Why was he so badly affected by an accident next door?

'Poor Mrs Shaw,' said Marie. 'We'll have to go and see her when we get time.'

'No point in that,' said Billy, too quickly for Abigail's liking. 'She's unconscious and they don't know whether she'll ever come round. They'll probably let nobody in unless it's family.'

'Them little kiddies,' said Theresa.

'She was never a mother to them,' said Ellen by way of comfort. 'They're settled where they are, Theresa.'

'Yes, but your mother's still your mother, no matter what.'

Ellen smiled at her daughter. 'I suppose you're right, lass. Well, there's nowt we can do. Off you go, girls, and get to bed. There could be another warning yet, so we might as well get all the sleep we can.'

Abigail lingered while the other three went upstairs, then she followed her father through to the front room.

'You've done something,' she said. 'I know you have.'

'Eh?'

'I can sense it. You've been up to no good.'

'Don't talk stupid. Air raids always make me nervous. Don't forget, I've still got shell shock from the last lot. The doctor said I have to take things easy.'

Abigail inclined her head, her eyes travelling the length of his body. 'You've no fear of bombs, not really. I know you got a bit shaken up by the one that actually fell round here, but you're quite happy to stay in the house when the bomber planes come over. No, it's something else. You're terrified, aren't you?'

'And you've got what's known as a vivid imagination.'

'Have I? We'll see about that.'

He stared at her disappearing back as she left the room. His throat was as dry as sandpaper, while his heart leapt about in his chest like a trapped wild animal. God, he would be a damned sight better off without that eldest daughter! Hadn't Marie said something about a fancy nursing home and Dr Harrison? He wished he'd listened. Marie had come back full of it after her lunch break, she'd been telling one or two of the customers about Abigail getting made up to a matron. When, though? When was he going to be rid of the one who could see straight through him? Not soon enough. Yesterday would not have been soon enough for him.

Marie and Abigail sat on the top stair where the other two girls could not hear them. 'So, what do you reckon he's done?' asked Marie. 'He's been in the shop nearly all day, never even came home for any dinner. He's not had the chance to get up to mischief.'

Abigail, arms wrapped round her shins, studied her knees closely in the dim light from a single mantle at the top of the flight. 'It's just a feeling. He's very nervous all of a sudden.'

'Not as nervous as our Theresa. She's begged me mam to let her go into service like they did in the old days.

Imagine that, though. She'd rather be a servant than live in a house with her own dad.'

'He's horrible,' pronounced the older girl. 'My mother never said much against him, just that he'd gone away and left us poor. But she must have hated him, and so do I.'

'I'm not that keen on him myself. It won't be the same here without our Theresa. And I'll miss you and all.'

'Will you?' The tone registered real surprise. 'I've never had a female friend before, not since I was at school. Look, if you get really fed up in that shop, come and see me. I'm sure you'd make a good nurse, and I'll be needing auxiliaries.'

'I can't leave Mam. She'll have to run the Derby Street shop on her own as it is, and we can't let him loose by himself in Deane Road, couldn't trust him. I caught him trying to make off with a pound today, shoving it in his pocket right under my nose, he was.'

'But you said he'd done nothing.'

'I'd forgotten that. Anyway, it's only a little thing. He wouldn't be nervous about that, because he still likes to think he can do whatever he wants in the shop. Anyway, I put him in his place good and proper.'

Abigail grinned broadly. 'Good for you. No, you're right. It's bigger than that, whatever he's done. Probably criminal, from the looks of him. I mean, he's got no conscience, so what's it going to be? You know, Marie, I'm concerned about myself, because I'm so like him. I can't seem to worry much about other people. That's how he is, completely bloody selfish. Yes, the only person I ever worried about was Mother.' She nodded. 'Oh, he's like me. So whatever it is that's making him so worried, it has to be a big item.'

'Like what?'

'A massive robbery, murder, fraud – who knows?'

'Happen he's going to light a beacon on Winter Hill, show Hitler where to land if he wants to take over the cotton mills.'

They both burst out laughing. Theresa put her head round the door. 'Shush,' she said. 'He might be trying to sleep. You know how mad he gets if we wake him.'

'Theresa,' sighed Marie. 'How many times do I have to tell you? Them days are over. Mam's in charge now. She might not say much, but she's got him right where she wants him.'

Theresa sniffed. 'Well, I'm not taking any chances. I'm sixteen, old enough to go away, and it's time I had some peace. Are you coming to bed, or are you going to talk all night?' She didn't like to admit it to herself, but she felt a small pang of jealousy each time she caught Abigail and Marie in a huddle. It was as if Abigail had taken her twin away – they had used to be so close until the other two had turned up. She would pray tonight that her envy would disappear. After all, Theresa had a whole new life to look forward to. A life apart from him.

Tishy hummed a little tune as she prepared herself for bed in the room she shared with her sister. It had been a funny night, a mixture of enjoyment and confusion. The shelter had been lovely, everyone singing songs and laughing and jigging about. Someone had taught her 'Sally, Sally, pride of our alley', and it was this tune that lingered on her lips as she pulled on her nightdress. She loved the music from round here. Most people in Noble Street liked a good old sing, and she was picking up 'She's a Lassie from Lancashire' and other local ditties.

So, why did she feel uneasy? Ah yes, the hand. It had been hard work, staring out of a black bedroom into an even blacker night, but her eyes had got used to it eventually. And she'd seen a dark figure falling in the next yard, and a white hand reaching out to push that figure. There hadn't been a glove on the hand, which was strange on such a cold night. A tiny light had grown in the hand, like when Mum used to strike a match for the gas, like when Ellen lit a mantle. Tishy knew about someone who never wore gloves, but she couldn't remember who it was. The hand hadn't had a body attached to it either. Perhaps the body had been hidden at the time by the wall, or perhaps the hand had belonged to one of Abigail's ghosts. Tishy hadn't stayed by the window. The siren had been very loud, that awful noise that always sent her scurrying off in search of Abigail or Ellen. It was all very confusing, hands and bodies and dark shapes falling. She had better not think about it any longer, or she might have more bad dreams.

Fortunately for Billy London, his second daughter did not connect what she had seen earlier with the report of Vera Shaw's accident. Tishy was not one to linger over unsavoury concepts. She simply got into bed, hummed a few more songs, and committed the unpleasant little incident to the back of her mind. After struggling to remember a few extra words of the songs that were new to her, Tishy fell into a deep and dreamless sleep.

Percy Shaw sat howling his eyes out in Ellen Langden's kitchen. He'd had a shocking war up to now, and he was emptying his soul into the apparently patient ear of his next door neighbour. 'I were running along with this leg in me hand, Ellen, and I didn't know whose leg it was. "Whose is this one?" I kept shouting, and some clever bugger told me to shove it in the bin with the others, they'd try and match it for shoes and socks once they'd got all the limbs together. Fair sickened with it, I was.'

'I'm sure you must have been, Percy.'

'Then I got one feller in the ambulance with a big bandage on his head. He kept thinking I was his dad, kept hanging on to me hand something merciless. Any road, we gets halfway to the hospital, and his bandage slips off. Honest, I'd never seen nowt like it in me life. Half his head had gone. He'd only one eye and one ear, then there was a load of grey matter showing through where his skull had been. Died in me arms, he did. Now our Vera's in the same state. I've had enough, lass, I can tell thee that for nowt. There's nothing like the smell of fresh blood. Like rusty iron, it is. It sticks in your nose long after you're off shift. She'll go the same road as him that only had half a head, I know she will.'

'Don't say that, Percy. You've got to have hope. Despair is a sin, you know. And Vera wasn't left with only half her head, was she?'

He sniffed and dabbed at his eyes with a handkerchief that had seen cleaner days. 'It's all inside with our Vera. Subdural, it is.' He prided himself on having picked up a few medical terms that he scarcely understood, and he used them at every opportunity, even when such terms were inappropriate. 'She's concussed, traumatized and having haema . . .' He struggled for the word. 'Haematomas, that's what she's undergoing. Inter-cranial haematomas.'

Ellen patted his hand. 'Listen, lad. You're going to have to pull yourself together. We want no more of this. If you're thinking of carrying on in this state, you'll find you're no use to Vera or to anyone else. Look at yourself. When did you last have a good scrub? Have you been visiting the hospital like that? Whatever will they think of you at all? You smell, Percy Shaw, and smelling isn't going to make anybody better.'

Percy stared at her. She had changed almost beyond recognition, had Ellen Langden. Why, in her quiet little way, she was quite a bossy woman all of a sudden. 'It's not easy,' he said lamely. 'I've been used to running hot water and a proper bathroom—'

'Have you indeed? Well, there's no such luxury round here, lad. There's the public baths, only they're being used mostly for scabies cases. Still, I think they've the odd cubicle free in an evening. That's where me and the girls go once a week. Or you could bring the tin bath in like most folk do. You'd catch no harm boiling a bit of water and cleaning yourself up. I'm sorry, Percy, but I'm not keen on talking to you till you smell a bit sweeter.'

'But I mustn't get cold. Not with me heart murmur.'

'Don't you be giving me that tale. You've been through more bomb sites than I've had hot dinners, out in all weathers you must have been. So why worry about catching cold now? Get away with your bother, I've a meal to see to.'

'Ellen?'

'Hello?'

'She's been unconscious weeks now. Do you think she'll come round?'

'Nay, you're the one with the medical training. All I can do is pray and light a candle for her at church. Just try to keep your spirits up, do your best for Vera.'

He sighed, his breath heaving with sobs. 'It's the kiddies, see. I want me children back. What chance have I without a wife?'

Ellen closed her mouth firmly. He had no chance at all if Vera did come back into the picture, because the authorities knew that she was completely unfit to care for young ones. Her house had always been a midden. Vera's attitude to cleaning seemed to be rather like a drunk's excuse for hitting the bottle – no need to bother getting sober if you know you'll be tipsy again in half an hour. Aye, cleaning was too repetitive for Vera.

'What'll I do?' he wailed.

'To get the little ones back?'

'Yes.'

'Just clean the house up.'

His jaw dropped. 'What? Have you seen the state of that place? You can't find a floor, never mind clean up. I wouldn't know where to put everything. I'd be better off trying to nail jelly to a gate, I'd have more chance. It's hopeless.'

She tutted under her breath. 'You're the one that's hopeless. If you'd given her a hand when the kids were babies, she might have stayed on top of the job. But you just left her to it, same as most menfolk seem to do.'

'Hang on, Ellen. Them two youngest likely aren't mine. I don't want them back, do I? And I lost heart when I found out how she was with the men.'

Ellen rounded on him. 'The two youngest – the ones

you say aren't yours – are with Vera's mother, and they'll probably stay there. Now, if you want the others back, get out of here and do something with your life. I can't carry you, Percy Shaw. Nobody can live life for you.' This was all said softly, yet it carried more weight than it would have if she'd screamed it.

'Nay, Ellen Langden,' he said lugubriously. 'I never thought I'd hear you talk so hard. Specially to me when me poor wife's took badly. Whatever's got into you at all?'

'The smell of you, for a start. Now get home, get washed, then go down to that hospital and see your Vera. Don't forget to shave.' She pushed the little man out of the house, then picked up a rolling pin to deal with the pastry.

Things were getting sorted out here, anyway. Theresa had landed a job at the top of Bradshaw, helping some rich woman to look after evacuated mothers and babies. She would like that, would Theresa. Aye, she was very fond of babies, too fond to ever think about making herself into a nun. She was due to start next Monday, and the girl's relief about leaving home was so marked as to lessen Ellen's grief at losing her.

Abigail had recently kicked off at the Hollywell Nursing Home up Chorley Old Road, and she only visited the Langden household on an occasional day off. Ellen was glad about that. She didn't want Marie getting any fancy ideas off Abigail, who, Ellen felt, was no better than she ought to have been. Though perhaps she wasn't quite that bad, Ellen had to admit, somewhat begrudgingly. She was a hurt girl, was Abigail. Marie was still running Deane Road with her dad, leaving Ellen with the prospect of working alone in the larger shop. Still, at least her twins were in occupations approved by the government. They wouldn't get called up at eighteen, not while one was looking after babies and the other was running a food shop.

She was going to miss Theresa in more ways than one. Theresa was quick, quiet and efficient at work, very good with the customers and always on top of the job. She was also a mother's girl, had clung to Ellen right from birth, and the final severance of this close tie was going to affect Ellen greatly. Marie was more resilient, more independent. Marie was the sort of person Ellen admired, the sort Ellen herself was deliberately becoming.

The door opened quietly and Billy stepped into the kitchen. 'I've just popped home for a bite,' he said.

'I'm still cooking.'

'How are you going to do the cooking when Theresa's gone?' he asked. 'There'll be nobody to serve in the shop while you come home.'

'It'll be seen to,' she replied quickly. 'If push comes to shove, the teas will have to be late and we can take carry-outs for our dinners.'

He cleared his throat, just as he always did when about to make a calculated statement. 'You can have Marie. I can run Deane Road, it's not a big shop.'

'No.'

'What do you mean, "no"? Haven't I done it for years? I know all the travellers, all the wholesalers. Can't we go back to the way things were?'

'No,' she said again.

'Why the hell not?'

'Because I say so.'

His temper bubbled, so he inhaled deeply. 'Is it always going to be like this? Me dancing to your tune?'

'Yes, till the girls take over.'

'Why? Bloody why?'

She shrugged her shoulders, then got on with making the pie.

'Why?' he shouted now.

Ellen picked up the rolling pin and looked him straight in the eye. 'Long enough I listened to you saying "because I say so". For years I did as I was told, acted the good little wife. But that's all it was, an act. Because in the first place, I wasn't a wife at all. And in the second place, I got just a bit fed up with listening to your orders. And in the third place, it's my turn to say "because I say so". I'd shut up if

I were you. No point in carrying on an argument you can't win.'

'I feel like packing my bags,' he yelled.

'Then get on with it. Nobody's stopping you.'

He strode towards her and she raised the implement in her hand. 'I'll do it,' she whispered. 'Don't think for one minute that I won't.'

He backed off. 'There's nothing for me here. Nothing.'

'There's lentil soup.'

'You know what I mean.'

'Yes.'

After eating his snack, he leaned back in his chair and studied her. She had changed greatly, not just in her attitude, but also in the way she looked. There was a new vibrance about her, a glow in her cheeks and a sheen to her hair. Yes, she had won. For the moment.

The other worry entered his thoughts, so he asked casually, 'How's madam next door?'

'No change.'

'Still in a coma?'

'That's right.'

He sighed, feigning sadness at Vera's plight. 'Looks as if she won't pull through, then.'

Ellen stared hard at him. 'I wouldn't say that. God works in some very mysterious ways. She could make a full recovery if we pray hard enough. Aye, God is good.'

He swallowed deeply. How much did she know? Why was she looking at him so strangely? Had Vera mumbled in her sleep, had she told stupid Percy what had happened? No. The police would have been here by now. But why did this one keep staring at him like that?

'I'll . . . er . . . get back to work, then.' He rose hastily to his feet.

'Yes, you do that.'

As he walked out of the room, he could feel her eyes boring into his back. They were damned clever, these women. Sometimes, they knew things they couldn't possibly know. And the annoying thing was that the creatures were so often proved right.

She followed him into the yard. 'You've forgotten your hat,' she said, passing the bowler to him. 'First time you've ever done that. Amazing how having something on your mind can affect you, isn't it?'

'Eh? What would I have on my mind?'

She raised her shoulders. 'Only you know that. Only you, your Maker, and happen the devil himself.'

He marched off, leaving Ellen standing in the yard. Tishy joined her after a few seconds. 'Can I play my piano now?' It was really exciting having a piano of her own at last, even if she was restricted to playing it just when he was out. This second-hand item was pushed behind the sofa in the front room, so Tishy could only use it when her father was not in residence.

Ellen smiled at the girl she thought of as a 'poor thing'. 'Tell you what, lass, if I could tinkle on the ivories like you can, I'd be off all over the place. You want to go in for one of them talent contests that they have at the Grand Theatre.'

Tishy glanced down at her gloved fingers. 'My mum used to say that I have clever hands. She said everything had gone into my hands.'

'Why are you wearing gloves all the time?'

'I don't know. He never wears them, does he?'

'You mean your father?'

Tishy nodded. 'I saw a hand without a glove on once. In the cold too, and in the dark. We must look after our hands, Ellen.'

'Aye, but there's no need to keep gloves on all the while. You even ate your dinner with them on yesterday, didn't you?'

'I take them off to play the piano. Doctor Harrison's piano is the best. Two of the patients gave me sweets yesterday, real sweets. And a nice old man gave me half a tin of Horlicks tablets. Wasn't that lovely of him?'

Ellen put her arm round the girl's waist. 'You're a good

142

lass, Tishy. There's summat about you, as if you were made out of angel-dust. God gave Lilian a great prize when He sent you to her.'

Soft blue-grey eyes stared solemnly down at Ellen. 'Are you my mother now?'

'Yes, I suppose I must be. You can call me Mam if you like, I wouldn't mind.'

'I love you, Ellen. You're one of the best people I met in my whole life. And I love Marie and Theresa too.'

'What about Abigail?'

'No. Abigail doesn't love anybody, and it's hard loving someone who doesn't love you back.'

'Do you care what happens to her?'

Tishy thought for a moment. 'Yes, I do. She mustn't get hurt.'

'That's love, sweetheart.'

'Is it?'

'Yes.' Ellen led Tishy back inside the house. This girl had been a terrible burden, sitting in the shop every afternoon so that she could be watched, following Ellen like a little dog every time she went through to the back for stock, singing her weird little songs, sitting in corners scribbling on scraps of paper. But some burdens, decided Ellen, were precious. And this was probably the most precious of them all.

CHAPTER SIX

Abigail

The flat was nice enough, Abigail thought. She had a furnished bedsitting room that measured at least eighteen feet by twelve, her own tiny bathroom with toilet, and a small kitchen which contained a gas cooker, a fold-away table, two stools, a meatsafe with double mesh doors, and the ultimate luxury in the form of a minute but effective refrigerator. The furniture in the living area was old and comfortable. There were two over-stuffed armchairs covered in chintz, a sofa of similar ancestry and with a similar cover, a proper dining table with four ladder-backed chairs, and a little padded foot stool with a hinged lid. Next to the gas fire stood bookcases on one side, and a display cabinet with a small wardrobe on the other. Her bed was under the French window, giving the room a cluttered appearance which she intended to rectify at the earliest opportunity.

She would go to the market when it was open, perhaps she might find some acceptable second-hand ornaments for the cabinet. As for books, she had little time for them. She would no doubt place her nursing manuals on the shelves, but Abigail had no collection of novels and no desire to acquire such objects. The novel was not for her. Reading was a waste of time, an activity to be reserved for people who wished to escape from the actual here-and-now world. Abigail wanted to conquer real life, so she wasted neither money nor energy in the pursuit of the written word.

The house was a large black and white detached that

pretended to be Tudor. There were timber beams outside and inside, and several balconies upstairs, one of which was attached to Abigail's quarters. She had visions of herself sitting out there on a summer's day with a jug of fresh lemonade and ice cubes from her own fridge. In such visions, she was not alone. There was always a figure by her side in a second deckchair, and that person, she thought, would probably be Clive Harrison.

He hadn't said much, had not got round to inviting her out, yet she sensed his interest. Clive talked a great deal about his mother, who had died a year earlier, and Abigail gathered that the late Mrs Harrison had almost dominated her son's existence. His father had been dead for many years, so his life had contained just himself and his mother for a long time. That he had never married was not a source of wonder to Abigail; she guessed that any potential wives would have needed to pass the Mrs Harrison entrance examination before getting over the doorstep.

And now, he needed a wife. He lived alone on Derby Street, in a large terraced house that also contained his surgery, and he was tended only by an aged housekeeper and, more recently, by Tishy who was learning how to polish properly when she wasn't playing the piano. This was no life for a man like Clive. He needed a prod now and then, a push in the right direction. Even when it came to simple things like clothes, he clearly required advice, for he was often seen in black suit with brown shoes and, occasionally, in odd socks. It was time for someone to take him in hand.

The fact that he had money was plain enough, otherwise he could not have afforded to buy a property of this size and equip it as a nursing home. Why he needed to do this puzzled Abigail. Could he not have used his money directly to do the research into vitamins? Perhaps this place salved a rather twisted socialist conscience, then. Perhaps he needed to convince himself that rich had served poor, and that he had been some kind of Robin Hood who had brought about this miracle.

Then, of course, there was his tendency to accept charity cases, people who would never have afforded the Hollywell's fees. The first of these was to be Vera Shaw, Ellen's next door neighbour from Noble Street. The hospital could do no more for her, so Clive had decided that he would take her in as soon as the home was opened. This generous gesture he had made in order to give Mr Shaw the opportunity to rearrange his home in accordance with his immobile wife's needs, and from what Ellen had said, it would be a cold day in hell before that particular house would be ready for any creatures except cockroaches and mice.

She looked at herself in the mirror, turning her head from side to side as if seeking the best angle. It was not a particularly wonderful face, but the brown eyes were lively, and she had taken plenty of soot from Ellen's house to mix with Vaseline as a substitute for mascara. This she applied now with little brush, sweeping the long, thick lashes with a practised upward movement that made them curl towards the plucked eyebrows. Her hair was her best feature, thick, dark as it could be without actually attaining blackness, and falling in rich, natural waves right down to her shoulders. Of course, she would have to pile it on top of her head for work, but work hadn't started yet.

She rubbed some lipstick into her thin cheeks, then applied the same to the narrow lips. There was little she could do about her nose and mouth. Now that she had met her father, she realized where she had got her hated nose with its large nostrils and slightly hooked bridge. He was the one to thank for the lips too, because he had the same ungenerous mouth. However, when she was all put together in what she called the war paint, she didn't look too bad. A little severe, maybe. She pulled the shiny curtain of hair over her right cheek and winked seductively. No, she was all right. She was not an apple-cheeked Marie, nor a saintlike Theresa. Nor was she a supremely beautiful Tishy. She was an Abigail, and Abigails were few

146

and far between. It was a rare name, a name to live up to. And she intended to do just that.

He knocked at the door. With one swift movement, she swept all the beautifying equipment into the lidded foot-rest, then, after one last glance in the mirror, she threw herself into an armchair and called, 'Come in.'

Clive entered the room and looked around. 'Very nice,' he commented. 'The chintz covers look good on that old suite. Is the wardrobe big enough?'

She grinned. 'You must be joking. For three dresses, one coat and two costumes, who needs space?'

'Oh, I see. Want some of my clothing coupons?'

She studied his somewhat bedraggled appearance for a moment or two. 'No, thanks. I think you ought to use those for yourself. When did you last have a new suit?' Was that gravy on his tie? Or had he been careless with medicines again?

He glanced down at the crumpled jacket. 'Mother's funeral. Anyway, enough about me and my lack of dress sense. I've got some wonderful news. Auntie Harrison has agreed to do the cooking. She's my father's sister, and a rarer character you have yet to meet. What that woman can do with a grain of flour and a spoonful of marge is nobody's business. She lives just a few streets away, so she can get here quite easily. The staff will have to see to the breakfasts, though. She likes her beauty sleep, does Auntie Harrison.'

Abigail pondered. Would this aunt throw her weight about because of her blood relationship to Clive? 'Strange name,' she muttered finally.

'Yes. I gave it to her, can't think why. Everyone else calls her Martha. She's a fierce old soul, but there's the heart of an angel underneath all that whalebone. I'm so glad we got her. So, if you simply hand her all the old dears' ration books, she'll make mountains out of mole-hills for you.'

'Sounds terrifying.'

He glanced at her quickly. 'You're afraid of nothing. I

shouldn't have thought you'd worry about old Auntie Harrison. Besides which, you're in charge here. If you don't like her, she'll have to go. But please try to like her, won't you?'

'I'll do my best.'

He scrutinized the floor, bending to assess the condition of the rather bedraggled and faded Axminster. 'You could do with a new carpet.'

'Most people could do with a new carpet, Clive. There's a war on, no carpets to be had. And I'm delighted with the flat, really I am. This is my first place, I've never been alone before. Oh, I've had a room in a nurses' home, but that wasn't the same. Girls giggling in the corridors, someone else's hair floating in the washbasin, people taking one another's make-up and toothpaste.' She gazed round the room. 'This is my own. Can I have visitors?'

He sighed with mock impatience. 'Are you the boss?'

'Yes.'

'Then bring the army in if you want to.'

'Wouldn't you mind?'

'No.'

'Oh.'

He shuffled about a bit, then perched himself awkwardly on the edge of the sofa. 'It's going to be an onerous task. Of course, you've got the registered nurse who'll do two nights a week for you, then there's that other newly trained girl, the one with the baby – she's happy to put in a couple of afternoons. Even mothers with youngish babies are expected to do their bit now, though there's no official call-up as yet. But apart from that sort of help, you'll be almost a prisoner here. We can't leave the place in the hands of untrained staff, can we?'

'I don't mind, honestly. I don't have to be on duty all the time. Once I've trained the auxiliaries, I can come up here and wait on call, look at a magazine, listen to the wireless you kindly got for me.'

He tried to look at her, and discovered that he couldn't quite manage it, so he stood up and fastened his eyes to an overblown rose on the wallpaper. 'What about your shopping?' he asked. 'And visits to your family?' Like a very awkward and extremely overgrown schoolboy, he shifted his weight from foot to foot, suddenly aware of his discomfort in the presence of this young woman. If he hadn't stopped biting his nails some years ago, they would no doubt have been down to their quicks by this time.

She spoke firmly, deliberately choosing to ignore his obvious embarrassment – though she did make a mental note of it before replying. 'Two afternoons and two nights – that's plenty for me. I can get my shopping in one fell swoop – not that there's much to buy these days – then I can go and see Tishy overnight. It will all work out splendidly, you'll see.'

'I knew you were the type,' he said.

'And what type is that?'

He blushed. 'The kind who doesn't mind responsibility. You're a strong woman, Matron, I knew that as soon as I met you. Not the sort to balk at a little bit of hard work.'

'That's me.'

He didn't know what to say next. She wasn't a pretty girl, not really, but she was . . . alive. Yes, that was the word. There was something vital, something elemental about Abigail. There was passion in her, he could sense that. And he was a doctor, a man whose standards must be high, a person whose morals should always be above and beyond question . . .

She smiled encouragingly before clearing her throat. 'Well, we've two diabetics and I can deal with those as long as they remain stable. There's a lady with particularly nasty ulcers on her legs – perhaps the hospital should have another look at her. We can keep the sores dry and dressed, but she really has been neglected by her doctor. It amazes me how these wealthy people fail to obtain proper treatment.' She inhaled sharply; he was still avoiding eye contact. 'Some cancers, two with angina, one with severe osteoarthritis of the hips.' She paused. 'And a blind man. Glaucoma, I think.'

'I beg your pardon?' He frowned deeply, determined now to concentrate.

'One of the patients is partially blind.'

'Oh. Good.'

She folded her arms. 'He won't think it's good.'

'I'm sorry?'

'The blind man. He won't think there's anything good about having glaucoma.'

He thrust his restless hands deep into jacket pockets. 'I didn't mean that. I meant it's good that you've studied the notes. No, there's nothing wonderful about growing old. These people will spend their last years with us. They're burdens, most of them, from families with more money than love. We have to be their families now.'

She inclined her head thoughtfully. 'I know that. I was going to specialize in geriatrics anyway after the end of this silly war. Most of the girls seemed to want the dramatic side – midwifery, theatre and so on. But I like old people.'

At last he looked at her. 'Do you? Why?'

She grinned. 'Because they're such fun.'

His eyebrows shot upward. 'Fun?'

She wriggled forward to the edge of her chair. 'I was training, halfway through my final year. My friend and I did six weeks on what most nurses called death row. My word, you should have seen what went on behind closed doors! There was a thriving poker school, a hint of something unseemly between an eighty-year-old ex-plumber and a woman of seventy who brought him stolen flowers every day, then there was my young man.'

'Oh?'

She lowered her chin, allowing him a sight of that truly lovely hair. 'He was ninety. His body had shut down completely – there were catheters everywhere. In fact, you had to battle your way through a jungle of equipment to get to him. His mind was so alert. He didn't always think in a straight line, if you get my meaning, but he knew every word ever written by John Milton. "Come pensive nun devout and pure, Sober steadfast and demure", he used to quote at me. Every time I went near him, he would wax lyrical about my appearance. Which was, of course, extremely flattering. Except for the fact that he couldn't see me, because his eyes had gone on strike too.' She paused. 'I stayed behind after shift to get him through his last couple of hours. Such a special thing to do, don't you think? To be there at the end.' She stared at her shoes. 'A blind schoolteacher of ninety thought his nurse was beautiful. And I knew then that I would work with the old. It's not a romantic notion. It's just that I find them so entertaining.'

He nodded slowly. 'Do you believe in God?'

'No.'

'Then where do they go after you've nursed them?'

Her shoulders were raised fractionally. 'Into the ground, into the fire. But if they believe, I allow them to imagine that I share their faith. Whatever helps, I use.'

He turned his back on her and stared through the window. She was so like himself! Though he wasn't quite an atheist. Like many in his profession, he hedged his bets by investing in agnosticism. When a child survived diphtheria against the odds, he suspected the intervention of a divine hand. But every time he wrote a death certificate, he doubted God.

He hesitated before speaking again. 'Abigail?'

'What?'

'Do you have a . . . a boyfriend or a fiancé?'

'No.'

'Ever had one?'

'Several friends.'

'I see.' He paused, deep in thought. 'I had somebody once. A lovely girl, very quiet and pleasant. I thought the world of her. She died two years ago of pernicious anaemia. That was when I decided to research deficiencies. Almost broke my heart, did Dorothy's death. So, when I'd picked myself up again, I decided that I need someone made of sterner stuff. Dorothy was frail. I have avoided frail women ever since.'

She sat very still and waited for him to continue.

'In my line of work, a man can't afford the luxury of an ailing wife. A doctor's missus needs to be fairly tough and resilient. I've been looking for that toughness ever since I recovered from the losses of Dorothy and Mother.'

'Ever found it?'

He paused for almost ten seconds before answering. 'Yes.'

'And?'

'And I have to wait and see what develops. There's a small item called love that needs to be an element in the mixture we call marriage. I could never marry for less than love. Could you?'

She touched her hair pensively. 'Yes. I could marry for security, a home, money, a decent future . . .'

'My, you are honest, aren't you?'

'In my experience, there's no other way to be. Oh, I know your average romantic novel is full of guile and winsome ways and love scenes. Magazines are the same. But life isn't about love, Clive. It's about settling for what you can get and making a go of it. So. Shall we tour the kingdom?'

He stared at her for a long time. 'What was that?' he asked eventually.

'The rooms, we need to look at them. I've positioned the beds, but they may not be to your liking. And I still need three commodes and some linen. Apart from that, we're ready to open.' She smiled to herself. He was beginning to fall in love with her, and he had not the sense to hide it. Like many people of good education, he had attained little real wisdom along the way.

She smiled as she pondered the possibilities. She could play with him, reel in the line, then throw back the fish, just as she'd done once or twice before. Or she could pretend to fall in love with him, make all the right noises, dress up for him, fuss over his every need. Or she could carry on as she had started, honest and direct. Whatever she did, he was probably hers for the taking. The idea of

152

becoming a doctor's wife was fairly appealing, though she would have preferred someone even richer than Clive appeared to be. But there were so few eligible men about, she had perhaps better snap him up while she seemed to hold the option. 'Coming?' she asked sweetly.

'Yes.'

They walked through the house together. It was a warren of a place, full of corridors and corners and unexpected little rooms. One such small bedroom had been set aside for the nurse who would be on call during Abigail's free nights, and they examined this first. From there they progressed to rooms four, five and six where twelve residents would live. Each of these rooms had four beds, four lockers and four small wardrobes. Rooms seven to twelve were singles, and it was in the singles that the richer folk would live.

Downstairs, they toured the vast kitchen with its huge double-ovened range, the large table at which staff would take meals, the very modern stacking dishwasher and the specially sectioned compartments for residents' trays. These were built to waist-height, and their tops provided a good working surface, though Clive did express his reservations about staff having to bend for patients' trays. They visited the scullery, the outside sluice, Matron's office, then the ground floor rooms one to three which had been prepared for a further twelve patients.

'Will four bathrooms be enough?' he asked.

'I should think so. They won't all be able to walk, you know. Most of them will use commodes, and a few will be incontinent. Some poor workers are going to spend a lot of time in that freezing sluice. Don't worry. We'll have our fair share of teething problems, many of which won't show until we actually open. The main thing is we've got a full list of applicants. If you weren't so stubborn about Mrs Shaw, we could take another one.'

'I'm going to be stubborn.'

'I know you are.'

His chin dropped as he thought of Vera Shaw. Never a

day's illness as far as he could remember, and now this, poor soul. 'She'll be doubly incontinent, of course. She has just a slight amount of movement in her left hand. No speech, either. Her brain was very badly damaged in that fall. Mr Shaw's quite amusing, thinks he's a medical man because he drove an ambulance for six months, but he'll have his work cut out, I fear. Until I've given him some counselling, and until his house is in a better state, we're going to be stuck with Vera.'

They stood at the front door, he unsure of whether to go or stay, she reluctant to be left alone for yet another night in this mansion. 'I could make us both a cup of tea,' she suggested.

He coughed self-consciously. He enjoyed her company, yet he did not want things to move too fast. He needed to think; he also needed to safeguard his reputation as a doctor, while she, a qualified nurse, would have to maintain a fairly strict level of self-discipline and decorum. 'Yes,' he said at last. 'A cup of tea would be lovely.'

She held the door wide and, as he passed her, he caught a whiff of her unusual perfume. This was no Evening in Paris, no Californian Poppy. Indeed not. Abigail Langden's scent was subtle and expensive, something she had saved for, a black market item, no doubt. He fingered his collar.

'Are you hot?' She forced a note of surprise into her tone as she fought to conceal her amusement. The man was mature, well over thirty-five, yet she felt as if she were the older of the two of them. 'Never mind, I can open a window upstairs.'

He followed her slowly, allowing her to reach the landing while he was still halfway up the flight. Her dress just about touched her knees, its length dictated by the wartime scarcity of good cloth. She had wonderful legs, long, slender and supple. And there was something endearing about the way she had painted them so carefully with a dark line pencilled up the backs to give the appearance of fully-fashioned stockings. She was tough, yet she was so young, so vulnerable.

Abigail felt almost shy as he watched her pouring the tea. There was something in his eyes that rather reminded her of a doting old mongrel they had once kept in London. She sympathized, yet was amused to think that a man of such obvious intelligence could fall in the love trap. And she was no raving beauty, so she still wondered what he saw in her. 'Sugar?' she asked.

'Just one. Thank goodness it is sugar and not that awful substitute. By the way, give most of your ration coupons to Auntie Harrison and she'll do your meals. Just keep your tea, sugar and sweets to register with a local grocer.'

'A practical soul, aren't you?' She passed him the cup. Strange how such a romantic fool of a man could worry about the little everyday wartime problems.

'During these troubled days, my dear, a bachelor is always practical.' He stirred his tea, then swallowed it in one gulp. 'I was ready for that,' he commented. 'Right. What do we do now?'

She crossed her legs. 'There's nothing more to do, Clive. Not till the rest of the equipment arrives. We could play cards. I gained a certain reputation as a poker player while nursing on Nightingale. That was the geriatric ward.'

He jumped to his feet. 'Notes to write up,' he mumbled hastily. 'Suspected TB, whole family coughing. Though the children have had whooping cough, so it could be the aftermath of that. Have to make sure, all the same.' He was gabbling and he knew it. 'The mother's lost a lot of weight,' he ended lamely.

She uncrossed her legs, stood up, then smoothed her skirt. 'You can find your own way out, then? I'll run down later and fasten the bolts.'

'Yes.' He backed away slowly. What had Ellen said about Abigail? Something about her putting up a front, or putting on a show . . . oh, he should have listened. But he hadn't known then that he was about to become . . . what? Interested, that was the word. He was definitely enthralled by this apparently tough young woman. Because behind the visible mask, there was a lot of life in that thin, brittle body. And there was some pain in the eyes too. She needed to be treated as special. Because she was special . . .

'Do you think we need to discuss anything else?' she was asking.

'Er . . . no, not at the moment. You seem to have everything well in hand.'

'Thank you. I'm glad that you appear to be satisfied with me thus far.'

He pulled the car key from his pocket. 'I'm more than satisfied,' he said quietly. 'You seem to be eminently suitable.'

She laughed. 'I'm a long way short of perfect, very like my father. Do you know my father?'

'Of course. I have a file on him thick enough to fill a drawer. He's not a well man.'

'And he's not a nice one. He and I are very similar. But, you see, I hide the darker side of my nature. Except that I can't help rejoicing in the fact that Daddy-Dear has lost everything. Revenge is sweet, Clive. I am taking my mother's revenge.'

'And I would have done the same.'

'Would you?'

'Yes, given your circumstances. You were abandoned by your father and you watched your mother struggle. If my father had done what yours did, I would have hated him. Your mother was brave, coming up here to find her ex-husband. She did that just for you and Tishy. A mother like that is worth defending. Don't keep putting yourself down and thinking of yourself as . . . cold just because you hate that man. Nobody likes him. Even his second wife doesn't like him.' He was glad that there was space between them, because he wanted to reach out and comfort her, needed to hold her close, to tell her that somebody cared, that he cared . . .

She tossed her head, causing a cascade of hair to fall over one cheek. She could trust this man, that fact was eminently certain. 'It's worse than that, Clive. I want him dead. If I could be instrumental in bringing about his end, if I thought I could do it without endangering my own freedom, then I would. Yes, I would and could kill that man quite happily.'

He took another small step away from her. 'That's all right.'

'Is it? How can you, a doctor, say that?'

'Because I know and understand strong feelings. I have strong feelings.' He paused momentarily. It would be so easy and so foolish to say too much. 'Just one thing, though. Don't kill him. He is not worth it.'

She smiled at him. 'I'm too much of a coward anyway. How's Tishy, by the way?' she asked, seeking a change of subject. After all, the ground had become unsafe these past few minutes – never before had she confided her deepest thoughts, not to anyone.

'Better. She's entertaining my patients every day. A lovely girl.'

'She was Mother's favourite.'

'And you're mine,' cried his mind's voice as he reached the door. But his lips remained set in a pleasant smile as he waved and stepped out to the landing.

Alone once more, Abigail listened as carpet-muted footsteps marked his progress. Shivering, she reached an old cardigan from a chair and draped it across shoulders that seemed frozen. He would be back. In a day or two, he would no doubt find an excuse to return to the Hollywell. Why did she suddenly feel so cold, so lonely? It would only be a matter of days – weeks at the most – until the inevitable proposal. He was not a man for dalliance, so there would be nothing unseemly about this situation.

A car door slammed while Abigail fought the urge to run out and call him back. She was not lonely, she refused to be lonely! And, given a chance, she would have wagered all her poker winnings on an early proposal. She hugged herself and grinned broadly. The odds against her refusing would have been very long. Very long indeed . . .

* * *

Ellen felt a bit guilty about Lilian's eldest now that she had left the house. When the girl did return to spend the odd night with her sister, Ellen went out of her way to make the situation as comfortable as possible. The fear that Abigail might lead Marie astray was fast diminishing, mostly because the opportunity for this to happen had been visibly lessened, and partly because Ellen was beginning to feel a degree of sympathy and trust for Abigail. She was also aware that Lilian's older child had always been jealous of the 'special' Tishy, and she sought to compensate for this by making a fuss of the visitor. She usually made her best weekday meal for Abigail's sake, a strange concoction called cheese soufflé. This baked dish contained the minimum of cheese and plenty of bread-crumbs, but it always looked good with its topping of dried egg, sliced onion and tomato.

'Fruit tart to follow,' said Ellen proudly as she placed the dish on the table. 'I managed to get a few baking apples. Go on, tuck in. I can warm it all up again for the others.'

Abigail spooned a boiled potato on to her plate. 'Where is Tishy?'

'Delivering.'

'What?' Abigail's jaw dropped. 'Can she do that?'

'Well now,' Ellen placed herself in the chair next to Abigail's. 'That depends on what she's delivering. I couldn't send her out with food, she'd have her fingers in the jelly crystals before she got out of the door. But she's all right with her string things.'

'Which string things?'

'Ooh, she knits dishcloths, handbags, gloves and snoods. I got her some dye, and she's made some lovely snoods, one for a bride's mother. She decorated it with some little pearls that the woman had, it was really nice. So I let her make her own deliveries – as long as it's just round here. She's coming on a treat, you know. I think she needed a little bit of independence.'

'Thanks, Ellen.' Abigail's voice was quiet.

'What for?'

'For looking after her, for looking after both of us. It must have been awful for you, having three strangers knocking at your door, especially in view of the . . . relationship. And the way you cared for my mother when I couldn't face it. Well, all I can say is that you must be one of those saints you're always talking about.'

'Nay.' Ellen shook her head slowly. 'I'm not. Lilian was dying, anybody could see that. You'd have needed to be a bad beggar to turn a dying woman from your door. Then I took to her. You see, after a few days, I started feeling as though I'd known her for ever. By the time she got to the end, she was likely my best friend.' Ellen swallowed her tears. 'She was all right, your mam. She talked to me, told me all about her life. I learned a lot from Lilian. It's me that's grateful, lass.'

'How has he been?' There was no need to speak his name.

'Getting drunker and nearer to stepping out of line, I'd say. He's not best pleased with your mother's dying wishes.'

'Neither was I, but the more I think about things, the more sense it all makes. What I don't understand is why he never tried to fight it. After all, it's a long time since he took that money. It would be a difficult crime to prove against him.'

'There were letters. Then there was Aunt Abigail's will – you know – that little gambling woman who left the money to your mam.' She took a deep breath. 'And, of course, there's his bigamy.'

Abigail's knife hit the plate with a clatter. 'What? I thought they were divorced.'

Ellen took several deep breaths. 'No. Now listen, you're the eldest. If anything happens to me, and if your dad tries to get the properties back, go and see Mr Simpson or Mr King on Deansgate. They've got all the papers including my will. Not that I own anything, unless we count that deed of gift thing on the six houses, but I needed to get it

159

all written down again. I've had to tell somebody in this family the truth in case I die, and I trust you.'

Abigail's jaw still hung loose. 'What?' she cried eventually. 'He ran off up here and married you while he was still married to Mother?'

'Yes.'

'Who knows about this? What about Theresa and Marie?'

'They think he was divorced. The only folk who know are him, me, Mr King, he's the lawyer chap, the priest, some old fellow in London called McDade, and now you. But I had to tell one of you. What if I popped off in my sleep, eh? If he could find a way round Mr Simpson's very old papers, he'd take everything back and likely marry some other poor fool, then who knows where he'd leave it all?'

Abigail took a quick gulp of water. 'And you've decided to trust me. Why?'

'Because there's no nonsense with you, Abigail. You're a hard one, but I think you're straight enough underneath it all. Besides, there's nowt you can do about my twins' claim, because him and me are married proper now. They're only sixteen, my two – well, near seventeen, I suppose. But I can't be telling them things like this. It was hard enough for them to understand divorce, they'd never cope with bigamy.' She pushed a damp curl from her forehead.

'They might have to one day.'

'Aye, and happen they'll be old enough.'

Abigail chased the cheese and breadcrumb mixture round her plate for a few seconds. 'I'll kill him for this,' she said softly. 'First Mother, then you, two lives ruined. I'll swing for him yet.'

'Don't talk like that.'

'Why not?' The brown eyes seemed to flash sparks of fury. 'You are one of the few people who understood my mother, who cared enough to understand. Most of the time, she was written off as fat and ugly. You took me in, took my sister in, found her something to do, something that stops her being completely bloody useless. You listened to my mother, really listened. I know you sat for hours with her just because I couldn't face watching her die. Ellen, you are the best thing that's happened to me and Tishy, apart from our mother. And he did this terrible crime to both of you. How do you expect me to feel? Happy? Forgiving?'

'Stop it, lass, before you make yourself ill.'

'I HATE HIM!' she screamed now. 'He spoils everything. I came here today to tell you that I'm getting married, and even that is spoiled.'

'Married? Who to? Eeh love, I wish you could cry some of this away. Who are you marrying?'

'Clive.'

Ellen's eyes were wide. 'Doctor Harrison? Our Doctor Harrison?'

'That's right. Registry Office, not quite sure when. Will you come?'

The older woman juggled her thoughts quickly. She wasn't supposed to attend any marriage except a Catholic one, it was a law of her Church. But there were times when laws were best ignored. Or broken, then confessed about later . . . 'I'll be proud to come, lass. What about him?'

'If he goes, I won't.'

'Then we shan't have to tell him.' Ellen thought quickly. 'Listen, I've got Mrs Tattersall starting in the Derby Street shop next week. She didn't like her canteen job, so I'm going to train her up to help me in Theresa's place. By next month, I should be able to put her in charge for a couple of hours. We'd be best leaving the twins out of this altogether. I can get Tishy dressed up one way or another, and I won't tell her where she's going. Will that do, love?'

'Thank you.'

'Feeling a bit better?'

Abigail shrugged. 'I'll never feel better about him. Never. How do you manage to live with him?'

'I don't. I sleep with Tishy now and he lives down here. You don't think I went and married him again out of choice, do you? But a mother will do nearly anything for her children. You know that.'

'I'm going, Ellen. I think I've had enough for one day.'

'Eh? What about Tishy?'

'She won't miss me, she scarcely knows what day it is.'

'Don't you be too sure of that, now. There's a lot more to that young madam than meets the eye. Have you read her poems? They're a bit on the fanciful side, but they all rhyme. And you should see the stuff she makes, beautiful, it is.'

Abigail stared at Ellen. Here was another one who had fallen head over heels for Tishy's odd charm. Still, perhaps it was a good thing. If Ellen would keep Tishy here, then there would be no need to offer her a home in the soon-to-be formed Harrison household. 'Theresa will be gone in a few weeks, I take it?'

'Aye,' sighed Ellen. 'She's off to some big farmhouse north of Bolton. She's already been up to look at the house a couple of Mondays ago. I'll miss her.' She found herself praying that Abigail would not take Tishy away. If everyone but Marie left, there would be too much exposure to him, too little to distract Ellen from the fact of his presence. 'Where will you be living?' she asked casually.

'In the nursing home. We're going to have all the attics converted, but that will take a while. Until the place is ready, I suppose we'll flit about a bit. Clive will look for a partner to live on Derby Street eventually, but he'll be keeping the practice on, he'll still run his surgery. You won't be losing your doctor, Ellen.'

'Good. He's a great doctor, you know.'

'Yes.'

Ellen studied the girl covertly. 'Do you love him?'

'I like him,' she replied without hesitation. 'Look where love got you and my mother. I suppose you did both love him at some stage. I've no time for such nonsense. We'll have a good marriage, one based on things more tangible than love. Like mutual interests and trust for one another.'

'I wish you luck, then.'

A timid knocking at the front door was followed by, 'Hello? Can I come in?'

Ellen raised her eyes to the ceiling. 'Come in as long as you're not collecting.'

Cedric Wilkinson stumbled into the room, his face bright red, hands moulding his cap into an impossible ball, eyes watering and blinking at a speed that betrayed his terrible nervousness. He stood by the table, mouth moving as if to frame words that obviously refused to be released from his throat.

'I forgot about him,' said Ellen to Abigail. 'He knows and all. About your dad, I mean.'

'Hello,' managed Cedric at last. 'Better weather this past few days.'

'What do you want?' asked Ellen with an air of resignation.

'Just to see how you are. I noticed yon feller in the shop, so I went round to the other and Theresa said you'd come home.' This all came out in a rush. 'I've been worried about you, like.'

Abigail began to laugh, great loud chuckles that shook her thin frame. 'See, Ellen, that's what it does.'

'What what does?'

'That four-letter word, the one you asked about.'

'Eh?'

'You asked if I had a certain feeling for Clive. I told you it was nonsense. Look at the proof of my point.' She dried her eyes. 'You keep telling me to cry, but a good laugh beats everything, Ellen.'

Ellen looked severely at Cedric. 'What are you doing calling on me in the middle of the cooking? Coming in here and interrupting while I've got a bit of company. Did you wipe your feet? And leave that cap alone, else I'll have it for the rag bag.'

Cedric stared at Ellen so adoringly that Abigail had to turn away and study the picture over the fireplace. It was a grim sepia affair portraying Jesus carrying a large storm lamp, and it had THE LIGHT OF THE WORLD printed at the bottom, and she suddenly found this funny too, so she fixed her eyes on the oven door while Ellen carried on behind her. 'I'm fine, Cedric. I don't know why you won't believe me when I tell you I'm all right. He's not been so bad since we got it all sorted.'

'I hear he's drinking again,' said Cedric mournfully. 'What if he kicks off again?'

Ellen sighed. 'If he does, I'll send for you. And if you're out painting, I'll send for the cavalry like they do at the pictures. Keep still. If you knock that dresser again, we'll have the Sacred Heart on the floor and I had that statue blessed by the Bishop of Salford himself. Where's your van?'

'Outside.'

'What? Outside here? I'll be getting a name, Cedric Wilkinson. They'll be having me in the same bin where they put Vera Shaw before she was took badly. Kindly remove your vehicle from my door.'

'I'm sorry, Ellen.'

'And stop saying you're sorry all the while.'

'Sorry.'

Ellen ground her teeth. 'Get gone, lad. If anything happens, I'll send a message with one of Mr Armstrong's pigeons. See, look where you're going. How you manage to bang yourself into that doorway every time, I'll never know. Put your cap on, it's cold. And try and look as if you've been here on business, we'll be having the priest round.'

Abigail's mirth had subsided to an acceptable and controllable level by the time Ellen returned from seeing Cedric off. 'He's daft, you know,' said Ellen. 'He could fall over his own shadow in the dark, that one. Yet he hangs from these great high ceilings on a bit of string, painting girders and rivets, never a slip. He seems to have a fair head for heights, he's just no good at ground level.

Should have a warning printed on a card and hung round his neck. Or happen we should give him a bell like they do with lepers. He's a health hazard, he is.'

'He's in love with you.'

'Yes, I know.'

'And he's a lovely kind man.'

'I know that and all. I wasn't born yesterday, miss. But I'm a married woman. I can't just jump into Cedric's van and drive off into a shepherds' delight sunset. I've got responsibilities. Any road, it's a sin, is all that kind of stuff.'

'Would you marry him if London was dead?'

'Eh? Now listen, you. Don't be thinking along them lines. I'm not having you walking about with your soul covered in mortal sin. What are you bothering for? You've a wonderful new life in front of you, a nice fiancé, that nursing home to run. You mustn't worry about this end of things, I've got it all under control.'

'Have you?'

'Yes.'

'You've changed a lot, haven't you, Ellen? Such a cowed and frightened little woman you were when we arrived.'

'And you've changed too. You might not be able to see it yourself, but I can tell you've altered. You're more . . . settled. Do you know what I think?'

'No.'

'I think you're in love with Doctor Harrison and you don't even know it.'

'Don't be silly.'

Ellen grinned. 'No use lying to yourself, lass. Time will tell. Go on, then, I won't hold you up any more. Shall I give Tishy your love?'

'If you like. I'll see you next week, Ellen.'

After Abigail had left, Ellen sat by the fire thinking about her. She wasn't as black as she tried to paint herself, that one. There were chinks in the armour, little holes of vulnerability that had started to show now and then. Aye, but she was a deep one. A lot of Lilian in her, and some of him too. But Ellen sensed in her heart that Abigail was in love. The girl probably didn't know it, likely didn't even recognize the symptoms, but she'd left her hanky and a scarf on the table, and Abigail wasn't one for forgetting details. Ellen grinned to herself. He was getting quite a catch, was Clive Harrison, a good worker and a woman of great loyalty. No more than he deserved, and good luck to him.

She sighed. If Lilian could have lived to see Abigail settled, if she could have known what Tishy was really capable of . . . Ah well. If was a very big word, possibly the biggest in the dictionary. And, instead of iffing, she'd better get the meal warmed up for the rest of them.

Miss Martha Harrison was a woman of large proportions. She always wore exactly the same style of dress, but in a variety of colours. It was obvious that she had discovered this pattern some years ago, that it suited her needs and that she had therefore cut all her cloth to suit this particular arrangement. There was a shallow V neck with a small collar, a belt covered in matching material, three gored pleats to the front and a kick-pleat at the back, and each dress had three buttons on the tight-fitting bodice. That she was very rigidly corseted beneath the dress was plain, because the lengths of whalebone required to encase her flesh showed through in places. At her throat she wore three strands of good cultured pearls, while her chest was decorated by a fobwatch of which she was inordinately proud.

Her new job dictated that she must cover her hair, and this she did thoroughly with a huge white mob cap that left not one single grey curl showing. The only other concession she made to her position was to wear an apron round her waist. She refused a full pinafore, as this would have made her 'too hot to concentrate'.

'Meals,' she informed Abigail at their first meeting, 'are important to elderly people. Many of their pleasures are curtailed by infirmity, so they look to food for comfort.'

She adjusted her steel-rimmed spectacles while Abigail stood very still, fascinated by the vision before her. It was like being back at school, like being lectured by a rather benevolent headmistress. 'Unfortunately,' continued this formidable lady, 'we are in a period of rationing. However, I can offer a reasonably varied menu of main meals because I have collected recipes since the war began.' She took several Ministry of Food leaflets from her capacious handbag. 'I do a good cheap fruit cake called Cut and Come Again. It improves with keeping in an airtight tin. Then there's my famous lentil roast and my carrot tart. These I shall cook each week, so that there will be something to eat if supplies dry up.'

'Good.' Abigail was feeling stupid and nervous, so she assumed an air of tight professionalism. 'Do you have the first week's plan, Miss Harrison?'

'Of course. For main meals we shall have potato hash on Monday, tripe and onions on Tuesday. You will find that they like their tripe and manifold, Matron. On Wednesday I plan sausages and toasted cheese, potato and onion pie for Thursday, fish cakes on Friday. Saturday . . . let me see . . . Saturday will be rissoles. On Sundays, of course, there will be roast meat with vegetables and potatoes. We shall not allow our standards to collapse completely just because of the war.'

'Hmm. Yes. What about the other meals?'

'I shall prepare a pan of porridge each night, and that will do for breakfasts. Teatimes will be scones, buns, bread and butter, crystal jellies and the like. Suppers will have to be toast and tea until further notice. It all depends on what I can lay my hands on. No black market, of course. It's just that sometimes coupons can be exchanged.' The steel glasses were removed and snapped into a case. 'Does that seem satisfactory to you?'

'Yes. Oh yes. Very good, very well thought out.'

Auntie Harrison looked her up and down. 'You need feeding, get your strength back,' she pronounced. 'I'll bring you a tin of pilchards.'

'Thank you.' To refuse would have seemed churlish, even though Abigail hated pilchards. And to refuse this particular lady might be next to impossible anyway. 'I've always been thin,' she added.

'Just lost your mother?'

'Yes.'

'Off your food?'

'Well, not particularly—'

'Are you regular? Your bodily functions, are they keeping time?'

'What? Oh, yes.' Who was the nurse here?

'Very important to keep the clock ticking over, you know. I have a friend who lost her mother recently, stopped eating, went into quite a decline. Finished up with bleeding piles, my dear. Quite shocking, a terrible state she allowed herself to get into. Though you are young. The young tend to recover more quickly from life's knocks.'

'Yes.' She needed to think of another word, and quickly. These 'yeses' were getting a bit repetitive . . .

'So.' The small, beady eyes travelled slowly over Abigail's form. 'You are to marry my nephew?'

'Yes.'

'He's a good enough lad, as long as you show him what's what. I find that with most men, don't you? Silly creatures on the whole, need a lot of kindness and understanding. Rather like children in my opinion.'

'He's an excellent doctor,' ventured Abigail.

'Oh yes, I'm sure he is. Many of them can be quite good at certain things, you know, as long as they're properly trained.'

Abigail struggled to squash a grin. 'You make him sound like a dog.'

'Do I? Well, that's all right, then. I've always had a lot of time for dogs. Intelligent animals, good companions.'

Abigail didn't know what to say next. This aunt of Clive's was an odd sort, like something out of a different era altogether. Though her feminist views were not exactly Victorian . . .

'Yes, I'm sure that you'll make him a good wife. You seem to have common sense, and that's the main requisite. I shall, of course, pass on the watch. It was left to me by my mother, and as Clive is my only living relative, I suppose it should go to his wife.' She looked with sadness at the watch on her bosom. 'I have worn this every day of my adult life.'

'Then continue to do so. I have a watch of my own, one of those new upside-down nurses' things. I don't need your watch, Miss Harrison. You clearly get a lot of pleasure from it, so keep it.'

'Really?' The eyes disappeared completely into deep folds of fat created by a huge smile.

'Really.' Yes, this businesslike approach would probably be best. She summoned up her supposed authority, straightening her shoulders as she spoke. 'Now, I must get on with my duty lists. As soon as the first patient arrives, I want this place working like a well-oiled machine. You can manage the kitchen, I take it? You don't want anything altering or moving?'

'Everything will do splendidly, my dear. May I call you Abigail as we are to be related? I shan't do it front of the staff, of course. I can see that you have high standards.'

'Yes, call me Abigail by all means. What am I to call you?'

'Why, Auntie Harrison, naturally. It has always amused me. My name is Martha, but I bear so poor a resemblance to the good sister in the Bible, don't I? Quite a dragon, I am supposed to be.'

Abigail decided to go in for the kill. 'And are you? A dragon, I mean?'

Auntie Harrison threw back her large head and laughed. 'I only breathe fire when there's a full moon. Ah, here's Clive. I have met your fiancée, and yes, I approve.'

'It wouldn't matter if you didn't.' He turned to Abigail

and kissed her on the cheek. 'How many staff have you got for Monday?'

'Three from eight till four, then two from four till ten.'

'Is two enough for the afternoon?'

'There's always me.'

'But you'll have to be on hand for the medical side, for doctors' visits and so on. You can't be a carer as well.'

She shook a finger at him. 'If I need more, I'll get more. Mornings, I'll serve breakfasts on to trays and the staff can carry them through. Before breakfast, they'll have half an hour to start their duties. There'll be one for locker tops, flowers and commodes, one for light beds and two for heavy beds.'

'You've counted yourself again.'

She nodded. 'Yes, if I do heavy beds, I'll see who's getting sores, who needs special attention. Clive, most of these carers are untrained women. I can't leave them to do my heavy beds until I'm sure they can cope.'

'And what about in the night? When the bells ring, there'll be just you to answer their requirements. Imagine turning a twenty-stone patient to change a draw sheet.'

Abigail looked at Auntie Harrison. 'Was he always such a worrier?'

'Yes, but he's right. You ought to have someone staying here with you.'

'I'm stronger than I look.'

Clive held up his hand. 'May I speak?'

'Feel free,' said Auntie.

'I'm getting a deputy matron. Sorry, Abigail, but I can't let you carry this on your own. It's going to be far too much for you. I'll put an advert in the paper, offer a good wage and sleeping accommodation. You are not to be worn out before we even get to the registry office. I want a wife in one piece, not a shattered wreck.'

'He's made up his mind,' said Auntie. 'There's no doing anything with him now. I remember when he was a child—'

'Don't start that,' shouted Clive. 'She doesn't want to hear about how wayward I was.'

'Don't I?' Abigail was laughing. 'I may need it all to use in evidence against you at a later date. Come along, Auntie Harrison. You and I shall go into a little huddle in the scullery and you can tell me of all his misdeeds.'

Clive drew up his shoulders in a gesture of helplessness. 'How am I going to manage with all these bossy women?'

'You love it,' said Auntie. 'Come along, Abigail. I shall tell you of the time when he stretched cotton across the avenue to knock gentlemen's hats off. Oh, then there was the case of the missing mousetraps. Ever heard a teacher scream when its hand gets caught in a trap? A terrible sound, I am sure it has haunted Clive all down the years.'

As she followed Auntie, Abigail looked back at Clive. He was staring at her with such naked adoration in his eyes that she suddenly found it hard to bear. It wasn't funny, this love business. What poor old Cedric Wilkinson felt for Ellen wasn't funny either, and Abigail should not have laughed at him.

'I love you,' he mouthed before turning to leave.

She made no answer, yet her body felt chilled as soon as he closed the door. Perhaps it was her imagination. After all, there was a draught from the scullery. Yes, that would be it. Just a drop in room temperature, no more than that.

CHAPTER SEVEN

Marie

'Mrs Banks, I'm sorry, honest I am. Only there's nowt I can do about it, is there? I mean, it's not my fault, and I can't give you what I haven't got. Look round the shelves if you don't believe me – I've got nothing new, have I? Where's your ration book? You should have it with you, no use leaving it in the house.'

The old lady leaned against the counter, one hand gripped tightly at her throat to hold together the two sides of a voluminous black shawl, which covered her whole body except for a small crack where one eye and a hairy nostril peeped through. 'There's plenty you can do if you want, if you shape yourself. I bet you've loads of stuff hid under that there counter. I'm having nowt more to do with them bloody books and their bits of points. I've told you, I've got none. Why do they have to have these new-fangled things all the while? Ninety, I am this year. Ninety years old, and I'm supposed to start messing about with books at my age.' With her free hand, she waved a stained clay pipe. 'Can't even get me baccy, I'll be smoking dandelion leaves next news. And snuff is like gold dust. Where's me comforts, that's what I want to know. Country's gone to the dogs, no time for us old folk, no care for our needs.'

Marie clicked her tongue. 'Look, we've had rationing for ages now, you should be used to it. Everybody's the same, you know. It's not just you.'

'Aye, but they keep changing things, don't they? Like you can have four ounces of summat one minute, then all of a sudden, you get two ounces. I don't know whether I'm coming or going, I'm that mithered with it all. Sick to death of turnips, I am. And when did you last have a decent onion in this here shop? Fiddly little things you've been selling – why, I remember proper onions, big as footballs and tasty with it. And I could do with a banana. Long time since I had a banana. They've stopped fetching them in, you know. And us without teeth has to be careful what we eat. You can get pain in your stomach when things is too hard to chew.'

'Mrs Banks.' Marie spoke slowly, firmly and as loudly as she could without bringing the street in. 'This country is an island, it's completely surrounded by water.'

The eye flashed. 'What's that to do with the price of fish?'

'A lot. And we don't sell fish any road.'

'You know what I mean, don't start getting clever. What's being an island got to do with me having nowt on the table and no baccy for me pipe?'

The girl behind the counter gathered her shattered patience together and smiled as sweetly as she could. 'There's ships at sea, war ships that stop stuff coming in the docks. Fetching food in is a dangerous business. England isn't self-sufficient, it's only a little country.' She remembered that from geography at school. 'Government can't go risking lives just to fetch a bit of tea and sugar in, there's trouble enough. Now, I have to have your coupons so I can get more stock. I can't get things without points, same as you. See, I'm very sorry, but it's just one ounce of cheese, four ounces of bacon and two ounces of tea every week. Happen I might find you an extra bit of dried egg, but you can't have any more marge, you've had your eight ounces for this week. I'm doing me best for you, and for everybody, but there's restrictions—'

'Well then, I suppose I must starve. Stands to reason I'll die if I don't get no food. I do have money, you know. Look, I'll give you a bob on the side for a tin of salmon and a scrape of marge. I just fancy a nice bit of salmon, it goes

173

down easy. Now, can I do fairer than offering you a bit extra cash?'

Marie shook her dark brown curls and looked over her shoulder into the room at the back of the shop, checking herself almost immediately. Why should she care if he was listening? He carried no clout, this wasn't his shop any more, he'd no right to interfere. 'Mrs Banks,' she said clearly. 'There's no black market in this shop. As far as I know, there never was any funny goings on here. If there was a bit of favouritism in the past, it was nowt to do with me.' She sniffed meaningfully. 'I don't agree with black marketing, 'cos it's not fair on them that have no money. I've told you before, fetch your book in here and I'll mind it for you, save you getting confused. I'll not see you starve. You can have half my fat for this week and I'll let you know when I've got some salmon. You will be the first to know when the tinned stuff comes in.'

The old lady grinned, displaying a single tooth that stood like a lone gravestone in the centre of her lower jaw. 'You're a little flower, what are you?'

'A little flower,' sighed Marie. 'Though it was my twin sister who was called after Saint Theresa the Little Flower. Now. Can you get yourself home all right? Here's your bits and pieces.'

'Course I can get home,' snapped the mouth from the gap in the thick shawl. 'Listen, lass, I know these streets like the back of my hand, saw some of these houses going up, I did. Aye, and I've seen a few of them come down and all. What's up with these folk that they've got to go and start a war? Waste of bloody money, that's all war is. We're all taxed up to the eyeballs, then they go and chuck our brass away on bombs. Have they nowt better to do? Daft buggers, the lot of them. We should have kept our noses out of it, shouldn't we? None of our concern if foreigners wants to go about blowing each other to pieces.' Without waiting for answer or comment, Mrs Banks clattered out of the shop, worn clogs scraping the floor as she staggered along on age-bent limbs.

'Going soft, are you?' He leaned against the door frame, ankles crossed in an attitude of nonchalance. 'That woman's got more food stashed in her meatsafe than we've got in six houses. And she's not without money. You could have sold her some stock. You know damned well there's plenty of everything put away.'

Marie lifted a small side of bacon from the floor and began to cut carefully at its muslin wrapper, which would make a good dishcloth.

'Can you hear me, lady?'

'I hear you. And me mam's having them houses altered so's folk can have a proper upstairs bedroom like what they should have. Any spare stock will go to them that need it, like folk with kiddies and old people and them that's sick. No point in hoarding while there's shortages. Me mam says it's a sin.' Not that he'd know about sin, she thought as she sliced through the cloth. He'd no idea of right and wrong, this fellow.

'What? She'll never get all that stuff stored in one room. What does she think she's playing at? You need both bedrooms for all the surplus. Listen, I struggled for years to get that lot together. Nobody listened when I said there was a war coming. What's she going to do? Sell it all at once and let things run down?'

'Why should you bother? It's not yours to worry about any more. Anything that's not on points will be sold off, specially all the ironmongery, it takes up too much room. Me mam says the folk in them houses have got to lead normal lives. You threw them out if they had a baby, didn't you? Only space for two, you said, no children, you said. Anyway, me mam's sorting it all out. She'll likely tell the Ministry about all that salmon and tinned fruit. I'm not selling it till I know it's cleared proper.'

Anger and frustration caused him to take a step towards her. He raised a hand as if to lash out, and she picked up the ham knife, holding it out at waist height in front of her body. 'I'll do it, I will,' she said. Her voice was quiet like her mother's. 'Go on, hit me. You've been hitting us for

175

years, so why stop now?' He lowered his arm. 'I'll tell you why you'll stop,' she went on. 'Because for one, I'll stick this in you. I hate you, do you know that? I hate the sight of you. And for another, you're not in charge any more. This is my shop, mine. I might be only nearly seventeen, but I know what happened, I know you took Lilian's money and left her with Abigail and Tishy. Now she's turned on you. She might be in her coffin, but she's made you sign everything over to us. I've heard of folk turning in their graves, and that's what Lilian's doing. You can't do anything to anybody now. You're finished.'

He stared at her, his eyes almost popping from his head as he fought the urge to hit out. Yes, she was nearly seventeen and going on forty-five, this one. She had brains and guts and cheek, all the things he hated to see in a woman. If only he could get rid of her. But he'd have to get rid of all of them, all five. Plan and scheme as he might, he still hadn't been able to work out a way. And there was still that bloody woman in hospital hanging on till she could split on him.

Oh, if only he could work this out! If he got rid of them all, that damned solicitor's papers wouldn't be worth a scrap, because everything would come to the sole survivor. Yes, he needed to make a plan that would leave him a childless widower. Was it beyond hope now, beyond reach? It had all gone so wrong, hadn't it? Was this really the end of the London empire, or could it be retrieved even now, at what seemed to be the eleventh hour? He turned on his heel and walked out of the shop, slamming the front door behind him.

It was eight o'clock in the morning. They had been open for just a few minutes, and already the day promised to be grim. Marie leaned on the counter and watched Linda Tattersall mopping the outside flags. Linda Tattersall had, it seemed, one ambition in life, and that was to work for Mr London in his shop, to serve customers and handle money and be trusted. Things were so uncomplicated for the Linda Tattersalls of the world, no imagination, no ambition, no dream.

Marie let out a heartfelt groan. She was, for the first time ever, jealous and discontented. Life hadn't been easy, not with him for a father, but Marie had always managed somehow to make the best of it. Now, all she could see was more of the same, a future that would consist entirely of making the best of things. Theresa had escaped at last. She had gone up to a big farm in Bradshaw, a grand place from all accounts, where evacuees stayed until their babies were born, where bombed-out folk got temporary accommodation. Abigail was doing an interesting job, while even Tishy seemed content enough.

Would poor Marie be standing here in fifty years' time, a bent old lady with a croaky voice and hands too stiff to count change? Surely not! No, once she had reached twenty-one, she would persuade the others to sell, then she'd go off on a world cruise and marry a very dashing man from foreign parts. Though she wasn't really sure about who owned what, was she? Mam was holding the shops and the houses in trust, but Marie hadn't managed to work out whether or when she and the other three would become outright owners. And there was Mam to consider too. Still, happen Mam would have had enough of shops by the time Marie and Theresa got to twenty-one.

Twenty-one. That was ages off yet, over four years away. And she couldn't just walk out, couldn't leave Mam to cope with two shops and him as well. Because he took some coping with, did London. She never referred to him as Dad any more. Only Theresa called him Dad, because Theresa didn't think it was nice to call anybody by a second name that wasn't even their real second name. But then Theresa was soft, always had been. It had been Abigail's idea to call him London after she'd grown tired of Daddy-Dear, and it had stuck with the three of them. Tishy just did what others did, Tishy was a copier. And Tishy was getting on Marie's flaming nerves, and

Marie knew it wasn't Christian to allow a poor soul like Tishy to get on her nerves.

She lined some Dolly Cream up on the counter while she thought about Tishy. It was getting near spring-cleaning time, and Dolly Cream would be favourite for putting life back into lace curtains. She was daft, was Tishy, and that was the top and bottom of it. There were a few screws loose in her head, because she could think just so far and no further. But Mam was making such a fuss of the girl, saying how clever she was with her knitting and her sewing. Mam missed Theresa, that was plain to see. Happen Tishy had taken Theresa's place, and Marie felt envious about that. It was all right being self-sufficient, but everybody thought you needed no time and attention if you could think for yourself.

She straightened a pile of gas mantle boxes, then gazed round the shop. She was the one condemned to work here, the one who couldn't escape. It should be hers by rights. If the others wanted a piece of it, then they should be forced to come here and share in the watching of London. Yes, she would tackle Mam about this at the earliest opportunity. After the war, this shop could be great again, worth keeping or worth selling, and she would own only a quarter of it. And the other shop on Derby Street was even more valuable; any money from that ought to be Mam's. Tishy would never need anything except a roof and a piano. Abigail had proper training, could earn money doing a real job. The shops should come to Marie – and perhaps to Theresa – because these two had worked in them from infancy.

All these thoughts made Marie uneasy with herself. It was as if she were changing, becoming hard and selfish and all the things she'd been brought up not to be. But Abigail had told her to look out for herself, and she was clever, was Abigail. 'Always think of number one first,' she had said to Marie. 'Take your chances and make the most of them.'

Linda Tattersall dragged the heavy mop bucket into the shop. 'Shall I sweep?'

'No. Get yourself off, have some breakfast.' Yes, the girl looked as if a mug of tea and some hot toast with beef dripping would not go amiss. 'You can finish the jobs at four o'clock, after school. There's nowt that won't wait.'

Linda stood there looking foolish, the thin blonde hair tumbling over rounded eyes. 'But I always sweep at ten past eight. Mr London said it were important to have a routine, like. I mop, then I sweep, then I dust some shelves. And at four o'clock, I finish the dusting and fill the shelves and—'

'Never mind. Just empty your bucket and go.'

Linda heaved up the bucket and staggered through to the back yard with it. When she returned she looked reproachfully at Marie. 'What will Mr London say about the dust on them shelves? It's all thick and greasy. What will he say?' she repeated.

'Nothing. This is my shop and I do what I like in it.'

'Oh.'

Marie struggled with her own impatience. After all, there was no point in taking out frustrations on this undergrown girl. 'Linda, I don't mean to be nasty, love. It's just that I've had Mrs Banks in with another of her sob stories and I gave in because she's so old. That one gets round me at least once a week. She's took off with half my own margarine.'

Linda sniffed and rubbed her cold nose. 'Mr London was telling me mam about that last night.'

Marie's ears pricked up. 'Was he? What was he doing round your house? You've no need of help now that your mam's working in our other shop. My mam will make sure your house doesn't go short. Whatever's available on ration or on special, your family will get a fair share. What's going on?'

The younger girl pulled at the cheap blue skirt that was beginning to tighten round her slight but developing frame. 'Well, they sit near the fire, have a cigarette and a talk.'

'What about?'

Linda scratched her pointed chin while she thought for a moment or two. 'I'm not rightly sure, 'cos I'm usually at Nan's when he comes. But he likes us, does Mr London. He looked after us that night when the bomb came and me dad died, and he's been keeping an eye on us ever since.'

'Listen, he helps nobody unless there's something in it for him. And don't take anything from him, do you hear? The folk in the six houses know now that they've to give him nowt. That stock's not for giving away, and it's not for black market. Them days is over and done with. Things have got to be shared fair and square during war, that's what me mam says. You'd best watch him, Linda. He's a bad beggar if ever there was one. Don't trust him, and tell your mam the same. He'd sell us all for five bob.'

The girl's jaw fell for a fraction of a second. 'How can you say that about your own dad? You don't know how lucky you are, having a dad. I wish mine was here, I can tell you that. I think you're awful, Marie. How would you feel if he died, eh?' Before Marie could warn her any further, Linda turned and fled from the shop, her eyes filled with tears.

It was a terrible day. Because the butcher next door ran out of meat after the first ten minutes, everybody started to panic about what they might have for their tea. There were people begging for an extra ounce of bacon, folk almost in tears because they'd run out of coal and Marie had no coal bricks, and an impromptu coupon-swapping group occupied a whole corner of the shop for the best part of half an hour. Two women nearly came to blows over the last pound of pudding rice, and Marie finally separated them by explaining that she had more, that it was in storage, and that she would deliver it personally to the loser's house by two o'clock.

At dinner time, she had to close because he hadn't come back. Mind, she thought, it was just as well, since he did most of his petty pilfering when she was on her break. After calling home for a quick bite and a short chat with her mother and Tishy, she set off for the Derby Street shop on the pretext of getting rice.

Marie stood in the doorway of the shop and watched Cissie Tattersall dealing with the customers. The woman had a pleasant enough manner, and seemed quite capable when it came to money and points. When the shop was empty, Marie approached the counter. 'Can I have some rice for Deane Road, please?'

'Help yourself, love. Write it down in this here book, though.'

'I will. I do know how to go about things, Mrs Tattersall.'

Her business completed, Marie studied the woman behind the till. She half-prayed that somebody would come into the shop and save the situation, but the doorbell remained silent.

'Anything else?' asked Cissie.

'Yes.'

'Well, I'm sure you know how to handle it. Shall I go and put the kettle on the gas ring?'

'No. I want a word with you, Mrs Tattersall.'

Cissie leaned on the counter, hands spread wide on its polished surface. 'Oh, I see. Well, your mother seems quite satisfied with me. Have I been doing summat wrong?'

'That's for you to know and the rest of us to wonder about.' Marie's voice trembled. She was still young enough to be timid while tackling a true adult.

'Eh?' She could feel the flush rising from her chest and over her neck. 'Whatever's the matter?'

Marie inhaled deeply. 'What's going on between you and London?'

'Me and . . . oh . . . you mean your dad.' The down-turned hands slowly curled into tightly balled fists.

'I mean him they call Billy London, yes. He's been no dad to me, not if you think about what the word "dad" means. How come he's always round at your house? Is he still fetching you the sweepings? I thought you were getting your rations here now. Didn't you get your registration changed to this shop?'

'I did. Makes things easier with me working here, like. I can pick the stuff up, you see.' The stiff smile faded. 'I've took nothing I wasn't supposed to take. I just get our rations here, that's all. Your mam doesn't allow any favouritism.'

Marie leaned forward from the waist. 'Then why does he come to visit you? Come on, Mrs T, there has to be a reason. That man never did anything without a reason.'

Cissie all but squirmed. She put Marie in mind of a fish on a hook, wriggling and doing its best to get safely back into the water. 'I don't know what you're getting at, lass.'

'Mrs Tattersall, I'm sure you do know what I mean. You've gone as red as a beetroot for a start. Your Linda let it slip this morning, told me that he's round your house a lot. Well, I'm seventeen next month, and I know what's what, I can tell you that for nowt. I've asked you a very easy question and you're not giving me any answers.' She wished she'd never started this. It would have been better to take the rice and run, because she didn't really want any answers, did she?

'Well . . . we're friends, like. He wants . . . somebody to talk to.'

'I see.' Marie tapped the floor with the toe of her clog. 'Does my mam know about this? Does she know that you and London are good friends?'

'I . . . er . . . I couldn't say.'

Marie's heart was banging like the bass drum on walking day. 'No, I'm sure you couldn't. Well, let me tell you this, missus. My family's had enough trouble lately what with one thing and another. We don't need you shoving your oar in and making things worse for Mam. You can tell him that he's not to come to your house no more. Have you got that?' She could feel her cheeks glowing. That was the trouble with being fresh-complexioned – you always got two pinkish spots on your cheeks when feelings would have been best hidden.

'Yes, but . . .'

'But what?'

Cissie mopped her warm face with a rag that had used to be the tail of her husband's shirt. 'I don't know how to stop him, Marie. I mean, I've told him, like. I've said it didn't seem right us being friends and all that. But he won't listen. I might as well talk to the fire back. I'm not very good at telling men what to do.' Her voice faded to nothing.

'Why?'

'I don't know, it's just the road I am, it's how I'm made.'

A customer came in, so Marie stepped back while Cissie sold some bread and lard. When the bell had clanged shut, Marie stepped closer to the counter. 'Do you like your job here, Mrs Tattersall?'

'Aye, you know I do.' With shaking fingers, Cissie closed the wooden cash drawer.

'Is the money good enough for you?'

'Yes.'

'And does my mother treat you right?'

Cissie sniffed while her eyes watered ominously. 'Your mam is one of the finest women I've ever known, Marie. She's a wonderful person. You don't need me to tell you that, love.'

'Good, good.' Marie nodded in time with her words. 'Then get shut of him. If you think so much of my mam – my mam and your boss – then tell him to sling his hook as far as he can throw it.' Preferably into the nearest river, she mused.

The large-boned woman turned her broad back on Marie while she sorted ration points into a sectioned tray. 'Marie?' she threw over her shoulder.

'What? For goodness sake, don't start crying.'

The wide shoulders drooped. 'I'm scared of him. There's summat about him, a thing I can't put me finger on. It's as if he's took over my house, I can't shift him. He won't listen to me, won't take no notice. I do want shut of

183

him, I do – honest! But what if he turns on me?'

Marie laughed mirthlessly. 'Oh, he will. He's turned on us and our mam that many times, I can tell you now that he won't like it. He has to have all his own road. Now listen to me, Mrs Tattersall. Wherever he goes, he makes trouble.' She pondered for a moment. 'Tell you what, carry on as normal. You just leave things as they are for a bit till I get something sorted out in my mind. He's clever, the worst kind of clever. The thing is, we have to be cleverer. I'll work it out. I can see you're too scared to do it for yourself. And I can't say as how I blame you, either.'

Cissie swallowed audibly. 'Nay, whatever are you thinking of doing?'

'I've thought of nowt yet. The only thing I can think of is getting this rice round to John Street before Mrs Turner kills Elsie Burns. Near came to blows over it, they did.' She reached a hand out to the distressed woman. 'Look, I'm sorry I came in like a bull at a gate. I should have known you were frightened of him. That's what he does to women, he terrifies them till they do as they're told. I'll get rid of him for you.'

Cissie turned and smiled through her unshed tears. 'I wish you would, lass. It's been bothering me since it started, but there's been nowt I could do. And with him employing our Linda, I were right grateful to him. It's like I owe him summat. And he makes damned sure I remember the debt.'

Marie raised her chin. 'You owe nobody anything. We've always liked you, me and our Theresa. I remember you putting us right over babies when we thought they came out of ladies' belly buttons. No. Don't be thinking you're less than him just because he's a man and you're a woman. Them days are over. Anyway, I'd best get back before there's murder done over a bit of rice pudding.' She walked to the door.

'Marie?'

'What?'

'Go careful now, love. With him, I mean.'

Marie smiled. 'We've been careful for years. The time for being careful is long gone. No, it's time he got a taste of what he's been dishing out. I'm not feared of him, not any more. He's just a man, and not a very big one.' She stalked out with her head held high and ran down John Street to deliver the promised rice.

When she got back to the shop, there was great confusion. A few people had gathered outside for their bread, so a few others had joined the queue in the vain hope that there might be something worth queuing up for. By the time the shop was due to re-open, a rumour had spread the length of Deane Road that London's had oranges, loads of white bread, Virginia tobacco and tinned pears in heavy syrup. Marie addressed the multitude. 'What are you lot doing here?' Honestly, she thought, if two people stood for a chat outside a shop, there was always a queue within minutes.

'Salmon,' shouted a stout woman with a shopping basket.

'Proper ciggies,' called another woman.

'I've got nothing I didn't have yesterday,' yelled Marie.

'No oranges?' asked a sad-faced old man as he waved a green ration book. 'I promised my grandkids some fruit, even brought their coupons.'

'No oranges, no Virginias, no salmon. I don't know who starts these ideas, I really don't. Anyway, if you're here for normal stuff with points, come in. If you're after something special, try the Co-op.' She was suddenly weary. With tired eyes, she watched the crowd disappearing in a blur of legs and arms and waving baskets, all pushing and shoving to be the first at the Co-op. And she didn't care. She was the guilty party this time, she had started the rumour. But at least she'd got rid of them and they could go and be hysterical or patient or whatever outside somebody else's shop for a change.

It was gloomy and cold inside, so she lit the paraffin heater and sat almost on top of it, pulling her stool close to the heat and hitching her frock above her knees. The bell rang, and she hastily rearranged herself into a more decorous state before turning to look at the customer.

'Hiya, Marie.' It was John Duffy from school, only he was all done up in the uniform of a telegram boy. He looked older and wiser than he had used to, and his hair, which had always stood up like a dry haystack, was plastered to his head with oil. She grinned at him, 'Hiya, Ginger.'

'I don't get called that any more since me hair went darker.' He removed his cap so that she might examine the smooth, flattened thatch.

'That's not darker, you daft lad. That's greased up. What have you put on it – the lard out of your mam's chip pan?' He wasn't a bad-looking boy in spite of the freckles. He had what could be best described as a cheerful face, homely, open and welcoming. At school, he had performed like a proper clown, forever in trouble, forever stuck in a corner with the dunce hat covering his spiky red hair. Mind, he had been fed up, come to think, because he'd been a few months older than everybody else in the class, so he had apparently needed to act big. 'What do you want?' she asked now. 'Have you brought me a telegram?' She wasn't nervous; her family had no-one serving abroad.

'I just thought I'd come and have a look at you. I'm on me dinner, so I can do as I like for the next half hour.'

She handed him a peppermint from her apron pocket, and he accepted this with a smile of gratitude, pushing the sweet between strong teeth and crunching it noisily.

'Why don't you suck it?' she asked. 'They last a lot longer if you suck instead of chewing.'

'Best to live for the moment, Marie. In a job like mine, you do things quick, enjoy them while you can. I hate this bloody job, can't wait to join up. I'm forever knocking at doors with bad news. They see you coming on your bike, and they all run in and lock their doors. They think they can stop it being them if they shut me out. But they can't stop it, can they? So I knock and I wait and the curtains twitch. They're usually already crying before they read the message. They start saying things like, "no, not our Jimmy, please tell me it's not him", and I stand there feeling proper daft 'cos I can't do nowt. I mean, I don't even know what's in the message, so I don't know if it's Jimmy or Bert or whoever. Then they look at me right sad, as if I've done summat to them.' He shook his head. 'I can't stand it, I'm joining up.'

Marie felt so sorry for him that she went and placed a hand on his shoulder. 'It's not your fault, John. You can't help what's in them telegrams.'

'I know. But with me being so big for my age, they stare at me as if they're thinking it should have been me instead of their lad. I can't help it if I'm not old enough to be in the war. But I will be old enough soon – remember I'm nearly eighteen – I did an extra year at school after all the months off with diphtheria. And that was flaming Sister Hunchback's fault, persuading me mam that I was clever. Very handy with the cane, was old Hunchback.' He studied his hand as if he still expected to see the red stripes. 'Didn't even have to bend, did she? Doubled over all the time into killer position, she was.' He shrugged. 'Any road, as soon as I'm eighteen, I'll go and beat hell out of them Germans.'

'Army?'

'Aye.' He grabbed her hand with a suddenness that surprised both of them. 'Come out for a walk with me tonight, Marie.' Even his ears were blushing.

Her mouth hung loose for a split second. 'Eh? What for? We can't go out, there might be a raid. Me mam would go mad if I went out at night.' She retrieved her hand with difficulty. She would have to get rid of him, he might just cause a scene in front of customers. 'Tell you what, we'll go for a nice walk in Queens Park on Sunday afternoon. Will that do you?'

He smiled, his mouth growing wider than ever, seeming to threaten to split his face into two halves. 'I like you,' he mumbled, his face reddening now to the roots of his carrotty fringe. 'I always did. And before I go away, I want to find somebody as'll write to me. I know me mam'll write, but I wanted a girl. Just a friend, like.' He turned his head and stared through the window. This had taken a lot of courage. How many times had he cycled past this shop lately because he hadn't had the guts to face her?

'I'll write to you, John.' The day didn't seem so bad now. Here was John Duffy all ready to go to war, yet he had come round specially to see Marie first. 'When are you going?'

'Oh, it'll be a while yet. Me mam wouldn't let me lie about me age, see, so I have to wait till I'm really turned eighteen. She's like that, me mam. A right fusspot.'

The door burst open to reveal Mrs Pickavance from Emblem Street. Mrs Pickavance was famous among the grocers of Daubhill and Deane, because she always had a lot of points, far too many for just herself and her husband. She was carrying a handful today, probably hoping that a young girl like Marie would be taken in. 'Four lots of bacon, four lots of cheese, two pounds of marge,' ordered the huge lady breathlessly.

Marie picked up the ration tokens. 'Who are these for?' she asked pleasantly.

'Myself, me husband, our Diana, our Beattie, our Joan and our Lizzie.'

'Oh. Aren't the four girls at the ordnance depot at Euxton?'

The woman bridled, folding thick arms across her enormous chest. 'Aye. They come home at weekends, though, so their books are registered in two places.'

'I see.' She spread the coupons on the counter. 'And this is not weekend, is it? They've gone back to the hostel now. Did the hostel release some extra points for last weekend, Mrs Pickavance? Has there been a new arrangement? You see, I have to be told. There's forms and stuff to fill in, chitties to sign.'

The woman scowled fiercely. 'Well, I had a bit in from

the week before, and now I'm replacing it. I'm nobbut getting back what's rightly mine.'

Marie nodded. She knew all about the 'bit in from the week before'. Everybody knew about it. The four Pickavance girls were forced, every weekend, to live on thin potato stew so that their greedy mother could save their food points for herself. Mrs Pickavance thought her girls were fed well enough at the hostel, and she regarded their weekly contribution of rations as her due. The fact that her children were working in dangerous circumstances, to produce munitions for the war effort, meant little to Gertie Pickavance. She was a hungry woman who needed her strength, and her girls were all right, somebody else was getting their dinners for them.

'I can't do all this,' said Marie, still pleasantly. 'I can fill yours and your husband's, because the two of you are on my register, but I've not enough stock to do the girls as well. Try the Co-op if we can't satisfy your . . . needs.' She smiled to herself – the Co-op would bless her today.

Mrs Pickavance cursed under her breath, picked up the paltry heap of merchandise that Marie was willing to allow her, then stamped out of the shop on her massive feet.

'Well done,' said John Duffy.

Marie's round cheeks dimpled. She liked the idea that John Duffy approved of her. In fact, she quite liked John Duffy. He might have been daft at school, but he was more serious now, more thoughtful and grown-up. After all, he was nearly eighteen, almost a man. 'I've met her sort before,' she said. 'They fleece their kids and eat it all themselves.'

'Will you miss me when I've gone, Marie?'

'Don't talk so stupid.' But she was blushing and she knew it. And she knew that he could see her blushing. He would think she liked him. The thought that he would think she liked him made her blush even more. And she didn't care. Not about blushing, anyway.

London didn't come back to the shop at all that day.

When four o'clock arrived, Marie welcomed Linda, apologizing for upsetting her earlier. 'Let's be friends,' she said. 'Tell you what, I've one or two frocks I've grown out of. Shall I fetch them round your house tonight just after the shop shuts? I can nip home and get them, it won't be any trouble. And if we get a warning, we'll go in the same shelter as Mam anyway, so she won't mind me being at yours.'

Linda smiled, eager to be forgiven for the earlier disagreement. 'Ooh, I'd love a couple of frocks. Me mam's made me a nice skirt since she got work, but I'd like something for best. What are they like? Are they short or long? I like the new short frocks—'

'They're plain but good. You can soon dress them up with new collars and a bit of lace, happen a few buttons. Now, you do your dusting, Linda, while I see to this queue. It's been happening all day, has this. They seem to think my ship's come in, I can't work out what's the matter with them at all.'

She went off resignedly to explain, yet again, that she had no salmon, that there had been no delivery of white flour and that she had no cheese rinds to give away. What they managed to do with cheese rinds she had never been able to work out, but the nasty, rubbery items were always in great demand, probably because they were free.

Six o'clock arrived at last. Linda went on her happy way with an extra shilling in her pocket, while Marie put up the blackouts, doused the lights and locked everything securely.

She rushed home, wrote a quick note for her mother who had not yet returned with Tishy from Derby Street, grabbed two dresses from her wardrobe, then dashed round to Emblem Street. Mrs Tattersall was still out, probably helping Mam to close the shop and count the takings.

Marie heaved a sigh of relief, picked up Mrs Tattersall's rag bag and sewing box, then dragged Linda off upstairs. 'Come on, hurry up,' she admonished gently. 'Let's do a good job and give your mam a surprise. If she doesn't hear us, think how pleased she'll be when you go downstairs in your new frock. See this blue one? Light the gas and I'll show you. I've only worn it twice. We got it when I was going through one of my growing phases. Right. Let's try it on, then we can look in the rag bag for bits to liven it up.'

They became absorbed in their task; even Marie got caught up in it, fitting a bit of broderie anglaise to the collar, finding a set of paler blue buttons, tacking some red felt together to make a sleeveless waistcoat. 'See,' she said, sitting back on her heels to observe her handiwork. 'If we put that waistcoat on our sewing machine tomorrow, and make some holes down the front with our hole-puncher, you can tie the front up with white shoe-laces. Then you'll be in red, white and blue, ready for the end of the war.'

Linda looked at herself in the pock-marked mirror. 'That's really beautiful, Marie. It's the most loveliest frock I've ever had in me whole life.'

Marie, one ear cocked towards the stairs, put a finger to her lips. 'Let's do the pink one as well,' she whispered. She felt sorry for little Linda, partly because she had never had a decent frock in all her born days, mostly because the poor girl was being used at this very moment. 'I've brought some navy blue rick-rack braid from our house. We've got loads of it, I think Mam swapped something for it ages ago. We can put it all around the skirt and at the neck too. It'll set off that pale pink something lovely. Then I'll machine it all on proper tomorrow. You start tacking while I go to the lav.'

Linda paused, needle in hand. 'But me mam'll see you. She thinks I'm at Nan's. You'll spoil the surprise.'

'No, I won't. As long as you stop here, I'll tell her we're looking at *Picturegoer*s. She'll still get her surprise, don't you worry.'

Cissie Tattersall got her surprise all right. She was lying on the sofa with Billy London on top of her when his daughter sallied into the room.

Marie stood and surveyed the scene. She knew what went on between men and women, but she'd never actually seen it before. It looked ridiculous, she thought. London was panting like a train getting up steam, while Mrs Tattersall just lay there studying the washing until she spotted Marie, whereupon she let out a scream the force of which seemed to hurl her partner on to the floor. He knelt there, frantically trying to cover himself against Marie's expressionless stare.

'Well, don't we meet some queer folk in some queer places?' asked Marie. 'Got another woman in your clutches, London?' In spite of her acute embarrassment, she managed to keep her tone as cold as ice.

He struggled with his buttons while Cissie sat up and closed her blouse. 'Eeh, lass,' she breathed. 'You gave me one hell of a start then.' Her face was scarlet as she straightened her ruffled hair.

'Linda's upstairs,' snapped Marie. 'She knows nowt about this, and you'd best keep it that way, both of you.'

Cissie finished pushing her hair into some sort of order. 'But she's supposed to be at me mother's with Tony.'

'We were trying clothes on. And I just came down to go to the toilet. I never expected to find him here.' She pointed at her father. 'You had better get home,' she said to him. 'And if I find out you've been here again, I'll tell Mam. If she hears about this, you'll be out of our house before you can blink. You're nothing but a lodger any road. See if Mrs Tattersall will take you in.'

He staggered to his feet. 'You've no right here,' he said breathlessly. 'Have you been following me? This is none of your business.'

'Isn't it?' She took a step nearer to him. 'I'm making it my business. You've brought enough trouble on our family with your divorce and all that carry-on, without starting this caper with my mam's friend. You come near this house again, and your feet won't touch the ground. I'll tell everybody you've been coming here, and I'll tell them what I've just seen. You're disgusting, that's what you are.

And if my mam turns you out, you'll have no wage, no food and no clothes to your back. So get home now.'

'You bloody little bitch.'

'You dirty, horrible, ugly, nasty old man. I can call names as well, you know. Raise one finger to me, and I'll tell on you. I will.'

He moved towards her, obscenities pouring from his lips. Cissie began to weep softly. 'Shut up,' hissed Marie. 'That girl up there is not old enough to hear any of this. Neither am I, come to that. But I have heard it and I have seen it. Remember that, both of you.' She looked him straight in the face. 'One step more, and I'll go straight to my mam.'

He stopped dead in his tracks, hatred for this girl seeming to ooze from every pore as he sweated from recent exertion and from shock. He had to get rid of her, get rid of them all. With a last futile demonstration of his rage, he grabbed his hat, slammed it on to his head, then stormed out through the scullery.

'Thanks,' said Cissie.

Marie sank into a chair, swallowing the bile that rose in her gorge. 'Why?' she managed at last. 'Why did you let him do . . . that to you? It's . . . it's a thing that should only happen between folk that's . . . well . . . in love and all that. He's horrible.'

Several moments passed before the answer came. 'At first, I were grateful. It seemed to be what he wanted.'

'As payment? For dirty sugar and a bit of tea?'

Cissie nodded mutely.

'I feel sick. I don't want things to be like this, Mrs Tattersall. I didn't know you and him were . . . like that. Well, I wasn't sure. I must have had some idea at the back of my mind, but it still came as a shock, seeing him doing that to you. I still can't believe that a nice, kind woman like you could do that with him. And you've gone behind my mam's back and she gave you a job and all.'

Cissie stood up and approached the fireplace. 'It started before Ellen took me on. After it started, I couldn't stop it.

193

He frightens me, Marie. I don't know why I'm frightened of him, but I am. Will you tell Ellen? Will you? I don't think I could ever look her in the face again if she knew.'

Marie shook her head. 'I'll do nothing to hurt her. She's had her share without being the laughing stock round here all over again. It was bad enough when the neighbours and customers found out he'd been married before, bad enough when they started asking about Tishy and Abigail. I can't put her through this, I just can't. But, God forgive me, I want that man dead before he can do any more harm in this world.'

Cissie sighed. 'I wish my man could come back, love. If he'd never gone and got himself killed, I wouldn't be in this mess now. But I'll tell you one thing, Marie. I've learned something. I think I've just learned how to say no, how to stand up to a man. If he comes here again, he'll not get over my doorstep.'

'I'm glad to hear it.' Marie shook her head sharply, as if deliberately pulling herself together. 'Now, I'm going for Linda. Dry your face and try to look happy for her. She's all excited with her new frocks.'

Cissie stared at Marie. 'How old are you?'

'Near seventeen.'

'Aye, and with twice my sense. You'll go far, lass. There's wisdom in you, and you got that from your mam. I'll never be able to tell you how grateful I am to you. A good girl, that's what you are. Right. I'm ready. Go and get our Linda in her finery. Life's got to go on, hasn't it?'

If Marie Langden had ever been asked to identify the day on which she actually became grown-up, she would have nominated that March Tuesday in 1942, the day when she found her so-called father fornicating with Linda Tattersall's mam. She felt strangely calm once she'd recovered from the initial shock, as if it had all happened to somebody else. And the funny thing was, she didn't blame Cissie Tattersall in the slightest way, didn't ever consider that the woman might have been sinful or guilty or even weak. It was his fault, all of it, just one more black mark to add to all the others he'd collected over the years.

Another symptom of the girl's quick maturation was the fact that she decided to say nothing to Ellen about her feelings concerning the shop. It suddenly didn't matter any more that she had to work there, that she had worked there since infancy, and that the shops were now owned four ways. It was as if everything had become relative, and she found herself looking with new eyes at other people, folk who had little to their names, nothing to fall back on. Marie felt lucky. She had food, clothes, a home, a good mother and, last but not least, it looked as if she had a boyfriend too. So her naturally sunny nature won through after all, and she forgot the jealousies she had felt so strongly during those few brief days.

John Duffy had access to a tandem, an ancient and creaky machine that belonged to an uncle. On fine Sundays, he and Marie would set off with a few sandwiches in the bike's basket, some quiet words from Ellen about getting in before dark, and with the vain hope that the machine's rusty chain would stay in place just this once. They returned each time covered in oil, faces wreathed in happy smiles, and Ellen would serve up tea, toast and more soft words of warning about getting stuck out on country lanes on a rickety bike in the middle of a world war.

Marie found that she was growing to like John, that she liked him a lot. Some of the best days in the shop were those on which he managed to put in an unscheduled appearance, however brief. When London was behind the counter, the two young people would slip outside for a few moments, and when London was absent, they ran the shop between them, like a pair of big kids acting out a grown-up game.

They visited Theresa at the farm, and the newly-married Abigail at the Hollywell Nursing Home. They went to Haslam Park, Queens Park and Rivington Pike, where they rolled themselves down from top to bottom like they had used to every Easter as children.

John had invented several methods of beating sweet rationing. He often carried jelly crystals into which they would dip their fingers, becoming gloriously sticky in the process. From the chemist, he would buy liquorice root, cinnamon sticks and black spanish. This thick, dark stuff was too strong to eat, but it made an excellent drink when mixed with water. On better days, he appropriated some Horlicks tablets, a luxury that Marie thoroughly enjoyed.

They sat at the bottom of Rivington Pike one Sunday, eating Victory V gums and staring at the surrounding countryside. 'I might never come back,' he said suddenly, as if the thought had only just occurred to him.

'Don't say that.'

He grinned hugely. 'Why not? Does it upset you?'

'Yes,' she said gravely. 'They never have Horlicks tablets at our chemist shop. I'd miss the Horlicks tablets if you didn't come back.'

He rolled over on to his stomach and pulled at some tall strands of grass. 'Are you my girl now?' His face was hidden from her as he spoke.

'I suppose so. I'm nobody else's, I can tell you that much.'

'Yes, but do you want to be my girl? I mean, do you go with me just because I'm here like Rivington Pike's here? Or do you go with me because you like my company?'

'Yes.'

He groaned aloud. 'Did anybody ever tell you what an annoying woman you are?'

'I'm not as annoying as you. I never bought coloured sweeties and passed them round the class knowing they were worm tablets. I never sent everybody to the lavatory for three days. You were the one always in trouble, not me.'

'Well, it saved us from getting bored, didn't it? I think I've still got the cane marks from the worming tablets do. She couldn't half whack, that there Sister Hunchback. I can't see her getting to heaven in a hurry, the road she treats children. Suffer little children to come unto me? It was suffer little children all right, I never sat down for a week.' He paused. 'Well, are you or are you not?'

'What?'

'My girl.'

'Depends.'

'Eh?'

'Depends what you're after.'

He sat up and pushed his face near to hers. 'I'm after nowt, Marie Langden. If you think I'm wanting to marry into money, you can shove that shop up your jumper.'

She struggled not to smile. 'Who said anything about getting wed?'

His face coloured. 'Well, I thought that were what usually happened. To people. To people that go out together. After a while, like. They get married to one another and all that stuff.'

'I'm too young.'

He sighed heavily and somewhat dramatically. 'Aye, and I might not get much older.'

'Stop it.'

'Why? Listen, the number of telegrams I take out every day just goes to show how many men aren't coming back. I might be one of them.'

'And you might not. We can't rush off and get wed just because you're going away. We're only seventeen. My mam wouldn't let me get married at this age, she'd never give permission.'

'I just want you to be my girl, somebody to come back to. Like we're engaged.'

'Do I get a ring?'

He shrugged. 'I might manage a curtain ring. But you know what I mean, Marie. I want something to live for, hope for. I feel as if I'm going out there and there's only me mam to care if I die. I want . . .' He struggled for the right words. 'I want . . . a future, to know I'll have kids of me own, a woman of mine to come home to, somebody waiting for me, writing to me.'

'You're frightened, aren't you?'

He turned his head away briefly. 'Between you and me, I'm scared to death. Scared of death, more like. But I want to go, I have to go. There's lads my age already out there. I could never look them in the eye if I found an excuse not to go.'

'I don't want you in the army, John.' Her voice was no more than a whisper. 'And I will miss you and I will be your girl.'

'Thanks.'

'It's not because I feel sorry for you, and it's not because you've asked. I want to be your girl anyway. As long as there's no funny business. That's what I meant before, when I said it depended what you were after. I didn't mean money. I meant . . .'

'I know.' He covered her hand with his. 'I'll never hurt thee, lass. I'd swim the bloody Atlantic for Marie Langden. When we were at school, all that daft stuff was just so I could show off to you. All the time I was doing them things, I was cringing inside, knowing I was just making meself look stupid in front of you. But I couldn't help it. I had to get you to notice me some road.'

'You did! You were about the most noticeable thing in the whole school. Specially when you pushed that little nun over in the corridor. Our Theresa thought that was terrible, seeing a nun's long bloomers.'

'Ah but,' he shook a finger at her, 'that was a real accident. I'd pinched some of Tommy Whelan's marbles, and I was on the run. I'd never have knocked a nun over on purpose.'

'That's what I said to our Theresa.'

'Did you?'

She nodded. 'I always stuck up for you, but not to your face. I thought you were very brave, answering the teachers back and always going for the cane. You said all the things I wanted to say and you did the things I daren't do.'

'So, you like me, then?'

'A bit.'

'That'll do for starters. Come on, we'd best be getting back.'

He hadn't even tried to kiss her, and Marie had very mixed feelings about that. She wanted him to try, but she didn't want any of that stuff she'd seen London doing with Mrs Tattersall. Yet she felt safe with John, was sure that he would never go too far. So why didn't he kiss her, then? They got on the bike, stopping several times to fix the chain during the long ride home.

Outside her house, he gave her a quick peck on the cheek, his face flushing brightly with embarrassment. 'Don't forget, you're my girl now.'

'I won't forget.' She placed one hand on each side of his pink face and stood on tip-toe to kiss him gently on the lips. 'You're a good lad, John Duffy. Even if you did give out worm tablets.' Then she fled to the safety of the house, the heat in her face telling her that she too was blushing.

Ellen was waiting in the kitchen with Tishy. 'Nice time, love?'

Marie nodded. 'Chain came off a few times.'

'You look a bit hot. Has he behaved himself?'

'Yes. And I think I'm sort of engaged.'

Ellen sighed and nodded her head sagely. 'Eeh, love. Don't you think you're a bit young for all that? Time enough to think about getting married when you're over twenty.'

'He's going away soon, Mam.'

'I know. But you shouldn't be tying yourself down.'

'He's good. He's what I want.' And Marie suddenly knew that John Duffy was what she wanted, kind, generous, down-to-earth, friendly and lovable. 'I shall marry him when the war finishes.'

A stab of fear hit Ellen's chest. If the war finished soon, she'd be alone here with him, just him and Tishy who had neither wit nor strength with which to defend herself if and when he did revert to type.

Marie seemed to read her thoughts. 'It's all right, Mam.

We'll stay near, me and John. I'll still do the shop, and happen he can help me instead of London.'

'As long as you know what you're doing, Marie. I thought I knew what I was doing. Mind, John is a nice lad, I've always thought so. And his mam's a lovely woman too. Mind, she could mither all four legs off a horse . . . Aye, I reckon you could do worse, lass. But give it time. Promise me you'll give yourself plenty of time. Don't be . . . getting yourself in any trouble and having to get wed. Understand?'

'Yes, there's no danger. What's for tea?'

'Fish pie. And don't tell your dad you're engaged.'

'Don't worry, I'll tell London nowt.'

'I wish you wouldn't call him that. He doesn't like it, it only riles him.'

'Good.'

Tishy looked up from her sewing. She was, as usual, wearing gloves. 'London's burning, London's burning,' she sang happily.

Marie laughed. 'Wouldn't it be easier to sew without your gloves on, Tishy?'

Tishy frowned. 'Bad hands wear no gloves. Hands in the dark, hands that push.'

Ellen shook her head. 'She's keeping them nice for her piano, aren't you, love? Some funny ideas about hands, she has. As if there's summat she's seen and forgotten.'

'Oh, I've not forgotten,' said Tishy sweetly. 'I just don't think about it. I only think about nice things like making bonnets and playing music. Marie, would John teach me how to ride on the back of that big bicycle?'

'I'm sure he will. Has Abigail been?'

Tishy smiled benignly on a world that was good to her. 'I enjoyed being a bridesmaid,' she said. 'Abigail's wedding was such fun.'

Marie ate her meal hungrily. 'Where is he?' she asked when she had finished.

'Front room. Says he's tired.'

Marie smiled to herself. He was fed up, that was what

he was. Everything had been taken from him, even his lover. He was a man in a corner, though. And, like a cornered rat, he might just go for the nearest throat. Yes, she would keep an eye on things while John was busy at the war. That would be her job, to keep an eye on things.

CHAPTER EIGHT

Theresa

Moor Bottom Farm was situated exactly as its name indicated, at the edge of a gentle sloping group of moors. It was a long, tall and extremely large house set right next to a lane that wound its stone-walled way through thick wedges of lush green pasture and arable land on the north side of Bolton.

Behind Moor Bottom Farmhouse, there was a vast square of cobbled yard which was bordered by the house itself on one side, then, forming the other three almost perfectly even sides of the rectangle, there were barns, store sheds, stables, pig styes, and a massive white-painted dairy shippon. In the centre of the yard stood an iron pump with a deep trough for animals' drinking water. Beside the gate leading to the first field, there was a huge muck midden that was used for collected animal waste. Strangely enough, this latter item gave off the smell that most comforted Theresa, a cleanish-dirtyish country scent with which she somehow managed to sympathize right from her first day at Moor Bottom. Though, as she told herself at frequent intervals, she had not yet spent a summer here. Perhaps the muck midden would come into its own in hot August weather, and the smell might well become completely unbearable.

Mrs Carrington was a well-built, solid and comfortably-off widow whose husband, a man of considerable military standing, had died in the saddle some years previously while riding to hounds. She was not, in Theresa's books at least, typical of the rich, because she pitched in with everybody else, and was regularly to be seen in old overalls and tall, mud-caked Wellington boots whose tops reached right up to cover sturdy knees. Her clothes, too, were disreputable, mostly dun-coloured jumpers worn with tweed skirts or blue coveralls, all of which were nearly threadbare with age. It seemed that Mrs C, for all her money and position, took little or no interest in personal adornments. She talked posh, though, and had a wonderful home full of paintings and sumptuous rugs and the sort of ornaments that Theresa hated to dust for fear of breaking them.

'Elbow grease, m' dear,' Mrs Carrington pronounced on Theresa's first nerve-wracked day. 'Scrub the damned shelves and to hell with the toby jugs, brutish ugly articles. Belonged to the Galloping Major, don't you know. Yes, my husband had a tendency to collect and hoard things. Till he collected a broken neck, and that was the end of him. Anyway, if you smash something, that's too bad, no sense in tears. This house is for living in, great barn of a place. No children of my own, couldn't have them for some reason or other, never did get to the bottom of it. So I'm using the war as an excuse to borrow everybody else's offspring. Are you by any chance good with children?'

Theresa rubbed her nose with the heel of her hand. 'I think so. They usually like me any road, always did when I worked in the shop, used to talk to me and that.'

Mrs Carrington patted steel-wool hair that looked as if it had been ironed into a shape from which it would never have dared to attempt escape. 'Fine, glad to hear it. But we've got a pair of terrors up from London, I call them the diabolical duo. Their manners are deplorable and, while their mother has been incapacitated, they have enjoyed no more than a passing acquaintance with soap and water. No-one can catch them, you see. In fact, we're wondering if they might represent Britain once the Olympics are resumed.'

Theresa strangled a rising giggle. 'I might be a bit lame,

but I reckon I can collar a pair of lads for you all right. We're used to tearaways where I come from.'

The older woman thrust her hands deep into her pockets. 'Good, good. Their mother married a Lancashire chap, second marriage. He went off to basic training or some such unavoidable foolishness, and she's been left with the two urchins and another on the way. They got bombed out a few weeks ago, so I took them in for a while. She's been up north just a short time, and her children obviously didn't take well to being uprooted from the East End. Lucky to find another husband, I'd say, with those two awful brats in tow. These little boys don't seem at all grateful to have a step-daddy and a brand new life. They're rather young, possibly pining for their real father, not exactly well-adjusted.'

Theresa raised her chin slightly. 'Do you mean they're naughty, Ma'am?'

A long, whistling breath was forced from between thin lips. 'Naughty would be an understatement, Theresa. Wicked might be slightly nearer the mark. Speaking of marks, watch your shins, these two are a pair of kickers. I'm black and blue underneath.' She pulled at the leg of her dungarees to display a thick, lisle stocking. 'Their mother's in bed most of the time, having a difficult pregnancy. We are all having a difficult pregnancy because of Ernest and Harold, so see what you can do with them.' She paused. 'If anything.' The grey head shook slowly as she walked away.

Ernest and Harold, when viewed from a safe distance, gave the impression of a brace of newly-descended cherubs, with their tight blond curls and pretty pink complexions. On closer and more courageous observation, Theresa discovered that they were indeed beautiful boys, each with huge blue eyes surrounded by thick lashes that rested on peach-down cheeks whenever they blinked. Ernest was four, Harold was three.

By the end of her first day, Theresa wondered whether Ernest would ever become five, and she was downright certain that Harold would not attain the age of four in a state of bodily integrity. She had rescued them from the trough, the bull, the geese and from the pig sty where a huge mother sow had threatened, rather loudly, to serve these offending humans as a meal for her squealing offspring.

Theresa, breathless after the final chase, sat the boys at the kitchen table. 'You have to be good,' she admonished mildly while scraping pig-dirt from her clogs. 'Otherwise, you will very likely get killed.'

Harold stared at her roundly, then spat across the table with an accuracy plainly born of long and arduous practice. The spittle flew past her left ear, and Theresa worried vaguely about its eventual destination.

'Killed,' said Ernest.

Theresa's eyes wandered round the kitchen while she pondered her next move. It was an enormous room with an oak-beamed ceiling and a big black range in which a cheerful fire crackled. The floor was sprinkled with fine sand ready for Theresa to do the evening sweeping, but she couldn't do the evening sweeping because of these two. 'I have to do the sweeping,' she said to herself.

Harold spat again.

'Sweeping,' said Ernest.

Mrs Jones, the bustling Welsh lady who was in charge of cooking and washing, came through from the scullery. 'Have they been at it again?' she asked in her pleasant, lilting tone. 'There's naughty boys, they are. Look you, Ernest, Theresa is new and she wants to help you. And the floor needs doing before I can set the meal for all Mrs Carrington's ladies.'

Harold spat.

'Look you,' sang Ernest.

Theresa fixed her gaze on the delinquent infants. They weren't going to get any better unless somebody did something about them. She set her mouth in what she hoped was a determined line, picked up her broom, and began to sweep, sending clouds of sand into the air. After a few simulated sneezes, Ernest dropped from his chair and performed a clog-dance in the sand. Harold, who forgot to spit, leapt down quickly and joined in the merriment. Without warning, Theresa swept the pair of them off their feet, then carried on cleaning as if nothing untoward had occurred.

They picked themselves up and resumed the cavorting until Theresa swept them aside once more with the long-handled broom. The flagged floor was very hard and, after four or five falls, the younger boy was beginning to look decidedly quivery about the lower lip. Mrs Jones watched, her buxom form rigid with fascination. 'How long will you keep this up, Theresa?'

Theresa glanced up from her task, not a trace of malice in her expression. 'Till they learn, Mrs Jones. Till they learn that they can't go through life making bother and getting all their own road.'

After countless tumbles, Ernest made a grab for the brush. Theresa, adequately prepared by now for this frontal attack, fixed him with a steely stare. 'Get your hand off that,' she whispered.

'No.' The reply arrived clear, strong, and without the slightest hint of fear or respect.

She turned to Harold. 'And if you spit again, you dirty little boy, I shall wash your mouth out with nasty red carbolic.' All this was very strange to Theresa, who had never felt so positive about anything before. Even twenty-four hours earlier, she could not have envisaged herself in such a situation. Was she going to win, though? It was somehow important to win.

Harold spat. His directional radar was less than accurate this time, and Theresa's new apron became the unhappy recipient of a large, wet blob. For want of a better and quicker solution, she allowed Ernest to keep the sweeping brush, gathered up the smaller boy and heaved the kicking, screaming bundle through to the cream-distempered brick scullery. At the shallow slopstone, she turned on the tap, then proceeded to poke soap-covered fingers between teeth that were keener than razors. He bit her. She slapped him sharply and carried on with the soap. The slapping continued until the biting stopped, whereupon she rinsed out the child's mouth before carrying him back to the kitchen and placing him next to his belligerent brother.

Ernest kicked her hard on the ankle, so she gathered him up, pulled down his shorts and held him face down on the table. With the flat of her hand, she delivered five hearty smacks to his bare bottom, then, after heaving up trousers and braces, she dumped him into a chair and resumed the sweeping as if nothing of particular moment had taken place.

Ernest and Harold bawled their eyes out in a very professional and well-rehearsed chorus while Theresa cleaned and Mrs Jones lingered in the scullery doorway stirring a pan of gravy.

Mrs Carrington rushed in. 'What on earth is going on?'

'Nothing,' answered Theresa in a mild tone that belied her grim resolve. 'I've just . . . showed them who's the boss. They've been very bad, both of them.'

'Given them a pasting, have you?' Mrs Carrington's straight eyebrows were raised in an expression of shock and surprise. 'Didn't know you had it in you, m' dear. Well done. If it works, I'll treat you to a glass of wine at the weekend.'

The others came in then, two with shawl-swathed bundles, and more girls at various stages of pregnancy who were sheltering at the farm while they awaited babies' arrivals. They were a nice lot on the whole, youngish Lancashire women with the flattened accents that Theresa understood thoroughly. They teased her gently, asked her when her baby was due, and giggled at her blushes.

Theresa dragged the now subdued Ernest and Harold to a small, low table in a corner next to the fire. The two boys looked so sad and downcast that she almost wanted to comfort them, but she held herself back, deliberately remembering the spitting and the kicking. 'Eat,' she commanded firmly. 'There'll be nothing else till morning. Chickens don't grow on trees, you know.'

Ernest blinked rapidly. 'I seen a chicken in a twee one time,' he said.

Harold's mouth hung open, displaying no visible collection of salivary ammunition.

'It didn't grow there,' said Theresa patiently. 'It grew in an egg.'

Ernest took up his fork and stabbed a slice of breast meat. 'Eggs is little,' he announced. 'Chickens is big.'

'They grow.' She picked up a spoonful of vegetables and pushed it into Harold's gaping mouth. 'Hang on to them peas,' she advised quietly. 'Remember the soap.' He swallowed the lot with a noisy, unchewed gulp.

'But not on twees,' said Ernest.

'That's right.'

'Was it stopped in the twee so it wouldn't gwow?'

She scratched her head. 'Eh?'

'I seen a chicken up a twee,' he persisted. 'Was it sitted still not gwowing?'

'No.'

He shrugged. 'So it gwown in a twee.'

Theresa tried not to smile. Ernest was obviously bright. He hadn't 'bested' her by kicking, so he was simply taking a cleverer tack.

'It wasn't stuck to the tree like a leaf,' she explained hopelessly. 'It was just visiting the tree.'

A girl at the large table laughed. 'Nay, don't take him on – he'll only trip you up, love. Pair of little buggers, they are, not worth bothering with.'

Theresa stared directly at the speaker of these words. 'They're people,' she said. 'Just little people like your babies will be. You don't know what's happened to them. Children turn when they're frightened. Sometimes they go quiet, sometimes they go naughty.'

Harold, sensing that he had gained an ally, pushed a sliver of chicken into Theresa's hand. She transferred it to her mouth, patted him absently on the head with a greasy hand, then picked up his mother's tray. 'Behave,' she breathed. 'Otherwise, nobody will like you – ever.'

When she arrived upstairs, Theresa found a person with another familiar accent, southern this time, almost definitely cockney. 'Evening,' said the woman in the bed. 'What's the grub tonight?'

'Chicken and veg.' She deposited the tray on a bedside table. 'Are you from the East End of London?'

The pretty, if somewhat bloated, face broadened into a cheeky smile. 'Yes. How did you guess?'

'My dad comes from there, only he lives in Bolton now. What's your name?'

'Alice. Alice Anderson. Well, it was, but I keep forgetting – it's Crawford now. I married a lad from Bolton, see. I used to be married to a Londoner till I gave him the elbow. So I got the divorce and I married Tom. He's stationed down south, but his mother lives in Bolton, so he sent us packing up here to be safe.' The grin widened even further. 'Safe? We got bombed out after a month, and Tom's mum's still in hospital, poor old duck. She got a fractured hip and a smashed foot. And I was sent to this farm with the two horrors. Like their dad, they are, bleeding terrible. They could start a war in an empty room, my two.' She seemed inordinately proud of this concept. 'Spirited, that's what they are. I called them after my two grandads – they were tartars too.'

Theresa opened the curtains. 'Are you in bed all the while?'

'Most of the time. Something about blood pressure. That doctor's got a bee in his trilby about blood pressure, daft old fart.'

The younger girl, unused to such vulgarity, blushed hotly. She crossed the room quickly and placed the tray of food in Alice's rounded lap. 'Er . . . I have to tell you something.'

'What's that?'

Theresa groped for words. 'Ernest and Harold. They were awful today. I had to . . . deal with them.'

'Oh?'

Theresa swallowed painfully. 'I had to smack them. Both of them.'

Alice put her head on one side and thought for a moment. 'Well, I suppose you're forced to look after them while I'm out of order, so you must decide what's best. I never hit them, you see.'

'Happen that's what's wrong with them, then,' gabbled Theresa nervously. 'Now meself – I got clouted as a child, bashed too hard and too often, I was. Not by me mam – it's me dad who has the temper. So I don't agree with battering children, it only makes them frightened. But sometimes, you have to slap a kiddy. Not hard, and never in temper, just to show them they've gone far enough, like. And they had gone far enough. Twice round the world, they went, made everybody's life a misery. I reckon they'll never be good lads till somebody shows them how to carry on proper.'

Alice shrugged and spoke through a mouthful of potato. 'All right. As long as you don't knock them senseless.'

'I wouldn't do that.'

'I know. I can tell from your face. What's your name?'

'Theresa.'

Alice pondered. 'I don't like that, it's too fancy for you. I'll call you Terry. Come up and see me some time, Terry. God, I sound like a film star, don't I? Wish I looked like one, though. Have you ever seen a belly the size of this?' She stuffed a slice of chicken into her mouth, chewed thoughtfully for a second or two, then said, 'I think I'm going to give birth to five or six. It won't be a birth, this one, it'll be more like a launch.'

Theresa laughed. She wasn't going to feel lonely after all, wasn't going to get time or chance to really miss Mam. 'I'd better go and see to Ernest and Harold. I've got to give them a bath.'

'Then Gawd help you, make sure you wear a raincoat and some wellies and take a brolly in with you. They're both good shots with a wet flannel.' Alice chuckled loudly. 'Good luck, you'll need it.'

In the vast white-and-blue-tiled bathroom, two shiny-clean naked little boys splashed about in that special haphazard joy that usually arises when any young animal meets water. Theresa, wet to her own skin, showed them 'this little piggy' and 'one, two, three, four, five'. When it got to 'which little finger did it bite?', she grabbed at their slippery hands and pretended to snap. They were delighted. 'Good boys have fun,' she said seriously. 'And they don't get smacked, and they never, ever spit.'

Ernest frowned. 'Can Hawold spit when he bwushes his teef?'

'Of course. It's nice to spit when you clean your teeth, but it's not nice to spit in the kitchen.'

The older boy allowed his tongue to stray along the bar of green soap, then pulled a comical face. What his brother had endured in the scullery must have been unpleasant. 'Can he spit at the pigs?'

'No.'

'The cows?'

'Never.'

'Chickens and geeses?'

Theresa shook her head in great solemnity.

'Wight. Hawold not spit, then.' He touched his small brother's shoulder. 'Hawold,' he said severely. 'No spitting.'

And at that moment, Theresa realized that she didn't want to go into the convent any more. No, this was what she wanted, little children, preferably little children of her own. She wanted a houseful of them, six or seven at least.

Theresa was going to be a mother, the best mother in the whole world.

At Moor Bottom Farm, Theresa gained a first real sense of freedom, an awareness of space that she had never encountered before. Whenever she managed a few hours off, she would walk for miles across farmland and open

211

moor, seeing rabbits and hares, cows, sheep, hedgehogs, and, occasionally, a rare lone fox.

There were birds she did not recognize, and wild plants whose names were foreign to her, though Mrs Carrington did give her a book about flora and fauna, and from this Theresa learned to identify a few species. Her affection for the countryside was immediate and passionate. Although she missed her old neighbours, she had no desire to return permanently to the mean streets of her childhood. That she was now an adult could not be doubted. She was calmer, relatively fearless, while her body had filled out with good farm food and fresh air. Even her limp had improved and, if she chose her shoes and clogs carefully, she could walk for over half an hour without resting.

The work was not difficult. There were three girls on the staff at Moor Bottom, and the other two did most of the work simply because Theresa seemed to be the only person who could control Ernest and Harold. She therefore spent most of her waking hours in the company of these terrible children. They became less terrible with each passing day, responding gladly, gratefully and with a degree of devotion to the open warmth of their temporary nanny.

Theresa loved those boys, just as she loved all infants, and they would accompany her on shorter walks, sitting silently beside streams while fish darted and splashed, waiting in the evening light at the edge of a wood until a blur of black and white announced a badger's presence among lush greenery. Like Theresa, they flourished on the moors, their skin darkening healthily, bright blue eyes seeming to reflect the clarity of the skies.

They asked questions, and Theresa found the answers for them in Mrs Carrington's library, translating stilted adult prose into language that was comprehensible to babies of nursery age. Together, the three of them painted, sailed paper boats, sang songs, played games. If one of the boys became afraid in the night, he would run to Theresa's bed to seek her gentle reassurance. Their mother was out of bounds, out of reach, so Theresa became surrogate parent, teacher, friend and nurse. It was a role that suited her, and her serenity showed.

'You're good with them,' said Alice one night when Theresa brought in her cocoa. 'They asleep?'

Theresa nodded. 'I told them stories till their eyes closed.'

The mother smiled. 'Beautiful when they're asleep, ain't they? Pair of pink and white angels, they are, till they wake up. Mind, it's not been easy for none of us, the way their dad was.'

Theresa perched on the end of the bed. She and Alice had become firm friends during the past few weeks, and there were not many secrets between them. 'Tell me,' she said simply. 'I know you didn't like him, but you've never said why.'

A puffy hand plucked at the top quilt, the ring finger still marked where a wedding band had cut in until Theresa had removed the circle of gold with warm, soapy water. 'It was women. There was loads of them, because he was what you might call a good looker. I had a rotten time with the kids, both births were difficult with me being so small.' She patted the huge mound of her belly. 'Only thirty-four round the hips without this lot, you know. Well, I came home one night after visiting an old school friend. The babies were both with me, one in a pram, the other just about staggering. And there he was with her from next door. Big blowsy piece with dyed hair and tits like barrage balloons.' She nodded, her eyes glinting with a mixture of anger and amusement. 'Stark naked, they were, on the rug in front of the fire.'

Theresa let out a slow breath. 'Ooh heck. What did you do?'

Alice gazed past Theresa. 'Nothing. At four foot eleven and with two babies, what could I do? But I am very good at doing nothing. He got no meals, no washing, no ironing and no other comforts for three months.'

'And then?'

Alice raised a careless shoulder. 'He moved in next door with henna-head and her bolster chest. A senior fireman, he was, so he got let off the war when it started. One day, he just moved on, packed his bags and left the area.'

'Oh. And what about her with the bosoms?'

'He left her too. Went down Spitalfields, took up with a butcher's daughter, probably got more than his weekly rations there. I divorced him. Last I heard, he'd been killed under a pile of masonry down the West End, some hotel or other.' She bit into a green apple, grimacing against its clean, sharp taste. 'In the papers, they said he was a hero. I don't think he was much of a hero.'

Theresa leaned forward. 'Hey,' she whispered. 'I bet her with the chest wouldn't give him any medals either.'

Alice guffawed, almost choking on her Granny Smith. 'You are a caution,' she declared when she had regained her composure. 'Making me laugh when I'm nine months gone. Anyway, you listen to me, my girl. When you get yourself a man to marry, make sure he's not a stunner. I had a stunner, and he left me and the boys without a single backward glance. My Tom, now, he'd never go off except in times of war and pestilence, as they call it.'

She waved a hand at the small framed photograph of a very ordinary, dark-haired young man. 'And if this baby don't hurry up, it'll miss its dad's embarkation leave. He'll be home tomorrow, and we've nothing to show him. A carpenter, is Tom. Got called up late because he was on gas-proofing, then they put him on the sites once the bombs started, told him to shore things up or knock them down, whatever seemed best. They've put the older men on that work now. All the ones who can stand up straight are being sent abroad, and my Tom's one of them.'

'I'm sorry. It must be awful for you.'

'I manage.' She groaned and patted her belly once more. 'I'm overdue, you know. Must be nearly a fortnight late. Shall I start running about and taking hot baths?'

'In four inches of water? Even the public baths only get

214

a bucketful now, except for scabies cases. No, you just sit there and pray. Shall I go and fetch you a bit of toast and some more cocoa?'

The tiny woman pulled a wry face. 'No, ta. I'm swollen to bursting as it is, and I feel a bit iffy at the moment. She don't half feed us up, this Mrs Carrington. I've never eaten so well in years. And the boys are blooming, aren't they? Looking really well. You're doing a good job, I couldn't bring them up better myself.'

Theresa straightened Alice's crumpled bed cover and plumped up the four pillows in an effort to create some comfort. She was enormous round the middle now, was poor Alice. And the little face was even more stretched and bloated, as if it might be full of fluids or something. 'Mrs Carrington's a very kind woman, isn't she? I didn't know rich people could be kind, I always thought they'd be like misers.'

'Everybody's different, Terry, just depends on how they're made. Get off to your bed, now. I'll see you in the morning.'

Theresa walked to the door, turned, then smiled at her new friend. 'Behave yourself,' she said, shaking a finger. 'No midnight walks, and no dashing off to the dance at the Palais.'

A rueful smile covered the small, puffed-up face. 'You're a good mate, Terry. I feel as if I've known you all my life.' She paused, her face suddenly serious. 'I'll not forget you, dearie. Get that string of beads out and say a few for me.'

'I will.'

'See you in the morning, then.'

'Yes. I'll bring your toast and tea, then we'll get you ready for Tom.'

'That's right. You get me ready for Tom.'

Theresa slept like the proverbial log. When morning began to filter through the curtains, she stretched luxuriantly in her comfortable bed, resolving to enjoy a few moments of solitude before going along the corridor to lift the two boys from their cots.

It was nice here – wonderful, in fact. She lay with her eyes closed against the bright fingers of a May morning that threatened to pierce the heavy drapes of lined pink brocade. Outside, the wild birds celebrated another new day, while Geronimo, the farm cockerel, began his morning strut by crowing loudly so that all his wives would know who was the boss.

This was the life, all right. New-laid eggs, fresh milk, home-grown vegetables, mile upon mile of open green and filled by nothing but crops and pasture. It was becoming difficult to remember the shop with its clanging bell and querulous customers, though she did feel the odd pang of guilt whenever she thought about Mam and Marie. They should be here to enjoy the air, the sunshine, the blessed God-given freedom.

She opened an uneasy eye. There was something wrong this morning, something different. Opposite the end of her bed stood a Victorian washstand with a white marble top. In front of this, there was a wooden chair, a plainish item of the kitchen variety.

The chair was occupied. A pair of broad shoulders in an ugly khaki brown jumper, a cropped, steely-grey head of hair . . . Theresa's heart pounded as she achieved consciousness. No, it was not a man, it was Mrs Carrington. What was she doing here, and why was she sitting so still? One of the shoulders sat lower than the other; it was obvious that the lady of the house was leaning forward, elbow on the washstand, a hand to her forehead.

Theresa raised herself into a sitting position and focused on Mrs Carrington's reflection in the small, square, mahogany-framed mirror. Mrs Carrington was crying. Although she sat rigidly still, no sobbing, no movement in her face or body, great tears were pouring down the drawn cheeks, tears that were probably obscuring Theresa's answering image in the glass. What was happening? If Mrs C had to cry, then why did she need to come in here to do it? And it didn't seem right, this weeping. The high-born and educated lady was not one for tears. Life had already dealt its severest blows to the middle-aged woman, leaving her too tough for open grief, too strong for hysteria.

Theresa crept from the bed and stood by the forlorn figure of her employer. 'Ma'am?' she whispered.

A cuff of the coarse jumper was quickly pulled across a pair of streaming eyes. 'Ah, Theresa.'

'What's . . . what's the matter?'

The substantial lady heaved herself up from the chair, took Theresa's hand, then led her to the bed, pulling her down so that the two of them were seated side by side. 'How old are you? Is it seventeen?'

Theresa nodded mutely.

'There's a letter for you.'

'Oh.' She fought the dull thud of fear in her chest. If anything had happened to Mam, somebody would have got on the telephone. 'Who's it from?'

Mrs C's voice was unsteady. 'It's from . . . from Alice Crawford.' The woman doubled over as if in great pain, fixing her eyes on her flat brown brogues. 'You are so young for this, child.'

Theresa frowned. 'But why would Alice write to me? Why?'

'The letter was written days or weeks ago – there's no date. We found it in the night, after . . . after . . .'

Theresa jumped up, but Mrs C, too quick for her, pulled the girl into her arms, rocking her gently to and fro. A terrible dread filled Theresa's heart, while the smell of sweat and horses, which rose in comforting abundance from the rough jumper, invaded her nose. 'Is she dead? Is Alice dead?' She felt Mrs Carrington's head as it moved against her to form a silent 'yes'. 'When?' asked Theresa. 'How?'

'My fault.' Though the tone was quiet, her distress was plain. 'Should've got her to hospital, should've fetched the doctor earlier. I suppose . . .' she sniffed loudly, 'I mean I think Alice knew. She must have been aware, because

217

there were three letters. One for her husband, one for me, one for you.' There was a crackle of paper. 'Haven't opened yours. Thought about it, don't you know, with you being so young. But – well – dying wishes and all that. I have never felt so completely bloody useless.'

A horrible high-pitched sound filled the room, and several moments passed before Theresa realized that this noise was being made by herself, that she was screaming like an injured cat. Wildly, she beat her fists against Mrs Carrington until she achieved freedom, then she pulled herself up and fled to the window, dragging aside the curtains as soon as she arrived. 'But everything's the same,' she wept. 'Cows are getting milked, eggs are being collected. It's as if she was never here!'

'Everything always remains the same. People come, people go, and scarcely a ripple in the tide of life.' These sad words arrived from the bed. 'We make few marks, Theresa. But poor Alice left three. For their sakes, we must endeavour to carry on as normal.'

Theresa's sobs were stifled as she asked, 'Three?'

'The baby is alive and well.'

'Oh.' She walked back to the bed, her limp more pronounced due to a sudden, almost overpowering weakness. 'I'm sorry I hit you just then. I didn't mean it – it's not like me.'

'Quite all right. Shock, you see. I understand only too well, dear.' She shuddered as she remembered a grey morning, leaden skies dripping down to the fields, her husband's body arriving home on a flat farm cart, the scream of a crippled horse echoing across acres until a single report had ended the creature's torment. She pulled herself together, tightening the leather belt at her waist, hoping that this physical movement would restrict the wanderings of her mind. 'The letter. Would you like to read it now?'

'I don't know. I mean no – you read it to me if you don't mind.'

'Are you sure? It may contain a personal message.'

'I've nothing to hide, Mrs Carrington.'

The grey head drooped. 'No. I'll do it now, shall I?'

Theresa nodded swiftly. 'I'd sooner not be on me own. I want you with me.' She stumbled across the room, sat down at the washstand, then stared at her own pale face in the mirror. 'I'm ready,' she said.

The envelope tore. Mrs C cleared her raw throat and began to speak. '"Dear Terry. If you are reading this, then that means I'm not around any more and I'll miss our chats and giggles. Will you? Anyway, I had feelings about this right from the word go, because the doc in Stepney said I shouldn't have more babies after Harold.

'"Tom wanted children, and I hoped I'd be all right. This one's a girl, I can tell. She's a quiet little thing, doesn't jump about much. Call her Alison after me. Tom's a good man, one of the best, but with this war we just don't know what will happen. Please look after my children, Terry, till everything gets sorted out. There's nobody at home, my parents are dead, and I never had brothers or sisters. As I told you, my first husband died, and his family was never any good to anybody.

'"Tom will get married again, he's that sort. He'll find a nice girl and settle down once he gets back safe from the fighting. Take care of Ernest and Harold and Alison till Tom meets somebody decent to take my place. If I'm wrong, and if Alison turns out to be a boy, call him Tom after his dad.

'"I know I'm leaving you in a pickle, girl, but I don't know where else to turn. There's something wrong with me and I know it's bad, which is why I'm writing all these letters. I've just got to lie still till she's born, give her a chance. If she doesn't make it, bury her with me, put her in my arms. Don't cry for me, Terry. I'm not scared, just worried about my kids and Tom. Do what you can for him, he's a real sweetheart. Keep your chin up. Love from Alice."'

Both women sat in a long, heavy silence after the letter had been re-folded.

'Well?' said Theresa at last. 'Was she right?'

'I beg your pardon?'

'The baby. Is it a girl?'

'Yes.' Mrs Carrington placed the letter on Theresa's pillow. 'She was so brave, so . . . cheerful.'

'I know. She had me in pleats every day.' Tight knuckles pressed themselves against her lips as she remembered her last conversation with Alice.

'A real mother,' sighed Mrs Carrington. 'Now, the midwife says she can place the baby quite easily, get her into a temporary foster home.'

'No.' There was little emotion now in Theresa's voice. 'I'll keep her. It says in the letter that I've got to mind all of them. And now, I have to do Alice's face.' She swivelled as far as the straight-backed chair would allow. 'Last night, I promised to get her ready for Tom, and I will. He's arriving today, and she wanted to look nice for him.'

The stout lady leapt to her feet with an agility that belied her size. 'No, let me do it.'

Theresa smiled sadly. Mrs Carrington looked as if she didn't know the first thing about powder and rouge. Not that Theresa was well-acquainted with such items, but she was bound to have some clearer idea. 'It has to be me,' she said firmly. 'Because I promised.'

They made their way along the landing to Alice's room. Mrs Carrington sat, straighter than any ramrod, in a chair by the bed, her anxious eyes never once leaving Theresa's stricken face as the sheet was drawn back to reveal the still, pale form. The swellings had reduced, leaving Alice serene and almost beautiful in death, her tiny, gamin features neat and clear. It was as if all the worry and terror had drained away too, as if the woman in the bed knew that her mission had been accomplished, that Alison was safely delivered.

The flesh was cool but not stiff, reminding Theresa of a doll she'd once owned, one with a soft, unbreakable head. She smoothed powder and rouge on to the ashen cheeks, coloured the lips in a soft shade of coral, then brushed the light brown hair into pretty waves. 'Ready for Tom, love,' she whispered. 'You're lovely now. I've read your letter and I'll do my best.'

Theresa turned from the bed and, for the first time in her young life, fell in a deep faint on the rug. When she came to, she was stretched out on a chaise in Mrs Carrington's bedroom, and Mrs C was waving a bottle of something foul-smelling under her nose.

'Are you all right?' The anxious voice arrived from above. 'I shouldn't have allowed you to go in there.'

Theresa turned her face away from the smelling salts. 'Where is she?'

'Where we left her, dear, waiting for her husband to arrive. The undertaker should be along shortly. I shall pay for the burial, of course.'

Theresa coughed against the strong odour. 'Not Alice. I don't mean Alice. Where's Alison?'

'Ah.' At last, Mrs Carrington straightened, taking with her the smell that was almost unbearable. 'She's with the other mothers. Someone's giving her a bottle.'

'Please bring her to me. I have to be the one, I have to look after her. Alice said so.'

'But you're not well enough.'

Theresa fixed her employer with a stare that fell just short of steely. 'I'm in better shape than Alice is. She gave up her life for that baby. The least I can do is to take over now. Bring Alison, please. And I'd better see Ernest and Harold too, introduce them to their new sister. They'll have to be told, of course, but perhaps Tom will do that. Does he know? Has he had the news?'

The older woman shook her head. 'No, he was already en route when I phoned the barracks.' She suddenly looked truly aged, back bent as if weighted down by a great burden. 'He will arrive full of great expectations, and I shall have to dash his hopes before he crosses my threshold. What a mess. What a bloody awful mess.'

Theresa sat up. 'There's none of this your fault, Mrs Carrington. God willed it.'

'Did He?' The large head bobbed about on its short, squat neck. 'Willed a war, willed that a young mother should die and leave three children? Oh, don't misinterpret me, Theresa, I'm a churchgoer and a strong believer. But why? Why poor little Alice Crawford?'

'This is when our faith gets tested.'

'It is indeed.' Mrs Carrington inhaled deeply, then went out to fetch the baby.

Alison was perfect, a tiny, placid, blonde child with pink cheeks, balled fists, and those deep purple eyes which are lent but briefly to the very new while true colour is decided. Theresa could never have explained, nor even described the feeling she experienced at her first physical contact with the infant girl. To say that she was overwhelmed would have been an exaggeration, because she remained calm and steady when the child was handed over. But her breast was invaded by a warmth she had never met before; she simply knew that she would never find it easy to relinquish the hold. It was almost as if the child were really hers, as if she had laboured and sweated to bring this life into the world.

A boat-shaped bottle with a rubber stopper on one end and a teat on the other was handed to her. She hesitated fractionally before offering the milk, then tilted the container like a real expert, pushing the fluid to the end so that the child would swallow no air.

In pensive silence, Audrey Carrington studied the scene before her. This girl was a natural mother, that was plain enough to anyone with normal vision. And the little one was already struggling to focus on Theresa's face, violet eyes blinking rhythmically while milk was gorged, while scents were inhaled to be filed away in the tiny brain for future reference.

The country woman had seen such sights before, a mother animal adopting a baby as its own, the orphan clinging and demanding . . . This would have to be dealt with quickly, before a real bond could be formed. It would be necessary to consult the father without delay. Perhaps he would have plans for the family, perhaps he could remove Alison before Theresa's maternalism surfaced completely.

Yet even as she entertained these thoughts, Audrey Carrington sensed that it was already too late. Theresa was in love; the tie between infant and substitute mother was being woven right now, in this instant. Indeed, the picture presented by the two of them was reminiscent of an updated Madonna and Child, so perfect did they look together. 'Don't get too fond,' was all the older woman managed before leaving the room.

Ernest and Harold were quite interested for a while, until they realized that Alison had brought nothing with her from heaven – no train sets, no building blocks or toy soldiers. The pregnant girl who had brought the two boys in to visit their new sister dragged them off for breakfast as soon as their interest waned visibly. There had been no awkward questions, not yet.

Theresa, fully recovered now from her fainting spell, crooned and sang until the satisfied baby slept. Holding a newborn was truly wonderful; she did not want to leave the child in its lonely crib. And this was a piece of Alice, the very last piece of a treasured friend. The warm bundle slept while Theresa cried her final tears for the little dead mother. She must stop weeping. Alice had ordered her not to weep.

A loud crash from the landing caused Theresa to jump, though the child showed no sign of stirring. Several thuds were followed by what sounded like the cry of a mortally wounded animal, then hurried footsteps pounded unevenly along the carpet. Theresa placed the baby on the chaise, packing the edge with cushions for security. On tiptoe, she moved to the door, opened it and peeped outside.

A man howled. His head was thrown so far back that he almost faced the ceiling, while the noise he made now was like nothing on earth. In front of the man stood Mrs Carrington, arms and legs set wide and square as if to block his path. Theresa caught a few of the woman's words. 'Mr Crawford . . . calm down . . . very sorry . . .'

So this was Alice's Tom. The sound of his terrible grieving seemed to cut like a knife through Theresa's chest. A black beret with a shiny gilt badge lay on the floor, so she retrieved this item and moved towards the pair outside Alice's room. She touched Mrs Carrington's shoulder, and the lady jumped, thereby demonstrating her own state of nerves. Mrs Carrington was not a jumper. 'Has he seen her?' whispered Theresa.

'Yes.' Mrs C wasn't going to tell this young girl the truth, not all of it. She was too innocent to hear of a man picking up a corpse, talking to it, kissing it, trying to stand it up so that it would walk. 'Give me the hat, dear.'

Theresa reached across and touched the soldier's arm. 'Tom?'

He stopped screaming and looked at her. Though he wasn't really looking at anything, Theresa thought. He was looking through her, past and beyond her. 'The sea is rising and the world is sand,' he said distinctly.

Theresa chewed her lip. 'Eh?' she asked softly.

'Wilfred Owen,' said Audrey Carrington. 'War poet, died about 1918.' She faced the man squarely. 'Mr Crawford.' Her tone was not severe. 'In the same verse, Owen bids us "go forever children hand in hand". You have a child. In fact, there are three of them, because I understand that you have legally adopted the other two. They are all here . . .'

'"Better our lips should bruise our eyes",' he quoted.

Theresa's eyes were fixed to him as if by a magnet. 'More Wilfred Owen?' she asked.

'Yes.' The lady of the house glanced down at her watch. 'Stay, Theresa,' she commanded. 'You seem to calm him. The police will be here directly, and the doctor too.'

'He doesn't look right, does he?'

'Indeed not. Probably shock, you see. No doubt he'll come out of it in a day or two.'

'Did you have to fetch the police, though?'

'Yes. He was impossible in there.' She jerked a thumb

in the direction of Alice's door. 'The girls were holding him back, and I can't expose pregnant women and nursing mothers to this kind of danger. However short the duration of this phase, Mr Crawford is currently a hazard.' She pushed an unusually wayward strand of hair from her forehead.

The man continued to mutter, this time about dead bodies being used to mend a wall.

'Shakespeare.' Mrs Carrington's voice was weary. 'One of the Henrys, I believe. I hope those two boys stay in the kitchen. Yes, that's definitely Shakespeare. He must be a reader, though I understand he's a carpenter by trade. Still, no reason why a working man shouldn't enjoy the literary fruits of his own culture. He knows his stuff, all right.'

'I wouldn't say he was enjoying anything, poor man. Why is he like this? What's he doing messing about with bits of poetry while Alice is dead behind that door? And he's not seen Alison. Shall I fetch her, see if that'll bring him round?'

'No!' This word was spat sharply. 'I'm sorry, dear, I don't mean to shout. But I wouldn't trust him at the moment. He smashed quite a lot of ornaments before embarking on this strange soliloquy. Best left, I believe. We'll just stand here until the police arrive, try to protect the rest of the household.'

So they waited for at least fifteen minutes while Tom Crawford recited lines of verse and speeches from plays. 'He's getting very confused,' murmured Mrs Carrington at one point. 'That's quite a pot pourri – *Lear*, *Macbeth* and Wordsworth's "Westminster Bridge", unless I'm sadly mistaken.' She lifted her voice. 'Mr Crawford?'

He gazed at her blankly. 'Alice?'

Theresa felt faint again, knees trembling, an icy hand making its invisible way along the length of her spine. Alice was dead and her husband wouldn't allow himself to know about it. Alice was dead and her new baby lay all alone on a chaise longue with no-one to hear her if she cried. Breathing deeply through her mouth, Theresa propped herself against a wall just as the police arrived, three burly, middle-aged men with blue uniforms and black truncheons held out at waist height.

He made no protest as they led him away, but his head swung around when he reached the top of the stairway. 'Alice?' he yelled, despairingly. Theresa swallowed a sob. She would not cry, because Alice wanted her not to cry. He shouted 'Alice' all the way to the front door, then he was gone, leaving in his wake a terrible and hopeless silence.

Mrs Carrington drew a drab sleeve across the end of her nose.

'Don't cry,' said Theresa.

The lady sniffed. 'Shit,' she said softly.

Theresa was past blushing. 'He'll be back for the funeral,' she said.

But Audrey Carrington simply repeated 'shit' several times before striding away with all the purpose she could muster.

Tom didn't arrive for the funeral. After a brief service in a Church of England chapel, Alice Crawford was buried and sadly mourned by all the residents of Moor Bottom Farm. But there was no sign of her husband, even at the end of a week. His mother sent a wreath and some matinée jackets, but she was unable to leave her hospital bed. According to Mrs Carrington, Tom's mother had suffered some appalling fractures in the bombing, and she would be fortunate to walk again without assistance.

Ernest and Harold were heartbroken. Because they were heartbroken, they took out their childish frustrations on anyone and anything that crossed their path, and Theresa found that her hands were completely filled by Alice's children.

Ellen came to visit once the funeral was safely in the past. She sat with Theresa and Mrs Carrington in the larger of the two drawing rooms, and Theresa thought

226

how hilarious the situation would have been if Alice hadn't died. Yes, she and Alice would have enjoyed a hearty laugh about this. Not a cruel laugh, but a good old giggle all the same. Mam had arrived all decked out for the big house, the bottle green swagger newly sponged and pressed, hair in a careful, even roll, a neat little black hat with a spotted veil, black gloves, polished shoes, a marcasite brooch pinned to her collar.

The lady of the manor, meanwhile, looked like a bag of dirty washing. She sported Wellington boots, her dead husband's moleskin trousers, a collarless shirt and a broad leather belt with a small axe threaded through it. 'Doing a bit of wood-chopping,' she said, removing the weapon and tossing it carelessly on to a Persian rug. 'Trying to knock some sense into the orchard, though it's the wrong time of year. I need the fruit for my wines, Mrs Langden. Supposing I can get hold of the sugar, that is. Well . . .' She raised an eyebrow at Theresa. 'Would you kindly pour the tea, my dear? My nails are too dirty for the handling of consumables.'

Ellen emptied her cup quickly, grateful when the smelly stuff was finally swallowed. What anybody wanted with these posh perfumed teas she couldn't work out at all. More to the point, what anybody was doing with posh perfumed teas in the middle of worldwide conflict . . . She crossed her ankles and leaned back in the chair. Rationing didn't touch some folk, she reckoned. And Theresa was in bother, and here sat Ellen Langden thinking like a grocer again!

'The tea is old, from a precious cache I saved years ago. It's lost a little of its flavour.'

Ellen forced a smile. Could this woman read minds? 'I've come up about our Theresa and this here pickle,' she said. 'Only I wondered if you'd managed to contact the father. Our Theresa says she can't visit us at home now, because the lads fret without her. Aye, and the baby too. So I thought I'd best call round and find out what's what.'

Mrs Carrington placed her saucerless cup on a table

while Ellen winced as she thought of the cost of french polishing. 'He's in hospital.' Mrs C patted her carefully corrugated hair. 'The military police took him back to barracks, but there was no improvement. The poor man is locked away.'

Theresa coughed. 'No, he isn't,' she said carefully. 'They call him a voluntary patient.'

Audrey Carrington grimaced knowingly. 'They haven't committed him, not yet. But there's nothing voluntary about it, Theresa. In the first place, the man is a soldier, and soldiers have no free will, not in wartime. Secondly, Tom Crawford is not fit to volunteer for anything.' She turned to Ellen. 'A complete mental breakdown, I'm afraid. And there's so much of it about, people pretending to be unstable just to avoid combat. So they're testing him to make sure he's genuine.'

'And is he?' Ellen removed her hat. It was stupid, sitting here in a hat while the landed gentry wore wellies and a filthy shirt.

'He's not putting it on,' said Theresa.

'Well? What about these children?' Ellen fought to keep her voice steady. 'Who's going to be looking after them if he's not up to coping?'

'I am.' The girl folded her arms, her face setting as solid as a closed door. 'And I'll have to go in a minute. Ernest and Harold like to see me at tea time, and Alison is used to me giving her a bottle. She takes it better from me.'

Mrs Carrington, sensing an imminent storm in the atmosphere, snatched up her axe and leapt forward. Partway across the room, she hesitated as if to say something, then, having clearly chosen non-involvement, she lengthened her stride. 'I'll see you later,' she called before going out.

'She won't put them in a home or an orphanage,' said Theresa. 'Them kiddies are stopping here, and I'm staying with them. We've talked about it, me and the missus. Whether I go or stay, she'll not put Alice's children out. And I'm not coming home, Mam. You can sit as long as

228

you want with that look on your face, but I made a promise.'

'To a dead woman? I'm sorry, love, I didn't mean to—'

'She's still my friend. Just because she's dead, not breathing and talking – that doesn't stop her being my friend, doesn't stop her being Alice.' She stared past her mother and through the window. 'That morning, her soul was still in the room, Mam. She heard me, I know she did. And I promised before God, 'cos He was there and all. No.' Her head shook fiercely. 'Them babies need me.'

Ellen fixed her gaze on an untouched cucumber sandwich. 'You're seventeen, lass. You can't go lumbering yourself with somebody else's problems.'

'You did.'

'Eh?'

'You took Abigail and Tishy in when Lilian asked you. Why are you preaching at me for doing something you've already done yourself?'

'I wasn't seventeen! And Tishy and Abigail were grown up!'

'Tishy will never grow up.'

Ellen could think of no answer to this statement.

'You couldn't have refused Lilian, Mam, it's not in your nature. Listen to me. My friend was a lovely, beautiful person. She stopped in bed weeks to give Alison a chance. Happen if she'd run about a bit, she might have lost the baby and saved herself. She bled to death. Here, upstairs in this house, she bled to death. Alison's . . . well . . . she's like my own. And the lads love me, they really do.'

'But it's all wrong!' cried Ellen. 'What if their father never gets better in his head? Who'll marry you with three young ones fastened to your skirts? You can't go round picking up children as if they're dolls or summat. It's for ever, Theresa. Children are a forever thing.'

'I know. And happen I don't want to be married.'

'But you can't mind children without being wed.'

Theresa shook the blonde waves back from her face and looked at her mother with large, sad eyes that had darkened with emotion until they were almost navy. 'Mother,' she said. 'I can do exactly what I want.'

She had never called her Mother before. Ellen watched the poised and graceful young woman and knew that she, Ellen, had lost. She had lost because this was definitely a woman, nobody's daughter, nobody's sister. Theresa was suddenly a person in her own right, an adult who was fully capable of making her own decisions, good and bad. There were shallow lines of worry on the face, yet these seemed to make Theresa more beautiful than ever, as if the picture had finally been coloured in. Ellen rose to her feet and reached out a hand to touch Theresa on the shoulder. 'I shall pray for you, love. And you know what?'

'What?'

'You're not feared any more. Of him, I mean.'

'Eh?'

'Your father.'

'Oh, him.' No, she wasn't frightened of him, but that was because he wasn't here. All the fears and confusions were currently centred round Tom Crawford, a man she scarcely knew. Because if Tom got better – and she prayed that he would – then she would lose her little family. The thought of that was unbearable, so she pushed it to where it usually lurked, at the back of her mind. 'I'll show you out, Mam.'

That night, in her sleep, Tom came and took the children away. Their distant voices called her name and, on legs that were leaden, she pursued Tom along dark, narrow corridors, but she did not catch him. When she woke, her face was wet with tears. She sat in the blackness, a hand straying to the nearby cot to touch the sleeping Alison.

If necessary, she would follow Ernest and Harold and this baby to the ends of the earth. Nothing and no-one would ever separate her from the people she loved. The details might prove difficult, but she would manage somehow.

Because these were her children.

CHAPTER NINE

Visits

The huge nurse wobbled along grotesquely, sometimes in front of them, sometimes breathing heavily down their necks, unlocking each door as she reached it, turning keys again once everyone had passed through. Every time they approached another section of the hospital, Abigail and Theresa flattened themselves against walls and windows to allow the mountainous figure to move ahead and lead the way. She seemed to enjoy being in charge; she fingered with love and reverence the massive chain that hung from her vast waist. On the end of the chain there dangled a bunch of keys, an assortment that would not have looked out of place in the company of a prison officer.

Theresa stared along the corridor. This was a prison, because each window was barred and meshed over, while the doors were thick and heavy. Tom had been here for three months now. Yes, he had served a thirteen-week sentence for something he hadn't done, for reacting strongly to circumstances outside himself. Poor Alice must be spinning in her grave, Theresa thought. And this was the first time he'd had a visit here, because his mother, a long-term patient in Bolton Royal Infirmary, had been unable to see her only son.

Theresa sniffed the unpalatably stale air. 'Ta for coming with me, Abigail. I'd not have liked to come here by myself. Isn't it horrible? I never imagined anything like this. It's worse than a nightmare, worse than the last hospital he was in.'

Abigail raised a casual shoulder, though the words

which followed belied the careless gesture. 'These psychiatric places are always sad. Something soaks into the walls – I think it's called misery – and they just painted over it, usually in green and brown. But it's still there, breeding in the plasterwork.'

Theresa sniffed again. She was a funny girl, was Abigail. Very commonsensical, yet sometimes she came out with things that showed she was sensitive and caring underneath the hard mask she chose to wear. She had insisted on accompanying Theresa. 'You're not going alone,' she had said firmly when Theresa had announced her intention to visit the children's father. 'Clive will take us there in the car. He can talk to the psychiatrist while we visit Mr Crawford. And I know about these things, because I've had experience. Visiting him in that military establishment was one thing, Theresa, but you'll need support this time.'

So here they were, tracking along endless passageways while Clive sat in an office studying case-notes.

'We've arrived,' breathed the enormous nurse asthmatically. 'Try not to disturb any of them. They're not used to visitors, you see.'

'Why is that?' asked Abigail.

'Most of them are too far gone for visitors, and a lot of families don't want to know about their own crazy folk. We locked the worst up when we heard you were coming, but we couldn't remove them all because we haven't enough staff. There'll be two male attendants standing by in case there's any problem. Make sure you don't talk to anybody except Shakespeare and whatever you do—'

'His name's Crawford.' Abigail's tone was serrated. 'Mr Thomas Crawford.'

The fat woman bristled, her uniform seeming ready to scream in pain as she threatened to burst out of it. 'They all have nicknames,' she said, her many chins disappearing into a red, swollen neck. 'The job would be murder if we didn't try to make light of it. We call him Shakespeare because he reads a lot, sometimes aloud to the others. And he writes, scribbles on bits of paper about somebody called Alice.'

Abigail shook a finger dangerously close to the bloated face. 'The somebody called Alice was his wife. If you had read his notes, you would have known that.'

'But I've—'

'It pays to learn about your patients. You can't treat them without studying background.'

'I've only recently moved to D4!' The jowls were turning an interesting shade of magenta. 'I've just spent three weeks on baths. Do you have any idea of what it's like to be locked in a room with twenty screaming, howling, naked women, trying to keep the water at the right temperature, trying to stop them from drowning themselves or killing one another?'

'Indeed,' snapped Abigail. 'I did some psychiatric training in London, and I was involved in warm water therapy.' She tilted her head knowingly. 'Yes, I've been locked in with the so-called insane from time to time.'

'Oh.' The face seemed to shrink like a balloon with a slow puncture. 'I didn't know you were a nurse. Nobody told me, nobody said . . .'

Abigail stretched her spine. 'I am a matron of a geriatric unit. The mentally ill do not frighten me, nurse. They deserve attention because their condition is usually attributable to great pain, the sort of suffering I hope you and I will never endure. It isn't nicknames they need, it's a bit of care, understanding and bloody research into their histories. Above all, they want respect.' Her lecture duly delivered, Abigail removed her gloves, folded them neatly, and placed them in her bag. She fixed her eyes on the nurse, making no obvious effort to conceal the animosity that had set in her narrow features.

The purple-faced nurse adjusted her ridiculously small cap, then opened the final door, stepping back to allow the other two into D4. It was a long room with tall, sticky-taped windows and a row of beds on each side. Two of these were occupied, while four men in shabby clothing sat at a scratched and stained centre table.

At the far end, in one of a group of three dilapidated armchairs, sat Tom. He wore slippers, baggy corduroy trousers and a shirt of indeterminate colour. Abigail cupped Theresa's elbow and steered her through the ward. Two white-garbed men entered from a side door, one wafting at the air to disperse the cigarette smoke that still emerged from his nose and mouth. Abigail stood and stared at this sorry-looking pair, pulling at Theresa's coat until she, too, stopped in her tracks. 'Is it the war, I wonder?' Abigail's voice was not muted. 'Or are these a typical example of psychiatric nurses?' She glanced over her shoulder at the obese female who continued to dog their steps. 'I shall write to Parliament about this place,' she declared vigorously. 'And God speed some kind of organized health service.'

One of the men at the table began to rock violently, almost banging his head against scarred wood each time he threw himself forward. The man opposite the rocking patient tugged tentatively at Theresa's sleeve. 'Can I have a penny for a bun, Mam?'

Theresa pulled an apple from her basket. 'Here. That's better than a bun.' He bit into the fruit greedily. 'Ta, Mam,' he said, spitting splinters of apple down his pullover. 'I'll play out after.'

'You do that,' answered Theresa, wishing they could all go outside in the fresh air.

Tom, a timid and undecided smile hovering on his lips, rose to greet them. 'I'm better now,' he said, a touch too eagerly for Abigail's liking. Theresa's heart plummeted. He looked greyer, older and sadder than when she'd seen him at the military hospital in Cheshire.

They sat one each side of him and, after a few seconds of uncertainty, he lowered himself into the middle chair. He smelled unwashed, and there was a heavy growth of stubbly beard on his chin. His eyes were dead one minute, falsely alive the next. Theresa handed him the basket of fruit and cakes. 'Mrs Carrington sent them,' she said. 'But they're really from Alison and the boys.'

He reached out for the gift, and both girls noticed the bruising on the wrist. Although it was fading to ochre, it was plain that there had been some quite deep and angry weals just below the frayed cuff of his shirt sleeve. Abigail winced visibly. It was obvious that the man had been restrained at some point, tied up, probably with rope or thick twine. 'How is it in here?' she whispered.

His dark-ringed eyes strayed to the fat nurse who hovered within earshot. 'All right,' he answered mechanically.

'You've got books?'

'Library trolley comes once a week.' He glanced fearfully at the men in white. 'And I've a pad and pencil sometimes. You can have a pencil if you don't shout, but you've got to make sure nobody pinches it off you.'

'They can do a lot of damage with pencils.' This unwanted announcement was pushed from between the blubbery lips of their self-appointed guardian. 'Poke one another's eyes out with them, stick them in their ears – and in other places too.'

Abigail spoke sweetly to the large, blue-clad woman. 'Could we have a cup of tea, Sister?' she asked. 'We have come a long way, you see.'

The nurse, flattered by her sudden elevation in status, smiled before stamping heavily on flat feet towards the two male attendants.

Abigail grabbed Tom's hand. 'Tied up?' she hissed.

He nodded jerkily.

'What for?'

'Shouting.'

'Why were you shouting?'

He stared directly at Theresa. 'Because there's no hope. Because there's no Alice.'

Theresa took his other hand. 'There's Alison.' The words almost stuck in her throat as she confronted head-on the concept of this man taking away her baby. Yet she deliberately twisted the knife in her own chest by adding, 'Please get better, Tom. You can't stop in here, it's not right.'

Two great tears slid down his haggard face. 'I can't always think,' he said. 'Sometimes, I can't get straight. There's nothing in my head most days. When there is, it's just Alice. But I'm better than I was, I am, I am.' A desperate, pleading note had entered his words, while pale hands plucked repeatedly at the front of his shirt.

Abigail fell to her knees and put an arm round the thin, trembling shoulders. 'Let go, Tom,' she said gently. 'Please stop holding on like this. The past is not our jailer – the past is our mother – it gives us life, but we have to move on.'

He smiled sadly. 'Lovely words. That's all I've got, words. No feelings. All empty inside.' He pushed a closed fist against his ribs, turning the knuckles sharply, as if trying to externalize his suffering. 'I just want to feel again,' he said, almost to himself.

A terrible crash broadcast that the rocking patient had gone too far. Abigail and Theresa jumped to their feet just as the large table overturned completely on top of the fallen man. The other three who had been seated at the table began to scream and moan, one rolling on the floor, another hopping from foot to foot, hands clamped over his eyes. The third yelled, then disappeared under a bed where he began to sing a hymn very loudly and with no discernible sense of pitch or rhythm. The noise was dreadful, and Theresa covered her ears to muffle the cacophony.

Like well-trained circus beasts, the male attendants pounced. Within thirty seconds or so, the two howling patients were straitjacketed and fastened in their beds with leather straps. The rocking man lay still, silent and possibly concussed beneath the upturned table. From underneath the bed, 'Abide With Me' faded to nothing.

'That's it.' Abigail's voice was almost strangled by fury. 'I've seen enough.' She turned to Tom who was sheltering behind the thin, bruised and inadequate shield of his own forearm. 'Empty your locker,' she ordered. 'You are coming home with me.'

He made no move, so Abigail doubled over until her nose all but made contact with the top of his greasy, unkempt hair. 'Listen to me, Tom. You're out of the army, declared unfit. But you are not certified. Do you hear me, man? You are, technically speaking, a voluntary patient in this hell-hole. And a voluntary patient should never be confined in a ward like this one. You need to get better, and that won't happen here.' She straightened and spoke to Theresa. 'He wants peace, peace and a pattern to his life, some sort of framework. There's nothing wrong with him that can't be put right by pulling him out of this mess.'

Theresa dragged Abigail to one side. 'But he was bad when I first saw him, very bad. I've never seen anybody look so poorly. He was smashing things, shouting and—'

'What did you expect?' mouthed Abigail, pulling the younger girl into a corner. 'He lost his wife and got a baby all in one night. More than that, he was left with the responsibility of two adopted sons and a mother with a smashed leg and double pneumonia. On top of all which, he was expected to abandon the lot and go off to fight this bloody stupid war. He got all his shocks at once, Theresa. But this . . .' She waved a hand across the grey room. 'Breathe it, smell the fear in the air. If we hadn't been here, those poor devils sitting in the middle would have been beaten, I'd guess. These are the cattle sheds that finish people. Some spend all their adult lives in such institutions. Theresa!' Her voice almost cracked, but she dropped her tone, spacing the words evenly. 'This is where Tishy will end up if she lives and I don't.' In the small and terrible silence that followed, Abigail was sure that she could hear her own heart beating.

'Oh, my God!' Theresa covered her gaping mouth with a hand.

'For years I have hated myself for feeling the way I did about her. She wasn't normal, and that embarrassed me. She took all my mother's attention, and that made me jealous. Even lately, I have been cruel to her, tried to instil some . . . ordinariness into her. Because I am scared of . . . of seeing her here. And is this what you want for Tom, for the husband of your friend? Is it? Do we turn our backs and leave him here?'

Theresa shook her head vehemently. No, this was a hateful place and Tom would never recover here. Her own pain, her own fears didn't matter any more, not if Abigail was right, not if Tom could be cured. 'Tishy won't come to this, not while I'm alive, or Mam or Marie.' She cleared her thickening throat. 'I'll root round and find his locker,' she said. 'They seem to have names on. As long as you're sure you can manage him once we get him out, Abigail.'

'He'll be a pussy cat.' Abigail's tone was tailored to disguise her own apprehension. She went back to him. 'Tom? Are you a carpenter?'

He blinked.

'Will you work for me? I need some shelves putting up and a lot of stuff altering in the attics. Clive and I are going to live in the attics at the nursing home – they are fine, big rooms. We can put a bed up there and Clive can get you a radio. Will you come with us? Today, this minute, will you come out?'

'I'm a lot better now,' he said again with that forced brightness. 'But my mam's house got hit, didn't it? Nowhere to live, nowhere of our own. She's in hospital with a bad leg, you know. And there's something wrong with her chest too.'

Abigail, pleased, nodded at him. He was capable of remembering, calculating, reasoning. 'Live with me. See.' She pointed across the ward. 'Theresa's getting your things out of the locker. We'll go in the car. My husband's a doctor, he'll look after you and see about getting a house for you and your mother when she's better. There's lots to do, Tom, and we even managed to get hold of some new wood, nice timber that deserves a master carpenter. Come home.'

238

His eyes were glued to Theresa as she walked towards them. 'Terry,' he said quietly. 'Terry who looked after my Alice. I can't get her back, can I? There's nowt will fetch our Alice back. And me mam'll not walk again.' His gaze travelled back to Abigail. 'I do know what's going on outside my own head, you know. I've not gone doo-lally. It's more like . . . like . . .'

'An emptiness inside? A great big black nothing?'

He looked closely and gratefully at the thin, sharp-featured, dark-haired girl. 'That's it,' he said. 'That and the panics. I lose my grip at times and shout a bit.'

'Good.' She patted his hand. 'Let it out, then it can't turn inward. You can shout all you like in my attics. You can shout until you've worked it all out of your system, till you learn that nothing is your fault. We won't truss you up like a bird for the oven, Tom. I just want to get you out of this dangerous place.'

Theresa stood by helplessly with Tom's pathetic bundle of possessions. There wasn't even a toothbrush or a facecloth. She'd found a grubby pad of paper with two blunt stubs of pencil, a couple of mud-coloured vests, some torn underpants and a shirt that was still trying to remember to be blue in spite of ingrained grime.

She felt sick and dizzy. Three times she'd fainted just lately, and she fought against collapsing here. This was not a place to lie down in, this was a place to escape from. They were going to get him out now, this very minute. She steadied herself against the end of a bed, breathing deeply through her mouth. The air tasted foul, but she would concentrate on the fact that they were getting him out, and that he would be better soon. She gripped the hollow, metal bed-frame. Once he'd got better, he would take away Ernest, Harold and Alison. He was staring at her, couldn't seem to take his eyes off her. Fascinated in spite of sudden weakness, she met his gaze, seeming to soak up some of the misery that hung in the air between them.

Pale lips drew back from teeth that were only marginally

239

yellower than the sallow skin of his face. 'Terry,' he said. 'How is my baby?'

The terrible question hit her in the chest with all the force of a missile from a strongbow. Her knees trembled, while the lifelong pain in her hip, which had lessened of late, was instantly rekindled, as if her whole body were reacting against this poor, defenceless man. 'Pretty,' she finally achieved. 'She's very pretty and quite well, I think.'

He looked her up and down. 'Bad leg?'

She nodded. 'I fell. A long time ago.'

'You're all right, you are, Terry,' he said. 'Alice said so when she phoned me, and in her letters. And she were never wrong about folk, our Alice.'

The erstwhile hymn-singer crawled out from his hiding place. 'Can I have a bun, Mam?' he asked. Theresa tried to smile at him as he moved crabwise towards the basket of goodies. 'Tom will leave you all the food,' she promised gently. The rocking patient was seated once more at the righted table. He was immobile now, and the only evidence of the recent catastrophe was a bluish lump over his left eye.

The door at the end of the ward was suddenly thrown open. Clive, who was glowering like a mad bull, dragged a huge key-ring from the lock and thrust the resulting tangle of metal in the general direction of a white-coated figure that lingered behind him. He strode into the room closely pursued by a small, meek-looking man with a receding hairline, an indefinite chin and thick glasses that made the eyes tiny. 'There is no question . . .' A bony hand waved in the air. '. . . of any of these patients being given unsuitable treatment, Doctor Harrison. The procedures I mentioned . . .' He tripped over the crawling patient, righted himself inelegantly, then groped blindly at the back of a dining chair. 'It was just a thought. Little else seems to work with Mr . . . Mr . . . er . . .'

'Crawford,' snapped Clive, his teeth bared. 'And this lot . . .' He swept an arm across the ward, 'would be grand guinea pigs. No visitors, no-one to check. So, when do you start overdosing Tom on insulin, eh? Or is it already happening? Have you electrocuted him yet?' He paced about in a perfect circle, arms akimbo, face coloured by anger. 'You will release this man into my care now, Doctor. You know my qualifications – and my attitude. Abigail? Pack Tom Crawford's things.'

'They're packed.'

Clive stopped in his tracks and looked at the woman who was his wife, realizing with a jolt why he loved her. He loved her because she herself was full of love, fuller of understanding than anyone he had ever known. She was a good woman. In spite of boiling temper, he delivered a beaming smile, only to erase it immediately when he noticed the two figures strapped tightly to mattresses. 'Christ,' he muttered. 'Why don't you go the whole hog? Why not lock them up in cages and be done with it, let people pay to come and have a look! You could make a fortune, turn it into another Belle Vue Zoo.'

The pebble-eyed psychiatrist straightened pinched shoulders and craned his stringy neck, as if taking a vain stab at achieving an air of authority. 'If you think you can do better, then come and work here, put your time and energy where your mouth is.'

Clive let out a snort of derision. 'Listen, I don't pretend to be an expert in your field, but no decent-minded human being could possibly condone the deliberate creation of simulated epilepsy. It's positively barbaric.'

The shorter man stood his ground, though his demeanour was that of a man around whose ankles the quicksand is closing. 'Epileptics do not suffer psychotic or deeply depressive episodes. We merely seek to release these patients from endless misery by introducing a mild convulsion—'

'Mild?' Clive's voice rose in pitch and tempo. 'Poison them with insulin, force a rubber tube into their stomachs and bring them round with glucose while they thrash around in pain? Or are you going to cut corners by plugging them all into light sockets? Have you seen inside their minds, are you God, do you know what . . . ?' He stepped back, a hand pushing through his disordered hair. 'Oh, what's the use?'

'Then what is the answer?' asked the specialist. 'Leave them, dope them so heavily that they're no threat to us, to one another, to themselves? Be your age, Doctor Harrison. You treat their bodies, we'll scratch around till we find a way through all their nightmares.'

Clive loosened his tie and took a step towards Abigail. 'I deal with minds, Doctor Spencer-Ford.' The hyphenation was spoken with emphasis and in a manner that missed contempt by the merest fraction. 'Every day, I encounter disturbed people, and we who are condemned to general practice fight tooth and nail to shelter such sufferers, to harbour them in safe berths within their own communities. You are no more than a last straw, to be used only when all else has failed.' He decided on a different and more practical tack. 'Fresh air would not go amiss in here, nor would a bit of soap and polish.' Again, he changed the subject without warning, plainly attempting to keep the prey well within his sights. 'Are you sure that Tom Crawford has not been a victim of any of these treatments?'

'He was judged, on early assessment, to be unsuitable, though we are beginning to wonder . . .'

'Unsuitable, eh? Not ill enough? Ah well, there's hope for the man. I will take responsibility for him. He should not be in a secure ward anyway.'

'There was no room.'

Clive nodded, visibly beginning to climb down from his high horse. 'I know, I know, and I'm sorry.' He helped Tom from the chair and guided him along the room towards the door. Abigail followed after casting a few meaningful glances in the direction of the fat nurse and her two familiars.

Theresa emptied her basket on to the table, and the singer of hymns fell upon the bounty right away. She walked slowly to the doctor. 'Sorry,' she said. 'I'm sure you do your best, most of you.'

'We try.'

The spectacles were thick to the point of opacity, so Theresa wasn't completely sure, but there seemed to be a hint of despair in the pale, pin-prick eyes.

She walked out, the empty basket dangling limply from a hand. It was, she thought, a very sad world.

'Yellow is my favourite colour,' announced Tishy on entering the room. She liked coming here. It was a lovely, cluttered place, full of wood and sawdust and pretty curled-up shavings. 'Shall we be able to get some yellow distemper for the walls? I had a yellow dress when I was little. It had a huge satin bow at the back, and flounces round the hem. It's the colour of happiness, you know. Daffodils are yellow too, they're the nicest flowers. Abigail says I can stay ten more minutes, then Ellen's coming for me. Marie's in love with John Duffy, I heard her telling him. They kiss in the street, you know.'

Tom struggled with a bracket, inwardly cursing his disobedient fingers. He was all right now when drawing or writing, so the plans for the attics hadn't been a problem. But, given a screwdriver, he was like a first-year apprentice, all thumbs and watery eyes. 'Come and hold this, love,' he said. She sat next to him on the floor, placing a hand on the bracket, and he found that he could manage, just about, with both hands free. 'Thanks,' he said, once metal was secured against plaster. 'You're a good help.'

'Tell me "The Daffodils" again, Tom.'

He smiled ruefully at the beautiful waif who had dragged him back to sanity. It had been a long road too, because it was nearly Christmas, and he had been living here since August. The flat was almost ready for Clive and Abigail's occupation now. He would be moving on soon, living with his mam and the kiddies. He leaned back, sighing deeply as he remembered the blackest times, nights when Abigail had tended him, listened to him, talked, explained, sympathized. He owed a lot to this family.

Abigail had brought Tishy to see him every day, then someone called Ellen had collected the girl in the evenings. Ellen had never visited him, and he was not surprised. After all, who would want to call on a madman? Except that he wasn't mad – he knew that at last. This girl, this lovely, damaged girl had not seemed to notice his oddness, and she had somehow guided him along her own road, a special route paved with hope, song, poetry and love. Ellen didn't approve of the visits – Tishy had been plain enough about that. But Abigail, stubbornly constructive, had sent his medicine up the stairs at three o'clock each day. Today, his medicine wore a navy skirt, a pink hand-knitted jumper and a white pearl rosary as a necklace.

They sat on the floor while he recited Wordsworth.

'Clouds,' she said afterwards, 'are not always lonely. Sometimes, they're together and they can hold hands in the sky. So why did the man who wrote the poem say "lonely as a cloud"?'

He shrugged. 'Must have seen one on its own up in the Lake District.' The idea of clouds holding hands could only have come from Tishy, he thought. It was a pretty concept . . .

'Where's that?'

He waved a vague hand. 'North.'

'Will you take me to his daffodils?'

He nodded. 'Aye, when the war's over.'

She pouted prettily. 'Everyone always says that. When I ask for a whole bar of chocolate to myself, Ellen says, "when the war's over". Sally Manson down John Street got a full bar. That was because her mother had been with an American. I asked Ellen to go with one, but she wouldn't. They can get stockings too if they go with Americans. And bubble gum, pink and black. They shout and they talk funny and they're very, very clumsy.'

He scratched his head with the handle of the screw-driver. 'Eh?'

'Americans. They're always putting their foot in it, Abigail says. I don't care what they put their feet in if they can get chocolate. And they can't help having big feet, can they? I expect that's what makes them clumsy.'

He grinned inwardly. She lit up his life, this one. Never a dull moment, never a thought held for much more than two minutes.

'Are you lonely, Tom?' she asked, displaying yet again the unnerving perspicacity that was, strangely, one of the more noticeable factors in her particular type of brain damage.

'I miss Alice. And I'm on my own here a lot. But I'm doing a fair bit of writing and all this work for your sister. I'm not . . . scared any more.' He couldn't for the life of him fathom why, but he knew that she understood. 'And I don't mind getting up in a morning. Mornings were the worst, see. But I'm mending. Slowly and surely, I'm pulling through.'

Tishy patted his hand.

'I've been twice to the farm,' he went on. 'She's bonny, is Alison. And the lads are running round like a pair of wild things, brown as berries, they are. Terry looks after them, so does that there Mrs Carrington.'

'And your mother's better, so everything's nice now.'

His mother would never walk again without support. 'That's right, lass. Everything's a host of golden daffodils.' No, he wouldn't tell this particular fragile bloom the truth about the shakes in the night, the bone-deep ice-cold in his hands, the black thoughts that chased around in his head like a filthy coven of brewing witches. Abigail knew, though. Not that he'd said much since those first tormented weeks, but she seemed to have a knack of knowing when to come up with a brew of tea, a firm touch for a twitching shoulder, a few sharp yet strangely comforting words. Between them, these two sisters were knitting him together again, turning him into a different garment. Not a new one, no, because the threads were of used fibre, but they were managing to weave a fair cloth out of damaged and torn strands. 'I'll never know how to thank you,' he said quietly.

The alabaster cheeks stretched into a full and becoming smile. 'Barley sugar would be nice. Or Uncle Joes.'

'You're easy pleased, you are. Have you done any more of your poems?'

She jerked her head up and down vigorously. 'Can you think of a rhyme for Tishy that's not fishy?'

He pondered. 'Dishy?'

'Don't like that. Is the Alice story finished?'

'Yes.'

'Did you do the bit about her feeding the pigeons in Trafalgar Square?'

He smiled.

'And that woman saying she shouldn't waste food on pigeons and Alice saying the pigeons hadn't started the war and hadn't been given ration books?'

'It's all there, Tishy.'

She leaned a companionable cheek against his arm. 'She was right. Not the nasty woman – Alice was right. It's Germans, you see. They have guns and things. I never saw a pigeon with a gun.'

He laughed and shook his head..

The door opened. 'Tishy?' called Abigail. 'Ellen's here. Come on now, time to go.'

Tishy jumped up and ran across the room. 'See you tomorrow,' she called happily.

'Switch the wireless on, Tom,' ordered Abigail. 'Home Service – there's something on that might interest you.'

Tom sat and listened as the two girls clattered their way down uncarpeted stairs. Would he cope without the support of this place, would he manage in the house they'd been allocated, that decaying heap in Bromwich Street? He gazed around at the kitchen he had made, shelves, plate racks, cupboards. He would miss the nursing home. All he had here was in another, smaller room, just a camp bed, a tallboy and two orange boxes, but there were people downstairs, folk who kept him on an even keel. Just about.

Ah, well, it was time to move on, time to organize his own life. He was a big boy now, a man with responsibilities. He reached across the table and turned a knob. The news was just finishing, then the announcer introduced a new programme called 'Memories'. There was a bit of static interference, followed by another man's voice saying, 'Alice, by Tom Crawford'.

Tom Crawford's jaw dropped as he listened to his own words being poured from the mouth of a stranger, a talented man who had a gobful of plums one minute, a perfect cockney accent the next. 'I watched her walking towards me. She wasn't very big, but she was extremely angry. There's something powerful about a small, angry person. I suppose the temper is concentrated because it doesn't get made less by fighting for life through piles of flesh and bone . . .'

He screwed up his face, seeing her now, trim hips, ridiculous wedge-heeled shoes, red polish on nails she never quite managed to stop chewing. But the man on the wireless had moved on.

'Through the window of Lyon's, I noticed her putting a bun into her bag. The bun was for the pigeons. So I wandered into Lyon's. I suppose that's the sort of thing a young man does when there's a war on. Well, there was nothing else for it, was there? When you see the woman you're going to marry, you follow her into Lyon's and try to look casual about the whole business . . .'

There was a further ten minutes of it. He married her, impregnated her, sent her packing up north with two rumbustious little boys. And then she died. At the moment of her death, he howled aloud for the first time since Alice's actual dying. This was not the same as before, because he wasn't screaming mindlessly into inky darkness. No, this was right, this was going somewhere. As if a bubble had burst, the grief flowed from him in a horrible, wet, red-hot roar, filling the room, the whole floor, the house beneath him. With the heels of his hands, he rubbed at eyes that refused to be dammed, while his elbows pressed themselves close and tight against painful ribs. She was gone. With a last wail of acceptance, Tom let his wife slip away, finally laid her to rest in a grave he had not yet visited.

With his vision still blurred, he watched the door open to reveal a small figure. It wasn't Alice; it could never again be Alice. The woman was pretty, forty-ish, with blonde hair and kind blue eyes. When his sight cleared, he noticed that she, too, had been weeping. This, then, must be Ellen. This was Terry's mam.

She reached out her hands in a gesture of hopelessness that somehow held hope. 'Eeh, lad,' she whispered. 'There'll not be a dry eye in all England after that.'

He blinked, smiling as his fingers tightened around the handle of the screwdriver. The grip was strong. His hand was as steady as a rock.

'I heard your story on the wireless. You're a good writer, Tom. I believe Abigail got it typed up and sent in.' She shifted the now weighty Alison to her other arm. 'We all had a good old cry up at the farm. She was grand, was your Alice.'

He stooped to lay a small bunch of flowers on the icy patch of earth that covered his wife. 'More than grand, Terry.' He grinned wryly. 'She got stuck in a lift once down in the West End, her and three others in some big, posh shop. They were all panicking except Alice. She saw this spider up in a corner, and two flies buzzing round. So out came her purse, no messing. They had bets on whether the spider could finish its web before the lift moved, bets on whether the little fly or the big fly would get caught, bets on what time they'd all be rescued. She got everybody sitting dead still and quiet while they watched this blinking spider. That way, they breathed less oxygen. When the cavalry arrived, nobody noticed, they were all too busy trying to win money.' He laughed aloud. 'Thirty bob she got that day, bought a big, daft hat with it.' He straightened to survey the surrounding terrain.

'She'll be doing the same now at Peter's Gates, laying odds on who'll get in and who won't. Them with moustaches she'll have earmarked for downstairs. She didn't like men with hair on their faces, reckoned they'd something to hide.'

Theresa looked for Ernest and Harold. They were playing a noisy game of hide-and-seek among taller, frost-bedecked gravestones. Tomorrow, they would be gone. Her grip on Alison tightened slightly. From behind a stone cross, a magpie rose, crying loudly as he mashed the air with powerful wings. She remembered the day of the funeral when a skylark had soared, spilling his rainbow song into steady sunlight, offering a hymn far more beautiful than any church-organized chorus.

Her limbs were cold, while an icy fist clenched itself around her heart, forcing the blood to her head where it pounded dully and caused Tom's voice to arrive distorted, eerie and strange. To Bromwich Street, they were going. Tom had advertised for someone 'of mature years' to come in and care for his mother and the children. He intended to work in an ordnance factory somewhere near Chorley.

'I'll be sleeping up at Euxton week nights,' he was saying now. He sighed, pulled cold, crisp air into his lungs. 'The lads'll miss round here. There's a garden down yonder, but it's not the same. The whole world's a garden here.'

He looked at the rolling patchwork of snow-speckled moors, the wandering stone walls, the winding lanes that narrowed to ribbons at the skyline, then his gaze travelled back to Alice's tree-mantled grave that nestled at the edge of the cemetery, under the naked arm of a chestnut tree. 'She was good at keeping out of the rain, always did know where to find a sheltered spot.' He fell to one knee. 'Ta-ra, love,' he said, almost conversationally. 'You're gone now, lass, but we'll not forget.' He rose and turned to his companion, noticing how pinched the face looked behind the small cloud born of its own breathing. 'Are you all right?'

'Yes.' Her tone, she thought, was oddly normal.

Distant, but ordinary. 'We'd best catch them two.' She waved her free arm towards the boys. 'Get here, the pair of you,' she shouted. 'Before you turn them good clothes into washing or worse.'

He took Alison from her, finding a measure of resistance before the hold on the child was relinquished. 'Terry?' he whispered.

She turned away from him, arms akimbo, one foot resting on the rim of Alice's plot. 'Do you hear me? You'll get no pie and custard.'

They tumbled towards her, a tangle of colourful winter scarves and bright hair, each boy grabbing at her clothes and demanding immediate attention. Her face was beautiful and placid as she dabbed with a handkerchief at the many stains of childhood before planting a kiss atop each tousled head. She walked to the cemetery gate while Ernest and Harold danced round her.

Tom stared down at the ice-rimed surface of his wife's patch. 'Alice,' he mouthed. 'I know she's nobbut seventeen, and I know I'm still raw from losing you.' He glanced quickly towards the lane where Theresa waited patiently. That the boys' endurance was wearing thin was plain – he could hear them calling from behind the wall. 'But,' he straightened the recently laid posy with the toe of his boot, 'if I'd never met you, I would have followed her into Lyon's any day of the week.'

Theresa had grown to love Mrs Carrington. She was, on the surface, a tough old boot, but beneath all the tweeds and army jumpers, there beat a twenty-four carat heart. Mrs Carrington had sent for Theresa after tea. The lady of Moor Bottom Farm only sent for people after tea when she had a bone to pick, and Mrs Carrington could have laid bare an elephant carcass within ten seconds, because no bone was too big for her. Or too small. There had been The Case of The Missing Silver for a start. One of the pregnant girls had been salting away the odd knife, spoon, cruet, serviette ring, and Mrs C had dealt with her single-handedly and without interference from police. Smoking in the upper rooms was treated similarly; the size of the crime was not significant – sins mortal and venial were all handled with the same caustic exuberance.

Theresa wondered what she might have done. Not that it mattered; the ache in her chest was already huge – nothing could make it worse. She had bathed Alison for the last time, had promised the boys an extra-long story later on.

The drawing-room door hung open. Mrs Carrington was scanning the newspaper, a pair of one-armed reading spectacles balanced precariously on her nose. Ever since Theresa had arrived at the farm, Mrs C had been intending to have her glasses mended 'next week'. She removed them now and waved the paper at the opposite chair. 'Sit down,' she said. Theresa came and sat.

'You look tired. I've noticed lately that you get worn out from time to time. But the country air's good for you, best medicine ever invented. A few more months up here and you'll be fine.' She folded her arms and studied the pale girl. 'So. What are you going to do?'

Theresa pushed a lock of hair from her forehead. 'Eh?' she asked listlessly, pulling herself up almost immediately, 'I mean, I beg your pardon?'

'Are you going?'

'Where?'

'Back to the satanic mills. To Bolton, dear.'

Theresa frowned. 'Am I getting the sack?'

'No.'

'Then why do I have to go home?'

'I didn't mention home.' She paused thoughtfully. 'Ah, so you haven't been asked, then. Mr Crawford hasn't enlightened you about his proposition?'

'Eh?' This time, Theresa was too flummoxed to correct herself.

'He wants you to go with him as nurse for his mother, nanny for Alison and his adopted sons, housemaid, cook, bottle-washer, Jill of all trades . . .' Her voice faded as she watched, fascinated, while the transformation occurred.

Theresa's eyes lit up as if a switch had been used, and two spots of excitement glowed on the fine, high cheekbones. Even the blonde hair seemed to acquire new sheen and bounce, and the small hands were clasped against a bosom that positively heaved with emotion. 'Ooh, Mrs Carrington,' was all she managed.

'Calm down.' The tone was little short of acid. 'And think. You're happy here, aren't you?'

'Yes! Ooh, Mrs Carrington—'

'And you love the countryside?'

'I do, yes, I do—'

'It's a lot to give up.'

Theresa, unable to contain herself any further, sprang to her feet. 'The children,' she shouted. 'I can stay with the children. That's what Alice would have wanted.' She smiled down at the kind, weather-wrinkled face with its rigid frame of corrugated steel hair. 'Will you manage without me?'

'Yes.' A hand stained by blue veins and brown age-spots strayed along the arm of the chair. 'Will you manage? Think of yourself, girl. No fields, few flowers, plenty of hardware falling out of the sky.'

'They need me. I can handle Ernest and Harold. As for Alison—'

'You're the only mother she's ever known.'

'Yes.'

Mrs Carrington stood and placed an arm across Theresa's shoulders. 'People will talk, you know, about you and him living under one roof.'

The delicate chin was raised in happy defiance. 'I don't care. Anyway, his mother will be there. And there'll be nowt – I mean nothing – going on. It's the kiddies, see. All I want is to stay with them for as long as I can.'

'Then I can do nothing to dissuade you.' Her arm fell away and she walked to the window, standing motionless while she stared out at the garden. 'Is he . . . stable now?' she asked without turning her head.

'I think so.'

'And if he remarries?'

Theresa faltered. She couldn't imagine Tom married to anyone but Alice, didn't care to imagine him married. 'I don't know,' she said at last. 'That's a bridge we'll cross when we reach it.'

Mrs Carrington spread her hands well apart on the deep window sill, shoulders hunched so high that they almost touched her ears. This poor, beautiful youngster was going to give herself over to a life of drudgery. In her innocence, she could not see what was probably already written, that Tom Crawford would wait a decent interval before proposing marriage, thereby caging Theresa for ever in that damp, dirty, smelly town.

She forced herself to relax, straightening her back and pushing hands deep into pockets as she swung to face the girl. She hesitated, remembering a certain expression on Tom Crawford's face. Perhaps her thoughts had been unkind just now. He seemed to have a genuine and growing affection for Theresa, while Theresa clearly loved his children. 'Any time you hit a problem, come to me,' she said gruffly. 'And if you ever want to return, you need only arrive.'

'Thank you.' Theresa's face dimpled with joy. With that solid single-mindedness known only to the young, she skipped through the doorway towards a future that suddenly held promise.

The tweed-clad woman grimaced. In the skipping, there was that slight limp, and she prayed fervently that Theresa's path would be an easy one, a road without lumps, bumps or curves. With a steady hand, she poured a measure of pre-war Napoleon into a globe, sloshing the amber liquid round the base of the crystal, staring into its depths before swallowing the lot in one greedy, starved gulp.

Theresa Langden was a country girl. A person didn't need to be born in the wilds to belong there. Her hand strayed in the direction of the bottle, but she stayed its wayward journey, no more straighteners for her today. Ernest and Harold were squealing joyfully somewhere down the hall. Audrey Carrington licked the brandy from her upper lip. Theresa would be back.

It was a barn of a place, dark, dank, redolent of decay and rodent droppings. Attached to the huge kitchen at the back was a wide, walk-in pantry which had been converted into a toilet, so for this reason alone, the house had been deemed suitable.

While Ernest and Harold ran amok in the tangled rear garden, Theresa carried Alison through the ground floor of the house. There was a long brown hallway that led from front door to kitchen, its bare, uneven floorboards ingrained with filth. The upper half of the vestibule door was glazed in dirty colours, while the vestibule itself, square and tiled in mosaic, was shut off from the outside world by a door of heavy oak.

Halfway down the hall, side by side, stood two flimsier panelled doors with tarnished brass handles. The first led to the sitting room, a bay-fronted rectangle whose windows were encased in rot and layers of flaking, yellowish paint. A middle, possibly morning room, sandwiched between parlour and kitchen, stood in permanent twilight, its only window set in the side of the house. The view was sombre, as the next house was only feet away, and Theresa stood for several moments gazing into the blind eye of a similar empty room.

These dwellings had not been occupied for some time. They sat on Bromwich Street, grey, sullen, abandoned till the end of the war when, no doubt, sentence would be passed. Theresa sniffed, inhaling a variety of scents, none of them healthy.

Tom clattered down the stairs. 'Up there's no good,' he declared glumly. 'Stairs are safe enough and I can sort the bathroom out, but I wouldn't put furniture on the bedroom floorboards.'

'What about downstairs?' she asked.

He stamped round the room, causing the floor to squeak and jump in protest. 'I can patch it up with good wood from upstairs, but we'll have to shut the bedrooms off, lock them up. Fancy,' he raised his head and stared at a twisted wire that dangled from the ceiling, 'fancy putting the electrics in and the place half rotted.'

'He was eccentric,' said Theresa. 'A ruined man, used to deal in antiques. He's been dead six months, and nobody wanted to live here, not even them that were bombed out. And that lavatory off the kitchen's filthy. I don't think it's right, having a toilet next to the cooking.'

He raised his arms in a gesture of helplessness. 'But she's got to have a downstairs lav, Terry. Where else could we get one? She can only walk with that frame, and she'd never get it upstairs or down a slippy yard. And she doesn't want to live upstairs, she said she needs to see life.'

'I know.'

'Look.' He plastered a determined smile across his face. 'I'll get wood and coal somehow, we can dry the place out.'

Theresa eyed him steadily. 'What if the kiddies get ill with the damp?'

'They're tough,' he cried. 'They'll be all right.'

She shifted Alison to her other arm. 'And how do we all fit in? There's six of us counting your mam.'

He crossed the room slowly, leaning a weary elbow against the high mantelshelf. 'You can change your mind if you want, Terry, I'll get somebody else. But we have to be a family, me, Mam and the kids. If I leave them at Moor Bottom till the war's over, they'll not know me. And me mother's only got me.'

Theresa bit hard on her lower lip, trying to erase from her disobedient mind pictures of open fields, hedgerows, country cottages . . . 'I'll not leave Alice's children,' she said slowly. 'I'm just asking sensible questions, that's all. Like what about your mam just getting over pneumonia again? How's all this wet going to suit her and where will she sleep?'

He ran a hand through tousled dark hair. 'We'll clean

the dirt out first. Remember, I am a carpenter, I can soon sort the rot out, take some wood from next door if necessary – the place is empty.' He surveyed the room. 'Bit of distemper here and there, try and get some paint, a bit of varnish—'

'Mr Wilkinson,' said Theresa, suddenly inspired.

'Eh?'

'He's a family friend.' She smiled secretively. Cedric Wilkinson was the man who loved her mother, but she wouldn't tell Tom that, not yet, not till she knew him better. 'He's in paint, something to do with the corporation, I think. Mind, it is mostly green.'

'Beggars can't be choosers,' he quipped, encouraged by her lighter tone. 'So. Are you game, Terry?'

She raised a shoulder. 'Where do we sleep?'

Tom dropped his head and thought for a moment. 'You and Alice in the front room, me and the lads in here. Mind, I'll be sleeping at Euxton during the week, but I'll be here three nights. Mam will have to live in the kitchen – it's big enough.'

She took a small step towards him. 'Will you . . . be all right on munitions? Are you fit for it?'

He glanced away from the penetrating blue gaze. 'I'm fine. In fact, I could likely go back to the regiment, only they won't have me because I went doo-lally. Stress, they call it, stress and depression. Only I've got to do my bit, Terry. Seeing as they won't let me fire the bullets, I might as well make the damned things.' He cleared his throat self-consciously. 'And happen it's just as well. This way, the children won't be left orphans.'

'I'd never leave them, Tom. No matter what happens, they'll always have me.'

He stared directly at her now. She was an island of brightness and beauty in this nightmare of a room. Golden hair shone in soft waves like a halo round the perfect face, while the gentle eyes sparkled with the vigour of youth. What would Alice say if she knew how he was beginning to think already? It was too soon. Far too soon and far too easy. He almost smiled, knowing what Alice would say, hearing it. 'Get on wiv it, Tommy . . .' He stepped back, stumbling over a shabby brass fender. 'We'll manage,' he said, feeling foolish and clumsy.

Theresa looked at him with an expression he found totally inscrutable. 'Yes,' she said. 'We will.'

Cobwebs hung in the air between them, slender, misted threads that floated each time she breathed. She stood her ground, both arms folded around the dozing child. Something was happening, something she couldn't quite pinpoint, a situation that drifted, like the cobwebs, in an area of grey uncertainty. They had grown close, she and Tom, drawn together by the inevitable shared intimacies that are the result of rearing three young children. Yet the bonds that tied them could have no more substance than this spider's gossamer, because they both remembered Alice. Or . . . she blinked rapidly . . . was Alice in this, was she a part of it? She shook herself visibly, throwing off such careless thoughts. 'I bet it never gets warm in here,' she said.

'We'll warm it,' he said as she left the room. He looked through the window and across the narrow gap that separated this house from the next. How small the world was! His wife had died, Terry had nursed her, and now his heart was moving towards the nurse. It happened – he'd heard of it, read about it – but could he trust it? Was Terry just the next stop on the route, the nearest thing, separated from Alice merely by that small alleyway called death? It was only a stride from this house to the next, only a stride from Alice to Theresa.

A tinkling laugh echoed at the back of his skull, but he knew now not to turn and look. 'You'd like Terry,' he heard her say. 'No frills about her, very good with the lads, and she looks like something off a painting. Best friend I ever found, Tommy.' He heard a click and a buzz as the remembered phone call ended. That had been their final conversation, the last message from Alice. He hadn't written about it, hadn't put Theresa in the Alice story.

The cheque crackled in his pocket, twenty pounds for 'Double Trouble', the tale of a couple of lads who had been evacuated. It would be broadcast soon and he hoped that Ernest and Harold would not recognize themselves, since that would only make them even worse.

As he turned from the window, he smiled, suddenly knowing the answer. No, not the answer, but he understood the question now. Could he write Theresa down, put her on paper? Not for sale, not for general consumption, just for himself. Yes, once he knew her well enough to capture her in words, he would be able to assess the direction of his own feelings. And, perhaps, of hers.

John Duffy was performing a very precarious balancing act on a thick plank stretched between two ladders. His teeth were clamped around his 'fancy' brush, a half-inch item designed to get into nooks and crannies. At the end of his right arm, which waved with all the energy of an enthusiastic farewell, a distempered hand contained a larger brush with which he was painting the kitchen ceiling, any adjacent wall, the wooden pulley clothes line, and all humans who were unfortunate enough to cross his path.

Ellen wiped a white blob from the mantelshelf. 'Listen, you,' she said grimly. 'There's more distemper on folk than there is on that there ceiling, and I'll swear it's run right up to your armpit. I know you're willing, lad, and our Theresa's very grateful, but can't you spread it about a bit less?'

He beamed down at her, his carrotty hair frosted unevenly with splashes of white.

She grinned. It was impossible to get angry with John Duffy. He was like a puppy, full of amoral mischief and trusting friendship, no malice in him at all. 'How does your mother put up with you?'

He spat out his 'fancy' brush, which landed wetly on spread-out newspapers. 'She doesn't. Every Sunday, she gives me a paintbrush and tells me to ruin somebody else's house.'

Marie came in, the wrecked and twisted near-skeleton of a black umbrella opened over her head. 'All done in the other rooms.' She side-stepped some low-flying paint that threatened her blue dungarees. 'Tishy's done a great job with them old curtains, covered the settee and chairs a treat. She's putting patterns on the walls now with some sponges dipped in pink and green, it looks like proper wallpaper.'

John stopped painting. 'It's bad luck opening a brolly in the house, you know.'

'Worse luck still getting covered in your bird droppings,' answered Marie smartly.

He sighed with heavy drama. 'Oh ye of little faith,' he quoted, attacking the ceiling with renewed and messy vigour.

Ellen left them to their banter and walked into the hall. It looked bigger now with its cream walls and clean, varnished floorboards. She sat on the stairs, her eyes fixed to a monstrous hallstand that had been abandoned by the last resident. And no wonder, big, ugly thing, it was.

She leaned her head against banister railings. Well, there was no shifting Theresa, that was plain enough. She was coming to live here, in this house, with a young widower, his crippled mother and his children. Ellen had even brought both parish priests to plead with her daughter, but Theresa had withstood their quiet reasoning. There were children who needed her, and Theresa refused to see beyond these three motherless facts of human life.

Ellen drew the back of a hand across her aching, distemper-spattered brow. It had been time to give in gracefully, so she'd done just that, earmarking bits of furniture on second-hand stalls, rooting out old curtains, coming to Bromwich Street to receive items sent down by cart from Moor Bottom Farm. No matter what the cost, she would not lose her daughter, refused to alienate her.

Marie's laughter floated through from the kitchen, and

Ellen lifted her head to the sound. Aye, and there was another one on her way out, likely on the list for a wedding as soon as the war ended. He'd be going away soon, would John. He was a nice lad, no side or ceremony to him, just a good, ordinary boy with plenty of humour and a face plain enough to crack plates. She was bonny, was their Marie, could have got herself a handsomer fellow. But Marie obviously had the ability to see beyond the outer layers. Yes, as long as the brickwork was sound, Marie took no heed of decorative finish. Which was just as well, Ellen thought ruefully, since John, with a paintbrush, was about as much use as a concrete cushion, so Marie would probably get a plain and unadorned life.

What about Theresa, though? Living with a man who'd only just got his mind back? Did he have a permanent hold on his senses now, or was he just renting them for a while like he'd rented this house? And how would Theresa achieve a normal young girl's life? Nobody would look at her, not with three kiddies hanging on.

A shadow fell across her face. 'Mrs Langden?'

She looked up. 'Oh, hello.'

He placed a hand on the globe of wood that topped the lowest rail. His clothes hung on him carelessly, as if they would rather have been somewhere else, like on a hanger or over the back of a chair. 'I wanted to thank you for letting Terry help me.'

She studied the dark-haired, blue-eyed man. What sort of a person was he with his poetry books on the shelves and his stories on the wireless? A carpenter? Whoever heard of a carpenter reading verse and sending tales in to the Home Service? Mind, whoever would have expected a carpenter to rear the Son of God . . . ?

He was, she knew, a blinking good writer, no mistake about that. His stuff could make you laugh one minute, cry the next. She'd read a book once with a woman in it who'd made her giggle and weep all at once. What was the name of that book? There'd been a lad in it too, a lad with a daft name. And this criminal took a pie and a file, then left all his money to the lad with the daft name. The woman sat in a big house and never went out. Eeh, what was that book?

'Mrs Langden?'

'I'm Ellen. Listen, you'll know. A mad woman in a wedding frock, never came out of the house after getting jilted. Dickens, I think.'

'*Great Expectations*.' He nodded, his eyes crinkling at the corners. 'If a person was allowed to read only one book in his life, then it should be a Dickens. Do you want to borrow *A Tale of Two Cities*?'

She smiled at him. There was something in Tom Crawford's voice these days, something calm and steady that seemed to comfort her. 'Did Dickens write that one and all?'

'Aye, it's one of Charlie's.' He dropped to his hunkers. 'Don't worry about her, Ellen. I'll not take her life away.'

'Look after her.' She jumped up, not caring to consider the ways in which he might 'look after' her daughter. 'We'd best shape ourselves,' she said, businesslike once more. 'Your mam's out of the convalescent home on Monday, and this place stinks like a paint factory.'

He walked away, tugging at trousers that had slackened during his illness.

Squashing her misgivings, Ellen assaulted the coloured lights in the vestibule door, washing each piece of glass until it shone like a precious jewel. Both her daughters had focused their attention elsewhere, away from her. This was the start of the letting go that she'd heard about in the past from older mothers. 'You've got to let 'em go to keep 'em', and 'don't tighten the strings, you'll only strangle yourself'. Abigail was long gone and wed now, Theresa hadn't been at home for months, and if Marie got married young, then Ellen would be left with . . . with him.

Tishy poked a scarf-wrapped head round the door to the front room. 'Can I have a barley sugar now?' she asked plaintively.

Ellen chuckled and reached into the capacious pocket of

her apron. Aye, Tishy would still be there. 'Here you are, love.'

Tishy attacked the sweet with childlike joy, then returned happily to her paint-dabbing.

Ellen's hand paused on a rectangle of green glass. She would have Tishy. God and pernicious anaemia permitting . . .

CHAPTER TEN

Standing Together

There was a small sliver of light at the edge of the blackout curtain, and he fixed an unsteady eye against this crack, cursing soundlessly as his hipbone made sharp contact with a stone window sill. He'd been home after the pub had shut, expecting to find her there. She'd always been there before, especially at New Year. The last one had been a bit different, because of the beating that had put him in hospital, but it would be 1943 in a few minutes, and he was stuck outside in the bleeding cold while she enjoyed herself in the doctor's house with all her so-called family and friends.

They lived here off and on, Abigail and her husband, while their flat was being finished down Chorley Old Road. And they'd planned this party without him, deliberately ignoring him at a time when everybody should be celebrating together.

The crazy one was sitting at a piano. She wasn't playing; she was laughing and joking with someone outside his narrow scope of vision. But he could see his wife, all right, if she could be called a wife, wouldn't let him near her, paid him a pauper's wage, refused him access to money she'd stolen from the cellar and stuffed away in some bank under her own name. She was wearing a blue suit, one he'd never seen before, and her mouth was red. Was it coloured by the wine she held, or had she taken to getting herself noticed? He stepped back, beating arms against a body that was cooling for lack of sustenance. A hand groped in a pocket and pulled out a metal flask from which he drank deeply, toasting himself as the shouts from the house announced the arrival of midnight.

Well, this was a fine how-do-you-do, wasn't it? He was a man with a wife, four daughters, seven houses, two thriving shops, and he couldn't get a hand on any of them. Since the trouble, he'd only tried once for his marital rights with Ellen, and that had been an experience he would not care to repeat in a hurry. She'd bitten his ear and there'd been blood everywhere, then she'd threatened to sack him if he ever came near her again. He spat on the flags. Sack him? Him? It was his own bloody business, it was THE LONDON STORES! Still, he'd kept his distance since. After all, she'd a solicitor behind her, not to mention those strapping girls and the men that hung around them.

He swayed drunkenly, touching the yard wall for support. How many? How many against one man? Abigail and her doctor, Marie and the soldier-boy who was likely all dressed up in there, uniform on, ready to fight at the drop of a hat for king, country and a few measly bob a week. Then there was Theresa with her fancy man, big house down Bromwich Street . . . . He was losing count. There was Cedric too, wasn't there? A good mate, a lad from way back, from London, even. Yes, they'd covered a lot of ground together, him and old Cedric. Including the distance between here and Blackpool, at the end of which journey Billy had been dropped like a sack of potatoes, dumped in the road to rot for all Cedric cared.

An alcohol-tear made its slow, cold way down a stiff cheek as he walked through the gate and into the back alley, where he paused beneath an unused lamp to light a cigarette. 'See?' he said to the flaring match. 'I ain't done nothing wrong. That's what I don't understand.' He cast away the light just as his finger started to singe. 'It was mine, it bleeding was. It was me who did the running, me that put the old bat's money on her horses, me who collected her winnings and never a penny kept back. And what does she do, Miss Abigail McDade?'

He addressed the silent world loudly and with the air of a man confronting a large, rapt audience. 'Leaves·it all to fat Lil, that's what she does. An' I took it.' He nodded, the resulting dizziness causing him to resort once more to the contents of his flask. With a cuff of his coat, he wiped his mouth roughly. 'I admit I took it. But there was method in my madness, see? I would have sent her some, I would have seen to Lil once I'd got on my feet.'

His feet weren't too clever at the moment, so he embraced the lamp post closely. 'I'm going to get them,' he announced to the frost-slicked column. 'They don't know one thing, one very important thing. And that's the fact that I got brains.' He took one hand from the post, tapping his skull with a finger. 'I seen to old flap-mouth Vera Shaw, didn't I? She's not talked yet, and she won't – never! Oh yes, I'm not like this lot round here, you know, not a bleeding cottonhead. A London boy is what I am. Dragged myself up, I did, because nobody never wanted to know. When I've done, there'll be nothing to stand between me and what's mine. Solicitors?' He hawked this word from his throat like infected phlegm. 'I'll get him too, the lot of them, the whole scabby crowd.'

A gate opened. 'Who's there?' It was the doctor's voice.

'I'm looking for my family,' he said, spacing the words so evenly as to immediately betray his condition.

'Go home,' snapped Clive. 'You're not wanted here.'

''s my family!' he yelled. 'Not yours, not anybody else's. Mine! My house, my stores, my money . . . !'

'You're drunk. That's all that's really yours, Billy London – your drunkenness.'

'But you don't understand. It's New Year, I got to see my kids, I want to wish them—'

'What? Wish them what?'

He grinned into the heavy veil of midnight. 'All that's coming to them, Doctor, all that they deserve.' He belched, then emptied the contents of his stomach on to the cobbles.

'You're disgusting.' The gate slammed.

'Happy New Year,' yelled Billy. Then he spoke softly to his companion, stroking the lamp post as if it were a lover. 'Hope they enjoy it,' he said almost soberly. 'Because it will be their last.'

Inside the house, Clive threw a shovelful of coal on to the fire. Ellen touched his arm. 'Who was it?'

'Your husband. Don't worry, he's gone now. Ellen?' He drew her to one side. 'Why don't you see him off for good? He's no use to you, and he's still stealing bits and pieces for the black market – I know that from my patients. He must have contacts, because he's selling salmon and bacon – God knows where he gets it. Why not show him the door?'

She dropped her head and hugged herself with folded arms. 'I don't know, Clive. I suppose it's partly to do with pride and how it would look if I got rid, but mostly because with the way things are, I know where he is some of the time.' She inhaled sharply. 'I think he could be dangerous.'

'In what way?'

Her shoulders came up. 'I don't know. If I did know, then I could cater for it, fight against it. He's deep, you see, and there's something twisted in his mind. He thinks everybody's against him, thinks he has to fight the world and win. If I threw him out, I'd be forever watching my back.' She cast an eye round the room. 'Aye, and everybody else's backs and all. If you've got to have an enemy, you're best keeping him in view. It's like the circus, Clive. The lion tamer never turns away from the beasts.'

Marie, sitting on John Duffy's knee, threw back her head and laughed at some private joke they were sharing. Tishy ran her fingers over the piano keys, while Theresa, looking strangely lost now that Tom had gone home, nibbled at the edge of a scone. Abigail and Auntie Harrison stood in a doorway, heads together as they discussed the nursing home and its residents. 'You know,' said Ellen softly, 'at times like this – New Year and suchlike – you realize that it's just people that are precious, not things. I feel like giving the lot back to him, slinging my hook with Tishy and Marie, and finding a sane life somewhere. A fresh start, a clean slate . . .'

'But you can't, you're just a trustee. It's not yours to dispose of, is it, love?'

'No. I'm trapped by the whim of a dead woman from Mayfair, and by my husband's sins. I got a Christmas card from that Doctor McDade in London. It had a note inside saying that his Auntie Abigail would have approved of the way we've sorted things out. If only he knew what we're having to live with! Yon feller watches our every move, you know. I can't work out what he's thinking, but his eyes are all over the place like maggots on bad meat. He's sick in his mind, very sick. I wish he'd . . .'

'Die?'

She made no answer, but the shadows in her eyes spoke volumes.

'Hey, Mam,' shouted Marie. 'It's New Year – no need to look so miserable. Come here, everybody. John's got some new jokes.'

They all crowded round obediently while John, his face aglow with embarrassment, delivered an assortment of the least offensive stories in his recently acquired barrackroom repertoire. Martha Harrison, whose understanding of modern parlance was limited, stood next to Theresa, smiling when the others laughed, noticing that Theresa too was maintaining an attitude of pretended involvement.

When the jokes were exhausted, they gathered round the piano to sing while Tishy played. Martha Harrison, who, like Theresa, was to spend the night here, edged her way to Ellen's side. Under the cover of a heartily rendered 'John Peel', she whispered to Ellen, 'Theresa's looking pale.'

Ellen turned just in time to see Theresa's head disappearing behind the piano. The music stopped abruptly. 'She's gone again,' announced Marie, her voice tightened by concern. 'That's twice this week that I know of.'

John carried the limp form across the room, placing her gently on the couch. 'Light as a feather,' he muttered. 'I could have sworn there was more to Theresa.'

Ellen gripped Clive's arm. 'She's always doing it, always fainting. She never used to, but it started up at the farm, Mrs Carrington told me, round about the time that her friend died. And knowing our Theresa, she'll not have told us how often, because she'll not have us worrying.'

Abigail, who had left the room as soon as Theresa had fainted, returned now with a stethoscope. She knelt by the couch and listened to her half-sister's heart. 'She'll do,' she said abruptly. 'Take Tishy home, Ellen. This will only worry and over-excite her. We'll look after Theresa, so don't fret.'

Clive agreed. 'Time to break up the party, I'm afraid. John, you'll walk the ladies home, won't you?' He looked at Ellen's troubled face. 'It might well be something and nothing. I'll get to the bottom of it, never fear.'

Ellen grabbed Tishy's arm. Dear God, did Theresa have the same as Tishy, were there going to be two in this family with that dreadful disorder?

'No, Ellen.' Clive was plainly reading the thought. 'This is a different matter altogether.'

'Are you sure?'

He nodded, working hard to contain his sadness. He could have taken a reasonable guess at Theresa's trouble, had harboured suspicions for some time, but Theresa, in his books, was a woman now, and she therefore deserved the privacy deliberately provided by Hippocrates. 'I'll get her admitted,' he said quietly. 'Sort some tests out.'

Ellen stiffened. 'Hospital?'

'Just a few general procedures, just to find the answer to these fainting spells.'

'But . . .'

He placed a reassuring hand on her arm. 'I'm sure there's nothing to worry about. She'll be well cared for, in the best place. Bolton Royal's a damned good hospital. Ellen, you are going to have to trust the doctors for once.'

Auntie Harrison bustled about finding coats and bundling everybody into outdoor garments. When the door finally closed, she joined Abigail at the sofa. 'Has she come round?'

'I think she's drifted into proper sleep now. Clive? You'll have to pop round to Bromwich Street in the morning, tell Tom that Theresa will be out of action for a while.'

He measured Theresa's pulse, registering, not for the first time, how thin her wrist had become. 'Yes, sleeping,' he pronounced. 'And while she's in the ward, Abigail, we'll get this hip looked at. I'm not happy with the way she's walking.'

'It never rains but it pours,' said Auntie Harrison. 'I'll get to my bed.' She left the two of them standing over the sleeping girl.

'What is it?' asked Abigail.

'I'm her doctor, so I can't discuss it.'

Abigail gazed down at the ashen face, which was made paler by the colourful cushion on which it rested. 'Female trouble?'

He made no reply.

'She's not . . . pregnant?'

'Hardly.' He shook his head, and she noticed a few more grey streaks above his temples.

'What do you mean by "hardly"?'

'Abigail, I can't . . .'

'Don't, then,' she snapped. 'We've been through a lot together, Theresa and I. Remember the institution? We got one another through that. Because of Theresa, I finally faced my own nightmare about Tishy. I want to help her. Surely you can have some faith in me? After all, Theresa and I are related by blood.' She shrugged. 'Even if it is bad blood.'

He lifted a hand and stroked his wife's cheek. 'You will help her, my love. But there's no diagnosis yet. If my suspicions are correct, then there's something slightly awry here. If, on the other hand, I've missed the mark – and it wouldn't be the first time – then at least she will have a clean sheet. Now, let's get her upstairs. I have a feeling that the girl is going to need all the rest she can get.'

As they lifted her, Theresa opened her eyes. 'Alison?' she asked weakly.

Abigail's face was grim. Alison and her brothers would have to manage for a while. This was Abigail's sister, and no sister of hers would risk health unnecessarily. She forced a smile to her taut, unwilling lips. 'It's all right, Theresa. Everybody will be taken care of.'

The chairs were extremely uncomfortable. Marie and Ellen sat side by side in the gloomy green corridor, all efforts at conversation and mutual consolation finally abandoned. Theresa was in theatre. Her mother and her sister, having gained permission through Clive, were enduring what seemed like endless torture. Each time they glanced at the clock, they wondered about its apparently retarded mechanism. Nurses and porters trundled past with trolleys and carts, while doctors, wearing important white coats and sombre expressions, drifted about in their own special godlike way, noticing little, saying nothing.

Ellen, a hand in a pocket, counted Hail Marys. Marie sucked a peppermint, though it failed to take the taste of disinfectant from her tongue. How much longer were these surgeons going to be? 'Having a quick look', that was what Clive had said. Did a slow look take even more time, then? Clive was in there with them, supposed to be observing. Just as well, Marie thought, since it appeared as if they all wanted glasses if it took well over an hour for a quick look. At least Clive had good eyes . . .

Ellen drew the hand from her pocket and stared blankly at the palm. She had gripped the rosary so tightly that an arm of the crucifix had pierced her flesh, opening a wound that was almost stigmatic. Blood. They were cutting her child, her baby. She leapt from the chair just as Clive entered through swinging double doors.

'Is she all right?' screamed Ellen, terrified by the sight of him. He was dressed in a heavy apron and boots, looked as if he'd just emerged from a slaughterhouse, though there was not a mark on him.

'She's sleeping,' he said. 'Marie, stay here. I want to talk to your mother.'

Ellen followed Clive into a small, cramped room that contained six padded upright chairs and a low table scattered with an assortment of dirty cups. This was probably where the doctors had their tea when they weren't cutting people up.

'Well?' she asked, trying to trim the hysterical edge from her voice. 'What's up? What's going on, Clive?'

He pushed her gently into one of the leather seats. 'We can work on the leg,' he began. 'That limp can be minimalized, if not totally remedied.'

She stared hard at him; she could feel a 'but' coming.

'But she's a bit of a mess inside,' he finished.

She didn't know where to start, what to say, because she didn't want the answers. Like a child comforting itself, she rocked gently to and fro, arms clenched for protection across her chest.

He studied her movements while his mind shuffled words like a pack of cards, because there was no easy way to deal this hand. 'The main thing is that Theresa is going to be perfectly well.' He cleared his throat, as if seeking more thinking time. 'Ellen, we tried to blow through the Fallopian tubes, but they're too far gone.'

'Eh?' She was still now, rigid as a statue. 'Tell me in small words,' she said. 'I'm not stupid, but I'm not meself at the minute.'

He sat opposite her, elbows on knees, chin cupped in his hands so that his face was as near as possible to hers. 'The heavy bleeding has been caused by a small fibroid which has now been removed. That was no real problem, though she might be plagued by fibroids later on in life. However, her ovaries are intact. But there must have been infection in her womb at some stage, years ago, when she was an infant. This was not introduced sexually, Ellen. Your daughter is a virgin.'

Ellen nodded slowly. 'And them tubes you were on about – they bring the eggs into the womb.'

'Yes.'

'So she's got eggs and she's got a place to grow them, only they can't get there.'

'That's it. I'm sorry, love.'

Ellen stared into space for a few minutes. 'Like having a tram in the depot and no rails to run it on,' she said absently, as if nothing were sinking in. Then she sat up, eyes bright with questions. 'An infection? How would she get an infection if she's never been interfered with?'

Clive bit down on his lower lip before speaking. 'The experts in there . . .' He waved a hand towards the door. 'They can tell at a glance the age of scar tissue, adhesions and so on. As a small child, she must have had some sort of an accident, probably the one that gave her the limp. Internal bleeding probably occurred at that time, and the tissue obviously became infected. Her inside did its best to heal itself, but there were adhesions.'

'Things sticking to things.'

He jerked his head. 'The problem travelled to the tubes, which are always very narrow, and the scars have closed the gap.'

The small woman inhaled deeply. 'You are telling me that my Theresa can never be a mother.'

'Oh, Ellen, I am so very sorry.' He blinked rapidly, determined to be strong. Being strong was a doctor's lot, and it wasn't always easy. 'It must have been one hell of a fall downstairs to cause damage like this. The female reproductive system is extremely well-cushioned, and rightly so. But no system is ever completely foolproof.'

Ellen jumped to her feet. 'I want to see her.'

He rose and came to stand at her side, placing an arm about her shoulder. 'We revived her briefly – we always do that after a general. She said she wants Marie. I asked her did she want to see you, but she said no, she just wants Marie. Then she fell asleep again.'

She gazed past him through the window. 'Right, I

might as well go home, then. She needed babies, you know. She loves babies, does our Theresa.' She turned and walked out of the room.

Clive watched from the doorway while Ellen spoke to Marie. When she had finished, she drew the coat tightly about her small figure, dabbed at her nose with a handkerchief, then set off along the corridor. Silently, he backed into the room, closed the door and leaned heavily against it. Some days, Ellen looked even tinier than she actually was. This had been one of those days.

Marie stood in the grounds of Bolton Royal Infirmary, her eyes scanning the many windows with their criss-cross patterns of wartime sticky tape. She ought to be feeling something, but she wasn't, perhaps it was the cold. But the words she had just heard – she couldn't take them in. Her brain seemed to be closing down, shutting things out, refusing to function properly.

Unaware that she was displaying the signs of one in deep shock, Marie placed herself on a green-painted bench and studied a threatening sky. It hung like lead, touching the tops of mill chimneys, fingering the stacks with its cold, colourless hands. It was a grey world altogether, a bleak existence with no edge, no border, little sense of direction, no definition. Though perhaps it wasn't the grey. No, it was more likely to be the khaki that had narrowed the future down to nothing.

Theresa!

She bit hard on her lower lip, drawing blood, tasting its salty, metallic flavour. Mam had likely gone back to one shop, Mrs Tattersall was in the other. Theresa was stretched out on a bed, Marie was sitting on a rock-hard bench. She tried to make a song of this litany, filling her mind with words, groping for rhymes that wouldn't arrive, cramming her head with a nonsense that might preclude rational thought. Because she mustn't think, not yet, she wanted a minute to herself before the hatred moved in for the kill. He had done it. He had done this

273

awful thing, and she mustn't let the thoughts loose . . .

There were sparrows hopping about in a bare tree next to the bench. Theresa loved the country . . .

John was a soldier now, a soldier who could drive a lorry. He'd been a long time learning how to drive a lorry, so she'd been lucky. She was very lucky, and the lorry's wheels were mucky . . . God, she was going the same way as poor Tishy! There was a clock on the Infirmary buildings, stopped at ten to three. She'd heard a poem once, 'stands the village clock at ten to three?', something of that sort, then a line about honey for tea.

Mrs Carrington kept bees. She had a big daft hat with a curtain hanging in front of it, she looked like a bay window with it on. The honey at the farm was good, thick and yellow.

Theresa loved that farm. My sister . . . !

Mrs Banks had lost her ration book again, there were going to be all sorts of forms to fill in. And she'd decided she wanted bananas, had Mrs Banks, reckoned bananas would go down a treat while she only had the one tooth. There weren't any bananas. Such exotic fruits had to be shipped in from far-off islands, and no British seaman was going to risk his life so that Mrs Banks could have something to pour her evaporated milk on to. She had a cupboard full of tins, that old woman, enough to feed a family for a couple of months.

Theresa looked so beautiful lying there . . . Someone should strangle him, take his scrawny neck, squeeze and squeeze . . . Better not to dwell, better to force her imagination outward, away from the centre of her wounded soul. The wind curled around her ankles, and she drew them under the bench, crossing her feet for a chance of shared warmth. This was the coldest of cold days.

There were several great mysteries in life. Like when was Stan Laurel going to realize that Oliver Hardy was a bully and an idiot, and was a zebra black with white stripes or . . . ? The sparrows were squabbling noisily. Tom

Crawford was walking into the hospital, back bent, hands stuffed into his pockets, a thick scarf wound round his throat. He hadn't seen her and she was glad.

How could she be glad when . . . ?

'Marie?'

She turned, hadn't noticed Clive sneaking up behind her. 'Oh. Hello.'

He joined her on the bench, and she pulled herself away from him, didn't want his comfort, his warmth, didn't want anybody, not even John.

'Your lip's bleeding.'

'Yes.'

He reached for her hand, and she turned on him without warning, fighting and snarling like an angry cat. The hysteria burst from her, pouring its red-hot lava into the damp, icy air. She was a strong girl, so some seconds elapsed before Clive managed to restrain her. They sat, both breathing heavily, her arms pinned by his determined grip. 'Stop it,' he said as their exhalations mingled in a white, steamy fog. 'Your sister is going to recover completely. Didn't I explain that earlier to your mother? Well?' This sudden panic alarmed him, because Marie had always been such a level-headed girl. A thought occurred to him. 'You've seen Theresa. Did she tell you something? Something that has frightened you? There's nothing to fear, Marie, everything is going to be—'

'Leave me alone! I don't want you here, I didn't ask you to come, did I? This is my bench, my place. Nobody asked you to sit here. And what do you know about Theresa, eh? Any of you? Nowt, that's what.'

'Calm down.'

'That's my twin in there, mine! I love her. We've been together all the time, even before we were born, and you can't get closer than that.' Her words were tangled, arriving uneven, punctuated by deep, heart-rending sobs. 'Why did it have to happen to her? I'd sooner it was me, I would, I would. I could have handled it.'

His eyes pricked; he was just a hair's breadth from

expressing his own terrible pity. God damn Mother Nature and her tricks! He blinked to clear his vision. 'She will be well again, that's the main thing. I know it's been a shock, but Theresa must have been enduring some dreadful pain, Marie. As I said to Ellen, the trouble goes back a long way – it happens sometimes.'

'It's not that! It's not, it's not!'

'. . . and she'll never make you an auntie. But at least she'll be whole again, and she won't have to dread that awful business every month, because the fibroid is gone now.'

'You don't get it, do you? Neither did I, because she didn't trust me enough. But she's told me now, yes, she's told me all right.' Her head bobbed like a dark ball on elastic.

'What? That she'll never have a baby?'

Her mouth opened in a perfect O and she screamed in a long, drawn-out monotone that eventually faded to nothing for lack of wind power. She inhaled deeply, as if intending to repeat the process, but he shook her quite fiercely. 'You will come with me now, lady, into this hospital, and you will drink strong tea with sugar. Then we shall talk.'

She looked at him, her eyes suddenly steely. 'All right.'

He paused. 'Can I let you go, then? If I release you, will you attack me again?'

'No.'

He continued to hesitate. 'How can I be sure of that?'

'You can't.' The tone was even, giving the clear impression that the hysterical phase had passed. 'Let me go, Clive.'

He withdrew his hands and she stood and smoothed her coat. She was a mere foot away from him when she said, almost casually, 'I hate you. I hate all men.' Then she turned and fled at a speed that made pursuit superfluous. And besides, he had several patients to visit, and at least one of them was terminally ill.

Marie sped along Bradshawgate till she reached the

cinema. There were only ninepenny seats left, but she threw caution to the winds and bought one anyway. In the back row of the circle, boys and girls were pawing at one another, clutching and kneading at body parts, sucking at each others' faces with nasty, slopping sounds.

She stayed at the front, throwing herself into a seat, gripping the arms tightly, staring blindly at a screen where people in a black-and-white world pawed and kissed to the accompaniment of invisible violins. She wondered, briefly, where the black-and-white people kept their orchestras, then she closed her eyes and thought about Theresa.

When she had finished thinking, the matinée was over. So she followed them out, the girls with wrinkled blouses and shy smiles, the boys with streaks of lipstick on their faces. There were uniforms everywhere; it looked as if the whole of England and half the United States had come home on leave, while partners must have abandoned jobs for a desperate grab at pleasure.

Outside, she leaned on the window of Gregory and Porritts, watching as folk bustled past with bags and baskets, everybody looking for a queue to join, everybody anxious to hold together body and soul in a world that was still the colour of gun-metal. It seemed that ration points and the chance of a bit of fish were the only reason for continuing.

And Theresa would never be a mother; did this hurrying crowd know that?

She bowed her head against a whipping wind, turning her steps in the direction of home. Tonight, she would organize the words, write them down if necessary. Because tomorrow, she planned to do what Theresa should have done years ago. But Theresa had feared too much, had trusted too little, had eventually wiped clean a memory that hadn't coped with the truth. Tomorrow, Marie would tell Mam. And that might bring the roof down on them all.

'You're not to go anywhere near that hospital while you're in this state.' Clive pushed a teaspoonful of sweet tea against her teeth. 'Open your mouth, Ellen, or I shall fetch my tyre iron from the car and prise these jaws apart. That's better,' he said as she swallowed noisily. He placed the tea cup on the floor, then knelt at the side of the woman who was, he supposed, his stepmother-in-law.

Her mouth chattered, but no words came.

'How did you get here? Did you run?'

She nodded unevenly.

'Abigail's on her way, I phoned her. She picked up a second-hand bike last week. It's a man's, with a crossbar, but she manages. Well, you know Abigail, don't you?'

Her face was the colour of parchment. Looking at her now, he could see how she would be at the age of seventy. 'There's nothing you can do about the past, Ellen. You can't stop things that have already happened. And the good news is that she can be treated, manipulated so that arthritis won't chew at the bones. She may even lose the limp completely.'

'C . . . cut again?' she stammered.

'I don't know,' he answered truthfully. 'If the joint is seriously deformed – which it quite possibly isn't – then there will be some restructuring. But not yet. One operation at a time.'

He gripped her hand tightly. The story had tumbled out on the doorstep, reducing Ellen to a state that had reminded him of Marie. Ah yes, Marie yesterday. It all fell into place now. He glanced at his watch, knowing that the waiting room would be filling for morning surgery. As the worn cliché said, life had to go on.

Abigail burst in, thin cheeks aglow from pedalling against a bitter wind. She tore the scarf from her head, reaching immediately for the bottle clutched in Clive's free hand behind his back. She scanned the label, then tucked the container into a pocket. 'You've a full shop,' she said. 'Is Tishy coming to play the piano?'

'She's helping Mrs Tattersall.'

He hadn't said much on the telephone, because he had been anxious to return to Ellen, but there was obviously some trouble here. 'And London?' she asked quietly.

He shrugged, feeling useless. 'On his own. Marie's run off somewhere, I gather, probably to John's. I think he's got another day or so before he goes back to his training.'

Abigail drew a long breath. 'Oh well, no doubt Father will have a field day with no supervision, line his pockets while he has the chance.'

Clive stood up. 'He's running out of chances.'

She tugged at the white, starched collar of her uniform. 'What's happened now?'

'No time. Perhaps you can get Ellen to talk, but make sure she gets a dose of that.' He motioned towards her pocket. 'I would not like to be responsible in any small way for Ellen's reactions today.' He touched his wife's face, then walked out to do his job.

Ellen stared into the middle distance, a slight amount of colour arriving now in her drained cheeks. She was untidy; her hair had not been combed, while the green-and-white patterned work frock was incorrectly fastened, a missed button rising above collar level. She shifted in the seat, the familiar dark green coat slipping from a hunched shoulder.

Abigail removed the coat from the unresisting form, redid the dress buttons, combed the hair. 'You have to take a dose of this,' she said. 'It's just some extra vitamins to help you feel stronger.' The lie was delivered with a spoonful of moderately strong sedative, sufficient to keep Ellen offstage for several hours. Once Ellen was stretched out on the couch, her companion fetched an upright chair and sat stroking a pale hand until the medicine began to take effect. 'Is that better?' she asked after a few minutes.

'Yes. But why didn't Theresa tell me? I'm her mother. She never told anybody till yesterday, said she'd forgotten. Wiped it out, that's what she'd done. Scared to death.' They were good, these vitamins. She could think now, talk without tripping over the words, without screaming. 'What did he do to her, Abigail? What did he really do?'

'I don't know.' This, unlike the administering of the drug, was at least honest.

'I went out to my brother's, took Marie with me. She was the noisiest, especially when they were that age, about three, used to rile her father, so I took her out of his road. He was looking after Theresa.' She yawned and blinked rapidly. 'Theresa was no trouble. When I came back, she'd . . . fallen down the stairs. That was what he said, anyway.'

Abigail's spine stiffened, while the back of her neck pricked with cold gooseflesh. 'What did the doctor say at the time?'

Ellen all but smiled. 'Doctor Ferris?' Glazed eyes scanned the room. 'Used to live here, he did, with a bottle or two for company. Best thing he ever did for medicine was to step under a tram one day. He said she was all right, just bruised.'

'London did it.' This was not a question.

Ellen's irises and pupils were rolling upward now, threatening to disappear behind eyelids as sleep began to claim her. 'What else? Her insides . . . did he . . . do that . . . operation . . . all gone now.'

Ellen too had gone. Abigail took the green coat and draped it over the supine woman. She bit her lip hard, because she would not cry. The thought of him with a child, a little defenceless infant – no love in him, just hatred! The man was a psychopath, a schizophrenic freak! And he was . . . He was her father.

She walked to the window and stared blankly at the row of chimneys across the back street. Somewhere down the road towards Manchester, there was a hospital. And in a ward of that hospital there lived a man who sang hymns, another who asked for buns, a third who sat and rocked. They were locked in, tended by people who themselves seemed inadequate. Two or three times a week, those 'dangerous' patients were the victims of insulin treatment or electroconvulsive therapy. There was something very, very wrong with this world.

She pressed her hands flat against the glass. While those poor souls suffered unnecessarily, a criminal lunatic walked free, drank beer and whisky when he could get it, attacked women, threw little girls down flights of stairs. A dreadful sense of uselessness overcame her, and she sank to the floor, hands trailing down the window as she dropped. But she wasn't fainting – no – it wasn't in her nature. She was simply sitting down. He would be weighing sugar, patting butter, selling sticks of barley sugar to children. To children. She glanced over her shoulder at the unconscious woman. Clive couldn't keep Ellen here for ever, couldn't prevent her indefinitely from taking a mother's revenge.

He came in. 'What are you doing down there?'

'Resting. Thinking.'

'I've taken a breather to look at Ellen. Ah, she's had her medicine.' He stared at his wife for a long time. 'Do you think she'll . . . well . . . do something silly, Abigail?' he asked eventually.

'That's what I was thinking about. No, I don't. She would have dealt with him already – she wouldn't have bothered coming here. I take it that Marie told her?'

He nodded. 'The girl had the sense to wait until her father had departed for work. But then Marie's faculties deserted her and she ran off.'

'I don't blame her.'

He sat at the end of the couch near Ellen's feet. 'Theresa really had forgotten, I'm convinced of that. And, of course, when the attack took place, he probably threatened her, warned her not to speak of it. She simply rubbed it out, but the fear of him remained. The shock of the operation brought it back. She remembered as soon as she came out of anaesthesia.'

'Clive?'

'Yes?'

She swallowed. 'Did he do anything else to her? Ellen thinks – with this surgery and so on – that he might have assaulted Theresa in more than one way.'

'No, she was intact, and I told Ellen that. Not functioning, but not injured in that department. Are you going to stand up now?' For one always so poised and prepared, Abigail looked positively crumpled and child-like at the moment.

'In a minute. Let me pause and be grateful that my father is not a sex maniac.' She took several deep breaths. 'But he is a criminal, Clive.'

'I know.'

'What can we do?'

He rose, crossed the room and pulled her to her feet. 'Theresa can prosecute him.'

'She won't.'

'I know that too.'

'There's Vera.' She pursed her lips, remembering. 'She can't talk, but she can think. She hated me at first, you could tell by the expression in her eyes. That was because I look like him. Then I noticed the movement in her left hand, so I got her some chalk and a child's blackboard, told her that I knew who had pushed her. She's lying there now, trusting me, almost liking me, struggling to write his name. She still has her mind, but she's trapped in a body that won't obey. It's pathetic, because she's the only chance we've got of nailing him.'

He sighed and folded her in his arms. 'She's not going to make it, love.' He prayed silently that Abigail would let go, allow it all to come out at last. This hard, uncaring wife of his felt things too deeply, kept them in a place that was inaccessible, even to him. Even to herself, he guessed.

Her body was rigid in his arms. 'Clive?'

'I'm here.'

'I want him . . . to hang. And I want to be there when he does swing.'

'They don't have public executions any more, sweetheart.'

She looked past him to where Ellen lay, so quiet, so still and tired. 'Then perhaps we shall have to arrange a private function.'

'Stop this, Abigail.'

'I will. I will stop.'

'But will Ellen?' He buried his nose in the sweet-smelling dark hair. 'She loves her children. A female with children to defend or avenge can be an unpredictable creature.'

'Ellen will follow her God. Up to a point. But I wouldn't like to be in London's shoes when this drug wears off.' She sniffed. 'Underneath all that calm, Ellen has the most awful temper.'

'Are you crying?'

'No, Clive. You should know me better than that. I never cry.'

'Hello, Terry.'

She opened her eyes and tried to smile. 'Who let you in when it's not proper visiting? And why aren't you at work?'

He grinned, his fleshy face spreading outwards towards those ridiculously small ears. 'They gave me a couple of days to sort the family out. I came yesterday and all, but you were asleep.'

'Oh.' He had regained most of his weight, was looking more like the Tom in Alice's pictures. 'How are the kiddies and who's looking after them?'

He grimaced. 'Mornings, they get that Auntie Harrison, her with the funny frocks and the tight corsets – she was at the party with us at New Year. She's a right one, I can tell you. She's got me mother crocheting for the war effort – though I've yet to see a soldier in a crocheted scarf – and she makes the lads sing "Onward Christian Soldiers" while she looks in their heads for nits.'

'I suppose this will all go in one of your stories.'

He laughed. 'I'd be done for slander or libel. But she's got a thing about nits, that woman. If she goes near a child, I'll swear the first thing she does is to pull a fine-toothed comb out of her bag.'

There was a small, uneasy silence. 'What about the afternoons?' she asked.

'A girl called Elsie. Her mother's a nurse at that home of your Abigail's. Elsie's cross-eyed, so they won't have her in a factory or on a farm. Happen they think she'd do everything backwards, but she's a bright girl. I wish they could get her eyes right. Anyway, Elsie stops till they're all in bed, then Mrs Lawson from across the street sleeps the night. It's a bit catch-as-catch-can, but we'll manage till you get home.'

'Good.' She watched him as he gazed round the ward. A dark man with a round, amiable face, Tom was rather ordinary and totally non-threatening. She liked him because he loved his children. It was comforting to know a man who loved his children.

He placed one hand on each of his knees and focused his attention on Theresa. 'Yes, it'll be nice to have you back with us again.' He cursed himself inwardly. Conversations at hospital bedsides were usually stupid, but he had hoped to make this visit special.

'Not for a week or two yet, Tom. But I want to come straight back to Bromwich Street. Don't let them take me home. I'm not really scared of him, but I don't want to be near him.'

'Your dad? Alice told me you didn't like him.'

'Nobody likes him. Promise me you'll not let them take me home.'

'I promise.' He lowered his head, studying his hands carefully, as if he were reading a book. 'I've written a story about you.'

'Oh.'

'Well, it's not really a story, more of a description or a character study.'

'Thank you.'

'See, I had to get you down on paper.' His face remained downturned. 'I had to do that first.'

'I see.'

'It helped me to know what to do.'

There was a terrible pain in her gut, and it was nothing to do with the stitches. This was just an emptiness, an awful awareness of what had been done to her, of what she had lost years ago. She clenched her teeth, determined not to think. She didn't want to think about having no babies, didn't want to remember a man standing over her, pushing, throwing, kicking . . .

'Terry?'

'What?'

'Didn't you hear me? I asked you to marry me.'

'Eh?'

'This time, you heard.'

'Oh.'

He coughed and raised his eyes. 'Is that all you can say, "eh" and "oh"? I've been practising this all the way on the bus. I thought – you know – about how well we get on together. No, it's more than that. I love you, lass. And the kiddies love you too. What's up?'

She turned away from him, feeling like a swimmer who is swivelling to breathe.

'Terry?'

'I can't.'

'What? Speak up.' He stood up and ran to the other side of the bed. 'Say it again.'

She looked up at him, her eyes brimming. 'I said I can't.'

'Why? I know I'm no oil painting, but I'd look after you. And there's bound to be work in the building trade once this war's over, so we'll be all right. I mean, I understand if you don't love me, but we're good company for one another.'

She did love him. In that moment, as in many such earlier moments, she realized that she did. He was all the things a man should be, he was good and kind and generous and she was going to cry. 'Tom, I can't.'

'Why?'

She forced the knowledge to her lips, found words for it. 'Because I can't have children. Clive told me. I think I already knew, but I made him say the words.'

He clutched at her hand. 'You've got three children,

love. I understand what's happened here, you know. Oh, nobody's said, but I guessed. I love you, girl. I've always loved you, right from when we first met and I was crazy. It was as if I remembered you from the future, and I know that sounds daft. Don't get me wrong, I worshipped Alice and I would have stuck with her happily. But I love you just as much.'

Her fingers closed around the strong carpenter's hand. He didn't shake any more, he was steady enough for both of them. 'All right,' she said simply while the tears ran freely down her cheeks. 'I love you too, Tom.'

He whooped with joy, and a passing nurse put a finger to her lips.

'Keep it between ourselves for now, and I don't want any fuss,' said Theresa. There'd be enough fuss at home after what she'd blurted out to Marie yesterday. Would Mam be safe, would any of them be safe? She would tell Tom in a minute, would tell him all of it. Once she'd found a few more words. 'Just a quiet do, and he's not to come.'

'Your father?'

'That's right, the man who kicked me down the stairs. They call him London. Billy London.'

John Duffy opened the front door and guided Marie through it. He'd had a hell of a time finding her, finally bumping into her on the corner outside Timothy White's and Taylor's chemist shop in the middle of town.

He pushed her into a chair and threw some coal on the fire. 'Mam's stopping at our Shirley's tonight, her baby's expected any minute.'

'Oh.'

Well, at least she'd said a word, even if it was just a short one. He felt as if he'd spent the whole morning with a zombie, and there was nobody to tell him why his girl was in this state! Ellen wasn't available, Mrs Tattersall had nothing to say for herself, Tishy just knitted and smiled a lot, and Marie's dad hadn't cared a fig about any of it. 'I'll make a brew,' he said, rattling the kettle to assess its contents before setting it on the fire rack. 'And there might be a bit of bread for toast when the fire sorts itself.'

She sat bolt upright, looking as if she had a poker for a spine.

'Why don't you lean back? There's no extra charge for sitting comfortable, you know.'

'He did it.'

At last! 'Did he?'

She nodded just once. 'Chucked her down the stairs. Me mam'll get him now. I told her this morning, then I ran away. Happen I shouldn't have said anything, eh?'

'I wouldn't know.' If somebody was lying in a heap at the bottom of a flight of stairs, he had better find out pretty damned quick and do something about it. 'Have I to go round and pick her up?'

'You what?'

He knelt on the rug in front of her. 'Who's hurt, love?'

'Our Theresa.'

'Aye, she's in the infirmary. Who else?'

'Everybody.'

'I see.' He didn't, but it was as well to go along with someone in this state.

She stood up quickly, causing him to drop backwards, hands moving behind himself to take the sudden shift in position. Without another word, she crossed the small room and closed the curtains. While the fire fought for new life, Marie Langden removed her coat, unbuttoned the white blouse, took the pins from her hair. With movements that were almost languorous, she slipped out of her skirt and began to peel off a stocking.

His throat was parched. 'What the heck are you doing?' The voice was not like his own; it was dry and rusty. 'Marie?'

'I want you to take it all away,' she said clearly. 'Otherwise, I'll always feel like this.'

He gulped for air. 'Like what?'

'Hating,' she replied.

He ordered his thoughts to march into line quick-smart, no standing easy, eyes right and don't look! 'Listen. Don't you think I should go and find whoever it is that got pushed down the stairs?'

'Can you travel back fourteen years, John Duffy? Can you?'

'No, I can't.'

She finished undressing, and now he could no longer obey orders, could not take his eyes away from the riveting sight. She was truly beautiful, round, soft, kissed by pale yellow firelight that flickered over her like the tongue of a lover. His body was answering; the tension in the room was like a hidden spectator. 'It's only dinner time,' he said foolishly.

'Love me.' This was an order. She took a few steps, coming close enough to pull at his shirt. He stood woodenly while she undressed his upper body, jumping to life only when her hands strayed to his belt. 'You said . . . you said none of this, Marie.'

'That was before I needed you.'

He didn't want to be needed, didn't welcome this urgency that presented itself like an extremely unwelcome intruder. 'It's not right,' he mumbled.

She looked at him squarely. 'Did you have a dad?'

'Course I did. You knew him.'

'And did your dad ever throw your Shirley down the stairs and kick her so hard that she'd always have a limp? Eh?'

He shook his head dumbly.

'Then love me, John. Because I don't like the way I feel about things. Things and people.'

He wanted to cry. For the first time in ages, he wanted to bawl his eyes out like a kid, like he'd done when they'd brought his dad home after the scaffolding had given way. 'Theresa?' he asked.

'Yes.'

'He . . . ?' There was no language for this. Everybody round these parts knew Billy London for what he was, a cruel drunk, a black marketeer, a villain in the making. But to think of that lovely kid being near-slaughtered by him . . . His blood boiled, and his body was no longer prepared for Marie. Even though she presented the most exciting vision he'd ever witnessed, he turned from her, spreading his arms wide across the mantelshelf, head bowed low while grief and anger defeated him.

Her arms crept around his middle, and he could feel her sobs, stronger than his, shaking both their bodies, could feel the heat of her tears pouring down his spine. After several minutes, they sank together on to the rug, moaning and stroking each other's faces, whispering words of grief that became sounds of comfort, taking those easy steps from anguish to love. When they finally joined, even their tears seemed to have just one source, while the pale intruder that might have lain between them had been expelled for ever.

'I don't half love you,' he said.

She almost managed a smile, her eyes crinkling at the corners. 'I could do with that toast now,' she said. 'I've had nowt to eat since yesterday.'

It seemed that everybody from miles around had crowded into the room at the back of the surgery. There was Clive with his hair all messy again, as if he'd been running his hands through it. He had a habit of doing that, did Clive. Abigail, who had made sandwiches and many pots of tea, was staring outside a lot, thinking those deep thoughts of hers. It occurred to Ellen unexpectedly that Abigail was very fond of Theresa, that she was probably taking the whole thing on herself and hiding it away. Aye, she would have to be watched, that one, because she had her father's temper all right.

Tishy had a bit of paper at the table and was crayoning, tongue protruding from a corner of her mouth. God forbid that the child should ever reach a level of understanding where she could know her own father's true criminality. Cedric stood behind Tishy, a hand on her shoulder while he made suggestions about colour and pattern. He was a good man.

Ellen closed her eyes again, pretending that she was still under the influence. Well, she wasn't really pretending, because the pain hadn't arrived yet. Expecting the pain was a pain in itself, but it was dull, like a knife that had not seen a whetstone for years.

From splinters of conversation, she had gleaned that Clive's housekeeper had spilled the beans, announcing in the shop that Mrs Langden had taken a turn and was flat out in the doctor's sitting room. This news had been relayed via Tishy to John's house, and Cissie Tattersall had told Cedric when he had called in. Probably for firewood.

Peeping through small gaps in her eyelids, Ellen looked at Marie. Poor girl, having to come out with all that at the breakfast table this morning. And she'd even waited till he'd gone, then she'd sent Tishy out too, saying she wanted a word on her own with Mam. A solid girl, she was, a daughter to be proud of. John had his arm round her. He looked sad, yet important, confident and suddenly grown up. There was something going on there, like as not . . .

Then there was Tom, who had also been sent up by Cissie. He'd called in on his way back from the hospital, wanted a word with Ellen about Theresa's leg. So they all knew about it, then. Ellen wouldn't have to keep living it in words, only in her head. They were moving about now, all closing in together. Cedric was a right mess, paint splashes on his overalls, a dark donkey jacket spilling from his shoulders. Yes, he looked about as cheerful as a moulting crow at a funeral.

The more she squinted at them and thought about them, the more funereal the situation seemed. It was if she were a corpse, a subject for ceremonial treatment, and they'd gathered to talk about her and pay their respects. But she wasn't dead, not yet, not by a long chalk. She squeezed her eyes at the clock, it was only ten past two.

There was plenty of time for her to get her head sorted, to stop feeling so muggy. And she wouldn't be needing any more of Abigail's vitamins either.

When she listened properly, she knew they weren't talking about her. No, they were discussing Theresa and how well she was going to be. But the subject they were avoiding hung in the air like a cloud. There were only two missing; there was the victim and the perpetrator, though he'd been long gone as far as Ellen was concerned. Those who stood together against him were no doubt wondering what Ellen was going to do. And she was lying here wondering much the same.

They were shifting again, separating after standing for a while in a group whose closeness had physically expressed their accord. In ones and twos they stood over her; she could see their shadows even though her eyes were tight now. Doors opened and closed quietly as they left her to rest. But not in peace.

The stillness of the empty room was loud, like a new noise. It seemed to enter her, and she breathed it in gladly, feasting on the solitude. Her heart quickened, sending the last of the drug out of her system. Stealthily, she picked herself up, pulling the green coat round her shoulders. There was a sandpaper dryness to her mouth, and she slaked her thirst by drinking dregs of cold tea from an assortment of cups. Bachelor's cups, she thought, because nothing matched. Ah well, Abigail would soon sort that out.

The door opened. 'Where are you going?'

She did not turn to the voice. 'I bet Mrs Harrison was proud of this china before half of it got broke.'

'Ellen?'

'Don't follow me, Abigail. And tell the others to keep their noses out and all.'

'But—'

'Where've they all gone?'

Abigail walked right into the room, placing herself in front of Ellen. 'You must lie down. Even a horse would need to lie down after . . .'

'After being drugged to the blinkers? Nay, lass, don't preach at me. I've a thing or two to sort out, which you likely know about. And I want you to answer my question.'

Abigail sank into an upright chair. 'Clive's back at the hospital again, seeing somebody with a broken leg and not enough sense to stay where he'll be looked after. Cedric will be back at work, Tom's gone to visit Theresa again.'

Ellen fastened her buttons, noticing that her hands did not yet take instruction quickly. 'Marie?'

'Gone with John. I think it's his last day before he goes back to training camp. They've taken Tishy back to Mrs Tattersall.'

'Good.' She placed her hands apart on the table, leaning forward so that her face was just inches from Abigail's. 'If I don't think on it today, I'll fester over it till tomorrow. There's no way that things can go on as they have been doing. I've got to make changes. And I'll only say this once, so pin back your lugholes, love. This is my problem and mine alone. I don't want anybody else in it – none of the family, anyway.'

Abigail's near-black eyes stared steadily into Ellen's slightly enlarged pupils. This little woman was right, of course. Her life needed to change today, because tomorrow would be too late and far too treacherous. And no-one could draw a map for Ellen; she would have to plot her own route. 'What are you going to do?'

'If I had the answer to that, I'd be doing it instead of standing here gassing. I shall take advice. Pass me that sandwich off the sideboard, I shall be wanting some nourishment.'

She bit into the stale bread, chewing thoughtfully as she walked to the door. Before going out, she turned and tapped the side of her nose. 'Don't forget. Keep out of it.'

Abigail listened to the footfalls, the slamming of the back gate. Something akin to panic lurked in her gorge, and she gulped back the taste of it. Had she been a believer, she would no doubt have prayed at this point.

Grimly, she hung on to the knowledge that Ellen herself believed, that the mother, even while avenging her child, would remember what the nuns had taught her: That man was born with inalienable rights. And that the first of these was the right to life itself.

She cleared the dishes. Wasn't the second right something to do with wholeness of body? Another saucer smashed, appearing to jump out of her hands of its own accord. She trembled as she watched the chips of china flying in all directions. He should be afforded no privilege under any charter, because he was not human. She swept up the pieces and tossed them in the bin.

CHAPTER ELEVEN

Ellen

As far as Ellen Langden was concerned, there was only one place where she might go in times of dire need and confusion. No doubt Abigail would think a solicitor would be involved, especially after Ellen had stated her intention to seek advice, but a lawyer could not have found balm for a wounded heart, would not have the real power, the only power that might work for Ellen.

She prayed till her knees were sore, going round and round the rosary until the prayers became meaningless and the beads grew slick with sweat. Above her head, the statue of Our Lady reached out its succouring hands, while a dozen candles burned in the holders beneath the blue and white figure. Nothing helped, not yet, not while the drug was weeping its last vestiges through her pores.

She sighed, shifting her weight back and forth between aching joints. Whatever she did, wherever she looked, she saw his evil eyes and that nasty thin mouth, saw him hurting her child, heard the screams echoing down the years.

No wonder poor Theresa had been terrified of him. The little thing wouldn't have understood what had happened, it would have been just another pain, a terrible torture inflicted by him. Why hadn't Ellen realized? Why hadn't she insisted on having the child examined thoroughly by a proper doctor? And it was more basic than that – surely a loving mother would have recognized the signs? There must have been plenty of evidence at the time, symptoms to show that the child had taken more than a simple tumble down the stairs.

What had she been doing? What had she been thinking of? Probably him and his precious shops. Aye, she'd had to juggle with time all right. Even when they'd been babies, the twins had practically lived behind a counter, while she'd been mithered to death with it all, trying to bring up two babies, keep a home and run a business with only twenty-four hours to each day.

But she could find no comfort, no excuses for herself. She had failed her child, failed both of them, for she had been unsuccessful in protecting them from the evil in their midst. She'd read the Bible once, most of it. Catholics didn't use the whole Book very often, just tending to stick to the famous stories about prophets and Jesus, but she'd read some of it in her youth. What was the name of that book, that section of it? Revelations. Yes, that was the one. It said something about the beast having a number, and its number being 666. It was his number and his number was blinking well up.

She struggled to rise from her bruised knees, paid her penny and lit another candle, this time nominating it for herself. The first candle had been for Theresa, but this new bright light was hers, it was for Ellen Langden who would soon be calling herself O'Hara again. Yes, she would change her name and give the girls the chance to change theirs if they wanted to. Every bit of him was going to be expunged from her life. She would be clean from now on. The sins and omissions of the past could not be mended, but the future was in her hands from this moment. After blessing herself, she genuflected and made for the door where she blessed herself again with holy water. Even though she knew she was going to sin today, she made the Sign of the Cross before leaving to start the deed.

An unfriendly shower gave her a sullen greeting as she left the church; she did not feel the wetness soaking into her clothes. At the Derby Street shop, she stopped to check on Cissie Tattersall's progress. 'Can you manage without me?' she asked. 'I don't feel like coming in today.'

Cissie handed out some change, then came around the

counter, her eyes and voice expressing concern. 'How's she doing?'

Ellen took a deep breath. 'She'll be all right.'

'What have they done?'

'She'll have no children.' Aye, Clive had said that it might have happened anyway, this closing of her tubes, but they could all say what they liked, Ellen knew without question that Theresa's barren state had been induced by the impact of that so-called accident.

The larger woman tutted her sympathy. 'Eeh, what a shame. She was always me favourite, was little Theresa. I can see her now with her top and whip, all them yellow curls bouncing while she played. And her eyes, lovely dark blue eyes. I'm sorry, Ellen.'

'So am I. But we're neither of us as sorry as Theresa will be. And there's somebody else who'll not be happy when I've finished.'

'Eh?'

Ellen smoothed her hair and redid her neckscarf as if preparing for a special occasion. 'I'm going home now to have a clear-out. Fetch the keys round when you've done, and call at our house in the morning to see if I'm fit for work. I'll pay you double any road. And don't worry about Tishy, she'll just sit there doing her knitting till closing time. Won't you, love?'

The saintlike face was lifted. 'I'm making you a new scarf for winter, Mam. Something to keep you warm.'

A couple of customers came in, and Cissie went to serve them. She was in a funny mood today, was Ellen Langden. Still, it wasn't surprising. That must have come as a real shock, their Theresa being unable to have babies. Happen it was just as well that Theresa seemed to fancy going in the convent, then. There'd be no point in her getting wed if she couldn't have a family. When she next looked up, Ellen had disappeared. Cissie was a bit disappointed; she'd wanted to ask all about the treatment at the doctor's house, what had they given Ellen and how had it made her feel?

Cedric Wilkinson, supposedly on his belated way to paint a bus depot in Westhoughton, honked his horn as Ellen passed him, but she didn't seem to notice. Funny, he thought. She was supposed to be sedated, wasn't she? Supposed to be lying down, just as she'd been not twenty minutes ago when they'd all left her. Aye, and she was all of a rush too, head down as if she meant business, no time to give heed when a friend sounded his horn. This was a worry, so he turned the van round and headed for Noble Street. He wouldn't speak to her, he would just keep an eye on her for a minute or two.

Percy Shaw was up a ladder cleaning his windows. 'Hello, Ellen,' he called. 'I've near done at last. Honest, you could have filled ten middens with what I found in there. We'd newspapers from 1929. And I'd swear I've used enough black-leading to poison an army. Ellen?'

She looked up at him. 'Eh?'

'I were just saying, I'm nearly ready to have our Vera home. Spotless in there, it is. Mind, that cockroach stuff is no good. I reckon we get a sturdy breed round here, they just carry on with the powder on their backs, look as though they're wearing white coats. Happen we should paint numbers on them, get a race up and run a book, eh? Anyway, I think I've got rid of the bugs in the walls, right enough, miserable hangers-on, they are. They'll not be back till the hot weather comes, at any rate.'

'What? Oh yes.'

He came down the ladder two steps at a time. 'What's up, lass?'

'She's going to be better soon, our Theresa. And I'll be having her home. See, she won't come if he's here, so I have to get rid of him. I have to get rid of him any road after what he's done. And then our Theresa will come home for a bit of a visit, won't she? Won't she?' It was as if his answer would matter, as if she needed some sort of response.

He scratched his head. 'Aye, I suppose so. What are you on about at all, love?'

'I don't know.'

'Are you ill?'

'Sickened to death, Percy, that's what I am. Sickened to death.' She walked into the house and slammed the door shut.

Percy sauntered across to Cedric's van. 'I reckon yon missus needs her screws tightening today. She doesn't know whether she's coming or going or having her money back. The lass is in hospital, their Theresa, but she's going to turn out all right. I reckon it's put Ellen a bit on the strange side.' He pulled a wry face. 'In fact, I think she's what they call traumatized. Seen a lot of trauma in my time, I have. It means shock. Aye, I'd say she's in shock.'

Cedric fixed his eyes on the door of Ellen's house. There was something wrong with her, true enough, but he wasn't going to discuss it any more than absolutely necessary. Especially with this man, who looked as if he'd never hold his water, let alone a secret. As if to confirm Percy's spoken opinion, Ellen flung open the door and strode into the middle of the street with what looked like a bundle of washing. After glancing quickly at the van, she tossed the pile on to the cobbles and went back inside.

'What's she playing at?' asked Percy. 'Them's all his shirts.'

She returned with another load which she flung on top of the first.

'Socks, shoes and underclothes,' said Percy, who was clearly ready to catalogue everything. 'What the hell's she up to?'

Cedric opened the van door. Neighbours were beginning to gather in the street, clustering together in small groups as they discussed the odd situation in muted tones. She struggled out of the house with a chair. 'What are you doing?' shouted Cedric.

'Mind your own business,' came the firm reply. 'If you must know, I'm tidying up. This is the second fire I've had on account of His Royal rotten Highness. Now, get in there, the pair of you, and fetch the sofa out of the front room.'

'Eh?' Percy staggered back a pace. 'What for?'

'I want rid. He's slept on it. I don't want nothing he's sat on, worn, slept on, breathed near.'

'But you'll have no furniture,' said Cedric.

'I'll get some new. This Utility stuff's not that bad, I've seen it in town, I'll get some ordered. Till it comes, I'll buy some second-hand things, borrow them if necessary. Go on, what are you waiting for?'

They brought out the sofa and added it to the pile. 'You'll not get new furniture without special points,' said Percy, his eyes staring in the face of such high-handed audacity. 'You have to have a good reason for getting new furniture. Like a fire.'

Her eyes glinted. 'Really?' she asked, her face a picture of impassivity. 'Then let's give them what they want, lads. Now I need you to lift the mattress off the double bed. Tishy and me can sleep on the floor tonight.'

Cedric, who was not the world's best communicator, was beyond asking questions now. He walked towards the house, dragging Percy with him. Percy turned his head as he disappeared up the steps. 'If you don't want these things, I'll have them—' He was gone, pulled into the house by his stronger companion.

When the heap in the road was high enough to satisfy Ellen, she asked Percy for a match. He looked aghast. 'Nay, it's good stuff, is that. You can't go burning nice things – and we're not allowed bonfires because of the war. What if it starts raining again anyway?'

She looked at him steadily. 'I want it lit. I want it lit now.'

Cedric set fire to the pile while the two of them argued. 'If that's what you want, Ellen, that's what you shall have,' said the large man as he bent to his task.

'Thanks, Cedric.' She stood there, staring at the leaping flames like someone who had been mesmerized. The neighbours came nearer to the fire, drawn by the excitement of the moment. Ellen Langden had gone off her rocker, she was burning her life in the street. Cedric gripped her arm. 'Come inside, love. Come on, let's go in the house.'

She looked up at him. 'I'm waiting till he comes. He's not setting foot over that doorstep, Cedric. Percy, nip in and get me poker, there's a few things here want pushing in a bit further.'

When the poker had been handed over, she used it to make sure that every item on the pyre was alight. 'That's it,' she said, a note of pure satisfaction entering her voice. 'He's gone.'

'He's bloody not,' said Percy. 'He's bloody coming.'

The crowd suddenly melted away, each member flattened against the house walls. In the middle of the street, there was just the fire and the group of three who had participated in this bizarre charade. Percy coughed. The smoke wasn't doing his heart any good, so he sneaked away towards his house, positioning himself at the top of the steps and within the safety of the doorway. From here, he had a grandstand view without actually taking part in the battle that would surely follow.

She advanced with the poker in her hand. Each step she took towards the man who had been her husband seemed to lift her chin further, while her short spine apparently extended itself by several inches as she approached the intended target. 'Come no nearer,' she yelled at last. The neighbours, who had never heard her raise her voice, not even when London had been in his cups, muttered and whispered to one another.

'What the hell do you think you're playing at?' asked London.

She cast an eye over him, taking in the jaunty stance, the good suit, the watch chain, that silly-looking bowler that sat on his head like some sort of crown. Aye, he should have decorated that over the years, stuck a few jewels in it. 'This is no game. You are out of my house, do you hear? If I ever see you round here again, I'll set our

Jack on you. This time, he'll do the job proper.'

Feeling foolish, he looked around at the watchful faces. 'Is that all my stuff? And why are you burning furniture?'

She waved the poker. 'Because it stinks of you.' Her eyes wandered up and down the street, accounting for every person present. 'Listen, all of you. This man is a bigamist. He married me while he was still wed, and I never knew till his wife and girls arrived at my door. He's a thief too. He stole money from his first wife, then left her to die of cancer. You've been buying your food from a criminal. AND HE HAS HURT MY CHILDREN! MY CHILDREN!'

He lifted his foot as if to approach her, but she gave him no chance. With the poker held aloft, she went right up to him and dropped her voice so that only he could hear what she had to say. 'You ruined my daughter,' she said, the words hissing from between clenched teeth. 'When she was a baby. I left her in your care, and you threw her about, stamped on her stomach too, from the looks of things. They've had to open her up to find the damage you did to her.'

It was then that she committed her sin, bringing the poker down on his shoulder with such force that he collapsed in a quaking mass at her feet. With great difficulty, she stopped herself from delivering a second blow. The nuns had taught her in her last year at school about the basics of moral law. If she'd had a bit more education, she might have understood what they were going on about. But there was nowt in the ten commandments about coping with a situation like this one, so her teachers had probably been telling her about basic human dignity. Well, the man deserved none, so perhaps it was as well she'd been educated no further. She grinned without smiling.

He cringed when he saw the travesty of a smile. 'You're mad,' he ventured.

'Mad, am I? I never threw a child, never broke and

301

twisted her bones. No.' She shook her head vehemently. 'You're the one with the big boots, London.' And how many times had he fractured the laws of common decency? Was it right, then, an eye for an eye? Should she finish the job? Cedric prevented any further damage by snatching the weapon from her hand.

She turned to the frightened bystanders. 'Here's the guy for the bonfire,' she shouted. 'Burn him for all I care. Have a party, buy some fireworks if you can find any. Mind, you've all had enough excitement for one day, eh?' She spun on her heel and walked into her house.

Percy ran forward and helped the dazed man to his feet. 'Here,' he said. 'You'd best come in our house till things calm down a bit.' Aye, it was a rum do, was this. Umpteen years he'd lived next door to Ellen Langden, and never a peep out of her. It was as if she'd saved it all up and couldn't hold it in any more. 'Come on, lad, up the steps. I wonder if she's give you an injury? Shall we go to the hospital just in case?'

Next door, Ellen was shaking and shivering in Cedric's arms. 'I wanted to hit him on the head with it, Cedric. I wanted his brain crushed, his life over and done with. I prayed, I prayed for God to get me through this day, and He told me what to do. It came to me in church, if I did it in the street, I couldn't kill him, not with folk watching. If I'd let him in here, I would have been behind the door with that poker. Then I would have been a murderer like him.'

Cedric tightened his hold on her; it felt as if she might fall straight to the floor if he let go. 'How do you mean, he's a murderer?'

'He'd be on his way home for a cuppa,' she said to herself. 'He often has a drink about this time, leaves Marie to fend. Well, he got more than sugar in his tea today, didn't he?'

'Ellen. Who did he kill?'

She lifted her face and looked at him. He noticed the odd fleck of silver among the blonde waves and, underneath the clear blue eyes, her lower lids were stained, like the skin of bruised fruit. 'Tell me, lass. It'll go no further, you know that. I care too much . . .' No, this wasn't the time.

'He killed my Theresa's babies.'

'Eh? Did Theresa have a baby?'

'No, and she never will, neither.'

'Oh.' He waited.

'Must have thrown her about till she got ripped open. Her insides are no good to her, so the doctors have just patched her up the best road they could. She can never have . . . she can never . . . my Theresa. If you only knew how much that girl loves kiddies. She wanted to go in the convent you know, but that wasn't for her. I always felt it wasn't for her, that she'd make a good mother some day. And any road, she were only taking the veil to get away from him. See, somewhere inside herself, she's always known too much, that girl. And he's been and gone and ruined her life, so I'm getting rid of him for good, now, today. And I can tell you for nothing, the man's got off easy.'

Cedric swallowed deeply. He felt as if something nasty had got stuck in his throat. He'd been told about the belting, the throwing downstairs, but Ellen wanted to blame her husband for more than that. And she was a grand lass, was Theresa, beautiful like her mother. What was Ellen saying? He couldn't take it in, it was too much for him to cope with.

'When that Alice died, Theresa grabbed little Alison. It was like she knew that was her only chance, her last chance of motherhood. She lives with them now, down Bromwich Street. With this Tom and his mam and the three kiddies. She'll have to spend all her life borrowing other folks' children, 'cos she can't have none of her own. He did that, Cedric. Likely drinking at the time, and happen she was making a bit of a noise. He hates anything female. When we had a cat, we had to have a male, and they smell. Aye, he's took his revenge on women all his life. Summat to do with a woman that was cruel to him once, I reckon. But a little girl, a helpless child? He is Satan, I'm sure he is.'

'Will you sit down while I make a brew, Ellen? We could both do with something hot and sweet, I reckon.' The situation was well beyond him now.

'Just hold me a minute, lad. Stick hold so I know there's good men in this world. I know how you feel about me, I don't want to hurt you. But you're a comfort, Cedric. You've done your best, been as good a friend as you could be. Aye, even though you stood by him with his bigamy, you were never anything but kind to me. You likely didn't know what to do at the time any road, and you didn't know me proper. He's a frightening man, he brings the worst out in all of us.'

He began to cry, allowing huge man-tears to drip into her hair. 'Oh, Ellen. I'm going to kill him.'

'There's a long queue for that.'

'How could he? What makes a man go like that?' he sobbed.

'Evil. We're all among evil. There's good and there's bad, and we choose. He chose the black side. Come on now, this is no trouble of your making. Dry them tears and get to the table. I'll cope some road. I'll get us a cup of tea.'

He managed to fall over the rug, the table and the chair before finally seating himself. She steadied him along the way, guiding his clumsy body until it collapsed in a distressed bundle on the tablecloth. He buried his face in his hands. 'I should have stopped him all them years ago.' His voice arrived muffled. 'I could have prevented all this messing.'

'And I wouldn't have had my Marie and my Theresa. Aye, and Tishy and Abigail too. I've got my girls, Cedric. Now, do you think you can manage a drink without scalding yourself? I've never known anybody have so many accidents as what you have.'

He lifted his tear-stained face. 'It's only when I'm here,

near you. I'm not so bad on me own. Well, not quite as accident-prone.'

'Glad to hear it. Well, I feel a bit better now. As long as he keeps his face out of here.' She was making a brave attempt to lighten her tone.

'Where will he go?'

'Back where he comes from, I hope.'

Cedric shook his head. 'Nay, he'll hang about. I think he wants his shops back. He'd do anything to get his shops back.'

She stared hard at him. 'He'd have to kill five of us for that.'

'Watch out.' His voice was quiet. 'You're going to need eyes in the backs of your heads, all of you. After what you've just told me, I think he'd stop at nothing.'

She lifted the kettle from the hob. 'If anything does happen, remember what you've just said to me.'

'Why don't you go to the police?'

Ellen frowned as she pondered this question. 'They've had enough, my girls. I shall have to tell them now about him being a bigamist, 'cos I've told the neighbours. I can't put them through any more. No, he'll not do anything, Cedric. His reign's over.'

'Is it? Are you sure?'

She lifted her chin. 'Aye, and mine's just starting. There's nothing more that man can do to us.'

'I wouldn't know, lass.'

Her eyes flashed dangerously. 'Just let him try, Cedric. Just let him try, and next time he'll get the poker across his skull. Don't worry about us. There comes a time when you know God's on your side. Mind, I shouldn't talk about God while there's murder in me. Do you want a scone?'

'No. I couldn't swallow anything solid, just a cup of tea. This has fair sickened me.'

She smiled, but the smile did not touch her eyes. 'I'll go and find Marie in a minute. I'd best tell her about London before anybody else does it. She'll have to run the shop on her own now. Happen I can shift Cissie between the two shops, mornings in one and afternoons in another. She's not eighteen, my Marie. That business is a lot for a girl her age. And she must wonder sometimes if she's going to spend all her life on Deane Road. I'll work something out.'

He looked at her and marvelled that she could think of practicalities at a time like this. As if reading his thoughts, she said, 'We've got to carry on the best road we can, Cedric. There's forms and stuff to fill in, because both my girls are nearly due for registration.'

'Eh?'

'War work.'

His mouth gaped. 'They're only lasses.'

She waved a spoon at the sky. 'Aye, and they're only lads, them Germans that keep chucking bits of metal out of the sky. It's full mobilization, lad. Everybody gets to have a go.'

'They'll be exempted, Ellen.'

She puffed out her cheeks, exhaling through puckering lips that almost caused a whistle. 'Happen they will be. Our Theresa, when she gets right, will be tied down with kiddies so that a man can work. And she might be written off because of . . . because of her leg.' Her face had taken on that murderous expression again.

'Don't dwell on it.'

'I won't.' She smoothed the tablecloth with the flat of her hand. 'Marie's a grocery manager, so she'll be stopping where she is, I shouldn't wonder.'

'Aye, you're right. I just wish I lived a bit nearer, then I could keep an eye out for you. What if he stops next door with Percy? Have you thought of that?'

'He'll not stop. I won't allow it.'

'But—'

'I won't allow it. I've made me mind up, Cedric. He is out of Daubhill and Deane. One show of his face, and my brothers go for blood. I've kept them out of this since . . . since last time they were needed. And I can tell you now, if he comes in here, I'll get him myself.'

And Cedric knew from the tone of her voice, from the set of her jaw, that Billy London's days were numbered.

'What have you done about him?' Abigail's face was stiffened by lines of worry and tension. 'I thought you might do something ill-considered. Tell me. Come on, out with it. You've not come here just to look at the alterations.'

'It's going to be nice.' Ellen had wandered through the five attic rooms at the Hollywell Nursing Home, praising each one in turn as she viewed the new kitchen, bathroom, sitting room and bedrooms. 'Where will Clive do his messing about? You know, all them bottles and jars and stuff.'

'In the cellar. He'll be like a mad doctor out of the films,' said Abigail. 'He'll probably come out on Thursdays to be fed. No, seriously, he'll be carrying on with his surgeries, then I suppose he'll do his research at the weekends. He really is a crazy scientist at heart. Tell me about London, never mind Clive for now.'

'You love him.' This was not a question.

Abigail looked puzzled for a moment. 'Well, I married him, didn't I?'

Ellen placed her bag on the table and perched on the edge of a ladder-backed dining chair. 'Aye, but the love was all one-sided. I could see that, when we were at the Registry Office. He looked at you as if he thought the sun shone out of your face. But you were carrying on like it was just another day, any old day. I thought then that you'd married him to be safe. You thought that too, didn't you? Only you've gone and fell in love with him.'

Abigail sniffed. 'I haven't lost my head, if that's what you mean.'

'It's not your head I was thinking of.'

'Ellen Langden – are you being crude?'

'I am not. I was thinking of your heart. Aye, you've lost your heart to a man, and you so hard and clever. Any road,

307

as you said before, I've not come here to talk about your love life. I've hunted him out, burnt all his stuff in the middle of the street yesterday. And I clobbered him with me poker. Take that look off your face, I didn't kill him. That's what you were feared of, wasn't it?'

'I wasn't. Clive thought you might lose control and finish him. I knew you'd do something, but not that, not quite. It's funny, you're such a quiet woman, but I've always known there was a temper there.'

'Aye, the famous O'Hara fury. I don't know how I've kept it down all these years. Anyway, I gave the neighbours the story loud and clear. Not about Theresa, I couldn't let them look at her like she was a freak. Can you imagine how that would be?' She sighed heavily. 'He's in the cold now, all on his own. More to the point, he's on the loose. I couldn't have let him stay, not after what I've just learned. It doesn't bear thinking about. I keep trying not to think about it, only it's not easy to forget.'

Abigail placed herself in the chair opposite Ellen's. The sun shone through the little sloping window, and she looked almost beautiful, Ellen thought. The nose and mouth were still wrong, yet the whole picture was pleasing, as if Abigail had found herself at last. The girl was happy, and Ellen was glad about the happiness. 'I've told Marie,' Ellen went on. 'About your mum and the bigamy. She wasn't all that bothered, too wrapped up in her boyfriend going off for basic training and not getting many more leaves till embarkation. There's just Theresa now. I'll tell her this afternoon.'

'Not yet. She's had enough for the moment.'

'Aye, happen you're right. Does she know what the operation was?'

'Clive had to tell her, yes. It seemed that she already had her suspicions – female intuition and all that. They'll have put her in the picture properly by this time, I should imagine. It's a pity. If any one of the four of us is cut out to be a mother, it's Theresa. She worships that little girl. Yet it was looking after the children that finally wore her out.

But I'm glad it happened, Ellen, in a way. She must have been suffering untold misery, and the pain could have gone on for years. Still, at least that's over now. She'll have no more discomfort of that nature.' Seeking a change of subject, she asked, 'How's Tishy?'

'Fine. You're not thinking of bringing her here, are you? I notice there's two bedrooms.'

Abigail hesitated before replying. 'If you don't want her or can't manage her, we'll take over. I know she can be difficult. Though a lot of that is my fault.'

'Oh? And why do you say that?'

'I was jealous of her. I gave her a hard time. Even lately, I've been cruel to her. You see, I was told all my life that she was special, and that I had to look after her and make life easy for all of us. Everywhere I went, I had Tishy tagging along behind me. I was an unpleasant child, with very few saving graces. In fact, I'm not a terribly pleasing adult.'

'You're an honest one, I'll give you that. And I don't want to lose Tishy. She's part of my family now, and I can't imagine life without her. Oh, I know she can be hard work. Did you know she's got herself fixated with hands?' Ellen nodded, her eyes twinkling briefly with a merriment that hadn't shown for a while. 'Summat to do with a hand in the dark. She wears blinking gloves at the table, Abigail. She says nice people wear gloves. This hand in the dark must have had no glove on. I don't know. She has me potty at times. But I love her.'

'Yes. Everybody loves Tishy.' Was that a note of regret in her voice?

'We love you and all. You're one of mine too. Lilian left you to me, so you two are my daughters. Now, let's go and have a look at poor Vera. I seem to spend all my time at sickbeds just lately. Has she made any strides?'

'Not really. I'm massaging her left hand twice a day, trying to get her to write. She's still *compos mentis*, you see.'

'Eh?'

'I think you'd say she has a full set of chairs at home. Which is a shame, because she'd almost be better off if she didn't have any awareness. As things are, she must feel terribly trapped by a body that won't obey her brain. There's no speech. Although she is making noises now.'

'Will she get any better?'

Abigail shrugged and lifted her arms. 'Who knows? The human brain is a complex item. Perhaps she will improve in time. Come on, I'll show you where she is.'

Ellen stared down at the woman who had lived next door for more years than she cared to remember. She looked old, did Vera. Old, shrivelled and finished. 'How are you, lass?'

Vera grinned and salivated profusely. She gave the impression of a death's head, all teeth and bone, not much flesh covering her skull. But then, she always had been on the thin side. 'Ugh,' she managed.

Abigail picked up a small, wood-framed blackboard. A crude and wavery letter L was printed in chalk across its centre. 'It took her an hour and a half to do that. It's L for London, isn't it, Vera? Raise that hand to say yes.'

The hand flickered.

Ellen looked puzzled. 'What are you on about at all, Abigail? L for London? What does that mean?'

Abigail looked steadily at the woman in the bed. 'He did this to her. I knew it the night it happened, could tell from his face. It's my opinion that Vera threatened him, that she had some information he wanted her to keep quiet about. He crippled her. Isn't that right, Vera?'

The hand moved again.

'Eeh, good God in heaven,' said Ellen, a hand to her breast. 'Is she going to have him put away?'

'Make up your own mind about that,' said Abigail. 'There's not much she can do lying here, is there? I can't see her giving evidence in court. But she feels better now that we understand properly. And I'll look after her, she's not going back to that house. We're getting her a wireless tomorrow, something to occupy her mind. Because she does still have a mind, Ellen. Vera is fully aware of what's going on around her, she's still very much with us.'

Ellen patted the wax-like right hand. 'Vera, what can I say to you? He's a wicked bugger, and that's swearing, and I never swear. You don't know the full story, love. I can't tell you about all the awful things he's done, I can't bring myself to speak about them. But to leave you in this state – well – it's as bad as murder, isn't it? Shall I tell the police?'

'Waste of time,' said Abigail. 'Remember how icy it was that night? You'd have the devil of a job to prove that she didn't just slip, and he would deny any involvement, of course. Vera can't speak up, you see. So, we're unable to do much about this without a witness.'

Ellen's hand moved to her throat where nausea burned. 'Percy says London's staying at the Salvation Army. I wonder what the Sally Anns would say if they knew what they were harbouring? It's as if I find something out about him every day, another crime that he's committed. Will there ever be an end to it? I wonder what he'll try next?'

Abigail shrugged. 'There's only the family now, the five of us that stand between him and his precious shops. He'd have to pick us all off one at a time, wouldn't he? Even he won't try that, Ellen. He can't wander about Bolton leaving a trail of carnage and evidence. No, I think you'll find he'll disappear now. Perhaps he'll go back to London.'

'Aye, happen he will. Is there anything I can do for Vera? I feel a bit responsible.'

'I've told you, we'll look after her. The responsibility is a shared one, remember that. The man may be your husband, but he is also my father. Mine, Tishy's, Marie's and Theresa's. Whatever damage he's done, we share the burden.'

'You're a good girl.'

'Ugh,' said Vera, and they could tell from her eyes that she agreed.

A week after Theresa's operation, Ellen was walking through town, going to pay for some second-hand furniture. Pigeons flew around the civic buildings, and there was a false hint of spring in the air. Newness. Everything seemed fresh and wholesome. He had gone, disappeared into thin air, not a trace of him. Theresa was getting better, Marie was mourning the fact that her boyfriend had gone off to Manchester for more training. Abigail was doing well, while Tishy carried on much the same, quiet then suddenly excitable. Life was good. As long as she didn't think about Theresa at the age of three, life was satisfactory.

She was passing Gregory and Porritts on her way to Bradshawgate when she heard the clip-clop of hooves and the rattle of wheels. The vehicle drew into the kerb just as she reached the corner. 'Hey,' called a voice that made her shiver. 'Wait, I just want a word with you.'

He held the reins attached to a sad pony. His clothes were different; he was wearing a brown overall with a money-belt tied round the middle. On his head, looking ridiculously incongruous, sat the usual bowler.

'I've nowt to say,' she mouthed quietly.

He climbed down from the seat at the front of the flat cart. 'I never did it,' he said without preamble.

'Never did what? Are you talking about Theresa or Vera?'

He blanched and tripped backwards a pace. 'What?'

She glanced round. It was safe enough here, out in the open. 'Abigail says you attacked Vera. It'll go to court if Vera gets talking again. Abigail's always known you did that, right from the start. I just wish there'd been a witness.' She inhaled deeply. 'As for what you did to my daughter, don't talk to me about it, else I'll clobber you here in front of everybody. You did it. There's no excuse for you. God won't find any excuses for you either. Aye, you'll burn in hell. There's no punishment bad enough for you, I reckon.'

He was obviously trembling. 'I'm living in a shack,' he said, taking a desperate stab at pathos. 'On Dobson's land, near the gypsy site.'

'Good.'

He waved a hand towards the cart. 'I deliver peat.'

'As long as you don't deliver it up Daubhill and Deane. Keep away if you know what's good for you.'

He hesitated, unsure of what to say next.

'Have you finished?' she asked, her tone even and pleasant. 'Do you mind if I get on with my errands?'

'What if I'm sorry?' he mumbled into the check scarf that surrounded his neck.

'Eh? Speak up, I can't hear you.'

'I said what if I'm sorry?'

She shrugged lightly and hoisted the shopping bag up her arm. 'Makes no difference to me.'

'I thought your Church went in for forgiveness?'

She stared hard at him. 'Happen it does. And happen I don't.'

He bared his teeth like an animal ready to strike. 'I'll get you,' he said softly. 'You're not making off with my shops and my houses without me having some revenge. Watch out for me.'

'Shall I get the police now? Is that what you want? Shall I send them up to the Hollywell, see if Vera Shaw's any better? Shall I tell them to study registers from Bow and Bolton, look at marriage lines? And do I tell them you attack little girls? Eh? Or do you think Lilian's evidence of your thieving would be enough?'

He watched her as she turned and ran into Bradshawgate. The hatred frothed over again, making him catch his breath against the bile in his mouth. Vera Shaw hadn't said anything, she couldn't say anything, Percy had told him that. No, the specialists had agreed that Vera would be unlikely to utter another word as long as she lived. As for the other business – Lil, the money, the kid's 'accident' – it had all happened so long ago – why couldn't this stupid bloody wife just forget it? Ellen flaming

O'Hara. He would get her, he would sort out all of them.

His whole life had been spoilt by women. A dead mother, grandmothers who hadn't cared, aunts who had cast him out into orphanages. No matter where he turned, his existence was destroyed by the female of the species.

He would be meeting Percy for a drink tonight. Perhaps Percy could keep an eye on things for him, tell him what was going on at number nine. Yes, he could pretend concern about his family, find out when would be his best opportunity. For what, though?

The exhausted pony responded to the whip, pulling away as soon as his shanks were stung. The passenger on the cart steered the rein towards Breightmet. He would think of something, by hell he would.

It was an envelope larger than normal, about ten inches by five, buff-coloured and with no stamp anchored to the corner. Where the stamp should have sat, the words BY HAND were printed in neat, sloping capitals. Something turned in her chest, a warning, perhaps, and she kicked the item away from the door with the toe of her clog.

As this was Saturday, Tishy had gone to keep her regular lunch appointment with Abigail, so Ellen was grabbing a peaceful hour while Cissie coped. And this envelope had intruded on her promised solitude.

She picked it up, turned it, weighed it in her hand, then carried it through to the table while she made a cup of tea. But it seemed to have a life of its own, this message, as if it were ordering her to shape herself. Even before the kettle began to sing, she had slit the flap.

It was thick, whatever it was. She drew the bundle out, and a sheet fell away from the majority of the pages, which were secured by a metal clip. The separate leaf floated from her hand, and she bent to retrieve it from the rug. It was a letter, handwritten in the same angled style she'd noticed on the envelope. Lower down the page, there was a postscript in a hand she knew well.

The Hawthornes,
Bromwich Street,
Haulgh,
Bolton.

12 January 1943

Dear Mrs Langden,

I write to you formally, because it seems the right thing to do. After lengthy discussions with Theresa, it was decided that I should approach you in the proper manner.

The simple fact is that your daughter and I love one another and I am asking for her hand in marriage. As she is only eighteen, your permission is required, but we hope that you will, in any case, look favourably on our engagement.

Yours sincerely,
Thomas Crawford

P.S. Mam, we've done it this way because we never get you to ourselves. The hospital is busy, then when I get out of here, there will always be somebody round us, at Noble Street and Bromwich Street. I have read Tom's letter and I think it's very grand, like something out of a book. I love you, Mam.

Theresa

With the letter clutched against her stomach, Ellen slid into a chair. Married? Theresa getting married? Why, only yesterday, she was playing here with her top and whip . . . No, that had been a lot of yesterdays ago. How time flew. Still, it had to be a mistake, happen Ellen needed her vision testing. Or her head. But she held out the note once more, eyes narrowing over the stilted phrases until the gist finally soaked into her numb brain.

He was after Theresa. He was after that sick little girl, had gone for her while the defences were down after surgery, he was pushing her into becoming a minder for his brood.

She staggered to her feet and made a sloppy brew of tea, not warming the pot, spilling much of the water into the hearth where it sizzled as it slid towards the grate. She usually took her tea black and without sugar, but she threw in a few grains for the shock. Aye, she'd had more than her fair share of surprises just lately.

After a second cup, she picked up the sheaf that accompanied the letter. This was not handwritten. It was badly typed, obviously by a learner, someone who used just one or two fingers. There were extra spaces here and there, while many words were printed twice, first attempts having been crudely eliminated by a row of Xs.

The title was 'I Call Her Terry', and its author was, of course, Tom Crawford. She scanned the piece, her eye snagging now and then on a sentence, catching like the needle of a sewing machine on thick material.

'I was screaming, yet I could see peace standing there holding my hat. Peace has blonde hair and a face of unbearable sweetness . . . They thought I wasn't noticing, but they couldn't have been more wrong. When Blakey asked for a bun, she gave him an apple. She didn't think about giving him the apple – it was just something she did. That's how she is. She'll give you anything and she'll be happy with little or nothing . . .'

Ellen blinked rapidly. Here, in prose, was a photograph of her daughter's soul.

'In a brown room with no light, I knew I was in the presence of immense goodness. She speaks of ordinary things and colours them with love. I want to make a place for her. Above all, I want to make her laugh . . .'

Ellen's head lifted. Were it possible to capture the essence of a person, then here was Theresa's scent. Not in a bottle, but on scratchy, discoloured wartime paper.

She threw it down, rejected it, tried to deny all that she

had just read. It was there, black on white, the man loved Theresa. No-one could write like that without great affection. But he'd loved Alice too, hadn't he? And she'd only been gone nine months, poor thing. Was he fickle? Could he jump from one to another like some of them could, like London had? She shivered, drawing her chair to the heat of the fire.

'I knocked.'

She didn't move her head. 'Come in, Tom.'

He placed a flat cap on the table, his eyes riveted to the papers on the floor. She was blonde like Terry, lovely eyes and a smile that would melt the coldest heart. But she wore no smile just now. 'Terry told me to come and see you right away, and she said I'd likely catch you around this time of day. I think she's a bit frightened of telling you herself, like. And with her not being so well—'

'Who's Terry? I've got a brother called that, it's a man's name.' She hadn't intended to sound so sharp . . .

'Sorry. It was me wife – Alice – she took to calling Theresa Terry. I've never called her anything else, come to think on it. Except in writing.'

She poured the tea. 'Sugar?'

'Just one, ta.' He took the proffered cup and nursed it between fingers that were strangely slender. 'She looked after Alice, was with her when she died.'

'I know that. And I'm sorry you had to lose your wife in childbirth, Mr Crawford.'

He studied his shoes, unsure of whether to sit or remain standing. 'Terry needs looking after, Mrs Langden.'

Her eyebrows shot upward. 'I can look after me own, thanks all the same.'

He sat without asking, fiddling with the saucer, twisting it round and round on the table. 'You won't always be here.' He looked her straight in the face. 'I'm only twenty-six, I'll be around for a while yet. There'll be years when she'll have no mother. Not for a long time yet, but it'll come. She wants my three children and I think the world of her and all.'

She pushed a lock of hair from her damp face. 'What do you want to marry her for? She's already living at your house and seeing to the kiddies. She'll have none of her own, you know. And that's the reason for marriage, to have babies.'

His gaze did not waver. 'Is it? Who says so?'

Ellen dropped her eyes, unable to meet his searching stare. There was something about this man, an inner strength, a confidence that simply sat on his shoulders like a warm cloak. He certainly didn't seem the type for a nervous breakdown. 'It's in the marriage service. The main reason for getting wed is to procreate.'

He shook his head. 'Nay, that can't be right. The main reason for getting wed is because you care about somebody, care enough to change your life for them. She's such a good, honest girl. I want to be with her, Mrs Langden, I want to make sure she's all right.'

She sniffed meaningfully. 'You mean you want an unpaid nanny for your children and a nurse for your sick mother. That's all she'd be, a drudge. I stopped her going into the convent 'cos I didn't want her to finish up as a servant. She's been hurt and used for too long, has my Theresa. I can't give my permission for her to be your slave from the age of eighteen. You'd not be changing your life for her, Tom. Your life would stay much as it is now. She'd be the one with the changes, she'd be the one making all the sacrifices.'

'No.'

At last, she looked at him again. 'How do you mean, "no"?'

'We'll not be stopping down yonder in the Haulgh, Mrs Langden. Terry's got a taste for country life, you see. That there Mrs Carrington is going to rent her a cottage on the estate, a nice little stone house with four small bedrooms and a bit of space for the kiddies to run in. I'll just be a labourer on that farm. Aye, I'm willing to give up a good income for that lass of yours. I'm a carpenter, Mrs Langden, and a flaming good one. But if she wants fresh air, then she shall have it and plenty.'

'Oh. I see. All arranged then, is it? All done behind me back?'

He smiled at her. 'It's not like that. Mrs Carrington doesn't know we're wanting to get married. She's offered Terry a place anyway, and Terry asked if she could take the children and me mam. So Mrs Carrington said that would be all right as long as the children's father was prepared to do a fair day's work with her Land Army crew. She knows Terry's living with us any road. No. We've not talked to anybody before I came here.'

Ellen looked hard at him. He seemed a decent enough type, not the sort to put on anybody. But Theresa was so young, so vulnerable. 'Mr Crawford?'

'Yes?'

She took a deep breath. 'She's not strong. There's . . . a bit of a problem. I don't know as she'll be cut out for . . . the . . . the close side of marriage.'

He nodded slowly. 'Aye, I've reckoned that far meself. She's like a little girl in a lot of ways, is Terry, yet she's so grown up with it. Take the way she's sorted our Ernest and our Harold. Let me tell you, there's never been a couple of tearaways to match them. Like summat out of the wild west, they were. You've never had boys, have you? Well, them two could start a bonfire without matches, I can tell you that. She won't have any nonsense from them. Like a schoolteacher, she is, but a kind one. Don't worry, I've worked out what's what with my girl.'

'Your girl?'

He inclined his head. 'That's right. Even if we've to wait a couple of years, we'll get wed. And till then, she'll live with me anyway. Not as man and wife, there'll be none of that game. But she'll not leave them kids, I know she won't.'

Ellen knew now that she liked this man. He was kind, warm, generous and caring. Yes, he would do very well for Theresa, even though it was a shame that she must tie herself so early in life. 'I'll miss her, Tom.'

'I do realize that.'

'I don't want to let her go so young.'

'She's ready to go.'

'Aye, but only away from her father. He's not here now. She's been told he's not here.'

'She needs me. She wants me and the children. There's nowt we can do about the way she feels. And me mam likes her too. There's only you standing in our road, Mrs Langden.'

'Ellen.'

He placed the cup in its saucer. 'How can I shift an obstacle like you? Look, I'm just an ordinary bloke with failings like everybody else. I've had a rough time, lost me first wife, had a breakdown. There's not a lot I can offer, is there?'

She picked up the papers, gathering them into a careful pile, smoothing them flat with a palm. 'Only yourself, lad. Yourself and your love. You think a lot of her, don't you?'

'I do that.'

'Right. Then I'll sign your licence application. Just give her a few weeks to pull round. And I want her wed from here, from my house.'

He grinned from ear to ear. 'She said I could choose the church. So I'll see your Father about getting a wedding in Terry's parish. It'll be mixed, like. I don't want to turn. But I think she'd feel better if she got a Catholic wedding. And a white frock if we can run to one. Aye, I want her to have the best we can get for her. Happen a car to run her to church. And her sisters as bridesmaids and our lads as pages. And I want somebody to take some photos of her in her rigout.'

She began to laugh. 'Eeh, you've took the wind out of my sails, Tom. But I'll tell you this for nothing, my Theresa's got a good eye for people, doesn't pick up with just anybody. You must be a very special man if she loves you. And if you're what she wants, then you she shall have. Poor little beggar's never had her own road, happen it's time she did.'

His face reddened. 'I'll not . . . press her, Ellen. It'll all go at her own speed, even if it takes years. I know there's . . . well . . . I can tell she's been hurt some road. I won't ask questions, 'cos I can see that the answers might hurt all over again. But I do understand.'

She beamed at him. 'God sent you,' she said quietly. 'He sent you to mind my baby and for her to mind your babies. He works in some funny ways, doesn't He? She'll have a good husband and three children straight off, she won't mind having none of her own.'

'They're hers any road. Alice gave them to her just before she died. I reckon Alice realized that Terry would do for me and I would do for her. Like she were tidying up before popping off. She were very wise, my first wife. Same as a lot of women, she were clever. As if she knew things that men can't know.'

'Don't put us on a pedestal, lad. Remember feet of clay.'

He stood up. 'Will you come and see me mam? She'd come here and meet you, only she's not up to much walking since the bomb.'

'Aye, course I will. I'll come on tomorrow, see if I can find her a bit of boiled ham. How will we manage to get her moving at church?'

'Wheelchair. Though she says she's walking in for Terry. She'd do owt for her.'

'Good, I'm glad to hear it.' She shook his hand, a serious expression occupying her face. 'I know you're right for her, knew it as soon as I clapped eyes on you, even though I didn't want it to happen. She's only a bit of a kid, but she needs settling, specially now after what she's been through. And I can see how you feel about her, so I'm not worried now. Except about losing her, and that's selfish.'

'She'll be fine. Loads of country air, plenty to eat. What more can you want for her?'

'The best.' She clung to his hand. 'And it looks like she's found that for herself.'

*　　*　　*

321

Ellen sat in front of the fire, her bare feet stretched out to catch the warmth. Cedric Wilkinson had just left after doing his daily checking up on Ellen and the girls. He was a daft bat, he was. One of these days, he was going to get caught up in a raid on his way home. Love, she thought, does some strange things to folk.

Tishy and Marie were upstairs getting their things ready in case the siren went off. They shared a room now, Tishy sleeping in Theresa's bed, while Ellen had a brand new double mattress all to herself in the other room. It was nice being down here on her own, it gave her time to think. There was plenty to ponder over, too. Like which travellers were due tomorrow and how much chocolate could she get out of the Cadbury's man. And should she let that foreign chap from town put one of them fridges in at Derby Street. It was quite an honour, being asked to sell his home-made stuff, especially in the middle of a war. And they'd be able to make halfpenny ice lollies to sell when there wasn't any ice cream. It was worth a bit of thought.

She tried not to dwell on London. It was getting a little bit easier every day, though he did manage to enter her thoughts. The resulting murderous anger was frightening. No, she concentrated on the shops and her girls, all four of them. Abigail was blooming, and Ellen felt that there would be some good news from that quarter soon. Marie was a bit on the sad side with John Duffy spending a lot of time in Manchester, while Theresa was mending well in hospital. She wouldn't be coming to stop in Noble Street, not till just before her wedding. Theresa was going to stay with Mrs Carrington, get some colour in her cheeks again.

Then there was Tishy. When she thought of Tishy these days, Ellen couldn't help smiling, however low she had been feeling. She was a proper treasure, there was no other word for her. Aye, that girl's piano playing kept her new 'mam' going many a day. Then there was her knitting and her stitching and her messing about in gloves all the while. And Ellen had never seen a more beautiful girl in her life, large gentle eyes, shiny auburn hair, skin like mother of pearl. She hoped the lads wouldn't start noticing Tishy. Tishy probably wouldn't ever cope with a lad.

Marie came in. 'She's at it again.'

'Eh?' Ellen blinked in the firelight. 'Put the mantle on, love. What's she doing now?'

Marie lit the gas. 'Looking out of the bedroom window. She says the hand's in the street again.'

Ellen blew out her cheeks. 'What is she on about at all? And is she showing light? If she's showing light, we'll have our own little Hitler on the doorstep again. That ARP warden thinks he's a flaming dictator.'

Marie breathed heavily, almost moaning aloud. 'She's annoying, Mam. And I wish John was here.'

'I know, love. He'll be back, don't you fret. And you've years in front of you yet before you think about settling.'

'Theresa's getting wed. Why is she different?'

'She just is.'

'But why? Is it because of her operation?'

'Aye. There's some wouldn't take her on knowing she's not well. This Tom will look after her, he's a good man.'

'John's a good man.'

'I never said he wasn't.'

'Then why?'

'Don't start, love. I can't be doing with any more arguing.'

Marie slumped into the rocking chair. 'She's your favourite.'

'Rubbish.'

'She is. She's getting all her own road. Happen I should have an operation then I can get married.'

'Don't talk like that. You don't want to have what Theresa's had. What would John say if you couldn't have children, eh?'

Marie, ashamed of herself, dropped her chin. 'Aye, he wants children.'

'Then shut up and go and get madam, let's see what she's up to. Oh, by the way, I love you.'

The girl leapt up from the chair, round cheeks stretched into a smile. 'I know you do, Mam. And I love you and all.' She walked to the foot of the stairs. 'Tishy?'

'Yes?' The voice floated from the upper floor.

'You've to come down and stop messing with hands.' Marie faced her mother again. 'She sleeps in the gloves now.'

'Happen she's cold.'

The dark head shook slowly. 'No, she thinks gloved hands are good hands. Naughty hands, she says, don't wear gloves. Is there nowt you can do with her, Mam?'

'Not a lot, no. If anything could have been done, Lilian would have seen to it.'

Tishy walked into the room. She looked more ethereal than ever tonight, her lustrous skin whitened even further by the dark blue of her gaberdine. 'I'm ready for the shelter,' she announced. 'I want to go and sing. It's better to go and sing, in case it comes back.'

Marie squared up to her. 'In case what comes back?'

'The hand. It's gone, it was holding a cigarette. And it brought a face with it this time. I could see the face, but not what it looked like. Just white.'

Ellen stood up and lifted a milk pan from the warming shelf above the range. 'You'll have your cocoa, Tishy Langden, then you'll get back up them stairs. There's no need to be in the shelter unless we get the siren.'

Tishy studied them both. 'Nobody ever believes me,' she said sadly. 'It's a bad hand, a pushing hand. And I want a lot of sugar.' She lifted her head high and walked back upstairs.

'Well, that's telling us, I suppose,' said Ellen. 'Get some sugar out of the dresser.'

'She's daft,' said Marie.

Ellen stared into the fire. 'Is she?' she said to herself. 'I wonder.'

CHAPTER TWELVE

Tishy

She wasn't always thinking about hands. She thought about hands mostly at night, after it had gone dark, almost as dark as the first time. The darkness had always been her friend, but now she occasionally feared it, often requiring a night light to help her through the blackest times. During the day, she usually wore gloves, because her own hands were a constant reminder of something she could not piece together properly. Tishy only knew that she was sometimes frightened, that the thing that scared her was a disembodied hand, and that apart from the infrequent bouts of fear, she was happy.

Now that Mum had gone for ever, Tishy turned to Ellen, making her into a new 'mam'. She didn't call her Mam when Marie was about, though. Some instinct told Tishy that the 'Mam' part was a secret, something to be shared only with Ellen when the two of them were alone. Tishy, for all her shortcomings, was a sensitive soul, acutely aware of the feelings of others. She also realized that the people of Noble Street thought of her as a daft girl, but she was used to that, had known nothing else since childhood. Mum had always said that some minds were jealous minds, and that such envious people were often devoid of talent.

Tishy was talented, and she was fully at ease with her special gifts. The things she could not do she simply forgot about for most of the time, seldom bothering to remind herself that she really ought to learn how to count and do sums. Sums were a bore, they were for those who had no gifts. Mum had told her that. Mum had said that it didn't matter that she couldn't do her homework. Of course, Abigail hadn't been pleased. Abigail had tormented Tishy, because Abigail had been forced to Do Well, and people who had to Do Well always got angry with those who had talents instead.

Everything had gone into Tishy's hands, Mum had always believed that. Strange then that it should be a hand that haunted her, a hand from weeks and months ago, from a different cold weather time. Yes, it had been a winter hand, and she had written a poem about it. She had thought that writing a poem might make it go away, but it had started to come back of late. At first, it had just been in her dreams, floating around in the bedroom while she and Marie slept. But now it was back in real time. She recognized the difference between real and dream, because when real things happened, she could pinch herself and feel the hurt. She had pinched herself at the window last night, and she had felt it.

The poem was on her knee.

The hand, by Letticia Langden

I have two hands, one two
With fingers, so have you
But the hand is only one
And I think what it has done
Is bad out in the yard
Where the ice is very hard.

She looked through the window. There was no ice now, so she really ought to write some more, some lines about the hand coming back in the springtime, because it would soon be spring now. No, that wouldn't do any good. Writing about it hadn't sent it away the first time. She would go downstairs in a moment. Ellen would be there with the breakfast. Marie always went out earlier, because the little shop opened before the big one did. And today was to be a good day, the day of Tishy's stall.

She poked her head out on to the landing. 'Ellen? Are you alone?'

'Yes. Your breakfast's done.'

'Right, Mam. But what shall I wear?'

'Put your coat on. And that warm grey frock, the one with the long sleeves. You might get cold stood out in the street.'

Tishy did as she was told, adding grey gloves to the outfit once she was dressed. Ellen looked up as Tishy entered the kitchen. 'No, take your coat off till you've eaten. And your gloves.'

'But—'

'Take them off, Tishy. You're not supposed to eat toast with your gloves on, it's not nice. You'll get margarine all over them. Be a good girl, and don't start on about hands.'

'Can I wear them on my stall?'

'Yes.'

'And can I really keep all the money I get?'

'Course you can.'

'But I made my things out of your things.'

'That's all right.'

Tishy removed her outer garments, then sat at the table and fiddled with her toast. She didn't like eating, she was never hungry except for sweets. But eating was important, Ellen had said so many times. So she pushed a bit of toast into her mouth and chewed without enthusiasm.

Ellen stood on tip-toe in front of the mirror combing her hair. She had pretty hair, blonde and wavy like Theresa's. They both had kind eyes too, Ellen and Theresa, but Theresa's were dark while Ellen's were a gentler blue. Marie had what Ellen called 'sparklers', very bright sapphire eyes. But Ellen's were the nicest because Ellen was the loveliest person in the whole wide world and Tishy loved her.

'Come on, lass. Are you going to shape yourself? This is your big day, you're entering the world of commerce, starting your own business.'

'Oh. I thought I was just selling things.'

'That's commerce. And they're nice things, aren't they?'

'I made them myself. That's because it's all in my hands.'

'That's right. And tonight, we're going to the Grand Theatre, you and me. Our Marie will probably come too, and Clive and Abigail. Because you're making your debut, aren't you?'

'Playing the piano. Do they have a nice piano?'

'I should imagine so. There'll be other folk at talent night that need a piano, so they must have a good one. Now, go and do your teeth. I'll see if there's any more of your stuff to take down with us. I think we've already got most of it at the shop, but I'd best make sure.'

While Ellen went to look for saleable items, Tishy cleaned her teeth, then washed the dishes in the bowl that rested on the slopstone. She knew the routine by now, though she needed to be standing in the right place at the right time for her next move to be obvious. It wasn't that she was stupid. Abigail had told her that she wasn't stupid. It was because she was a dreamer with everything in her hands. It was her hands that drew the pictures, played the piano and made the things. It was her hands that wrote the stories and poems, but the dreams were in her head.

'Are you daydreaming again, Tishy?'

She smiled over her shoulder, Ellen often made her smile. 'Yes. I was thinking about my mum. Sometimes, I can still see her. Not here, I don't see her here. But in our old flat with the tubs in the garden. We had little trees in the tubs and flowers too. I see her standing there with the tablecloth after throwing crumbs for the birds. Then the bombs came.'

'Yes, love.'

'And we moved here and Mum went away. She died, of course. But I still see her in my head.'

'I know you do. I still see my mam in my head. She died when I was twelve, but she's with me all the time. You never forget your mam, Tishy. Right. Let's get you started, shall we? You've loads of customers coming, all wanting to buy your stuff. I bet there'll be a queue. If it rains, you'll have to come back in and we'll try and find you a corner on the counter.'

They linked arms as they walked up Noble Street and a few early shoppers passed them with their baskets. 'Hello, Mrs Langden. How's Tishy this morning?' And 'Have you anything special in?' and 'Nice day for the time of year'. Tishy was content. She was important today, she was going to show people what she could do. Ellen had made a sign about what Tishy could do, a big card with ALTERATIONS AND MAKE-OVERS, BONNETS, GLOVES, SNOODS, HANDBAGS written on it in big letters. No, she wasn't stupid. She could make things and people would buy them.

They set up the stall while Cissie Tattersall opened the shop. A trestle table had been borrowed from the Methodist church down the road, and Ellen covered the top with a sheet. On this they spread Tishy's store of goods. There were two little girls' dresses made out of skirts of Ellen's, beautiful items decorated with intricate smocking and rick-rack braid. Three Fair Isle pattern jumpers were laid next to these, colourfully yet tastefully crafted out of unpicked knitwear. It never failed to surprise Ellen that this girl could carry a pattern in her head, could make a complicated piece of knitting without ever counting or dropping a stitch.

But Tishy's chief raw materials were string and felt. With string she made gloves, handbags, dishcloths and snoods, all of which were now on display at the back of the table. The front of the stall was completely covered by felt bonnets. These were either pixie hoods, made by sewing two squares together, or fancier hats constructed out of four rectangles and lavishly embroidered with any thread that had come into Tishy's possession. It was plain that she had an eye for colour and design. Even the pom-poms on the pixie hoods were made to match or to contrast, little woollen balls achieved by winding wool round pieces of cardboard or milk-bottle tops. Handles on bags and ties on bonnets were of French knit wool or string which had been fed through an old cotton bobbin with four nails knocked into it.

They stood back and surveyed the scene. 'I like them crocheted mats,' said Ellen. 'And the round ones made out of French knitting. You're a clever girl, Tishy. I am that proud of you. I wish Lilian could see you now.'

Tishy smiled. 'But you said she can. You said she's in heaven with the lady and all her candles. When you took me to the church, you said that lady is Mum's best friend now. I like the lady, she is so pretty.'

'Aye, Lilian's likely got an eye on you. See, here's your first customer. I've put the prices on everything and if anybody wants change, just bring your money in the shop and I'll get it sorted.'

Ellen forced herself to step inside. It was important for Tishy to do this on her own, to get a sense of her own value. For an hour Ellen and Cissie sold groceries, newspapers, sweets and tobacco, each longing to look outside to see how the girl was faring. Cissie hovered by the window. 'Don't go out,' said Ellen. 'Let her find out what she's made of.'

'But she's not been in for change. They might have fleeced her.'

'No, they'll be helping her. You know how they all love Tishy.'

Customers came and went, often carrying things they had bought before coming into the shop. They pored over one another's purchases. 'That's too nice for a dishcloth,' said one. 'I'm putting it on me dresser under a vase. Look at them stitches, isn't she a little wonder?'

At a quarter to ten, an excited Tishy entered the shop. 'I've got nothing left,' she announced. 'But they've given me hundreds.'

Ellen grinned. Anything more than ten was 'hundreds' for Tishy. 'Here's a box. We'll put your money away.'

'No, no. I'm going on the market to buy some material. I know how to get to the market, Marie took me. It's down to the bottom of Derby Street, then turn . . .' She looked at her gloved hands then lifted the left one. 'Turn that way. And I've seen the stalls, so I can find some felt and string. And,' she said determinedly, 'Abigail told me I'm nineteen and at nineteen I can do things on my own. I want to go.'

Ellen thought for a moment. 'All right,' she said finally. 'You go and sort your business out, Tishy. Me and Cissie will be here when you get back. No dawdling and don't lose your money.'

Tishy fled gratefully, coat tails lifting in the breeze as she set off down the road.

By six o'clock, Ellen and Cissie were frantic. 'You stop here in case she comes back,' instructed Ellen. 'I'll go and look for her.'

Cissie wrung her hands. 'Eeh, that lass. She'll be the death of us all yet, Ellen. Wherever can she be all this while? And isn't she in the competition tonight?'

'Yes.' Ellen pulled on her coat. 'I'm sorry you're having to neglect your kiddies for one of mine, Cissie. But that's just what Tishy is, one of me own.' Yes, it was strange to think how quickly she had grown to care for Tishy. And for Abigail too, though in a different way . . .

'Nay, don't fret. They'll be up at me mother's anyway. I always give her money and bits for their teas. Go on, I'll stop here for as long as it takes. Our Linda will know where I am.'

The bell jangled and Tishy stepped into the shop. Ellen rounded on her. After a moment of silence that spoke volumes of shock and relief, Ellen asked, 'Where have you been, madam? We've been out of our minds since dinner.'

Tishy beamed from behind her parcels. 'I've been talking to people. It's lovely in town talking to people. And then I went on the market, then to the special shop. I was a long time at the special shop. It's wonderful there, isn't it?'

Ellen and Cissie exchanged a rueful glance. 'Tishy,' said Cissie patiently. 'You mustn't frighten Ellen like that. It's very, very naughty.'

'Oh.' Her face crumpled momentarily. 'But then I had to go to the Father man and get it blessed with water. He talked to me and gave me scones and lots of sweets and a cup of tea in his house.'

'Tishy.' Ellen leaned on the counter. 'What have you been and gone and done now? Have you been at the Catholic repository?'

The largest of the parcels was suddenly placed in Ellen's hands. 'It's for you,' said Tishy quietly. 'To go with the man with the bleeding heart.'

Ellen tore off the wrapping. It was an Immaculate Conception statue. 'Oh, Tishy,' she sighed. 'That's beautiful.'

'And it's been done with water,' said Tishy proudly. 'And I got it all by myself and material too. And beads as well, and the Father man showed me how to count on the beads, right up to twenty.' She produced a rosary from her pocket. 'And he told me about Jesus and the feeding of the five thousand, which is a lot of people, more than hundreds, and the wedding feast and Saint Peter the fisherman and a man called Judas who didn't tell the truth and it was all lovely.' She paused for breath. 'And I can go to church when I want, because the Father man says I am a child of God if ever he saw one and I can get water on my head like I had on the lady's head and then I can have the bread and then—'

'Tishy!' Ellen reached out a hand. 'Come on, slow down.'

'Then I can get confirmed,' finished Tishy, a smile of triumph playing on her lips.

'Well,' said Cissie. 'She's learned more about the Faith in one afternoon than I ever knew at school.'

'Tishy.' Ellen's tone was restrained, as usual. 'Your mother would not like any of this.'

'Wouldn't she? But I've brought her best friend to live

in our house. I even got some candles for the lady.' She smiled upon the blue and white statue. 'I am going to be a Catholic. Father Sheedy said I can be a Catholic if I want. And I want.' There was a stubborn set to her jaw. The girl's speech was becoming strange, Ellen thought. It was an absurd mixture of well-brought-up London and heavy Lancashire. 'I'm nineteen,' insisted Tishy now. 'And that's old, it's a lot of beads to count.'

Cissie smiled to herself. 'I think you've met your Waterloo, Ellen,' she said. 'She's made her mind up.'

Ellen frowned. 'But what will Abigail say?'

'I don't care,' said Tishy. 'I am old enough to know.'

'Well, there'll be no talent competition for you this week.' Ellen picked up the statue. 'We'll go next week instead. I'm not having you over-excited. And,' she looked at the perfect face of this lovely child, 'and thank you, Tishy. This is one of the nicest presents I ever got. Look a treat on my dresser, it will.'

Tishy seemed to glow with her new-found enthusiasm. 'It's Jesus's mother,' she said. 'That's who the lady is. Oh, and I managed to get some new wool. Won't it be lovely not having to unpick and wind the wool round a card? They let me have it without coupons. The woman on the stall said it matches my eyes and I could have it for three and sixpence. Is that a lot of money? And I've got some sequins for snoods and a lot of felt. And I prayed and lit a candle, but it was with my own words, the praying. Did I do it all right?'

Ellen inclined her head to hide the moisture in her eyes. 'Aye, lass. You've done it right. Come on, let's get Our Lady home.'

They were downstairs talking about why she hadn't gone to the Grand Theatre. She sat on the edge of the bed and counted the beads. A blackout at the window cut out the remaining light, so she was counting by feel, and through her gloves, which was quite a clever thing to do. She would not pull the blackout edge from the frame, she would not look out to see if the hand was in the street. It might be there and it might not. Looking and knowing would not make any difference.

'Tishy? Come downstairs now. Clive and Abigail will be leaving in a minute.'

She couldn't resist. Leaping forward, she pulled the heavy curtain back and looked out. There were no white bits, no floating hands and faces. Perhaps the thing had gone now, gone for ever like her mother.

In the kitchen, they had stopped talking about her. They were smiling as she walked into the room. Abigail said, 'Do what you like about that, Tishy.'

'Pardon?'

'About being a Catholic.'

'Oh yes. I shall do as I like anyway. I am nineteen now.'

Marie was staring into the fire. 'John will be home soon, Marie,' said Tishy. 'There is no need to be sad.'

Marie smiled at her. John was still doing a driving job at home, but everyone knew that embarkation could not be far off. 'Thanks. And what a lovely statue you bought for Mam and all with your own money.'

Tishy looked at the lady. She was so serene, so beautiful. As long as she could look at the lady, she would feel happy and calm. If she could stay in the church of Saints Peter and Paul, if she could just sit underneath the big figure of the lady, then she would always be safe.

'Are you eating?' asked Clive.

'Sometimes. There are a lot of things I don't like. There's cabbage and liver and tripe and beans. Then there's—'

'She likes sweets,' said Ellen. 'If I'd let her, she'd stuff herself with toffees and nowt else. Thank goodness they're on ration.'

Clive studied Tishy. 'Remember it's pernicious, Ellen. Get the cabbage and the liver down her if you can.'

'Am I supposed to force-feed her? You know what she's like, Clive. If she doesn't want something, then she just won't have it. I can happen get her some more fresh eggs, she seems to like an egg. But as for meat and veg, there's no chance of her eating them. Thin as a rake, isn't she?'

'But lovely with it,' said Tishy solemnly. 'That's what Mrs Banks said. That I'm a bit daft in the head but lovely with it. Am I daft in the head?'

'No,' said Abigail hotly. 'And if people say you are, then they're the silly ones. Next week, you'll get first prize. Think what you'll be able to do with five pounds.'

Tishy looked at Abigail as if for the first time. 'You're different,' she announced. 'The same, but different. Why didn't I play the piano for the audience tonight?'

'Because you're tired,' said Ellen, who sounded tired herself. 'And it's time we were all thinking about bed in case we get disturbed later on.'

Abigail stood up. 'Tishy?'

'Yes?'

'You're going to be an auntie. Clive and I are having a baby.'

Tishy grinned. 'Really? A real baby?'

'That's right,' said Clive. 'You're both going to be aunties. Come on, cheer up, Marie. There'll be plenty of days of happiness yet before John goes abroad. Aren't you pleased for us?'

'Course I am.'

Ellen was delighted. 'I knew it,' she said with a hint of satisfaction. 'When are you due?'

'In about four months. I know it doesn't show, but my clothes are getting tight.'

Marie rose to her feet and offered a hand first to Clive, then to Abigail. 'Congratulations,' she muttered.

Tishy stood to one side. 'How do you get a baby?' she asked. 'Because I want one. That can be the next thing, after I've learned to count and been made a Catholic.' She nodded, her face serious. 'Yes, I shall get a baby. I'm good at making clothes, you see. These days, they should give babies to the ones who can make the clothes.'

Clive coughed. 'Babies don't get given. They . . . grow.'

335

'Where?'

Marie giggled while Abigail shook her head. 'Don't take her on, Clive. She'll question you till the cows come home. And there are some things I would rather she didn't know.'

Ellen stepped forward and put her arms round Tishy. 'Never mind, love. You've got me and our Marie. Make a nice skirt for Marie, eh? Cheer her up for when John comes home.'

Marie stood and gazed into the fire once more. Everyone in the room could feel her terrible misery. Tishy clicked her tongue. 'Marie, I shall look after you. While John's away, I will take care of you for him.'

Marie turned, her eyes suspiciously bright. 'And you'll make me a skirt?'

'Yes. I'll make everybody a skirt.' She thought for a moment. 'Except for Clive. He would look silly in a skirt.'

Ellen wished that Theresa were here, that her other daughter could share these precious times that had arrived since London's leaving. And she said a silent prayer to Lilian, thanking her for a wonderful bequest, for leaving Tishy in her care.

She went to the door with Clive and Abigail. 'Watch her,' he whispered. 'She's running down again.'

'You make her sound like a clockwork toy,' said Ellen.

He nodded. 'Keep an eye on her spring, it could snap if she gets over-wound.'

Ellen closed the door. A terrible fear gripped her heart, seeming to squeeze it tight in an iron fist. Was Tishy ill? Was she? Then the voice floated through from the kitchen.

'You are my sunshine, my double Woodbine,
My box of matches, my Craven A,
My stick of candy for Tommy Handley,
Please don't take my coupons away.'

Ellen smiled to herself as she listened to the song Tishy

had picked up in the shelter. No, she wasn't ill. Nobody who could sing like that could possibly be ill. And even if she was a bit on the rundown side, Ellen would make her right. Even if she had to push the food down her throat, she would get that lovely girl right.

The theatre was filled to bursting point. Ellen stood in the wings with Tishy, her heart beating wildly as she thought about her vulnerable girl sitting all alone in the middle of that great stage, no-one to hold her hand, no-one to comfort her if things went wrong.

The comedian hadn't been in the slightest bit funny, and the ventriloquist had just been booed out of the theatre – the poor bloke was probably halfway to Manchester by now with the loud sounds of defeat still ringing in his ears. A weaver from Barlow's mill was singing 'Ave Maria' out of tune and the audience was getting restless again. 'Are you all right, love?' she whispered.

'Yes.' She didn't feel in the least bit nervous. She was going to go out there and make people happy. Her eyes shone with the sort of confidence that is given to very few, the few who do not question themselves.

Ellen held Tishy's hand tightly. The girl looked more beautiful than ever in the white dress, a simple garment with a high neck, long tight sleeves and a hint of fullness at the bottom of the long skirt. Aye, she looked like a bride. And she could never be a bride, and Ellen's eyes were filling up again. The first singer had been quite good. And the dancers too, the ones from a local school. Then there had been a couple of acrobats and a man who could do imitations of Churchill and Hitler and some actors off the wireless and the films. Happen one of the others would win, then. And it was important that Tishy should win.

'Don't worry, Mam. I'm going to be fine.'

'Yes, of course you are.'

As the audience clapped and hissed, the singer from

Barlow's fled into the opposite wings. 'It's you now,' said Ellen. 'Do your best.'

Tishy stepped out into the bright spotlight which followed her all the way to the piano. The stage gradually darkened except for this one bright light. It reminded her of the moon, so she started with Beethoven's Moonlight Sonata. There was a bit of shuffling at first, because these people weren't used to the classics, but once she had played a few phrases, a stillness descended upon the theatre as the pure loveliness of the music filled the great hall.

At the end of the piece, the applause was deafening. The manager waved from the wings. 'Play some more,' he whispered loudly.

She looked out, but could not see the audience. 'Do you want to sing?' she called.

'Yes,' chorused a hundred voices.

She led them through 'Sally, Sally', and 'Pack up Your Troubles', but when it came to 'Don't Go Walking Down Lovers' Lane', they let her sing by herself. They liked her. She could tell at the end that they liked her, because they wouldn't let her go. As a finale, she played two Chopin études, and there came not a single cough from the enraptured audience.

She stood at the edge of the stage bowing and curtseying until the curtains came down. The manager was shaking Ellen's hand. 'Friday nights,' he was saying. 'She'll get a resident's fee, proper wages. Just ten minutes each end of the programme.' But Ellen wasn't listening. She looked over his shoulder and saw Tishy walking towards her. 'Lass,' she said. 'You were magnificent. I'm that choked . . .' She dabbed at her eyes. 'I've never heard owt like it in all me life. It echoes here, doesn't it?'

Tishy folded her 'mam' in her arms. 'I liked that,' she said. 'Do I get the five pounds?' she asked the manager.

'Aye, you do,' he said. 'And a job. Would you like a job?'

'Yes. I'd love to come again. Will I get paid for it?'

'You will that. Start next Friday, half past seven. Just Fridays to begin with.' He turned to Ellen. 'Your daughter's a star in the making,' he said.

'Aye, but we've known that for a while. Haven't we, love? Eeh, I wish Lilian could be here.'

Tishy's pale face glowed for an instant. 'But she is. I know she is. Because I carry my mother in my head. You know, Ellen,' she said seriously, 'there is no gone for ever.'

Abigail, Clive and Marie stood with Ellen in the wings while Tishy claimed her prize in the midst of thunderous applause. She was a popular winner; several wolf-whistles reached Ellen's ears and she frowned deeply. The manager was still pestering. 'I run a small agency on the side . . . need people to entertain the workers . . . she'd be helping with the war effort.'

When the noise faded, Ellen faced him. 'Are you wanting her to go professional?'

'I reckon she could, yes.'

Ellen took a deep breath. 'Well, if she goes anywhere, one of us goes with her. She's . . . different.' Her spine straightened itself. 'Tishy is a genius,' she announced. 'And she will be treated as such. No men are to go near her, ever. I mean that, Mr er . . .'

'Morris. Geoffrey Morris, madam.' He handed her a card. 'At your disposal.'

'Well, you listen to me, Mr Morris. She'll do what she wants to do and what she's fit to do, no more than that. There'll be none of your contracts and legal doings. I won't have her tied down. This is her sister, our Abigail. And this is her other sister, our Marie. There's another one, only she's not here. There'll be one of us with her all the while. And it's up to her where she goes and what she does.'

'Whatever you say.' He rushed forward to bring Tishy from the stage.

'Ellen?' Clive's voice was ominously quiet. 'She's not well.'

'I know that. What do you say, Abigail? Marie?'

Marie swallowed. 'It's too good to keep to herself. What she can do should be heard all over. I think she should try, Mam.'

Abigail nodded. 'Let her do as she likes.' She looked thoughtfully and, Ellen mused, somewhat wistfully at her sister as she approached them. 'Yes, let her be happy, Ellen.'

She was happy.

Mr Morris, believing that he was investing in a famous future, took Tishy and Ellen all over the north west to play in factories, barracks, aircraft hangars and open fields. Tishy glowed. When the press caught up with her, she posed for photographs in Queens Park and was given rave reviews headlined 'Cockney Sparrow Turned Nightingale' and 'Keyed Up for Success'.

Tishy was a star. Like a star she twinkled and shone wherever she went, whether it was to practise at Clive's surgery on the good piano, or to play for the troops in Warrington and Manchester. But Ellen was worried. Like a comet in the heavens, Tishy might shine for a few brief nights, but would she burn herself out?

She questioned Clive who was visiting to do some sketches of Tishy for a portrait he intended to paint. 'Is she overdoing it?'

'Yes, but try stopping her.'

She glanced towards the stairs and hoped Tishy was resting out of earshot. 'Is she . . . going to die?'

He closed his portfolio. 'We all die, Ellen. She has a bad case of anaemia. Keep her warm and fed, that's all you can do for her until we isolate the deficiency.' He nodded, then said to himself, 'It's not just iron and it's not just the vitamin. If we knew what the hell it was . . .'

That night, Ellen concocted a pick-me-up consisting of raw eggs, milk, sugar, brandy and cod liver oil. After getting half of the mixture down, Tishy vomited quietly into the slopstone. Her stomach and her delicate nose refused to countenance such well-meant assistance. 'I'm sorry,' she muttered. 'But I don't like that drink. My mum tried too. She tried all kinds of medicine, but nothing stays after I swallow it.' She managed a tight smile. 'Except for sweets.'

'Don't worry, love.' And Ellen knew that Tishy's future was in God's hands. There was nothing anyone could do.

Theresa, who was recovering well and staying in Bromwich Street with Tom's family, went with Ellen, Tishy and Mr Morris to the concert at the munitions factory in Chorley. Tom met them at the door, pleased and proud to be associated with the people who would entertain his workmates. Tom had obtained permission to take the little group on a tour of the safer side of the factory, and Tishy soon made friends with the girls on the line. She laughed with them at the notice about not wearing corsets, ear rings and hairgrips, then she tried on the uniform, a ghastly coverall with a huge mob cap. 'Why can't you wear your ordinary clothes?' she asked once encased in the dreadful garments.

'Friction,' answered Tom. 'There are bombs and bullets made here.'

'What for?'

'To fight the Germans with.'

Tishy thought about this. 'Do we do the same as they do, then? Do we bomb houses and people?'

'Yes,' said Ellen. 'It's a war, you see.'

Tishy's eyes were round. 'I didn't know. I thought it was just the Germans that did bad things.'

Theresa took Tishy's arm. 'We have to defend ourselves, love. We have to get them before they get us.'

'It's wrong to kill people,' announced Tishy loudly. She was getting instruction at the church and had just learned the ten commandments. 'Thou shalt not kill,' she said now as she took off the hideous overalls.

The girl on the bench looked up at her. 'It's got to be done,' she said quietly. 'To save our children.'

This seemed to pacify Tishy. 'Well, in that case, it must be all right.'

The canteen was filled by workers, some dusty and yellowish-grey from working with cordite, many with bits of paper for Tishy's autograph. She walked the length of the hall as they cheered and whistled. Ellen sat in the front row while Mr Morris took Tishy to the piano.

She looked different, Ellen thought. As if she'd suddenly started to grow up, to think for herself. Tishy gazed at the audience, then got up from the stool. 'Thank you for inviting me,' she said.

Mr Morris grabbed Ellen's arm. 'What's she doing? We don't want no speeches out of her.' He had learned, over the weeks, that Tishy was 'a penny short of the shilling'. 'What the hell is she playing at?'

Ellen smiled and said nothing.

'I don't like what you're doing here,' Tishy went on. 'And I'm sorry that it has to be done. The things you make are killing German people and knocking their houses down. War is a terrible thing and I hope it will soon be over. But while it goes on, I am here to cheer you up.'

'Get on with it then,' hissed Mr Morris.

'Shut up.' Theresa glared at him. 'She's got rights, same as everybody else. If she wants a say, let her have it.'

Ellen's smile broadened. It looked as if Theresa could make her own mind up too, and not before time. Aye, he was likely good for her, this Tom.

Tishy took out her rosary. 'Before we begin, let's say a little prayer for the war to end.'

Mr Morris covered his eyes, slowly opening his fingers as he heard the workers joining Tishy in the Lord's Prayer. 'Dear me,' he said. 'She might have hit on something here.'

'She's hitting on nowt,' whispered Ellen. 'She's doing what she thinks is right.'

And thus began Tishy's Prayers For Peace. As she travelled round the area, whether to the Grand Theatre, to a factory, or to a public house, she got people to pray. Her simplicity, her clear faith and her ethereal beauty reached many hearts, and she was gradually hailed as a messenger from God, someone who could bring a ray of hope into days that had seemed so dark.

But all the time she was praying and making her little speeches, Tishy was aware that her true vocation was to bring fun into hard-working lives. So she would skip easily between holiness and impishness, from the classics to the music of the day, from a hymn to a bawdy music hall song and boogie-woogie.

Men fell in love with her; often, there was a sackload of mail to be answered in the evening. But Tishy, who seemed to be driven by a force too strong to be ignored, replied to every letter in the same friendly tone, managing always to maintain her distance. Never once did she allow herself to be steered from a goal that she seldom discussed, never once did she encourage the affection of an individual.

She grew paler and thinner than ever. The light in her eyes was clear and strong, yet Ellen knew that Tishy's body would not take the strain for ever. 'Can't you slow down, lass?' she asked on the morning when Tishy had just returned from church after being baptized.

'No,' came the reply. 'There is work to do. I've got some more bonnets ordered, then Mrs Fitzpatrick wants a Communion frock for Cecilia – I'm making it out of Mrs Fitzpatrick's wedding dress.'

'It's not that, it's the singing and piano playing. What about the shop? Cissie and Marie are on their own—'

'Then leave me. Let someone else go with me.'

'I will not.'

Tishy flicked through her mail. 'Another nasty letter,' she remarked. 'From somebody who thinks I want England to give up. I don't want anybody to give anything up, I just want the war to be over then there's no siren in the night. Why won't they understand? I am only praying for it all to be over.'

Ellen sighed. 'There'll always be warriors, lass, even in the most peaceful times. It's just in some folks' natures, like they can't help it. You see, there was another war, the war your . . . dad was in. Men lost their lives, some lost arms and legs. That was a German war too, so the old men want the young men to go out there and get revenge for them. That's how war gets carried on from one generation to another.' It was a simple explanation for the few impolite letters, but it would have to suffice.

They spent that evening at the Grand Theatre, where a free concert was to be held for local factory and munitions workers. The fact that she would not be paid was of no consequence to Tishy; the playing and singing of the songs was what mattered. That and the prayers. Now that she was a baptized Catholic, the prayers were very important.

Tishy's voice was not strong, but she could carry a tune, achieving high and low notes with some difficulty, yet the result was always acceptable. A small orchestra played while she stood in the spotlight, her piano abandoned for once.

She cleared her throat. Ellen stood still and tense in the wings. There was something very wrong tonight, something depressing about the way Tishy's shoulders drooped, the way her lovely auburn hair seemed to hang limply on her narrow neck.

Tishy sang. It was a complicated piece about a factory girl who was winning the war by proxy, making things out of strings and rings, a tribute to the many women who were currently oiling the wheels of war. It was plain right from the start that Tishy was not in good form, because she was mixing up 'string' and 'thing', while the more complicated words emerged from her mouth in a jumble of syllables which were covered, fortunately, by the audience's tendency to sing along with her. But Ellen noticed.

At one point, the girl actually stumbled forward, seeming to threaten to fall over into the orchestra pit. Ellen held her breath as Tishy righted herself. The conductor cued her in after a few extra bars.

Some women were actually dancing in the aisles, twisting and turning in time with the music's simple beat.

The resulting laughter drowned the fact that Tishy had stopped singing. She stood, her legs shaking visibly, hands clasped to her breast, mouth widening while she fought for air. As the final chord sounded, she fell to her knees. Ellen, heedless of the chattering audience, rushed forward and helped the girl offstage. 'You've done too much,' she whispered. 'Your head's on fire, love. Come on, we'll have to get you home some road, let's see if Mr Morris has his car.'

Tishy struggled feebly. 'I have to go back on, I have to—'

'There's no have to.' Ellen's tone was firm. 'I'm taking no nonsense from you, lady. You're ill, and if you're ill, you should be in bed. There'll be no more singing till we get you right.'

All the way home, Ellen held the girl in her arms while they both shivered in spite of the warm evening. They were frightened, and each seemed aware of the other's fear. 'I can see now, my eyes are working again,' said Tishy as they passed the market place.

A dart of pure terror shot through Ellen's breast. 'Did you go blind, then?'

'Yes, everything went away from me. I couldn't hear either. Just for a moment, I couldn't see or hear.'

'She's tired,' said Mr Morris. 'That'll be it, just a bit of exhaustion.'

'Of course,' said Ellen as bravely as she could. 'You'll be all right in a day or two, lass.'

When they reached home, Marie got Percy Shaw to help with bringing a bed into the kitchen. There were now five sleeping places upstairs, one for each of them in case they should ever be all together in the house again. The bed which was brought down was the one in which Lilian had died, and Ellen shivered as she watched it being erected in the very spot where the good woman had breathed her last.

Tishy sank exhausted on to the white sheet, her lank hair spread like a dull halo about her head. 'I feel better now,' she said. 'I'll have a nice sleep, then tomorrow I can go out again.'

'We'll see.' Ellen's voice was choked. She led Marie into the hallway. 'Go round to Cissie's,' she whispered. 'Give her the keys and tell her to carry on without me in the morning. I'll have to get Clive at nine o'clock tomorrow, before he starts his surgery. And be careful while you're out, there could be a raid.'

'What's the matter with her, Mam? She looks awful.'

'It's anaemia. Clive reckons she can't absorb her vitamins no matter what she eats. That's why I don't go on at her over-much. Even if she did eat the raw liver and cabbage, she'd still be more or less the same. Clive's been looking into it, it's supposed to be summat missing in her stomach. He says they'll be able to give her injections one day, only the stuff's not available yet. Aye, there'll be help for her. In time, like.'

Marie dropped her head. 'Will it come in time for her, though?'

'I hope so, love. I hope so.'

Percy put his head round the door. 'She fancies a dab of sherbet. Have you got some?'

Marie dug into the pocket of her coat which hung on the hall stand. 'I bought her some today. Here, Percy. Give her that and tell her not to get it on her clean bedding.'

Ellen looked at her daughter. 'You love her, don't you?'

Marie tossed her head. 'She's a pest, but you can't help liking her. It's like having a baby in the house, isn't it? I mean, I wouldn't want her to die, Mam. Or Abigail. At first, I didn't like having them here, but it's not their fault, is it?'

'No, it's not.'

'It's his fault, all of it. That bas . . .' She bit back a word that would not have pleased her mother. 'That . . . monster. He's brought all this on, years ago when he left Lilian. Abigail's a bit twisted up inside, like she has to hold everything in. Tishy's frail – anybody can see that she's poorly. Our Theresa's been scared to death, and as for me . . .' She shrugged as if lost for words.

'What about you?'

'I'm angry enough to kill him, mad enough to have a try. Sometimes, I want to go looking for him.'

'Well, you mustn't.'

'I know. But if I ever see him again, I don't know what I'll do.' She pulled on her coat and took the shop keys from her mother's hand. 'Right, I'll go and get tomorrow sorted out.'

'Eeh, love.' Ellen pulled the girl into her arms. 'You're only a child and with the responsibilities of somebody my age. You want to have some fun. When's John coming home?'

'In a few days. It'll be his last leave.'

'Then make the most of it. This war can't go on for ever.'

'Can't it?'

Ellen looked into the young-old face and said nothing. Sometimes, there were no words for sadness and anger like Marie's.

In the kitchen, Percy was perched on the edge of Tishy's bed when Ellen entered. 'She can count to twenty,' he said. 'She's just done it for me, her fingers and mine.'

'Twenty,' said Tishy, whose mouth was surrounded by orange sherbet. 'After that, it's twenty-one.'

'Thanks, Percy. I'll manage now if you want to go. How's Vera?'

'Much the same. I'll have to be getting some work if she doesn't come out of there. I mean, I'm only here as a nurse, and I've nobody to look after, have I? Any road, that there Mrs Carrington sent a message to Abigail, I can go up and help on the land, do me bit that way. It'd do me good, the fresh air, so I might take her up on it, get registered proper for the job. Will you see to the house if I go?'

'Course we will, Percy. And you want to be thinking

about getting them kiddies home now the house is nice.'
She turned to Tishy. 'Go to sleep.'

'I will.'

Percy pulled Ellen into the scullery. 'Hey,' he said in a whisper. 'Have you seen her colour? Isn't she a bit on the yellow side?'

'Yes.'

'And she's got tingling in her fingers, she said so when we were counting. And her tongue looks patchy—'

'I know, Percy.'

'That's pernicious, that is.'

'I know.'

'But there's no cure—'

'I know.' She dragged him into the yard. 'Clive's looking into it. There's doctors all over looking into it.'

'Aye, happen in peace time. But doctors is too busy to be looking into chronic disorders, Ellen. There's some at the front, and them that's left are all tied up with day to day stuff. It'll be after the war when they find a treatment.'

'I know,' she said yet again. 'And I don't want that poor girl to hear anything about this. If she's going to be took badly every so often, I don't want her worried on top.'

'I understand.' He left through the yard and Ellen stood for a moment, thinking about poor Percy and his lonely life.

Tishy was fast asleep when Ellen came into the kitchen. The pillow was dotted with sherbet and a bright orange finger poked over the top of the sheet. 'Eeh, lass,' she breathed. 'Whatever can we do for you? You look so thin – if you stood sideways behind a lamp post, we'd never see you. Still, at least you haven't eaten your sherbet with gloves, so happen you're learning.'

The back door latch rattled. 'Who is it?' called Ellen, hoping it wouldn't be him.

'It's me.'

Ellen's breath was released in a gush of relief. 'Come in, you daft bat. Honest, you had me frightened to death.'

Cedric Wilkinson stepped into the room. 'I left the van up the top and walked down the back way. I know you don't like me being seen . . .'

'Are you following me, Cedric Wilkinson? And what are you doing out at night when there's a war on?'

He stumbled over the end of the bed. 'I was at the concert.'

'Don't wake her up. What were you doing at the concert?'

'I was . . . I was . . . same as everybody else, listening and watching. And I saw her fall. I can go to the concerts, Ellen. I am a war worker.'

'Are you?' She looked him up and down. 'Did you used to go before?'

The cap slipped from mobile fingers and he bent to retrieve it. 'Before what?' he asked.

'Before Tishy started playing. Before I started going with her. Well?'

'No.'

'Oh, I see.' She leaned against the table, arms folded, ankles crossed. 'Then why have you started going now all of a sudden? Is it the prayers? Or are you keeping an eye on me, Cedric?'

He pushed the cap into his pocket. 'I'm only trying to help,' he muttered. 'Is she bad?' He waved a large hand in the direction of the bed. 'Shall I get that doctor as married her sister?'

'No, I'll fetch him in the morning. Cedric, this can't go on.'

'Oh.'

'Every time I turn round, you're on the doorstep. I mean, we've got past firewood now, haven't we? It's tapes of Aspros at the minute, isn't it? Do you get a lot of headaches? Because I do, and you're one of them.'

'I'm just trying to protect you, Ellen. He's not beyond hurting you—'

'Don't tell me, I lived with him for long enough. But the neighbours will talk. I've enough on without that, lad.

There's our Theresa living down Bromwich Street, likely doing too much for that family she's took on. She's supposed to be up at the farm having a rest, but she wouldn't stop above five minutes. Our Marie's past herself because her boyfriend's going to war, and Abigail's having a baby and she's too thin. Then there's this one . . .' She glanced at the face on the pillow. '"Look after them," Lilian said. If I hadn't looked after them, they'd have had to go back to London and all that mess with the bombs. And Abigail would have been stuck with Tishy, 'cos Tishy can't be left.' She turned and looked him full in the eyes. 'I've plenty on the plate without you adding to it.'

'But I'm not trying to add, I'm trying to help.'

'Why?'

He stared at his shoes.

'Why, Cedric? Let's have it out in the open, get the words said.'

'Because . . . I think the world of you.' His cheeks were bright red. 'I love you, Ellen.'

'Aye, and that's why you can't help me. If you love me, then it's as if I owe you something, something I can't pay back. I'm not a free woman, Cedric Wilkinson.'

'But if you were . . .'

'I don't know, and I'll never know. You're a nice man, a good man. I don't want you hanging about after me when there's young war widows out there that need caring for. There's Cissie Tattersall for a start. Why don't you start buying your Aspros off her, give her the sheep's eyes? Because I've things to think about, like Tishy here.'

He turned to leave, his shoulders drooping under the weight of great sadness.

'Cedric?'

'What?'

'Look after yourself.'

He stood in the doorway. 'If he were dead . . .'

'Stop it.'

'But if he were . . .'

'I don't know, and happen I never will. Don't be

350

thinking about folk dying, it's likely a sin. And shut that door behind you, there might be a draught on Tishy. And Cedric?'

'Aye?'

'Drive careful. Remember there's not much light.'

He placed the flat cap on his head. 'I'm not giving up,' he said softly. 'I might be shy, but I'm stubborn with it. If I can't have you, then I won't have anybody.' As if attempting to recover the shreds of his dignity, he straightened his shoulders, pulled his coat together and walked out smartly. She heard him as he tripped over the mop bucket in the back yard.

'Eeh, I don't know,' she said to herself. 'He's incurable.' The word stuck halfway down her throat as she bent to cover Tishy. Incurable was not a word she wanted to hear at the moment.

'Mam?'

'Hello, love. Go back to sleep.'

'If you kill a German, is it a sin?'

'No.' Here was another one going on about killing . . .

'So if you kill a bad person, it's not a sin?'

'I . . . I don't know. Some of the Germans aren't bad.'

Tishy thought about this. 'How do you know which is which?'

'You don't.'

Tishy sighed. 'It's all a muddle, isn't it? Can I wear my gloves in bed?'

Ellen passed the gloves over to Tishy. 'Your hands will get hot.'

'His won't. He never wears them.'

'Who?'

'The one in the yard.'

'Don't start all that again, lass. You know it only worries you and wears you out. It was just a dream, a bad dream.'

'Was it?'

'Yes. Here's your beads, do your counting and say a Hail Mary for me.'

Tishy stared at the big crack in the ceiling. Counting beads helped her to relax and she soon found herself drifting towards unconsciousness. As she took that last short step into sleep, a face floated above her, a mean face with thin lips and a hooked nose. It was fastened to the hand, that nasty white hand that pushed people in yards at night. She willed her eyes to open and saw Ellen at the range with Marie. It was just a dream, just a bad dream. Everything would be all right in the morning. Ellen would make it all better, and the hand would go away.

'Did she just faint, then?' Marie was asking.

'Yes,' answered Ellen. 'But she's doing no more concerts.'

Tishy smiled to herself. As long as Ellen cared, as long as Marie loved her, the hand didn't matter. She allowed her eyes to close and she slept for twelve full hours.

CHAPTER THIRTEEN

Tears

By the end of April 1943, Tishy had recovered sufficiently for the bed to be returned to its proper place. Forbidden by Ellen and by Clive to continue with her performances, Tishy was happy to sew and knit and to do her praying for peace in the relative solitude of the church of Saints Peter and Paul. Marie was still fretting about John Duffy, who would be leaving soon for foreign parts, while Theresa made quiet preparations for the imminent marriage to Tom Crawford. Tom, patient soul that he was, had waited long enough for Theresa, had given her several months in which to recover. In spite of the fact that she no longer appeared to fear her father, Theresa had remained in Bromwich Street, though no-one had caught sight of London for some months.

Abigail had become Ellen's most pressing problem. She had become drawn and tired, and Ellen was aware that this born work horse was doing too much for her own good. Now seven months pregnant, she seemed stubbornly unwilling to hand over the reins of the Hollywell Nursing Home. 'You'll be premature,' said Ellen on the last Sunday of the month. 'All this lifting and messing – you'll finish up in labour well before time. Isn't Margaret Hill supposed to be your deputy? Can't she take over while you get some rest?'

Abigail snorted her disgust. 'Ellen, you are worse than my own mother would have been. I am fine. In fact, I have never been so disgustingly healthy in my life. How's Tishy?'

'The same as always. She's like you, another donkey, won't do as she's told. That Doctor Sinclair says she'll never get any better if she won't eat. I've took her to see him a few times now. He's a grand old man, isn't he?'

'Clive wouldn't have any other kind living in his house and seeing half his patients. As my dear husband is fond of saying, the general practitioner is a layman's first line of defence.'

Auntie Harrison put her head round the door. 'Would you two like a cup of tea? I've a pot newly brewed, and some carrot cake too.'

Abigail turned sharply in her chair. She was learning fast to keep Auntie in her place. 'Auntie, I've told you already, I am quite capable of looking after my guests. And tea is always cold by the time you've brought it from the kitchen all the way up here. I shall make some in my own kitchen. Where's Clive?'

Auntie Harrison stepped uninvited into the room. She had made the decision some months previously to personnally supervise her nephew's marriage. The casual treatment of wedding vows, which had apparently been born with the war, should have no place in a decent Christian home. Like an evangelist with a mission, she was zealous beyond wisdom. 'He's in the cellar mixing potions. We shall be needing a potion for you, young woman, if you don't slow down. What's this I hear about you doing heavy beds again this morning?' She looked at Ellen. 'Lifting patients, Mrs Langden. This girl is actually heaving people about and moving furniture. There is no end to her naughtiness.'

Abigail took a deep breath. 'I am tired of this. I've got Clive moaning at me from one side, Auntie from another, and now you, Ellen, present me with a frontal attack. I only do what I'm capable of. There is no risk, none whatsoever.'

Ellen reached across and touched Abigail's hand tentatively. 'There's other duties, lass. There's light beds, them that can get themselves up into chairs, folk that's not too

354

bad. Why don't you see to them if you must work?'

'Because the heavy beds are the ones with the sores, the ones who need dressings and creams.'

'The ones Margaret Hill should be looking after,' snapped Auntie. 'But Margaret Hill is too busy looking after her own interests.' She looked at the ceiling. 'Loose little madam,' she muttered, her words still audible.

There followed a short silence. 'Well,' said Abigail at last. 'It's doing her no good, is it? She's getting nowhere with whatever she's pursuing.'

'With what?' asked Ellen. The air was taut with words that were about to be spoken.

'With my nephew,' answered Auntie Harrison. 'She's set her cap at him, which is why she wears it crooked and at a rakish angle. Head over heels, the woman is. She follows him round like a little lap dog. The whole thing would be sickening if it were not so ludicrous. Hmmph.' She spread her arms wide. 'Coming on duty with her face painted, smelling like an oriental flower garden, hanging on his every word. Hmmph,' she repeated. There was usually a lot of feeling behind Auntie's 'hmmphs'.

'What does Clive have to say about this kettle of fish, then?' asked Ellen, her heart seeming to miss several beats.

'Clive is blind when it comes to concerns of the heart, unless the matter involves actual medical treatment.' Abigail smoothed her hair. 'He laughed at me when I told him that Margaret is in love with him. Fortunately, he is a simple soul, so there's no danger of him running off with the better-looking woman. Also, I've got my little bit of insurance.' She patted her swollen belly. 'He's a family man, thank goodness.'

Ellen folded her arms resolutely. 'Sack her,' she said. 'Get shut once and for all.'

'And who would do her job?'

'Anybody.' Ellen's tone was stern. 'Don't tempt fate, Abigail. Be rid of her immediately if not sooner.'

'I can't. She's a registered nurse, and they're just a little bit thin on the ground these days. We're a rare breed, especially when it comes to the sort of dogsbodying that goes on here. No glamour, you see. And very few thanks.'

Auntie Harrison looked at the ceiling. 'And she does as little as possible. You don't need a registered nurse to wash bottoms, girl. Any damned fool can do what she does, anybody at all. I can change sheets and clean up a bit of mess every day. Give me a bottle of surgical spirit and I'll—'

'I need qualified help here, and they're all busy running the hospitals. We were lucky to get her in the first place.'

Abigail's mind-your-own-business tone passed unnoticed. 'You're asking for trouble,' insisted Auntie Harrison. 'Even the best of men can't resist temptation. I know he's a good boy, but that's all he'll ever be – a boy. In my opinion, they never grow up.'

'Stop it,' said Abigail. 'I won't have him watched and followed and worried about. Clive would not be unfaithful to me.'

'Oh aye?' Ellen's tone remained serious. 'It's not up to him, lass. That madam will make all the running, I can tell you that for nowt. When I came in just now, she was at the mirror in the hallway, titivating herself, smearing muck all over her chops. A pound to a penny she's in the cellar with him this minute.'

'She helps him.' Abigail struggled to her feet. 'Somebody has to do it – the poor chap has just one pair of hands. That's all she's doing, just assisting with the research.'

'Into what?' Auntie took a step forward and helped Abigail into a standing position. 'Heart problems? Now look, Abigail. He was a spoiled child and spoiled children expect their own way. He's not a wicked man, but he's as weak as the rest. Put your foot down.'

'Oh, stop it, I've had enough.' She walked through to the kitchen to make tea.

'Determined as a mule,' said Auntie. 'I'm afraid for her, Mrs Langden.'

'Ellen. Call me Ellen.'

356

'She does far too much and she's not watching that Hill person. I don't know a great deal about marriage, not at first hand, but my observations have led me to believe that women have to take charge if the system is to run correctly. She is giving him too long a leash. He needs his head pulling in before he starts to canter.'

'Clive won't leave her.'

Auntie Harrison chewed her lip and nodded slowly. 'But will she stay with him if he wanders? Ellen, I have seen him with Margaret Hill. He is plainly flattered to have the attention of such a handsome woman. There is no sense in men when it comes to this sort of thing.'

'Is she married?'

'Yes, he is serving abroad.'

'Children?'

'No.'

Ellen walked to the dormer window and stared out across the roof and into the garden. It was a lovely flat, bright and airy even though it was in an attic. Abigail had so much to lose. Yet Ellen understood this Margaret person too, because Ellen knew what loneliness was like. She didn't miss London, but she lacked somebody or something – she couldn't quite put her finger on the absent element. 'Abigail's hiding in the work,' she said now. 'The work takes her mind off Clive and the deputy matron. I'd better have a word with him, happen he'll listen to me. After all, I'm the nearest she's got to a mother.'

'I've tried. He laughed at me, said I was being a silly old auntie and not to worry my head about nothing. I felt like an absolute fool, standing there, as if I were a schoolchild being ticked off.'

'Do you think there's something in it?' Ellen turned to face the other woman. 'Is anything going on?'

'Not yet, not as far as I know. But if the relationship is allowed to develop, Abigail's pride will not take it kindly. Margaret Hill is very much in love. She finds all kinds of excuses to be alone with my nephew, and I'm sure that she intends to make off with him.'

'He won't go. He won't leave Abigail.'

Auntie smiled knowingly. 'There are several stages to go through before Clive might reach the point where a decision would be required, before he would need to make a choice. Those stages would not be tolerated by Abigail. If he is unfaithful, she will leave him.' She hoisted up the apron which had slipped below the level of her ample waist. 'I must go now and arrange for suppers, then I'm off to Saint Michael's.'

Ellen sat in thoughtful silence after Auntie had left. The woman was right. Abigail was too direct a person to tolerate any messing about from Clive. What could Ellen do? She suddenly felt terribly angry with Margaret Hill. Understanding her was one thing; agreeing with what she seemed to be doing was impossible. Why should she be allowed to get away with this? It was despicable, nothing less. Poor Abigail was pregnant, not herself at all. And the woman had waited until the pregnancy was advanced, until Abigail would have no energy, no fight. At best, Abigail would be boxing with one hand tied behind her back, and at worst, she would not even enter the arena. After all, the protection of the unborn would come high on the list of priorities.

As for Clive, Ellen wanted to give him a good hiding, which was, in her opinion, no more than he deserved. Oh, if she had him here right now . . . She bit her lip, not wanting, in her disappointment, to think about Clive.

Abigail came in with the tea tray. 'By the way, Vera Shaw is dying,' she said. 'I thought you might want to know.'

London's face flickered briefly in her mind, like a frame from a silent film. Ellen blinked against the unwanted vision. 'Percy told me yesterday. Pneumonia, isn't it?' She hoped that Vera wasn't suffering too much. Pneumonia was reckoned to be a fairly decent death, though what could be decent about cold-blooded murder? She shivered.

'Yes.' She gave the tray to Ellen. 'I wish she could have testified. I saw him the other day.'

'Where?' The older woman's spine stiffened as she placed the tray on the table. 'Where?'

'Outside here. He was on a cart selling peat.'

'Oh.' Ellen sank into a dining chair. 'I thought he'd gone back to London. Well, I hoped he had. Though I daresay if I'd listened properly to Percy's ramblings, I would have been a bit better informed.'

'No, he's very much with us, Ellen, large as life and twice as ugly. He should be in prison.'

And so should Clive, thought Ellen as she looked at the girl who stood so forlornly in front of the fire. 'Sit down, love,' she said. 'I'll pour. Then I want to go down and see Clive, ask him about Tishy.'

'He knows nothing new. It's more or less a digestive problem, that's becoming clear. She can't absorb the goodness in her food. You could give her the best food in the world and she wouldn't improve. And, of course, we can't get the best at the moment.'

Ellen poured the tea. She needed to say something, do something, didn't know where to start! 'Is everything all right? Between you and Clive, I mean.'

'Yes.'

'But what about—'

'Don't start, Ellen. Auntie has some stupid ideas, you know. Clive will never betray me.'

Ellen stirred her tea. 'What would you do if he did?'

'The question will not arise.'

'But if he did?'

Abigail raised the cup to her lips. 'I would leave him,' she said clearly before taking a sip of tea. 'If he placed no value on our marriage, then I would take myself off and rear the child alone.' She positioned the cup in the exact centre of its saucer. 'I could not bear to be second best.'

'Oh.'

'Stop worrying. The girl is infatuated, no more than that. He won't do it, Ellen. You must believe me.'

They sat without speaking for a few moments. Ellen

imagined Abigail's worry and fear; there was no need for the girl to say much. 'Theresa's wedding soon,' she said at last, seeking safer ground. 'Tishy and Marie are going to be bridesmaids, because Tishy has begged or stolen some blue material off the market.'

'Of course, I'll be too hideously swollen to be an attendant, won't I?'

'Don't be silly. We haven't got enough material, that's all.'

Abigail grinned ruefully. 'It would take a four man tent to cover me at the moment anyway. Why can't she wait till I've had the baby?'

'She's waited long enough. Living in the house with him – folk will be talking. Mind, he's a nice enough lad, and his mother's all right.' She fiddled with the handle of her cup. 'He'll be good to her.'

'Clive's good to me.'

'Did I say he wasn't?'

'No.'

'And you're sure he is?'

'Yes.'

'Abigail?'

'What?'

'If you . . . ever need me, you know where I am. I'm not saying that you will need . . . I mean . . .'

'I know what you mean.'

Ellen leaned forward. 'Your mam left you and Tishy in my care. I'm responsible for you, lass. If anything goes wrong – big or small – you've got to come to me and tell me. I don't want you ever to feel that you're on your own, because you're not. I can't be your mother, but I can always help and listen and . . . you know what I'm trying to say.' She stood up and grabbed at her bag. 'I'll go and see Clive now.'

'Thank you.'

'What for?'

'For being the nearest thing to a mother. For caring.' Her eyes were bright as if filled by tears, yet Ellen could have sworn there was a hint of . . . mischief? in their dark depths. 'It's good to know that you're there, Ellen. Especially for Tishy. If it hadn't been for you . . . well, who knows?'

'That's all right, love. Get a rest. I'll go and see his lordship.'

Ellen made her way through the home, passing several of the staff on her way. Outside Vera's room, she paused. Perhaps she should go in and say goodbye to the woman who had been her neighbour for so many years. The door was slightly ajar, and she heard two women talking almost in whispers. 'I tell you, they're at it like a pair of rabbits in that cellar,' said one.

'Don't be daft,' said a second voice. 'Missus upstairs would soon find out. There's no keeping anything from that one, eyes and ears of the world, she is.'

Ellen pushed the door with her foot. 'Watch yourselves,' she said softly. 'Careless talk costs jobs as well as lives.' She looked past the two assistants to where Vera lay propped up in the bed. Her breathing was loud and rasping, while her skin had achieved a colour that was nearly blue. 'You'd be best off seeing to her.' Ellen waved a hand towards the patient. 'Try doing the work you're paid for.' She stepped into the room. 'Can you hear me, Vera?'

The eyes opened.

'I'll tell Percy I saw you. Be good, now.' After saying a silent farewell to Vera, she cast a scathing glance in the direction of the two nurses, then marched out smartly. Poor Vera. And poor Abigail.

The corridor seemed endless. With resolution, she made firm her stride and went down towards the cellar door. Before pushing it open, she stood and listened. A girlish giggle reached her ears, and she stretched out an arm to the handle.

They stood at the bottom of the stairway, so closely intertwined as to appear eternally inseparable. Clive's fingers danced in slow ritual over the woman's spine until one hand broke free and pushed itself into a side pocket of the blue uniform, as if it were a lone hunter, a small animal seeking shelter and warmth.

Noiselessly, Ellen closed the door against this vile display, her heart rattling so fast and hard that she thought it might be heard by anyone but the profoundly deaf. Many of the residents had hearing problems – oh, what was she thinking of? She had no idea of what to do next. Abigail was upstairs with a baby in her belly. Clive was in the cellar with a loose woman. Ellen was in the hall with . . . ? With herself. She backed along the corridor and into the kitchen where Auntie Harrison ruled. In the kitchen, there would be a rum sort of sanity, but it would have to do.

The room was empty. Yes, Auntie would be teaching Sunday School, Lord help the kids. A hyacinth was dying in a pot on the window sill. On the long mantel, a clock lied about the time, its ticking hoarse and croupy. The mendacious timepiece was flanked by a brass candleholder on one side, a tarnished chrome cruet on the other. Herbs made some small effort to flourish in kidney bowls next to the dishwasher.

In a daze, she walked through the scullery, taking care not to breathe in until she had passed the open door of the sluice shed. The garden was long and wide, closed in by uneven and newly-pointed brick of a darkish pink. Plants prospered in an atmosphere of calculated carelessness. She recognized roses, honeysuckle and a triumphant magnolia in bud. The rest were a mystery; she had never owned a garden. An old man fumbled with a rake at the far end, a handkerchief knotted on his lumpy pate. He looked like a refugee from the sands at Blackpool, but he was probably the gardener. Good, youthful help was hard to come by these days. Everything was suddenly silly and meaningless, almost funny.

She leaned on the edge of a rain barrel. Abigail always did the last rinsing of her hair with rainwater. She didn't heat it, even when it was crusted with ice. A brave girl,

Abigail. She would need to be courageous. Her husband was committing adultery in the cellar.

Ellen pondered, tapping her teeth with a thumbnail. If she were to go upstairs now, if she were to tell Abigail the truth, then the girl might go into shock and premature labour. But if nothing got done about anything . . . Oh, what a muddle! That stupid, stupid man!

A shadow fell across her face. Abigail, smiling and breathless, stood in front of Ellen, feet planted wide to accommodate the new centre of gravity caused by uneven weight. 'You can come in now,' she said.

'Nice here.' Ellen's voice shook with thin defiance. Go in? To what? 'I was just having a look at the garden. Lovely flowers.'

'A jungle.' Abigail's tone had an indescribable edge to it. 'A jungle and a war zone.'

'Eh?' Ellen's heart missed another pulse. War zone? Did Abigail know, had she seen, was she on to him?

'Listen.' Abigail cocked her head to one side. 'Robins. They're killing one another. Territorial squabbles. Murderous little beasts, they are.'

'Oh.' A few more beats of time crawled past.

'I'll just have a word with Mr Benson-Bate.' She slow-marched off, hands pressed into her back as if to contain an ache. 'You go and pop the kettle on,' she threw over her shoulder.

Ellen fled while Abigail pottered off to talk to her double-barrelled gardener.

In the safety of the attic flat, Ellen failed to attain a sense of safety. She was angry. Temper boiled in the tips of her fingers and she knew that her cheeks were glowing, could feel the heat radiating from her own face.

She shut herself in the new bathroom, pushing home the snick on the door. Think, think. How to get to Clive without having to separate him from his clinging vine, without Abigail overhearing. Tomorrow. At the surgery, she would see him.

She held her wrists under cold, flowing water to soothe

the blood as it rushed through vessels near the surface. The bathroom was all shiny paint and fresh lino and newly-wed hope. It would be so easy to learn to hate Clive. She walked to the dormer and pushed at frosted glass. This was the back of the house and she could see the gardener with his rake. He was still working on the same square foot of soil, sifting out stones. There was laughter. Into view walked Clive and Abigail, arm in arm. Perhaps Abigail had no sense of smell, because that deputy matron was definitely the California Poppy type.

Ellen came out of the bathroom, through the tiny hall and into the sitting room. It was a pretty, peaceful area with nice blue-grey curtains and an old suite re-covered with pink, blue and cream chintz. There was a fitted carpet the colour of slate, re-cut from one of the bedrooms above the surgery. Pink cushions and lampshades made the room warm. Clive's grandfather's grandfather swung a proud brass pendulum in a corner. Her fingers were sweating again.

In the kitchen built by Theresa's Tom, she filled the kettle and set light to the gas. The pressure was low again, it would take an age to boil.

Back through the flat she walked until she reached the lemon room. They'd done it out in lemon so that the child's sex would not signify. There was a lamb transfer on the end of the cot. Tishy had been at the walls with her stencils, careful rows of yellow ducklings. An armless nursing chair squatted beneath the window. A blackout panel leaned against the tallboy.

Draught circled her ankles, then a door swung shut. They were standing behind her, so she arranged her features accordingly.

'I've done it.' Clive sounded triumphant.

Ellen made a half-turn. He was holding a hand out, stretching his fingers in her direction. 'Who's a clever boy, then?' There was laughter in his words.

Abigail brayed and snorted like a performing pony. 'Ellen, your face is a picture!'

Tablets, white like Aspros, sat in his palm. 'Three full quarter-grains,' he hooted happily.

Ellen would have worried for his sanity had she not decided to dislike him.

'And only God and Abigail know what I've been through to get them.' At least he was quieter now.

Abigail dug him in the ribs with a sharp elbow. 'No, it's common knowledge. The whole of Bolton knows that you are taking advantage of my deputy. It's disgraceful and careless, Clive. You will be struck off.' The 'off' came out as 'awf', as it sometimes did when she was acting what Ellen called 'cockney-daft'. 'I must go and sit down, somewhere away from Ellen. Put her out of her misery, oh husband of mine.' She sailed away like a galleon slowed by a sluggish wind. Ellen wondered briefly about modern marriage – happen Auntie Harrison was right . . .

'I can't stay,' he said. 'The police will be here shortly. I've been temporarily seconded, I do hope they give me a hat and a sheriff's badge.'

Her hands were cooling slightly. 'What the heck's going on with you two?'

He edged nearer, and she reversed unconsciously. Some folk weren't well in the head, it seemed. 'I've left enough about her person, of course,' he whispered, 'and I don't think she's any the wiser. I hope not. We don't want her to get the chance to stash it away, do we?'

He expected a response. She moved her head a fraction.

'But I had to be sure. And to be sure, I had to get close. Very close.' He rattled the tablets. 'My darling lover, alias Nurse Margaret Hill, is selling drugs at three bob a throw on her nights off. If the plan arranged by the Bolton Constabulary works, she will be in custody,' he looked at his watch, 'in about thirty seconds.'

A great rush of air entered Ellen's nose and mouth. She felt as if she had been starving herself of oxygen. 'Why didn't you tell me? I've been thinking all sorts.'

He grinned in a boyish and lopsided way. 'I was supposed to tell no-one. Abigail already knew, of course, it was she who aroused our suspicions. Margaret's attraction to me was a weapon too convenient to be wasted.'

'I should have been told,' she insisted stubbornly.

'Ellen,' he said soberly. 'Three people can keep a secret if two of them are dead. Remember that.'

Alone again in the lemon room, Ellen lowered tired bones into the nursing chair. A person was never too old to learn, she thought. And never too young to be a teacher. She felt foolish, isolated in her stupidity. How could she have doubted the solidity of this marriage? And was it her place to doubt, to believe, to meddle? She gathered up courage, scarf and handbag, then went to see Abigail.

'You weren't meant to be a witness,' came the greeting.

Ellen pursed her lips. 'How will you manage with no deputy?'

'I've got one. A detective sergeant's wife. Friends in high places, you see.'

Ellen fidgeted, moving from foot to foot. 'I didn't know what to think. There they were, bottom of the cellar stairs . . .' Mirth bubbled, exploded. 'They looked like . . . they looked . . . like Siamese twins! Ooh . . . I had to get out. The gardener . . . there's only the rake . . . holding him up.' She jackknifed against the pain of laughter. 'He's older than the residents!'

Abigail shrieked. 'He is a resident. It's therapy.'

'You . . . slave-driver! Looks like he needs crutches, never mind a rake.' She mopped her eyes, attempting to stand erect, failing completely as a series of pictures rushed through her head. 'And growing herbs in sick bowls.'

'They've been sterilized!'

Ellen, completely routed, sank in a graceless heap on the floor, her ribs aching. 'Even your plants die, so God help the patients.'

Clive put his head round the door, enjoying the scene. It was good to see Abigail laughing like that. She didn't often let go at either end of the emotional spectrum. He regretted having to spoil things. 'She's been arrested, found in possession.'

Abigail dabbed at her eyes. 'Good.'

'She made an excuse about having the medicine ready to administer, but the police are aware of our normal procedure. She would not have carried the drugs in her pockets. Ellen?' He was speaking softly, gently. She lifted her head, forcing a giggle to the back of her throat.

'I'm sorry,' he said, and his eyes were sad. 'Vera Shaw just died. Percy was with her, he did arrive in time. No, don't get up, Abigail, it's all in hand. Will someone get to that kettle before it burns to holes?' He disappeared abruptly.

Ellen struggled to her feet, an arm tangled in the strap of her bag. She remembered Vera's grey washing left to soak again in the rain, Vera languishing on the sofa, gin bottle at the ready. Children scattered to the winds, Vera singing tunelessly on her way home from the pub.

A dart of pure fear seemed to split her chest. She didn't feel like laughing any more. Her husband had just become a murderer, had been a murderer for more than a year. But now, the flickering candle called life had gone out, and he had gained his official status, was suddenly fully qualified.

'Ellen?'

'What?'

'She had a good time – in her time. Perhaps she wasn't everybody's idea of a homemaker, but she lived where she wanted to be, right at the edge.'

Ellen gulped. 'He finished her.'

'I realize that.'

'Ha! You're calm enough, you've changed your tune.'

'I've had to. Anger and hatred are no good in a hostess. And that's what I am to our little visitor.' She patted her abdomen.

Ellen went out to rescue the kettle.

Abigail continued to talk. 'Once I'm flying solo again, no doubt I shall find my temper.'

Percy would be in a state, like as not. 'Do you want this tea?'

'Make some for Percy, I think Clive will send him up.'

With the teapot at the ready, they sat side by side, prepared for the onslaught of Percy's grief. It would be terrible, Ellen realized that. A strange relationship, they'd had, a love-hate tangle that had somehow been as binding as glue. Vera would never have left Percy for one of her 'gentlemen', while Percy's bravado at going off to the Midlands still proved a source of wonder. Marriage was an odd institution, Ellen thought.

Later, she walked back home with the sad little man. Under his arm he clutched the latest medical dictionary, culled, no doubt, from the reference section of some depleted library. With such knowledge he had intended to cure his wife. In spite of all the world's learning, she had still died. Cut down by Ellen's husband.

'Will you step in for a cup of tea when we get back, Ellen?'

'Course I will.'

'And you'll come to the funeral?'

'Yes.'

He groaned deep in his throat. 'Tell you what. Every day's a bloody eye-opener, isn't it?'

It was. It definitely was. Yet again, the voices of the old ones returned, words pushed from between rotted teeth in heads encased by mouldy work-shawls. 'Aye, you've got to let them go . . .' She took Percy's arm and led him back to an empty life. The secret of which, she thought, was to put up and shut up. Her children were grown. It was time to stand alone.

It was a quietish week. The Germans were shouting about some bodies they'd found, four thousand Poles reputedly shot by the Russians and dumped in a hole. Churchill, certain that the threat of invasion was an empty one, had lifted restrictions on church bells, and York Minster chimes were due to be broadcast on the wireless. But the anger of the heartbroken Polish people did not reach Noble Street, nor did the cadence of bells. On that Thursday at the end of the month, Noble Street simply closed down. It was going to bury one of its own and nobody wanted bells.

Both shops were shut, blinds drawn and notices posted, OPEN THIS AFTERNOON. Tishy had made black armbands for all concerned, though she was not to attend the funeral. She and Abigail would stay in the house, would try to stretch two tins of salmon across a whole street. Even Mrs Banks had been moved to contribute, and her tin of luncheon meat, cut wafer thin, constituted the rest of the feast.

Percy had invested tuppence a week for Vera, just a penny for himself, right from the start of their marriage. A Wesleyan and General cheque would pay for the trappings, but Ellen had been forced to do a rescue job on Percy's suit, cleaning and patching and pressing well into the early hours. Even after all her efforts, the suit gleamed greenish in a weak morning sun.

Seven children, some old enough to stand, some in the arms of minders, were assembled at the bottom of Percy's steps. They stared at each other, strangers from the one womb, hair plastered down or plaited, a thumb in a mouth, some hands tugging at concertina stockings. The hearse grumbled, its exhaust spitting out the stench of inferior fuel. Vera's mother, a babe in her arms, wept for her wayward daughter.

Ellen watched as neighbours came through their doors, folk who had never had a good word for the dead woman. It was not a large crowd, because many were at work, but each house poured its human contents into the middle of the cobbles. In a sad grey line, they walked behind the hearse of a woman who had slipped in a December yard.

It was a short service. Even words of comfort seemed rationed in wartime, though the Methodist celebrant had probably never clapped eyes on Vera, so perhaps his brevity was understandable. There followed another short walk to a small civic cemetery, where the lean, black-garbed man spoke of glories to come. An older child sobbed while two others swapped cigarette cards between gravestones. Percy leaned on Ellen; he had been leaning for months and she'd hardly noticed.

A plain coffin of pale wood was lowered into the gaping maw. Small crumbs of earth were tossed in, first by Percy, then by the children. Ellen drew Percy's head down to her shoulder, sharing with him the scents of Brylcreem and hopelessness. She stiffened, her eyes riveted to movement several rows away.

He stood alone on a pebbled path between lines of graves, bowler clutched respectfully to his chest, head bowed in an attitude of thoughtful prayer. But there were no prayers in him, Ellen knew that. When he lifted his head, there was a stillness in his features, because he had deliberately frozen them in a shape that might accord with the sad occasion. But even from this distance, his eyes, reflecting a bright and watery sun, projected an expression that could only be termed triumphant.

Now it was her turn to depend, because her legs were offering no support. Percy, no doubt relieved by this small distraction, helped Ellen to a bench, pushing her down until her head met her knees. 'Blood to the brain, lass,' he said kindly. 'And breathe through your mouth – that'll stop the nausea.' Busy once more, needed and important, the grieving widower patted her hands and whispered words of solace, phrases designed not only for his neighbour, but also to assuage his own pain. 'Her's all right now, love. Our Vera can't feel no more hurt.' He nodded, almost excited by his new role. 'I shall watch out for thee, never fear. You've been good to me, and now it's my turn to pay you back.'

'Thank . . . you, Percy.' The murderer was standing there; he had come to make sure, to bury his crime. The thought of London's sickness overwhelmed her, making her sick.

A small hand insinuated itself into hers, sticky fingers

warm and strong. She looked up. This was Mickey, Vera's eldest. There was a shabbiness about him, a cleaned-up poverty that reeked of institutional life. His eyes, like his poor dead mother's, were at odds with one another, each greenish orb straying slightly towards the flat bridge of a snub nose. 'Are you all right, Mrs Langden?'

'Yes, I'll do.'

Eleven-year-old features were screwed up and mobile, fighting against a fear he attempted to disguise, a panic that undermined his supposed maturity. 'You'll not die like me mam?'

'No.' As he wandered off, soothed and near-adult once more, Ellen lifted her face to Percy. 'Get them kiddies home, lad. When the authorities learn you've such a big family, they'll cater for you.' She would not look across the graveyard. 'They need you, like Vera needed you.'

'Aye, we'll see.'

But she had to look, was pushed by elemental forces to look. He was gone, melted into the morning, leaving behind an unspoken threat that cast a cloud over Ellen's sun-warmed body. He was truly dangerous. Over the years, Ellen had caught only the edge of his menace, while the ultimate proof of the man's potential lay in a hole ten yards away.

Recovered, she stepped to the edge of the grave. The diggers stood by leaning on shovels, maintaining a respectful distance in spite of a desire to get finished and home to dinners. She took from her bag a carefully wrapped parcel of rosemary, tossed it on to Vera's box. Beneath her breath, she said, 'Vera, may God damn him to eternal torture.' Then, with this sin of loathing welded to her soul, she followed the rest of the party homeward.

As soon as the funeral party had disappeared around the corner, Abigail busied herself with bread knife and loaf, taking elegant, papery slices from the squarish cob. Tishy margarined the bread, then attacked two tomatoes, her tongue protruding as she counted with each division.

'Sixteen,' she cried. 'Out of two tomatoes. If I cut them in halves, I'll have . . . a lot more.'

'True. Now see what you can do with that lettuce. It looks to me as if it needs resuscitative treatment.'

'Eh?'

'Oh Tishy, you are so Lancastrian now! Not that it matters, I've grown quite fond of this strange dialect. Wash the lettuce, then open that tin of plums. Ellen's made a sponge flan and there's a jelly cooling in the kitchen. We need to put it all together for some sort of pudding. Don't forget to stone the plums.'

Playing with fruit stones was one of Tishy's favourite pastimes. She arranged them in a saucer, chanting, 'he loves me, he loves me not,' until she got to the last one – and he loved her. Then it was 'tinker, tailor, soldier, sailor—'

'Have you washed that lettuce?'

'I'll do it in a minute. What's a tinker?'

'Your father's a tinker. He travels about selling things in the street. That's what tinkers do.'

Tishy thought. 'Does he ever wear gloves?'

'I don't know.'

'Do they wear gloves, tinkers?' .

'If they have them, if someone gives them a pair. Go and see if that jelly's setting, we want it to pour.'

Tishy swished the cold jelly round the jug, then watched while her sister arranged plums in the flan case. 'Can I pour?' When Abigail nodded, Tishy poured, the fingers of her free hand crossed so that the jelly would not soak through the sponge. 'It's worked,' she breathed. 'And we've got Carnation to go with it.'

'Wash the lettuce.'

'In a minute.'

Abigail pressed a hand to her side as the child shifted, disturbing her bladder yet again. 'I'm going down the yard,' she said, removing her apron.

Tishy, who did not enjoy washing lettuce, picked out salmon bones and mixed the flesh with fine breadcrumbs to make it go further. She spread the concoction on the bread, leaving the sandwiches open to receive lettuce and tomato. When the salmon was used up, she began on the luncheon meat, trimming carefully so that spare bits could be jigsawed together for extra portions. Abigail had been gone for a long time. She was probably reading the bits of newspaper that hung from the wall.

In the lavatory, Abigail bit back a scream. There was no point in screaming, because the street was deserted, there was no-one to hear her. Except Tishy, and Tishy was useless. This, she thought grimly, was the result of doing heavy beds. She was weeks and weeks early, and the baby was coming now, probably dead, poor little thing. I am a murderer, she thought. After all my experience, I should have known better. My carelessness has killed an innocent child, and Clive will kill me.

Right. What to do? Tishy could go to the shop and get someone . . . no, the shops were closed and everyone was at the funeral. The surgery? Tishy knew her way to the surgery, she played the piano there. But it was gone eleven. The locum would be on home visits, Clive had an appointment at Townleys Hospital. The house on Derby Street would be deserted, because this was Thursday, and the housekeeper didn't do Thursdays. Thursdays were warmed-up soup from yesterday, cold meat and salad whatever the weather and . . . ooh, this was painful. Painful and quick – what had happened to that famous first stage, the stuff that was in all the manuals, those hours during which pains could be timed and counted?

She staggered up the yard, feeling her way along the scullery wall. In the house, she crawled past a round-eyed Tishy, making for the peg rug to lie panting and clutching at her abdomen.

Tishy hung over her. 'How does it get out?' she asked.

Abigail raised her legs.

'Ah.' Tishy's head nodded slowly. 'I know where the baby is. I've watched you getting fat.' She knelt beside her sister and peeled away the undergarments. 'Hold my hand, Abby.' She had not used this childhood name for years.

Abigail bore down. There was nothing else she could do, because the panting hadn't worked. The pains came thick and fast now, so close together as to be almost continuous. Lost inside the agony, Abigail ceased to care. There was a thin scream, and Tishy wasn't holding her hand any more.

In a daze, Abigail watched her stupid little sister, her sister who couldn't be trusted with anything beyond a bit of knitting. Tishy tossed the food on to the dresser, whipped off the tablecloth and wound it round a bloody bundle. With a long, delicate finger, she poked at the linen package, obviously clearing debris from a tiny mouth. The screaming grew louder and clearer while Tishy, perplexed, studied the lifeline that stretched from child to mother.

'Scissors.' Abigail's voice was hoarse. 'Knife – anything.'

Abigail propped herself against the fireguard and separated herself from her child, noticing that it was a very tiny girl. Exhausted, she keeled over, her eyes still fixed on Tishy.

The scene that followed would stay with Abigail for the rest of her life. With a bowl of warm water and some cotton wool, Tishy bathed the baby, paying close attention to eyes and ears. She wrapped the child in two towels, then fastened the miniature body against her chest, securing the buttons of her cardigan so that warmth could be shared. Wearing the baby, she emptied the bowl in the scullery, then carried it back to the kitchen.

Abigail reached up, received the container, wondering vaguely how Tishy knew that it was needed. With the afterbirth delivered, she lay back and closed her eyes.

Tishy looked round at the mess. There was no party, and everyone would be back shortly. 'What shall I do, Abigail?' she asked. 'What shall I do about the food?'

No reply was forthcoming.

She looked down at the pretty baby. 'I want her to be

called Patricia,' she said. 'Because that can be shortened to Tishy sometimes. Will you call her Patricia? Abigail?'

For an awful moment, Abigail knew that she was going to die. There was a terrible pain in her chest, the sort of pain that must surely herald some kind of occlusion, some dire trouble in her blood, perhaps a clot on a lung. The discomfort pushed its way up into her throat, but it was nothing simple, not heartburn nor any kind of reflux. No, this was much worse than that, and yet better, more wonderful, certainly powerful.

'You're crying.' The tone was almost accusatory.

'Yes.'

'Why are you crying?'

She was crying because she was alive, because her child had apparently survived thus far. She was crying because her sister, damaged though she might be, had retained all the age-old female instincts that are designed to guarantee the continuation of mankind. For ten full minutes she howled, careless of pride, setting her own precedent, almost baptizing herself. She lived, therefore she could weep.

Tishy was transfixed. 'You never cry,' she said.

'I love you,' answered Abigail in a voice unlike her own. 'You are a very clever girl.'

'And pretty too.'

'You are beautiful.'

Tishy patted her burden absently. 'Then why were you always shouting at me and hitting me?'

'I'm sorry. But impatience is a part of love, Tishy. I shall never, ever be able to repay . . .' She was off again, keening and moaning, hot tears pouring down her face.

Tishy watched her sister crying. She would never understand Abigail. As Ellen would say, never in a month of Sundays . . . oh dear. They would be here in a minute and the sandwiches were all squashed to bits, some of them stuck on the dresser mirror, one splattered all over the Sacred Heart. And the best tablecloth was ruined. Ellen would not be pleased.

The door opened. As Ellen stepped into the room, Tishy provided a descant to Abigail's main theme, her sobbing higher in pitch, faster in rhythm. 'Mam,' she cried. 'I never washed the lettuce.'

Percy, just behind Ellen, took in the scene quickly, then turned to steer all intruders out of the house. He split them up into groups, sent them into various houses, then came back to number nine, knocking hesitantly on the door to the kitchen.

Ellen poked out her head. 'Baby's here, Percy. Get to Townleys and find Clive, send for an ambulance first.'

He smiled. 'Is it a girl?'

'Yes, and she's struggling.'

He flew down the hall, cap in hand, rushing through the front doorway with a speed that was remarkable in a man with a bad heart. Vera had gone, and another little lass had come to take her place. He would get his kiddies back. Aye, even if it took all his time and energy, he would make a proper home for his family. And it didn't even matter who had fathered them, because they were Vera's children.

Theresa stood at the rickety gate, her eyes fastened to the front of the house she'd been visualizing all her life, a place she had drawn as a child at school, solid and safe, with tall chimneys, a fenced garden, a straight path to a stout front door. From some angles, she couldn't see Moor Bottom Farm, and there wasn't another dwelling in sight, because all the other farm cottages were on the far side of the main building.

She gulped greedily at the fresh country air, feeling drunk as it filled her chest. This was her own time, a few hours she had set aside after that sad funeral. She and Marie hadn't gone back to Noble Street for the . . . was party the right word? Marie had slipped away to steal a short time with John, while Theresa had come up here to stare at the top of the world. Well, it probably wasn't the actual top. The Pennines were taller than the distant moors, but these slopes provided the highest point of the life she'd known, a life that had been contained in a town that crouched in shadows cast by mills.

'Do you like it, then?'

She swivelled to look at the owner of the voice. 'Mrs Carrington.' Her eyes roamed back towards the house, her house, hers and Tom's. 'It is perfect.'

Mrs Carrington walked round Theresa and leaned on a gate post. 'Are you well now?'

'Yes, thank you. Thank you for this, for everything. And you've had your glasses mended.' They swung from the woman's short neck on a piece of string that was less than clean.

'Found a way to keep them within reach, hung the damned things about my person. Will Tom mind living up here?'

Theresa shook her head, then lifted it proudly. 'He's a writer. Writers need quiet places. And he's very good with animals,' she added hurriedly. 'He'll learn all he needs to know, Ma'am.'

'Who on earth told you to call me Ma'am? Sounds like bloody royalty.'

'My mother. She said I was to call you Mrs Carrington or Ma'am, and that I was to be respectful at all times because you're . . .'

'What am I?'

'Landed gentry.'

The grey head shook merrily. 'I certainly am, because I've landed in it many and many a day, mostly in the pig shed.' She swept a magnanimous arm across the garden. 'This is yours. Not to rent, but to keep.'

Theresa, dumbfounded, closed her mouth with a loud snap.

'The grim harvester will collect me one day, my dear, and the grasping fool government will collect my assets. Do me a favour, take this one small acre.' She strode away, then swung round, a Wellington boot crunching on a stone. 'Name's Audrey, dear. To my friends, that is.' She marched off, hands in pockets, shoulders set square against another day of toil.

Theresa opened the broken gate and propped its unevenness against the path. When she knew she was alone, she spread her arms wide as if to embrace the whole earth. Joy poured down her cheeks, and she danced shoeless on the grass, calling, 'I'm home! I am home!'

Audrey Carrington grinned widely, slipped from behind a broad tree, coughed the emotion out of her throat, then whistled all the way home.

They shared the liquorice water, counted out the wine gums, stared at the ducks. 'When are you going?' she asked at last.

'They've not told us. They don't say much, you know.'

She chewed thoughtfully. 'Where are you going?'

'Marie!'

A swan climbed out of the water and walked towards them, feet silly and clumsy on dry land. Marie tossed some bread and the bird swallowed it, a malevolent eye warning them not to expect gratitude.

'They can kill a child with their wings,' said Marie.

'Aye, if they choose.' He held out a sweet, and the creature took it, swallowed, and waddled away. 'I don't want you fretting while I'm gone. You'll be no use to me when I come back if you've fret away to nowt.'

She groaned, remembering the past hour. 'I hate funerals.'

'That's all right, they're not supposed to be funny.'

'John?'

'Hello.'

'Would you go now if you didn't have to?'

He fiddled with the toffee bag. 'I didn't have to.'

'What?' She sat bolt upright, indignation distorting her features. 'What did you say?'

He moved his shoulders lightly. 'I could have stopped, ferried lads to and from training in the truck. Yes, I could have watched them all going through their paces, then I could have chucked them on a train or a boat—'

'Then why? Why, John?'

He pointed to the swan, graceful once more as it glided soundlessly across the lake. 'See that?' he asked.

She nodded.

'That's summat to do with my reason for going.'

She shook her head.

'That's OK,' he said. 'Cos I don't understand neither.'

In a maternity bed, Abigail lay and waited. Everybody had rushed down the corridor, Clive with his hair on end again, Ellen carrying shawls and bootees, Tishy with new pride in her bearing. She ached from childbirth and from crying, and her feet were cold. In future, when she stood at the right side of the bed, at the other end of charts and thermometers, she would remember about patients' feet.

It was feeding time. Mothers around her had been given babies to hold. This was the wrong place for her, she should not be here. She would have been better in a side ward, away from all these healthy infants whose mothers had done the right things.

The Caesarian across the way was getting out of bed. It was easy to see she was a Caesarian, because she was bent like an old woman, though her face said about nineteen. A girl with twins was performing a balancing act, juggling with bottles and pillows. Both babies were screaming lustily. Their mother looked frayed.

She swivelled her eyes left, peering through the open door towards the nursery. Stealthily, she swung her legs over the edge of the high bed. The hospital gown had a split all the way up the back. This was to make life easier should the wearer become a corpse. The occupant of the next bed looked at her over the downy head of a suckling child. 'That's right, love,' she said. 'Go and see the kiddy, and to buggeration with the rules. There's some nappy pins in my locker. Twizz round and I'll save your dignity.'

Duly pinned, Abigail walked out of the ward. She

refused to creep, refused to keep her profile low.

Outside the nursery, Tishy sat alone. 'Mam's gone to the shop,' she said.

Through the doorway, Abigail saw her husband. He was smiling.

Patricia Lilian Harrison was curled in a heated cot, her blonde hair wisping as the right amount of added oxygen flowed over her head. She weighed four pounds and eleven ounces and she had a good chance. The world was a bright place, too bright for tired eyes. Hands touched her, washed her, pushed a teat into her mouth. The milk was good.

On the edge of sleep, Patricia sensed a change. It was just another hand, another touch, yet she remembered it. This was the right one, the one who would come back. Her mouth moved, gums fastening on to the proffered finger. With her mother by her side, Patricia Lilian Harrison decided to live.

CHAPTER FOURTEEN

Confessions

Everybody was up at the farm, supposedly helping to prepare Theresa's new house for the forthcoming wedding. The reception was to be held in Abigail's flat, but Tom and Theresa would be moving into the cottage on their wedding night. There were no plans for a honeymoon. Travel was restricted because of the war, and Tom's family needed constant attention, so any ideas the young couple might have contemplated were pushed back to make way for the immediacies of life.

Ellen, Abigail, Tishy, Clive and Tom were in the farmhouse drinking tea with Mrs Carrington and the four children. Marie and Theresa had opted to remain in the cottage where they climbed on stools and ladders to fit curtains at the small windows.

It was a lovely house, and Theresa knew that she was going to be very proud of it. There was a front-to-back sitting room with a view of open fields at each end, a kitchen with a dining area, four bedrooms with a bathroom leading off the largest, and an extra little bathroom tacked on to the back of the house next to a small conservatory. This would be ideal for the senior Mrs Crawford, who would need help to come downstairs each morning, though, in defiance of all prognosis, stairs were no longer a total impossibility. Mrs Carrington had donated a special sitting-room chair for Tom's mother, a high-seated item that was easy on arthritic bones.

'It's going to be lovely,' sighed Marie. 'A stone cottage, all on its own too. Think how long you've wanted a stone cottage, ever since we were at nursery school. And no rent to pay, no mortgage. You don't know how lucky you are, our kid.'

'I do.' Theresa smiled down benignly, her eyes resting briefly on her sister before fixing themselves on the rolling moors outside, verdant patchwork pieces all neatly seamed by walls and hedgerows. 'I recognize good fortune, Marie. And it'll be good for the children.' She bent her head against an amusing thought. 'Hey, Tom's in charge of cabbages and potatoes.' Her grin widened. 'He says he doesn't understand anything unless it used to be a tree and unless he can carve his name on it. He'll be giving up the chance of a good job, and all for me, Marie. Yes, he could have gone back into carpentry at the end of the war. I am a lucky girl, you're right.'

She glanced round the minute bedroom. 'This will just about take Alison's cot and a chest of drawers. We had to give Tom's mam the slightly bigger room, and the boys will share.'

Marie cleared her throat self-consciously. 'Are you going to be . . . all right? Being married, I mean. Like . . . you know . . . you and Tom and all that.'

'Yes.'

'Aren't you scared?'

Theresa ran curtain rings along the rail and pulled at the stiff brown fabric that would cover the window. 'I wish I could have got something with flowers on, something for a little girl's room. Still, Tishy does her best, doesn't she? These curtains are very well made and fully lined, even if it is with coffin-cotton.' This was the term invented by the family for the shroud material they had bought from a local mill.

Marie stared down at the patterned beige rush matting on the floor. 'You are frightened. I knew you'd be like this about it, unwilling to talk. There's nothing to be scared of, not if you love him. It's all very natural—'

'Stop it. There's more to life than that sort of thing.'

'Aye, but it's part of marriage, isn't it? I mean, you

always wanted to be a nun, and nuns don't . . .' Her voice faded, squashed by the faint glimmer in Theresa's eye.

'There's no need to be telling me what nuns do and don't do. And I know there's nothing to be frightened of with Tom. I do know him, I'm not getting wed to a complete stranger.'

'But—'

Theresa climbed down from her chair. 'I love him, Marie. If I love him, it doesn't matter. And I've got . . .' Her face reddened. 'I've got feelings for him. I want to look after him and get close to him. I mean, how would you feel if I asked about you and John, eh?'

'What about me and John?'

Theresa looked hard at her sister. 'You'd tell me it was private, I know you. You'd tell me to go away and mind my own business. Why should I be different?'

'Because I've always looked after you.'

Theresa placed an arm round the slightly shorter girl's shoulder. 'Thank you. For sticking up for me. You took a lot of clouts, and I haven't forgotten that. But I'm a woman now and you have to let me go. Tom will look after me, don't worry. And we'll be living in the country, in a lovely house of our very own, with fresh air and good food – it's all over for me now, all the trouble.' She waved a hand across the room. 'I still can't get over Mrs C giving us this place. It was like she was just handing me a bunch of flowers or a toffee, here's a house, I hope you enjoy it. Mind, she's like that, sees everything at one level. When there was trouble, she treated big things and little things all the same—'

Marie glanced through the window, interrupting her twin's flow. 'Is that Percy Shaw mending the fence out there? See – down yonder in that field.'

Theresa bent to peer through the bottom half of the window. 'Yes, he lives over the stables most of the time, then he goes home for his days off. Mrs Carrington is talking about renting him a cottage too. The country's good for his chest, makes him better. He'll be able to bring the kiddies to live up here.'

Marie pulled away and walked to the door, her head dropping slightly. It wasn't that she resented Theresa's good fortune, but what about herself, when was her life going to begin? 'It's all working out for everybody, isn't it? Everybody except me and John.'

Theresa's forehead furrowed in a deep frown. 'But he's home. Why can't you enjoy him being home for a while?'

Marie's shoulders lifted and fell. 'Because it is only for a while. If he'd had a bit of sense, he needn't have gone off to fight. They gave him a job here, Marie, a driving job, seeing to supplies, taking soldiers from one place to another. They told him he could stay in England. So what does he do, my brave boyfriend? He asks to serve abroad, insists on it. I thought you couldn't insist in the British army, but he got his own road at the finish. And I know he's going to die. I've always known that he was going to get killed in the war.'

'You can't be sure of that. Nobody but God can be sure of the future and who lives and dies. You're getting morbid, Marie. The Germans can't kill everybody.'

Marie leaned heavily against the wall, stubbornly determined to be miserable. 'I hate Sundays. Even the shop's better than this nothing day we get once a week.'

'It's not a nothing day. Anyway, you're here visiting me, aren't you? It's not as if you're stuck in the house with nowt to do. What would Mam say if she knew how downhearted you are?'

Marie said nothing. She was unbearably lonely, too isolated to reach out even to her sister. Nobody understood. Abigail had Clive; Theresa had Tom, Mam had Tishy. John was going away to fight a war, so Marie would soon have no-one at all, no partner, nothing to complete her sense of identity, no foundation on which to build her place in the world. All she had was work, just the shop, the day to day grind of humping potatoes, dusting shelves, listening to customers complaining about shortages. And she realized that she was not herself, that the usual 'good old Marie' was somehow absent without leave. She had always stood up to life, had been able to make the best of things for most of the time.

'Do you love him?' Theresa's voice was low. 'Is that it?'

'Yes.' Marie inhaled sharply. 'Remember what he was like at school? All that was to get my attention, because he's loved me a long while. He's clever, you know. Always reading books and magazines and newspapers. He knows everything about this war, and the last one too. It's because he's so clever and so brave that he'll get killed. If they're looking for a volunteer to do something dangerous, he'll stick his hand in the air every time. And whistle through his teeth so's he'll get noticed.'

'Just like he did at school.' Theresa held her head on one side, remembering. 'He could have got top marks if he'd tried. He used to do other folks' sums if they gave him sweets. And always the first in bother, Marie, always the one for the strap.'

'Yes. His mam feels the same way about him. She says he'll go into it with eyes closed and guns blazing. I don't know what to do.'

'What can you do?'

Marie lifted her arms in a gesture of hopelessness. 'I can tell him I'm pregnant,' she whispered.

Theresa's chin sagged. 'Eh?'

Marie walked past her sister and sat on the top stair. With her back turned, she said, 'It was my fault. I made him do it. It was . . . to get closer to him before he goes, to make sure I was the first. It's this terrible feeling that he's going to die, see. If he'd gone and died, and if we'd never . . . done it, then I would have been sorry all my life.'

She giggled, but the laugh was almost a sob. 'It was hopeless. I didn't even know at the time if we'd done it right. He'd never . . . you know . . . before, and I had no idea what it was all about. Mind, practice makes perfect.' She lifted her head. Her eyes were bright with tears and

385

memories. 'And I was the one who put my foot down in the first place, told him there'd be none of that sort of messing, yet it was me who started it. I needed to stop hating things, Theresa. I needed him. It was on the floor in their back kitchen, while his mam was out at Shirley's. And it was all over in a flash, so we never got caught by his mam.'

Theresa took a step forward. 'But you did get caught, love.'

Marie's head dropped on to her knees. 'No. I'm all right. Mind, we have . . . a few times since then . . . you know. But I'm going to tell him I'm not all right. If he thinks I'm having a baby, happen he'll be more careful about volunteering.'

'If you tell him that, he'll want to marry you before he goes.'

'Good. That's what I want, to be married.'

'But what about Mam? How will she feel when you tell her you have to get wed?'

'She won't bother. She's got Tishy to worry about, don't forget. As long as Tishy's all right, Mam doesn't seem to notice anything.'

'That's not true. You're Mam's right arm, and you know it.'

Marie sighed deeply. 'And who's mine, Theresa? Eh? Answer me that one if you can. I've kept the peace for long enough, standing between you and London, Mam and London, the customers and London. Who's watching out for me? Have you any idea what my life is like? Oh, I know it's easier than most, I know there's enough to eat and clothes to wear. But I want to be myself, to do things, go to see places, have experiences of my own. And a man of my own, somebody to be my right arm.'

Theresa knelt on the landing and touched the soft, silky, dark brown curls that hung down her sister's back. 'Don't be a liar, Marie. Only bad things can come from lies. You'd have him suffering all the while, worrying about a baby as well as about a wife. Then you'd have to tell him that it was all a mistake, that you'd lost his baby. Do you think that would do him any good?'

Marie thought for a moment. 'No.' She sighed heavily. 'The truth is, I wouldn't know whether I was pregnant or not. I've never been regular, so I've no way of judging. I do need to sort things out, though. I want something to look forward to, not this awful feeling of things ending. What'll I do when he does get killed?'

'Marie, you're going to have to learn to pray.'

The girl on the stairs snorted and tossed her head. 'Huh. Tishy does all my praying for me. I'd heard before that converts are always full of it, and it's true. She says her rosary every night for John. She likes him, 'cos he taught her how to ride a bike. No, there's enough praying goes on in our house without me turning it into high mass. And I'm not so sure I believe any more. I reckon Tishy's taken my bit of faith and swallowed it all up. I can't even . . .' She swallowed the tears. 'I can't even hope.'

'Despair's a sin.'

The sapphire eyes were large and round as she turned and looked at Theresa. 'I find it so hard. Please help me.'

'Oh, Marie, Marie.' She enfolded the trembling body in her arms. 'It's not one of them premonitions, love. It's only what every girl feels when her man goes to the fighting. They all fear the worst, it's only human nature to imagine all sorts. Just think, in a few months from now he'll be home, and he can live with you in one of the Noble Street houses. Mam's getting them all done up once the war's over. Then you and John can run the shops and have more money – I'm sure Abigail and Tishy will agree. And I want no part of them shops, love. Thanks to Mrs Carrington, me and Tom have all we need for a good start. So you look forward to running the business – you know you're the best at it. Then you can have babies . . .' Her voice faded away to nothing.

'I'm sorry, Theresa. Oh God, I never thought. Me and my big gob—'

'It doesn't matter.'

'It does, you would have made a smashing mother.'

'I am a mother. Tom and the children were sent to me. Why do you think I was there when poor Alice died? It was all a part of God's plan for me, all a part of the life He gave me. I love them three kiddies, Marie. They're as near my own as they could possibly be. I don't mind, honest.'

Marie freed herself and dried her eyes on a sleeve. 'Well, we'll be having your party soon, all girls together,' she said lightly, looking for a less depressing prospect. 'Mam's saved all kinds of coupons to make sure we have a good do. We're going to borrow a cot, so Abigail can bring Patricia. That'll be the last night that we'll all be together. You and me are having our own room. Abigail's going in with Mam and Tishy and the baby. Like old times, eh? When we used to lie awake and . . .'

'And listen to him hitting our mother,' Theresa finished for her. 'Thank God he won't be there. Sometimes, I wish . . . never mind.'

Marie nodded. 'Aye, I know. Come on, let's fix these beds up. They'll all be stuffing themselves over at the farm. We can give them a right showing up if we've done everything when they get back.'

They walked through to the main bedroom and picked up the spanners. 'You won't trick him, will you?' asked Theresa as they struggled with springs and frame. 'It wouldn't be right.'

Marie smiled and raised an eyebrow. 'No, I won't. Not now I've confessed to you. Don't tell Mam, will you? Don't tell her what I've been doing with John.'

'As if I would.'

When the bed was finally together, they stood back and admired their handiwork. 'Clever,' said Marie. 'Who needs men?'

The door flew open and Abigail fell in, eyes bright with laughter. 'Ernest has bathed Mrs Carrington's dead fox, that awful thing she puts round her neck when she's cold. He scrubbed it with carbolic in the trough. Now the trough has to be cleared or the animals will be sick. And

Harold has chased all the chickens out of the farmyard – Mrs Carrington says it'll be a miracle if she gets another egg before Christmas. She's a good sort, though. The house is full of women and babies. Theresa, what are you taking on with those two boys? I'm sure Mr Churchill could find a use for them, some sort of lethal weapon that would wipe Hitler out in a matter of minutes. Send them over with a couple of grenades, then it'll all be over in a week.'

Theresa laughed. 'They're good, really. It's because they're intelligent, they could do with being at school. How's the fox?'

'Even deader than it already was,' said Abigail. 'It's been relegated to the dressing-up box for the village church dramatic society.'

The twins stared at Abigail. She was bouncy, lively, full of vigour. Although she was far from beautiful, there was a new glow about her, a natural shine that needed and received no embellishment from a makeup bag.

She threw the mattress on to the bed springs, then dumped herself in the centre, stretching out like a tired cat. 'I'm exhausted,' she announced. 'And so's Clive. Patricia is fun, but she's hard work. That's why I admire you, Theresa. Taking three on in one fell swoop is no mean feat.' She looked at Marie. 'How's John?'

'Better. He has to go back.'

'Well, of course he does. He can't be discharged just because his girlfriend's moping and whining. Sorry.' She noticed the crestfallen expression on Marie's face. 'I sometimes forget how I must sound. He'll be all right, you just have to believe that. Otherwise, life will not be worth living. We all have to think that things will work out. I mean, look at me and Clive. I was all prepared to have a dead baby, and Tishy saved us both. Clive's been marvellous . . .'

The subject of discussion put his head round the door. 'Don't talk about me,' he said. 'I've got big ears. Ellen's giving Patricia a bottle. I've just been having a word with

Percy Shaw. It seems he sees a lot of your father, girls.'

Abigail sat up. 'He wouldn't if he knew what London did to Vera.'

'You've no proof.' Clive's tone was stern. 'Be careful what you say.'

'I'm sure, as sure as I could ever be,' she insisted. 'Ever since the night of Vera's so-called accident, I've realized that he was behind it. No doubt she knew about his bigamy. So he killed her.'

Theresa bit her lower lip. 'He can do anything,' she said. 'There is no sin too big for him. Sometimes, I wonder if he'll . . .'

'What?' Marie's eyes were wide. 'If he'll what?'

'It's too silly.' Theresa picked up the spanner and made for the door.

'Finish what you started,' said Abigail. 'Don't leave us all wondering about your wonderings.'

Theresa turned in the doorway. 'I worry about him getting Mam. When she's coming home from the shop at night, when she's in the house with just Tishy. He used to . . . kick her and throw her about. She's so small. I wish she could live out here with us, then she'd be safe.'

Abigail's lips drew back from her teeth. 'Just let him touch her,' she snarled. 'One move from him in her direction, and I'll fill the nearest hypodermic with the nastiest poison I can find.' She looked at the astonished faces around her. 'I know she's not my mother,' she said quietly. 'But I love her. The way she's looked after my sister, the way she worried about me and Clive when the drugs thing was happening, it's as if she really cares about us. Ellen taught me what love is.' She drew a hand across her face.

Clive helped his wife to stand. 'Don't start crying again.' His voice was gentle. 'Crying's a skill she's just learned,' he said to the twins. 'And she's determined to perfect the art. We are running out of handkerchiefs.'

Theresa came across and placed a hand on Abigail's shoulder. 'You cry all you like, love. Take no notice of

390

him, this is my house and you can do what you like in it. And it was Patricia who taught you about love. She has changed your life.' She glanced at Clive. 'Just be glad she can weep. She suffered more before she found her tears.'

He hugged Abigail and grinned over her shoulder. 'I know, I'm only pulling her leg. Listen, you two are expected at the manor to partake of tea with her Ladyship. She's made scones. Now, if you value your teeth, stick to the cook's cakes. Mrs Carrington's scones are one of life's more tedious and jaw-stretching events.'

Marie and Theresa walked downstairs together. A summons from Mrs Carrington was as good as a royal command, so they hastened their steps as they made their way down the flagged path. Theresa paused, a hand on the latch of the newly-mended and painted gate. Marie shunted into the back of her sister. 'What's up?' she asked. 'Have your brakes stuck?'

Theresa pointed across the nearest field. Percy Shaw was calling to someone, and the two girls caught sight of another man on a cart. 'It's him,' breathed Theresa. 'Look, I can see that daft bowler hat of his. He's followed me up here.'

Marie remained motionless. 'No,' she said at last. 'He's all over the place, I saw him in town last week. He's likely visiting Percy.'

'Why?' Theresa's face was a sickly white. 'I thought I'd got away, Marie. I really thought I'd seen the last of him. He can meet Percy in Bolton on his days off, no need for him to traipse halfway across Lancashire.'

'Happen he's delivering round these parts, then.'

Theresa shivered convulsively. 'I'm going to tell Tom.'

Marie nodded her agreement. 'Aye, and we should tell Percy and all, tell him what Abigail thinks. If he knew . . .'

'There's no proof. And Vera's dead, isn't she? It's only like an opinion, isn't it? I mean, we could get done for slander and stuff if we started on about that. He's dangerous and he's on our farm. I don't know what to do.

Except I'm going to tell Tom he's hanging about where he's no business.'

From across the meadow, London watched his twin daughters. Even at a distance, he could sense their unease, and he allowed himself a grim smile. Percy Shaw had turned out to be a useful if unwitting ally, always ready with tales of the family, always willing to gossip about weddings, illnesses, births. He arranged his features into an expression that was suitably doleful as Percy reached his side. 'My own children,' he said sadly. 'And they don't want to see me.'

Percy raised his arms and helped Billy down from the cart. 'No accounting for families,' he said. 'Specially when there's a separation. Your wife will have poisoned them against you, see. Don't forget, she's with them all the while, so she can fill their heads full of all sorts of tales. Not that she'd do it intentional, like. She's a good woman, even if the pair of you don't see eye to eye. I notice you've brought the peat, then. Come on, we'll stack it with the coal. She'll be glad of that come winter, will the missus. It's a barn of a place to heat, that house.'

While Percy took the pony's head, Billy London waited and stared at the two figures across the field. They stood very still, a pair of monuments to his own demise. And there were more of them, many more. There was Ellen and that rotten Abigail, then there was Lil's second child, the girl who was a bit slow in the head. And Abigail had given birth to a brat, another one to be removed before he could reclaim his rightful status.

The plan was almost complete. He would get them, all of them, the whole lot in one fell swoop. Whether or not it made sense had ceased to matter. The only thing he wanted now was his money's worth, and if he couldn't get it in cash, he'd have it in boxes, wooden ones with wreaths on top. Percy had told him the wheres and the whyfors. He raised his chin, then lifted his hat to the two girls, grinning to himself as they turned and ran towards the farmhouse. He would have his day, and his day had almost arrived.

The shop was empty at last. Ellen Langden lowered herself on to a stool, every bone in her body seeming to clamour for some ease, some rest from the endless standing. Cissie leaned against the counter, a hand to her heated brow. 'Why can't we get through to them, Ellen? Why are they always iffing and butting and telling us what we've got hid under this here counter? The road they carry on, you'd think we'd a king's ransom stacked in the cellar. And if old Mrs Banks doesn't have a bath soon, I'll chuck a bucket of water over her. She smells like the fishmarket when they've run out of ice.'

Ellen grinned ruefully. Cissie had certainly come out of her shell these past months. Such a quiet woman, she had been, so agreeable and subservient. Now, Cissie spoke her mind and was beholden to nobody. Labour had certainly given the woman some dignity. 'The day Mother Banks has a bath, I shall stretch bunting from Daubhill to Deane, all the way down Noble Street,' said Ellen. 'Right, we'd best tally these ration points and do the orders. Are you fit?'

'No.'

'Then that makes at least two of us. Nip through and stick that kettle on, will you? I reckon a brew wouldn't go amiss. Oh, and I want a word.'

Cissie paused on her way to the tiny scullery. 'Have I done owt wrong?'

'Not as I've noticed.'

While the kettle boiled, Cissie returned to wait by Ellen's side. 'Tell me,' she said at last. 'There's summat on your mind, Ellen Langden. I can always tell when things are weighing heavy, 'cos your face goes all still, like on a photo.'

'Does it? Happen me accumulator's running down. I know our Marie could do with charging up. And that's why I want to talk to you. How would you feel about being my manager, running this shop proper, having a girl under you? I think you know enough about the customers and the ordering, and I'd only be down the road. Good money in it, love. I don't expect you to do it for nowt.' She paused. 'Well? What do you say?'

Cissie swallowed. 'Eeh, I'm that grateful . . .' Her voice dropped away to nothing.

'See, I want to go and work with Marie. I know it's only a little shop, but it's still a lot for a young girl. I can see her going down, Cissie. And after the war's over, I'm going to knock that shop through to the back, make it bigger. She needs somebody with her. I know Tishy's gone up to keep her company, but Tishy's . . . well, Tishy is Tishy. What do you say, Cissie? Another three pounds a week?' She waited a moment. 'Three pounds two and six?'

Cissie nodded, her face suddenly white and drawn.

'What's up?' asked Ellen. 'Anybody would think I'd just slapped you in the chops with a pound of wet cod including ice. Don't you want to be my manager?'

Cissie's head dropped even further.

'Why the long face? Look, you're a good worker and I depend on you. There'll be a great future in retail once we've won this blinking war. There's no need for you to look so . . . I don't know how to describe your face at the minute, Cissie Tattersall. I suppose the nearest word would be mithered.'

'I don't know . . . what to say.'

'Yes would be a start.'

Cissie sniffed. 'It's him.'

'Oh, I see. Who's him when his mother shouts him for his dinner?'

'Your husband.'

Ellen put a hand to her forehead. 'What's he got to do with it? He can't touch these shops, not with what I'm holding over him. The fact is, these properties as good as belong to the girls now, because he'll not risk prison. Why the dickens should you worry over him?'

'I don't. Not now.'

The shorter woman jumped down from her stool. 'Listen, missus. Either you pull yourself together and tell

394

me what's on your mind, or I go home and leave you to the dinner-time rush. The mills will be out in a few minutes. Well?' She stood, arms akimbo and eyes blazing with curiosity. 'What's brought all this on?'

Cissie took a backward step. 'I had . . . I had a bit of a to-do with Mr London. Way back, before I worked here. He used to come round our house and he . . . I mean we . . . you know. I don't understand why I did it and I never will get the answer to that, not properly. I was grateful to him, now I'm grateful to you, so I'm all mixed up. You won't want me working here at all now, will you? I mean, I'm not a good woman . . .'

Ellen shook her head slowly. 'You mean you went and laid down with him voluntary, like?'

'I'm sorry.'

'So am I, sorry for you. I mean, it was in my contract, part of me job description, wasn't it? I had to do it, I was forced to put up with him on account of being his wife. Yes, you're a brave woman, Cissie. Did he make you pay for his bits and pieces, then? Is that the top and tail of it?'

Cissie gulped again. 'That's right, till your Marie found us one night. She planned it, I'm sure she did. And she never said a word to you, I know that. The poor kiddy kept it all to herself, and it's sat in my mind ever since, that sin. I've confessed it, like, only it won't go away, no matter what I do.'

'Our Marie? Found you and him doing . . . doing that?'

'Aye. I'm sorry, Ellen.'

'Well.' Ellen dropped back on to the stool. 'Well, I'll go to the foot of our stairs! No wonder she's grown up so fast, no wonder she hates her dad to blazes. And she's wise too, isn't she? Wise enough not to get me all worried and clever enough not to blame you, Cissie. And you can take that look off your face now, it doesn't suit you. Happen the wind'll change and leave you looking like a martyr. This makes no difference, you know. I still want you to take over here, and you can employ your own help.' She stared hard at Cissie. 'You've changed, haven't you?'

'I have, yes.'

'You can think for yourself now. We none of us need a man, remember that. We don't have to do what they say, and we don't have to have one in the background to make us into people. We've got the vote and we've got the earning power. All we need now is a woman in Number Ten, and we'll be away. There's no necessity for men, Cissie.'

The doorbell clanged and Cedric Wilkinson stepped into the shop, his large face bright with embarrassment. Ellen looked at the ceiling. 'See what I mean, Cissie? Who needs that?' She put a handkerchief to her face, using this shield while she arranged her features into some sort of order.

Cissie, torn between guilt and a strong desire to giggle at Ellen's inept suitor, ran through to the scullery.

Ellen composed herself, pushing the hanky into her pocket. 'Well?' she asked with mock sweetness. 'And what are you up to?'

'Prefabs.'

'Oh, I see. I hope it stays fine for you.'

He touched the neck of his shirt, wishing he'd thought to fasten a collar on today. 'Bit of what they call temporary housing up Tonge Moor. It's me dinner hour.' He was doing the usual job on his cap, mashing it into a wrinkled ball between his nervous hands.

'Right.' She tapped the ends of her fingers on the counter. 'And what can I get you?'

'Eh?'

She inhaled, then puffed out her cheeks. 'Cedric, watch my lips. What do you want? This is a shop. We sell things, folk buy them. I am selling, what are you buying?'

'Oh, well I thought . . .'

'Firewood? Another tape of Aspros? Or are you going to go all adventurous and buy a new bucket?'

'I don't need a bucket.'

'Good job, we haven't got any.'

'Oh, it's as well I don't want one then.' He fixed his

adoring gaze on a spot just above her head. 'I've come to tell you he's following everybody. Well, I think he is. No, now as I ponder, after these last few days, I'm sure—'

'Who?'

'London.'

'How do you know?'

He shifted his weight from foot to foot, annoyed because he couldn't seem to stand still, couldn't seem to express the simplest thoughts. 'Because I've been following him.'

'So.' Ellen pursed her lips while she pictured Cedric in his van pursuing London on his cart. She'd seen stuff like that in American films, daft men running in circles, mostly across tram tracks and railway cuttings. 'You've been following him following somebody else.'

'That's it. He keeps coming round here at night, as if he's watching and waiting for something. And he sees a lot of that Percy Shaw too. Then there's the girls . . .'

'What about them?'

Cedric shrugged helplessly. 'He goes and hangs round that nursing home back of Chorley Old Road, and I reckon he's been up at the farm and all. I've been skipping jobs to keep up with him – except at night. I can do what I want at night.'

Ellen glanced down at the counter. While her main thoughts were about London and what he might be up to, part of her mind was occupied by this man's obvious devotion to her. This was probably love, real love, the sort she had never come across before, not from a man. The thought that he would give up his few moments of leisure to watch and care for the Langden family was strangely touching and comforting. 'Cedric, don't be using your time on us. There's nowt we can do about him, short of getting him locked up . . .'

'Then do it.' His voice cracked, and he steadied himself against the counter. 'And I'm not wasting time, Ellen. You've got to remember that I've known yon feller for a long time, since I went to London looking for work. He's devious. He'd sell his own grandmother for half a crown, and he's not past hurting you, lass. I won't have you hurt no more.' He breathed in some confidence. 'The important thing is your safety.'

Ellen sighed. 'His crimes are old, Cedric. There's nobody will lock him up for a bigamy that happened years ago, specially now that Lilian's dead, though God knows I'd have a go at putting him away if push came to shove. Mind, there's evidence of theft with a Bolton lawyer, then papers down London way with that old doctor . . . But I'm still not a hundred per cent sure we could prove that he stole her money, not really. Then with me holding the shops for the girls after he signed the agreement – well – it looks as if he's paid everybody back, as if all's well with the world. So while we've legs to stand on, they may be a bit on the rheumaticky side.'

'The queer feller's not done. I can feel in me bones that he's not finished yet. Something up his sleeve, I reckon.'

'Such as?'

He coloured as she stared directly into his eyes. 'Something big. There's nowt he'd stop at, Ellen. I lived with him and I know . . .'

'I lived with him too. What do you expect me to do, Cedric? Leave the shops, run hell for leather, dig Abigail and Theresa out of their new homes? I can't do them things. And I don't want everybody frightened.'

He placed the mangled cap on the counter, pushed his hands into pockets and frowned. 'I'm only speaking me mind, you know. Long enough I've been tongue-tied near you. If owt happened just 'cos I couldn't open me gob, well I'd never forgive meself.'

'I'm glad you care,' she said softly.

'Are you?'

'I think so, yes.'

His eyelids blinked rapidly. 'I wish I'd met you afore he did. And I wish I'd spoke up—'

'Don't.' She leaned across and patted his shoulder. 'We can't mend it. What can't be cured must be endured.'

'Ellen?'

'What?'

He drew a breath. 'I love thee, lass.'

'I know, and I'm sorry.'

'I'm not.' He drew himself to his full and not inconsiderable height. 'It's not wasted, I don't want you to think my life's been wasted because of you. I've always cared . . .'

'Yes. And now you're getting your words out, aren't you? How many years have you stuttered every time you asked for firewood?' Struggling for her own self-assurance, she drew herself up to full height. 'Now listen. Don't worry about him, there's nowt more he can do. It's all legal and settled, so he'll not get back in here. And he daren't threaten us, because there's too many of us. Now, get yourself off to that job.'

'Right.' He hesitated briefly, crammed the cap on to his head and turned towards the door, kicking over a bag of potatoes as he moved. 'Back to normal,' he muttered to himself as he picked up the spilled vegetables.

She smiled and shook her head. Normal would do, wouldn't it? It was nice to know that somebody cared, that he was thinking about her and the family. If only . . . She picked up a cloth and began to dust the counter. There was no point in 'if onlying', her whole life had been spent doing that. There was no time for regrets, not with a business to organize.

The bell clanged again as the door closed behind him, and Ellen suddenly felt cheerless and lonely. It had been nice talking to him. He wasn't a bad old stick, wasn't Cedric. But she was a married woman, and married women couldn't afford to feel sad just because a man had gone outside.

Cissie brought the tea. 'He's gone, then.'

'Aye, he's gone.'

'Thinks a lot of you, Ellen.'

Ellen blew on her tea and stared over the rim of the cup. 'And I think a lot of him,' she surprised herself by saying.

'Yes, I do.' She looked at her companion and smiled broadly. 'Some men are not as bad as other men, Cissie. Happen you could find a good one if you looked hard enough.'

'I don't want one. I just want that job you've offered me, and a decent home for our Linda and our Tony. I'm sorry about the other business, though.'

Ellen clicked her tongue. 'Don't think about it. I've already forgotten about that.' And she had. All that occupied her mind was an unexpected consignment of tinned peaches and the look on a certain man's face. It was the expression in Cedric's eyes that somehow made life worth living, and Ellen's smile remained in place for the rest of the afternoon.

Tishy opened the small door and stepped inside. It was nice in here, dark and secret, and she could say anything that came into her head. Father Gorman was on duty this time, and he was the youngest of the priests, the man who took a special interest in Tishy's soul. She knelt on the low form and blessed herself, then sat back on her heels as she considered her sins. 'I've not done much, Father. I've made a cardigan this week, a red one with white rings round the bottoms of the sleeves. Then I started a black and white scarf for Bolton Wanderers, and a hat to match. Ellen's tired. She works too hard. And Marie's very sad even though John's still here.'

Father Gorman grinned to himself. This was a chosen child, a very special and lovely young woman, and he was fond of her capriciousness. 'What about the hand, then? Has it been back?'

'I haven't seen it, but I know it's there. Mostly, I don't look. Ever since you told me not to upset myself, I've tried not to look. You see, I want to be naughty when I see the hand.'

'Naughty?'

'Yes, I want to give it a good hiding. That's one of Marie's sayings, "good hiding". But that hand pushes

400

people. I saw it pushing somebody a long time ago, one time when it was icy. Do you think it's a ghost, Father?'

'No, it won't be a ghost.'

'A spirit, then?'

He swallowed a giggle – Tishy never failed to make him smile. 'A spirit is the same as a ghost. It's probably all in your imagination. Don't think about it. Try to concentrate on something more pleasant. Now, have you committed any sins this week?'

Tishy thought hard. 'I stole some of Marie's aniseed balls, and I dipped my finger in the condensed milk while Mam – I mean Ellen – wasn't looking.'

'Oh dear. Well, you can't do much about the milk, but you can try to buy some sweets for Marie. Is that all?'

She rummaged through her thoughts. 'Except for the cat.'

'Oh?'

'I've got a cat, you see. I keep him outside and save some of my dinner for him. This is a very thin starving cat, sort of grey with stripes. I think he's come from one of the bombed houses, so it's a shame, isn't it? Well, I have to steal food for him. Saint Francis of Assisi would have stolen food for him if he'd seen the state of the poor thing's coat, all bald bits. Every night, I creep out of bed and put the cat in the oven after the fire's out. I leave the oven door open, though, so he won't smothercate – that's another of Marie's words – and I put the cat on an old coat on the bottom shelf. In the morning, I get up first, before Mam and Marie, and let the cat out when he's had his milk. Mam doesn't know, so it's a sin, 'cos I'm taking milk and meat without telling.'

'I see.' Again, he stifled his laughter. After all, the confessional was no place for levity, though this girl made seriousness very difficult to maintain. 'Tishy?'

'What?'

'I'd tell Ellen if I were you.'

'Oh, I don't know about that, Father. What if she's like my mother? Mum couldn't have a cat, cats made her sneeze and she couldn't stop sneezing till she got away from a cat. If Ellen's like that, we'll have to take Tinkle to Vernon Street and have him put down. I love Tinkle. Tinkle hasn't got a home, so I've given him one like Ellen did for me and Abigail. It's called Christian charity, I've read about it in the Salvation Army's book. A lady in our street is in the Sally Anns. She wears a hat and bangs a drum. Why can't we have a band?'

Father Gorman stuffed his handkerchief into his mouth. Tishy's confessions were always confusing, but they made life worth living somehow. This was a true daughter of God, a beautiful flawed flower with an inherent goodness that put to shame many of the bowers and scrapers who comprised half of the congregation. 'Tishy,' he managed eventually. 'Please tell Ellen about your cat. She used to have one, I remember it.' Yes, she'd given it away after her husband had kicked it . . . 'A big orange tom, it was. She loves animals. I'm sure she'll take Tinkle in for you, give him a proper place to sleep.'

'Oh.' She paused. 'He has habits,' she said. 'Which is why I call him Tinkle.'

Father Gorman fled out of the back door of the confessional. In the church yard, he leaned against the wall and howled with glee. Some days in a priest's life were better than others, and he thanked God for sending him this little ray of sunshine. As soon as he was composed, he went back into the box. 'Are you still there?'

'Where've you been?'

'I went outside for a minute.'

She carried on as if there had been no interruption. 'My starling had habits. It was my mother who called them habits. Most of his habits went on to my shoes and Mum got cross. Ellen will be angry if Tinkle tinkles in the house.'

Tears coursed down the man's cheeks by this time. 'Ellen will get the vet to doctor him. That will stop his . . . habits.'

Tishy smiled in the darkness. 'Then the hand won't be

able to get him. If he lives in the house with us, he will be safe. Safe from peril.' She emphasized these last three words, separating them, colouring them with heavy drama.

It was probably best to humour her. 'That's right. So tell Ellen.'

'I will. What about my penance?'

'Just give the sweets back and say three Hail Marys. And visit me again next week, tell me about your cat.'

'Did God make cats, Father?'

'Yes.'

'Do they go to heaven when they're gone for ever?'

He scratched his head. The age-old question was asked by many pet-owning children, and this young lady was very much a child at heart. 'I don't know,' he said truthfully. 'Heaven is special, it's a happy and wonderful place. If you have loved an animal, then perhaps God allows it to come with you into perfect and eternal joy.'

'Perfect and eternal joy,' repeated Tishy, savouring the beauty of the words. 'That's where Mum is, with Our Lady. That's where I'm going.'

'Not yet, though,' he said.

Tishy made no reply. After making her act of contrition and receiving the blessing, she went out into the church and knelt beneath her favourite statue. 'Mary,' she said aloud. 'Don't let Ellen get rid of my cat. I will try to stop him tinkling, but he's only an animal and he doesn't speak English. Oh, and take the hand away. In the name of the Father, and of the Son . . .' She turned as a figure slipped into the pew beside her. 'Hello, Marie. I took your aniseed balls, but I've confessed.'

'It's all right, you're welcome. Is there anybody in the box?'

'No. Have you got sins?'

Marie sighed inwardly. Telling the priest about carrying on with John was going to be very hard.

'He's only giving three Hail Marys,' whispered Tishy.

'Even for condensed milk and cats. So it will be easy for you.'

Marie placed a hand on her half-sister's arm. 'You're too good for this world,' she said quietly before slipping into the confessional.

He was quite understanding for a priest, Marie thought. There was none of that business about keeping pure for marriage, no stuff about it being the most mortal sin for a girl. 'You don't want babies,' was the worst thing he said. 'There is no way you could rear a youngster without the support of a father. And you must not trap a man by having his child.' Then he told her to do five decades and not to sin with John again. He was a very lovely man, Marie thought as she rejoined Tishy.

'What did he give you?' asked Tishy when Marie pulled the beads from her pocket.

'A lot,' answered Marie.

Tishy thought about this. 'Did you steal a whole tin of condensed milk? Have you got a dog in the back street?'

'No, it's something else, a secret. Go and light a candle for me, will you? And say a prayer so that I will be good.'

Tishy stared at Marie. 'You are good,' she said. 'You and Theresa and Ellen are all good. Even Abigail's better than she was. I am very lucky with my family.' She went to light Marie's candle, then stared up into the benign face of the Immaculate Conception. 'It's only a little cat,' she said. 'Tell Jesus it's not a mortal sin. Oh, and ask Jesus to bring some more fish in from Fleetwood, Tinkle likes fish.' She dropped her voice. 'And it would help if you could take meat off ration.'

Marie grinned to herself. Tishy was a real caution – she talked to that statue as if it were alive. It was so easy for Tishy, all the believing, that unquestioning loyalty to her new religion. Marie closed her eyes and counted the beads. With a bit of perseverance, perhaps she would regain her faith. But all she could see behind her eyelids was John's face half-hidden in the smoke of combat, and she prayed for the image to be blotted out.

Trinity Street Station was dark, cold and filled with the smell of engines. John and Marie stood among many others, some with tear-streaked faces, others bearing their grief with typical British stoicism. Marie reached up and put her arms around his neck, burying her expression in the rough khaki jacket. 'When will it be over?' she mumbled. 'It's going on for ever. When will this blessed war finish?'

'Soon. I'm glad Mam didn't come, she'd never have stood this. It's a sad place, isn't it?'

Marie agreed with him silently. It was as if the sorrows of many partings had soaked into the very walls, into the flags beneath their feet. How many wives and mothers had stood here these past four years? How many would never stand here again with hope in their hearts? She could hear the train, so she clung to him with desperation as the large metal monster rumbled to the platform.

'Don't worry,' he said. 'They'll not get me.'

She did not dare to speak, could not tell him of her fears, of the near-knowledge that his final resting place would be abroad.

'Marie?'

'What?'

'Will you see to my mam? You know, if anything . . . I mean, nothing will happen, but if she gets worried . . . And go and see our Shirley sometimes.'

She nodded mutely. John was fond of his sister.

'Talk to me,' he said. 'You've got to say something, even if it's only ta-ra. Has that cat of Tishy's got your tongue?'

'No.' She pulled away from him with reluctance. 'John, I nearly did a terrible thing. I was going to tell you I was expecting, just so you'd marry me before you went.'

He smiled hugely. 'That shows how much you love me then, eh? So you'll wait for me, will you?'

'I will.'

'And we'll get wed when I come home. You've said

yourself that your mother could do with a man about the shops. That's something for me to look forward to now. I'll make sure I survive this bloody war even if it's just to sell spuds. And we will have a baby one day, Marie. Two or three if you want them. And a nice house too and a dog. Aye, I've always fancied a dog, one of them retrievers, a golden one. We could happen live up Bradshaw, somewhere nice like that.'

'John, don't let them put you in the front row. Stop at the back like you did at school. Tell them I said you can make a lot of trouble from behind. And make sure you've got plenty of bullets and one of them big guns.'

He kissed her, pushed her away and stepped on to the train. When he was settled, he made his way to a window and leaned out. 'Hey, you with the blue eyes,' he shouted.

She ran to his carriage. 'I'll write,' she said. 'I'll write every week.'

'And send me a parcel with your photo in.' The train began to move. 'And make sure you go and see Mam.'

She clung to his hand till the train was moving too quickly for her. Then, suddenly, the last link with him was severed and she found herself standing alone yet not alone, for she was surrounded by weeping women. It was the most terrible moment of her life so far, worse than London's beatings, worse than lying in bed and listening to him hitting her mother. Because this was her first love, her only love, possibly her last too.

People moved away, but Marie stayed on a bench outside the waiting room. There was still some steam from the train, from John's train, and she would sit here until it had all disappeared.

This was supposed to be a happy time – her twin was getting married in two days. There was a pretty blue dress to be worn, and Mam had managed to get hold of some silk posies as there were not many decent flowers to be had. John would not be there, John would not see the dress and the everlasting rosebuds. Her shoulders sagged, and she hugged herself against the unseasonable cold.

Tomorrow was going to be hard, the night of the party, the all-girls-together time that Mam and Tishy had planned so carefully.

She gazed along the deserted platform and wondered how they were all feeling, those people who had lingered here until just a few minutes ago. What were they doing, where had they gone? But she knew the answers. They had returned to their lives, to the day to day chores that would occupy time and take the edge off the pain. Getting on with life was the only way, the only balm for the sores.

Resolutely, Marie Langden jumped to her feet, swung the imitation silk scarf round her neck and pulled tight the belt of her coat. She would do what the rest had done, she would continue because there were no choices. To fail to achieve normality would surely mean insanity. So, like the rest, she would join in the charade that was called living. He might come home. She must hang on to the hope that he would not die.

Her echoing stride was firm as she walked away from the station. Anybody watching her might have thought what an ordinary girl she was, just another person going about her business. That was the picture she sought to present, and she did not intend to waver. Yet she stopped at the entrance to the station, casting one last look back towards the platform. It was as if a piece of her had died on Trinity Street that night. She was older and wiser, but a portion of herself would remain here on platform one. She nodded to herself. Perhaps this was what happened, perhaps folk died by inches, not all of a swoop at the end.

It was ten o'clock and the town was pitch black, but Marie knew every inch of the walk back home. Mam would be waiting, of course, anxious because one of her brood had gone missing during a blackout. There would be cocoa and toast and Tishy sitting by the fire with her knitting or with that scrawny animal she loved so much. And they would go into the shelter if the siren sounded, and Tishy would sing her songs and do those little dances she had learned.

Everybody was doing it, everybody was pretending. And Marie decided there and then that she would become the greatest pretender of all. From now on, she would be cheerful, even if the smiling broke her heart.

CHAPTER FIFTEEN

London's Burning

Theresa Langden stood in all her finery in front of the kitchen fire, her face glowing as everybody stared at her. She knew she looked nice. Tishy had made a special dress for her, a cream-coloured frock with a little collarless jacket that sat edge to braided edge with no buttons. Theresa felt that this was very stylish and unusual, especially when worn with the pillbox hat Mam had put together. That had a small bunch of feathers on one side, and a little cream veil that just about covered the young bride's nose. 'I'll sneeze,' she said. 'And the whole thing will shoot across the church like a bullet from a gun.'

'Eeh, love.' Ellen sat back on her heels after making some final adjustments to the hem of the dress. 'You look a smasher. I hope Tom realizes he's getting first prize in the raffle here. What do you say, Abigail? Doesn't she look lovely?'

'She does.' Abigail smiled. 'Definitely a great deal better than she used to look before the operation. You're positively glowing with health, Theresa. Or is it love?'

Theresa, still blushing, stepped towards the door. 'I'd best take this off and keep it safe, you never know what'll happen with all the food – and that wine Mrs Carrington sent. Isn't she good? She makes it all herself, you know, from blackberries and rhubarb and fruit picked in the orchard. Abigail, you come with me and check on Patricia. Is Tishy up there with her? That baby will get no sleep. All Tishy wants to do is play with her.' The two girls walked out together, leaving Ellen alone with Marie. The latter sat very still by the fire, an expression of pleasure deliberately printed across her features.

'I hope we don't get the siren,' said Ellen. 'We don't want to spoil the party, do we?'

'No.' Marie picked up the poker and prodded gently at the glowing coals.

Ellen folded her arms, setting her face into what she hoped was an expression of reassurance. 'Marie, love, he'll be all right. You can't spend every waking minute worrying yourself to death. What will he say when he comes home and finds you worn away to a shadow? A great mother he'll think I am if I let you go down.'

'I'm fine. I've decided just to get on with everyday life. It's . . . well, I wish he'd had a couple more days, that's all. It would have been nice if he could have been there tomorrow. But I'm not brooding, Mam. There's too much going on for me to brood. Shall I bring the plates in?'

'No, not yet. Cissie and Linda are coming later on, you know.'

'Yes.'

Ellen cleared her throat. 'Cissie was telling me you got a bit of a shock at her house.'

'Oh. What did she mean by that?'

After a short pause, Ellen said, 'Her and your dad. Why didn't you tell me what you'd seen, lass? Why keep it all to yourself?'

Marie's shoulders tightened against the unpalatable memory. 'There was no point in upsetting you, and no point in getting Mrs Tattersall into trouble. She needed me to help her. I had a good idea about what was going on before she told me, then when I realized how frightened she was, I decided I'd best take over and put a stop to it. So I did. There was nothing exciting about it, nothing to write home about.'

Ellen stood still and considered her daughter. This one was too old in the head, too controlled for her own good. Was it Ellen's fault? Had she allowed Marie too much freedom, had she placed on the young shoulders too heavy a load with the shop, was she guilty of neglecting her child? It was as if the girl had matured overnight, and John's leaving had somehow put the tin hat on things, had completed the metamorphosis from child to adult. 'Cissie's taking over Derby Street, we're getting an assistant,' Ellen said now. 'I'll be working with you on Deane Road as soon as things get sorted.'

'There's no need—'

'Yes, there is. You're old before your time, and you want to be going out and having a bit of fun. The factory girls don't stop in all the while because of the war, you know. There's still the odd dance, then there's the pictures and the pantomime. I know I kept you in when the war started, but you're older now.' She nodded slowly. 'Too old, Marie. I want you to be young, I want you to have some years before you settle down.' Aye, marriage was for life, though life didn't always improve after wedlock . . .

'Theresa isn't having any years.'

'She's different. Theresa needs a family, folk to look after. You're the one with the chance, Marie. You can't sit in just because John's gone. You're not engaged proper, are you?'

Marie smiled to herself.

'Well?'

'I said I'd wait for him, so I suppose I have made a promise. That means I can't go out.'

Ellen pulled an apple pie from the oven and placed it on the table, wishing, rather obliquely, that she had some caster or icing sugar, just to embellish the pastry a bit. 'It means no such thing. He wouldn't mind if you had the odd outing with a few friends from school.'

'I'm all right as I am.' There was strain in the voice, a slight impatience too. 'Leave me alone, will you? I don't need anybody telling me what to do, Mam. I know what I want and I know what I'm doing. I'm not Tishy, I don't want leading by the hand wherever I go.'

Ellen paused in the act of straightening the tablecloth.

'That's it, isn't it? You're jealous of Tishy because she gets a bit of attention.'

'I happen to think a lot of Tishy,' came the hot response.

'Aye, but you think I should push her in the background, being as she's not me own. Marie,' she dropped her voice. 'That girl's very ill. She only hung on by a thread last time, God knows how long she'll be with us, and—'

'I know. Oh, you don't understand at all. Look, Abigail's settled and married, and our Theresa's going to be the same tomorrow. Tishy only needs you, so she's got everything she wants. I'm . . . on me own, like. It's not your fault, it's not anybody's fault, unless we blame Hitler again. I'm ready for a life of me own, see. I'm only eighteen, I do understand that. But me and Theresa have been grown up a long while, and I fancy a fresh start with John. If – I mean when – he comes back, I'll be wanting to get married as soon as possible.'

'It is my fault, lass,' said Ellen softly. 'I let your father use you both as servants, and he damaged Theresa . . .' She cut herself off abruptly, refusing to dwell on the horror of it. 'He . . . frightened her,' she amended. 'And now you both want to run away from this house. Theresa hasn't been able to live here for ages. Now you're talking about going and all. I shouldn't have let him . . .'

'It wasn't up to you. He was the king of the castle, so you suffered as much as we did. Anyway, we'd best shape up for this party. No use having long talks and long faces at a time like this. I hope she'll be happy. All the time we were little, I just wanted our Theresa to be safe and contented. He seems nice enough, does Tom. Clever too, all that writing for the wireless.'

'Yes.' Ellen drew herself up, as if physically restoring herself to order. 'He's stopped in tonight to mind the kiddies while we have our party. There's not many men with a few days leave off work would do that. He's a kind lad, I'll give him that. As long as he goes easy on her.'

412

Marie tossed the dark curls over her shoulders, then stood up and smoothed her skirt. 'He's not London, Mam. Don't be thinking about your own life, 'cos Theresa's won't be anything like that. She won't get kicked and she won't get bullied. And she doesn't have to get married . . .'

Ellen dropped the pie knife. 'You what?'

Marie drew a sharp breath before speaking again. 'I've seen me birth certificate, and I can work dates out, Mam. You married him because you were expecting me and our Theresa. Don't look at me like that, it's something I've known a long while, ever since I found out how long it takes for a baby. You're not the only one who got caught that way.'

Ellen sank into the rocker. 'Well, I suppose I always dreaded this day, the day one of you would come to me and say what you've just said. I feel that ashamed of meself . . .' She turned her head, not knowing where to look, unable to face her own daughter, her own past weaknesses.

'Why?'

'It's wrong, that's why. You shouldn't do them things till you're married, but I . . . let that happen.'

'There's no need to explain to me, Mam. Everybody's allowed to make mistakes. Why do you think we have confession? All I'm saying is that our Theresa isn't under any pressure from Tom, so she's doing what she wants without being forced. I didn't mean to upset you. There's no need for you to feel guilty, you've been a good mother.' She spoke quietly, almost tenderly. 'We couldn't have had a better mam, me and our Theresa.'

'I don't know so much about that. Anyway,' she rose to her feet once more, a hand tightly clenched against her chest, 'you can fetch the stuff out of the scullery now. We want to give our Theresa a party she'll remember.'

The celebrations were indeed memorable. Tishy played the piano while everybody danced, and a great deal of Mrs Carrington's wine was consumed during the course of the evening. It occurred to Ellen that there was a sense of freedom about the event, and that this relaxation was caused by the absence of men. Even good men were a burden at times, she thought. The all-female atmosphere seemed to engender a joy that bounded on hysteria, especially when each of them was called upon for a party piece.

Abigail, looking very smart in a lilac suit, did a terrible monologue about bedpans. Her face never flickered as she recited the bawdy poem – even when she was drowned by laughter, she maintained her serious stance. Linda Tattersall, who was pretty enough in her new skirt and blouse, sang 'Greensleeves' in an unexpectedly sweet voice, then Cissie delivered a bit of Lady Macbeth that she had remembered from school. The result of this was that the whole company rubbed hands together for at least an hour, everybody convulsed with stupid laughter as the lines 'out damned spot' were repeated over and over again. Ellen, weeping with joy, said that she would never get through another washday without shouting 'out damned spot'.

Marie, who had the ability to lower her singing voice almost to bass level, gave them 'White Christmas', then Theresa sang 'Early One Morning', though she made a bad job of it because of giggles.

Ellen disappeared upstairs while Tishy played a medley of popular songs, then everybody recharged glasses and waited for Ellen to return. 'What's she up to?' asked Cissie. 'She's been on pins all day, nearly ready to give stuff away, she was. Linda, don't drink any more, you're too young. Are you sure you won't have a drop of wine, Marie? It's powerful stuff, I reckon she must put tractor fuel or summat in it.'

'No, thanks. I just don't like it. There's no use drinking it if you don't enjoy it.'

Tishy held up her hand. 'Ladies and gentlemen,' she said.

'There aren't any gentlemen,' shouted Theresa.

'And that's the truth.' Abigail hiccuped politely, putting a ladylike hand to her mouth. 'Gentlemen are a defunct breed like dinosaurs.'

'Hush,' chided Tishy. 'I want to introduce Miss Ellen Langden. She's come all the way from Paris to sing for you. Well, she didn't really, that's just pretend. Here she is – Miss Ellen Langden.'

While Tishy played the introduction, Ellen stepped into the room and everyone gasped. 'Mother!' yelled Marie, who, like her twin, reserved this formal title for serious occasions. 'What have you done?'

Theresa sank on to the rug in front of the fire. The wine had got to her, and now she was seeing things. After all, this couldn't be Mam, not this woman in fishnet tights . . .

Ellen simpered and smiled, balancing carefully on impossibly high heels as she raised the top hat and began to sing.

'I'm Burlington Bertie,
I rise at ten-thirty . . .'

Theresa flinched slightly as a white glove, waved by the performer, brushed her cheek. It was all very strange and she would never drink again. Mam looked about twenty, all legs and eyes, like a proper chorus girl.

Ellen pulled the gloves on to her hands and smiled at her daughter. She pranced about, then strutted along with a black cane tucked under her arm. She was Bert, Bert and she hadn't a shirt . . . Theresa swallowed hard. Her mam was beautiful, truly beautiful, and no-one had ever really noticed before. And she was funny too, she knew how to entertain folk. It saddened Theresa to think that such a woman had been hidden all these years, obscured by aprons and work dresses and cares. It was a pity that he was still alive, because Mam might have found herself another life, a second chance . . . Tears made their slow way down Theresa's cheeks as the song ended. Although the rest of the company cheered, Ellen stood motionless and stared at the girl on the rug. 'Nay,' she said finally. 'I know I'm not brilliant, but I didn't think I was that bad, not bad enough to cause a flood of blessed tears.'

'You were lovely,' moaned Theresa. 'You were grand and we didn't know.'

'That's right.' Marie bent and put an arm around her sister. 'We never knew what you could do, Mam.'

Ellen gazed at her twins. 'I borrowed the outfit out of Mrs Carrington's drama box,' she said. 'I thought it would cheer everybody up. I never expected to make folk miserable, not with that song.'

Abigail joined Ellen. 'They're seeing you in a different light,' she said. 'And wondering why they've never noticed this side of you before.'

'Happen it's as well,' muttered Ellen. 'I'd get meself carted off and locked up if I carried on this road every day. Now, who's going to finish these butties? Is there any more of that rhubarb wine? And who's that at this time of night?'

They stood still and listened to the knocking. 'It'll be that warden,' said Ellen. 'And I'll bet we're showing no light. He'll have heard the party and he'll want a drink. Ever since they gave him that badge, he's carried on as if he owns everybody's house. I'm not going to the door dressed like this. Abigail, go and see him off – growl if you have to.'

Abigail, gritting her teeth and attempting an imitation of a bulldog, went through to the hall. Twenty seconds later, she led in Cedric Wilkinson. 'He says he's worried,' she announced with a giggle. 'Though the word he actually used was mithered.'

'Worried?' screamed Ellen. 'Worried, is he?' She ran to the scullery and took a towel from the back of the door, wrapping it around her waist before re-appearing in the doorway. 'I'll worry him,' she said grimly. She turned on poor Cedric. 'What the heck are you doing interrupting our Theresa's party? This is supposed to be women only.

Well? Have you left your brain and tongue out in the van?'

He shifted from foot to foot, eyes wide, mouth opening and closing as he searched for words. 'I haven't got the van,' he said finally. 'I've walked here.'

'From Barrow Bridge?' asked Theresa.

He jerked his head in acknowledgement. 'It's hard, driving in the blackout. And there's not much petrol . . .'

Ellen folded her arms across her chest and tapped an impatient toe on the oilcloth. 'What are you up to now, Cedric? This is no time to be calling on folk, not while there's a war on. Have you no sense? How are you going to get all the way back up yonder? And you can't stop here, we've a wedding in the morning, in case you've forgot.'

Cedric drew a hand across his eyes. She was bonny, almost too bonny to look at. It would stay in his mind for ever, that picture of Ellen in her tailcoat, white shirt, little black pants and dicky bow. 'I'm not stopping nowhere,' he mumbled. 'It's yon peculiar feller. He's in the back yard at the Derby Street shop, drinking in the lav, he is, laughing and talking to himself and all. He's crackers, you know. I followed him from town. You shouldn't be together like this, not all of you in the same place.'

Abigail, who was beginning to feel the effects of the wine, reached up and put an arm round Cedric's neck. 'It's so nice to know that you care, darling,' she said in a sultry voice. 'There's safety in numbers, just remember that.' She stroked his shoulder. 'What a fine figure of a man you are,' she whispered before planting a kiss on his cheek, 'so extraordinarily . . .' She stuttered slightly, stumbling over the length of the word. 'So well-made,' she finished in triumphant tone.

Cedric's face was a picture, bright red and frantic. 'It's no joke,' he yelled, pushing Abigail away. 'The man's a dangerous bloody lunatic, and here you all are full of drink. Well, he's been at the whisky and all, so don't say I didn't warn you. He's bad enough sober, but drunk, he's a walking disaster.'

Ellen stared at the poor embarrassed man. He was

making a fuss over nothing again – what did he think London would do? Walk down here and attack her while she had a crowd with her? Cedric was a lovely fellow, but he had gone too far this time . . .

'He knows what you're all up to,' he said now. 'That Percy Shaw will have told him about this party—'

'And how did you know about it?' asked Ellen.

'Tishy told me,' he answered. 'When I called in at the Deane Road shop for a packet of dried peas. So I was ready for him. I knocked off work early and followed him. I've been at the back of him for hours, I have. It's not easy, this here detective work.'

Everyone except Marie seemed to find this statement very funny. They were no doubt picturing the sight of a huge man like Cedric skulking through town on London's tail. But Marie had taken no wine, so she caught the anxiety behind his words, sensed the man's desperate worry. She walked across and tugged at his sleeve. 'Will you do something?' she asked quietly while everyone else in the room continued to chatter and giggle. 'Will you help us?'

'Course I will.'

'Go for the police. Tell them there's a burglar in the shop yard, just say you were passing and you heard somebody moving about. They'll lock him up for the night, then we can all sleep sound. Don't come back here, though. You'll only upset Mam if you come back. There's not supposed to be any men at the party.'

'Right, lass. I'll do me best to get him put away.' He turned to leave, steering a careful path between dresser and table. They likely wouldn't lock that beggar up all night, though. Not once he'd proved that it was his own name over the shop. Oh heck . . .

'Mr Wilkinson?' shouted Cissie. 'Aren't you going to kiss your girlfriend good night? Come on, give us all something to talk about.'

Ellen dug Cissie in the ribs. 'Shut up, or I'll dock your pay.'

Cissie grinned broadly. 'It'd be worth it,' she said. 'Just to get a photo of your first kiss. I reckon he'd swoon. Wouldn't you, Cedric? Overcome, he'd be.'

The large man fled from the room, managing for once not to knock anything over as he went.

'You're wicked, all of you,' said Ellen sadly. 'He can't help it, and look at this lot, everybody laughing at him. Even Tishy's fair doubled up with it. Mind you, she's likely drunk. So am I, and so are you, Cissie Tattersall. It's a good job we're shutting the shops tomorrow, there's none of us could count past fourpence. Give us another tune, Tishy. Come on, we can't let daft men spoil our fun, can we? Give us a bit of Vera Lynn.'

Cedric listened to the piano for a moment or two, then he made his way up Noble Street, watching all the time for movement as he neared the Derby Street corner. At the back of the shop, he stood still and listened. Except for a couple of cats having an argument, there was no sound at all. Silently, he raised himself on to his toes and peered over the gate. The door to the lavatory seemed to be open, though it was too dark to be really sure.

He waited for several minutes, during which time he concluded that London had gone from the yard, then he climbed over the gate to make certain. The area was completely deserted. Undecided about his next move, Cedric sat on the lavatory seat for a while. It was no use getting the police, there was nobody to lock up. And they wouldn't lock him up anyway, not unless he was drunk to the point of disorderly. Where would London have gone from here? To the house? No, not yet. He was round here somewhere, hidden away like a rat, skulking in the shadows until . . . until when?

The night seemed to darken even further while Cedric pondered his predicament. He couldn't go home; if he went home, then the whole exercise would have been a waste of time. It would be stupid to stop here, because nothing would happen here, so he decided to make his way back to Ellen's. He wouldn't knock again. They were all drunk except for Marie, and another intrusion would probably prove less than welcome.

Slowly and with as much stealth as he could achieve, Cedric walked back down Noble Street, settling himself underneath the stone steps outside a cellar opposite Ellen's house. He tightened his scarf and pulled the collar of his coat high. It might be a long wait, but he was determined to sit it out.

The door of number nine opened, and Cissie came out with Linda. He listened to the 'good nights', shivering with cold as the wind picked up. For what seemed ages, he watched the house, seeing next to nothing because of the blackouts at the windows. It was hard to judge whether or when everyone had gone to bed, and the wind was biting into him by this time. He should have had some sense, he should have brought a blanket. For a so-called spring night, it was devilish cold. His mind began to go numb, and he could not manage the simplest thought. Although he fought to stay awake, the cruel chill had its way with him, and Cedric slipped into unconsciousness well before dawn.

In the back yard of Percy Shaw's house, Billy London peeled off his extra layers before climbing the wall. He'd read the weather forecast, knew the farmers had been warned to look out for frost even though this was May. By his reckoning, it was about three o'clock, and everybody next door would be fast asleep by now.

He dug deep into his trouser pockets, pushing the bottles well down where they would not break. He would show her how to make a fire all right. She was the one who favoured fires, setting light to all his stuff in the middle of the street, burning his suits and his bowlers in the grate too. Well, he had enough paraffin on him to make a proper blaze, and nobody would connect it with him. By the time the fire got going, he would be streets away.

He climbed over the wall, stopping to listen as he sat astride the top. There was no sound except for his own shallow breathing, and he cursed the weakness of his chest. Everything was magnified at this hour of night; it seemed as if the whole world could hear the noise of his labouring lungs. The house looked strangely huge in the blackness, and he had to force himself not to think of the enormity of his proposed action. They had to go, all of them had to die. Even the baby was inside, and this suited Billy, because he wanted no-one to survive, no-one who might enjoy his shops and the money that crossed his counters.

He landed on crêpe-soled feet, then took the few short strides towards the house until he reached the wooden flap under the kitchen window. This was the rear access to the cellar. It would be dirty inside, as he was going into the coal hatch, but he had deliberately worn his working clothes for this expedition, and they were already filthy from the peat. With due care and reverence, he removed his bowler before entering the black hole. The hat would have a better chance of survival out in the yard.

The cellar was pitch dark, so he stood for a while in deep gloom until his eyes had adjusted. He remembered where everything was, stepping carefully around the old mangle and a tin bath once he was past the coal, pausing alongside the loose bricks where he had used to put the cash. Yes, and she'd dumped it in a bank now . . .

At the top of the stairs, he reached for the door handle, almost praying that she had not changed her habits. If she had started to lock this door at night, then he would need to find an alternative entrance. The door swung open. He stood motionless, listening to the loud ticking of the front room clock. There was no other movement in the house; all was still except for the erratic beating of his own heart.

He crept through to the kitchen, grateful for the solidness of the floor. Flags did not creak, he thought to himself as he poured the paraffin on to the rug. It had to look like an accident, so he was starting the fire near to the embers in the grate, using as fuel a few newspapers from the stock Ellen kept under the dresser. It was so easy. His fingers trembled as he struck a match, then he stood fascinated for several seconds while the peg rug became engulfed in flame.

His knees trembled as he turned and fled quietly from the scene, not pausing to breathe or to think until he was outside again. He rammed the bowler on to his head, climbed the wall, picked up his extra clothing from Percy Shaw's yard, then sped down the back street to Deane Road, his mind beginning to spin when he reached relative safety.

It was done. The undeniable urge to laugh overcame him, and he stood in a shop doorway for a few moments while he composed himself. He had to hurry and get back to the shack he called home, that little wooden hut on his boss's land. If anyone wanted to ask questions, he would be tucked up in his bed fast asleep.

Before setting off again towards town, he searched the sky for signs of fire, but there were none yet. And that was just as well, he thought. It would be better if the house went up once he was well out of the area. But he had managed it, and that was the main thing. By tomorrow, he'd be a few steps nearer his goal, nearer to getting his shops back. And a damned good riddance to all those female schemers.

Marie moaned in her sleep. Because Cedric had made her uneasy, she hadn't meant to doze off at all, and she was struggling now to bring herself back to full awareness. There was something wrong, a strange smell accompanied by a vague crackling sound.

At last she surfaced fully, sitting bolt upright in her bed and reaching out to set flame to the nightlight on the chest of drawers. She saw immediately that the room was hazy, that white gaseous fingers were creeping under the door, and she jumped to her feet, yelling at Theresa, 'Wake up! We're on fire!' She dragged her sister to her feet and pulled a sheet from the bed. 'Here,' she ordered. 'Take this and wrap it round your face. Try to get out through

422

one of the doors downstairs, but shut it behind you.'

Theresa, stupid with sleep and drink, stood swaying slightly in the middle of the room. 'What about Mam and the others?' she asked feebly, hands coming up to rub at smoke-scratched eyes.

'I'll see to them. Now, get yourself out.'

While Theresa coughed and spluttered her way down the stairs, Marie ran into the second bedroom, grabbing Patricia from her borrowed cot as soon as she got inside. 'Fire!' she yelled at the top of her lungs. She hauled her mother into a sitting position, pushed her out of the bed, then forced her to the door. Abigail was already on her feet, but Tishy, in the other half of the double bed, remained still. Marie pushed the squirming infant into Abigail's arms. 'Get out,' she commanded. 'And take Mam with you. Here's your dressing gowns, stuff them over your faces.'

'Tishy . . .' began Abigail.

'I'll wake her. Go on, get out quick before that baby dies of fumes.'

Ellen was coughing badly by this time, so Marie wound the dressing gown round her mother's mouth and steered her through to the landing. 'Go careful,' she said to Abigail. 'Use the front, I reckon the fire's in the kitchen.'

Marie turned her attention to the still figure in the bed. Was she dead? Why wouldn't she wake? Tishy groaned softly as Marie leaned over her. It was probably the drink, thought Marie. Tishy wasn't used to drink, and nobody had monitored her intake. That rhubarb wine of Mrs Carrington's had smelled honeyish, so it was probably the sort of stuff that would suit Tishy's sweet palate.

Using every vestige of her strength, Marie lifted her half-sister from the bed, flinging the inert form over her shoulder in a clumsy fireman's lift. Although Tishy was thin, she felt terribly heavy because she had no movement in her body.

On knees that threatened to collapse, Marie made her unsteady way to the stairs. The smoke was thick out here, and she stuffed the collar of her nightdress into her mouth before beginning the descent. It was a nightmare. Every step she took was perilous, and the journey to the bottom of the flight seemed to last for ever. The stench of burning fabrics filled her chest, and her head was light, as if it were floating some inches above her neck.

Halfway down the stairs, she stumbled over something soft. It was the cat, that blessed Tinkle, the terrible creature that got under everyone's feet all the time, the animal Tishy loved. She sat down, picked up the unconscious cat, and dumped it on Tishy's back. The crackling sound was louder and nearer now, and she realized that the furniture was blazing just a few feet away.

The bottom few stairs were the worst. Tishy seemed to be gaining weight by the minute, the cat kept threatening to slip off his mistress's back, while the air was too thick to breathe. But at last, they were in the hallway. Marie, too tired to carry Tishy any further, placed the girl on the floor with the cat on her chest, then bent to drag the pair of them to the front door.

Hands reached out, and she was pulled into the night air, her mouth opening wide to take deep gulps of oxygen. The fire brigade had just arrived, and it was one of its members who brought Tishy and the cat into the street. Marie looked at her own saviour, trying to smile as she recognized Abigail. 'Thanks,' she said hoarsely.

Abigail was shaking. 'No, I must thank you,' she said. 'You have just saved my sister's life.'

'Where's Mam?'

'Across the road in Mrs Shipton's, having the hysterics. Mr Shipton went to the phone box and sent for the firemen. When he got back, he found Mr Wilkinson under the cellar steps, he's suffering from exposure.'

'Under our cellar steps?' Marie was puzzled.

'No, next door to Mrs Shipton's. It seems he was keeping watch, but the cold got to him. I'll swear it was warmer than this in February. Patricia and Theresa are both in the Shiptons' house too, but you and Tishy will definitely have to go to the infirmary. I think I'll come with you, get the baby checked over for smoke.'

Marie coughed while Abigail patted her back. 'You'll be all right,' said Abigail soothingly. 'Just a day or so in hospital . . .'

'You're trembling,' Marie managed. 'And what about the wedding?'

'Never mind that. Come on, let's get you warm.' She led Marie away to Mrs Shipton's while the fire fighters tackled the house. Mrs Shipton was brewing tea and making toast when Abigail and Marie entered. Ellen pushed the baby into Theresa's arms. 'My little heroine,' she cried. 'Marie, if it wasn't for you, we'd all be dead in our beds at this minute. You're a brave girl. Come on, get wrapped up.' She placed a cardigan of Mrs Shipton's round Marie's shoulders. 'How's Tishy – where is she? She's not still in the house . . .'

'She's with the fire brigade,' said Abigail. 'There'll be an ambulance here shortly. We'd better go to hospital, all of us.' She glanced at Theresa. 'The wedding must wait, I'm afraid.'

Theresa cuddled the baby. 'What? Oh yes, the wedding. Somebody will have to let Tom know – I'm not leaving him waiting at the altar. Can we phone Clive from the hospital? Will he go and tell Tom? Then there's poor Mr Wilkinson . . .'

'What about him?' asked Ellen, eyes wide with surprise.

'He's next door.' Abigail put an arm round Ellen's shoulders. 'He was asleep under some cellar stairs, apparently. The poor man will be suffering from exposure.' She nodded. 'We're all victims tonight, aren't we?'

'Whose victims?' asked Theresa.

Abigail looked at Marie. 'What do you think?' she asked.

Marie said nothing, partly because her throat was burning, mostly because nothing needed saying. It was his doing, all of this. She knew it, Mr Wilkinson knew it, and it was plain that Abigail was thinking along the same lines.

'Happen I didn't dampen the fire proper,' Ellen was saying now. 'After all that wine, we were none of us thinking straight. It must have been a bit of coal falling off, it must have got past the fireguard some road. It's easy done, but I blame meself. Now I've gone and ruined me own daughter's wedding day.'

'No.' Theresa's voice was strained. 'It wasn't you, Mam. Abigail and Marie know it wasn't you. This fire was deliberate. Who do we know that would want us all dead?'

Mrs Shipton paused in the act of pouring tea. 'Nay,' she breathed. 'Even he wouldn't . . . would he, Ellen?'

'I don't know. Cedric said summat about we shouldn't all be in one place. What did he mean by that, Abigail? Did he mean . . ? Oh no. Not his own children, not a little baby . . . Abigail?'

Abigail bit hard on her lower lip. 'We'll probably never know,' she said eventually. 'He'll have been clever, he'll have made it look like an accident. I'd wager a fortune that he's tucked up in bed miles away from here.'

Tishy came in with a fireman, her eyes red-rimmed from smoke. 'I've been on the engine,' she announced before slumping on the sofa. 'And my head feels funny and Tinkle's woken up and gone for a walk.'

Ellen ran to her side. 'Thank God you're all right.' She glanced around at all the worried faces. 'We must never be together again,' she whispered. Then, to the fireman she said, 'This was arson.'

He studied her. 'What makes you say that, love?'

'My husband wants us all dead. He likely got in through the cellar, and he's set fire to the house. If we all died, he'd be a bit nearer to getting what he wants. There'd only be a bit of paperwork between him and the money then. And I'd not be here to make sure he got his dues.' She lifted her chin. 'I want him prosecuted,' she said. 'He works for Dobson, lives on his land.'

The fireman removed his helmet and scratched his head. 'I'll tell the bobby, then we'll see what turns up when the fire's out. But I must say it's looking like an accident, as if it came from the kitchen range. Was the fire burning when you went to bed?'

Ellen's shoulders sagged. 'I don't know, and that's the truth. We . . . we had a few drinks, a bit of a party, and . . .'

'Does anybody smoke?' he asked.

'No. He does, though. If you find any dockers, they're his. It was deliberate, he waited till we were all in one place. He's been following us and . . .' Her voice died. There was no point. If they didn't find any evidence in the house, he would get away with it. Again. He was always getting away with things . . .

At the hospital, they were all questioned by the police. Mr Langden, it transpired, was at home in bed. There was nothing to indicate that the fire had been anything more than an accident. When morning came and everyone had been judged fit, they waited for Clive to ferry them in relays back to Noble Street.

The house was smoke-damaged, and the kitchen was a wreck, but it was not too bad to live in after cleaning. Theresa's wedding day was spent with buckets and mops, everyone scrubbing and scraping from dawn till dusk. The kitchen was filled by workers, while neighbours popped in and out with snacks, hot drinks and offers to lend bits of furniture. Clive rolled up his sleeves and tackled the ceiling, while Tom concentrated on the walls. Fathers Sheedy and Gorman, both in working men's overalls, scrubbed and painted alongside everybody else.

The four girls were upstairs going through the wardrobes. There wasn't much worth saving, and Theresa's wedding suit was among the discarded garments. Marie's dress would be wearable after a wash, and a debate took place about whether or not to try to save Tishy's blue frock. Abigail's navy costume was a definite ruin, while Ellen's new coat might just lose its smell after a day outside on the line. 'He's gone too far this time,' pronounced Abigail. 'No-one threatens my baby's life.'

'What are we going to do about it?' asked Marie. 'The

427

police think Mam's crackers, and we can't just walk up to the man and tell him we know what he did. We've not to go near him.'

Theresa sat on the bed with Patricia. 'He's too dangerous to tackle,' she said quietly. 'The main thing is we must never be together again, not while he's still around.'

Marie stamped her foot in fury. 'But we like being together. What about Christmases and birthdays? Are we going to stay split up because of him? Long enough he's run our lives. I reckon we should go, all of us, and face him.'

'Not Tishy,' said Abigail, glancing at her sister who sat on the other bed with her cat. 'She gets enough nightmares about floating hands and faces. No, it would have to be just the three of us. Does anybody know where he's living?'

Theresa nodded. 'I think he's in Dobson's shack. Dobson's the fellow who made a pile out of rags and peat. He started off living in the hut himself, only now he's got a great big house up Bradshaw. I think he lets one of the workmen live in the shed to guard his rag and bone place. That'll be where . . . you-know-who is living.'

'Right.' Abigail picked up her daughter. 'We'll go tomorrow while Ellen's visiting Mr Wilkinson in the hospital. I think it's important that she doesn't find out. And Theresa – you are coming. It's time you faced up to him. Now we'd better see if they need any help downstairs.'

Marie sat for a while after the others had left the room. She fingered her sooty new dress, and a terrible anger rose in her gorge until she was almost choked by it. The fury was directed at her father, yet the face in her mind's eye was John's. Where was he when she needed him? How could she rely on somebody who came and went like that, who actually volunteered to go off and get killed? But no, it wasn't his fault, she told herself determinedly. London was the one. He was the man who had terrorized her

428

sister, beaten her mother, burned the furniture in the kitchen. He was the one who had ruined this dress, who had postponed poor Theresa's wedding day.

She sighed, placed the garment on the bed, and made for the stairs. John! Where was he? When would he be home again? The stairs were filthy with soot. Her hand raised itself almost of its own accord. A few seconds later, she studied what she had written. DEATH TO LONDON was inscribed on the smoke-blackened wall. Perhaps Tishy was right, perhaps hands did work of their own accord sometimes. She rubbed at the message until it was obscured, then she walked down the stairs to join her family. She would see London tomorrow.

'They say he never did it.' Ellen placed the Eccles cakes on the locker, then sat in the metal-framed chair. Cedric looked terrible, all white and drawn, he was. She let out a deep sigh and smiled at him. 'There's no evidence, lad. What can't speak can't lie, so happen he didn't do it.'

'He did. He was up in the shop yard, then he must have walked down the back while I walked along the front. I've told you and you never listen. He's bloody dangerous, Ellen. Lilian knew what he was like, only she kept him down. Don't ask me how, because as far as I know, she never touched him. But he was scared, the coward, with her being such a whopper. If she'd wanted to hit out, she could have landed him straight in the middle of the week after next. Aye, a clout off her would have been like a kick from a young elephant, I shouldn't wonder. So he was sneaky, pinched her things when she wasn't looking, spent the kiddies' food money before Lily knew he'd earned it. Aye, he boxed cleverer with her.'

She patted his hand absently, her mind fixed on London and his latest doings. After a few moments, she dragged herself back into the present, grateful for Cedric's common sense. 'And you've found your words again. How are you feeling?'

'Warmer. I near froze to death, you know.'

'Yes. What for, Cedric? Are you going to spend the rest of your life watching me and mine?'

He smiled weakly. 'You looked bonny Friday night, lass. I could have wrote a poem about the way you looked, like a bloody film star.'

She sniffed significantly. 'You weren't supposed to see me like that. And then going and falling asleep out in the cold – you want your head testing, Cedric Wilkinson. You'll be off your work now. And I wouldn't be surprised if you caught double blinking pneumonia. When are you going to learn? You get dafter, I'll swear you do.'

He shifted in the bed until he was in a sitting position. 'Keep watch,' he said. 'And make sure they're not all together again, not at night. I've studied him, remember. Years ago, before you ever knew him. He took the kiddies' food from their mouths, sold all Lily's bits and pieces she'd inherited from her dad, ornaments and the like. And I'll swear he picked pockets at the races. Then he made off with that there Miss Abigail's money that was left to Lilian. I wasn't there when he did that, but I guessed once he turned up round here. There's nowt he won't do for money. Even murder won't stop him.'

She fingered her bag nervously. 'Well, the police won't listen and the fire brigade reckons it was all an accident. What more can I do?'

'I've told you till I'm sick of telling you, Ellen. You think I'm a pest, don't you? Daft Cedric making a fuss over nowt. Keep your eyes peeled. Don't be on your own in the shop, lock up at night. How did he get in? Through the cellar? Isn't it time you put some bolts on them doors and a padlock outside?'

She stared at him for a few moments. 'Happen you're not as daft as I thought, then.' No he wasn't daft at all. This was a sensible man, for all his stumblings. 'Just get yourself right, that's the main thing. What you did was . . . very kind. You were trying to look out for us, and I'm grateful. But I don't want you in danger because of my family. If he's as bad as you think, then steer clear of him.'

'No.' He sounded strangely certain of himself. 'You know how I feel about you.' His face showed signs of colour at last. 'It's a free country, and if I want to spend my time looking after you, then nobody can stop me.'

She bit her lip. 'You big soft lad,' she said. He was a lovely man, she thought. The sort she should have . . . no! There was no future in thoughts like these. 'I've brought you some cakes,' she added lamely. 'To have with your tea.'

He grinned. It was her turn to be tongue-tied this time.

She stood up and looked around the ward. 'I'll . . . get off then. Shall I come and see you tomorrow?'

'They'll have chucked me out by then, because there's nowt wrong with me. I've only come in for a warm and some free grub – if they've got any.'

'Oh. Right. I'll see you some other time, then.'

As she walked out, Cedric smiled to himself. She liked him. With the knowledge that she liked him, he turned over and closed his eyes. Bugger Billy London, he wouldn't get a chance like that again, not with the whole Langden family in the one house. There was nothing to worry about. So Cedric slept and dreamed of Ellen.

It was a horrible patch of land in a dip between Crompton Way and Breightmet, a hideous area of weed and scrub that would never look like a proper field. Abigail, Marie and Theresa stood on the edge of it, each of them seeming to hesitate to take the first step towards their father. 'I don't know why we've come,' said Theresa. 'We can't do anything. And I've left Tom to cope with his mam and the children. He'll never manage the Sunday dinner . . .'

'Shut up,' ordered Abigail. 'We've come to put him in the picture. Let me do the talking. It's time somebody set this awful man straight. Speaking of straight, stand up, Theresa. We are not going in there cowed. We arrive with our heads held high.' She inhaled deeply against the rising tide of temper. He had ruined Lilian's life, tormented Ellen, crippled Theresa, murdered Vera Shaw, set fire to a house where people slept. But worst of all, most heinous of all, he had almost killed Abigail's daughter.

Theresa forced herself into an upright posture. It was awful, coming here like this. She wanted to turn and run, even though she knew that she would be all right. After all, what could he do to her with Abigail and Marie standing by? She glanced at Marie, who seemed to be studying the grass round their feet. Marie had never been scared, not really. She'd taken some thumps, but she had never bowed to him. Yes, Marie was brave, so was Abigail . . .

Marie let out a huge sigh. 'Might as well get it over with,' she muttered. 'And I'm frightened. Not of him, he's only a little man with a bad chest. I'm terrified of seeing London, because once I set eyes on him, I'll want to set hands on him as well. Hands, feet, teeth and nails. You'll have to hold me back.'

Abigail frowned. 'We want to do this with dignity,' she said. 'There's no need to go over the top, Marie. I'm the oldest, so I'll take full responsibility. Come on, there's the hut.'

They marched in unison up to the door. Abigail knocked loudly. A chair scraped along the wooden floor, and Theresa stepped away, only to be dragged back by the other two. 'Stand your ground,' hissed Marie from between clenched teeth.

He was unshaven and dirty, and a Woodbine drooped from his lip. He had already heard from the police that they weren't dead, that the whole bloody lot of them had survived the fire, so he wasn't exactly surprised to see them alive, though he hadn't expected them to arrive here. He cleared his throat. 'Come to see your old dad, then?'

Marie held Theresa's hand tightly while Abigail stepped forward and grabbed the front of London's shirt. 'Bastard,' she spat into his face. Marie swallowed hard. If this was Abigail's idea of doing things with dignity . . .

'What the bleeding hell . . . ?' began London, but Abigail was shaking him, pushing and pulling him in and

432

out of the doorway. 'You tried to kill my baby,' she said. 'And all of us, all your children. Well, I am warning you now, watch yourself, because we are after you. Every last one of us bears a grudge. You are sick, sick, sick! There are people locked away who shouldn't . . . it should be you!' she screamed. 'In a ward without windows, without doors, padded, entombed . . .' She let her hand fall. 'They should throw away the key, you stinking rat.'

He pushed her away and straightened his collar. 'I don't know what you mean,' he mumbled.

Abigail planted her feet wide and craned her neck so far forward that her face almost touched his. 'I mean you murdered Vera Shaw, then you came for us. On Friday night, you got into the house and set fire to the kitchen.'

'Got proof?' he asked, almost cockily. 'The police have been, so I know what you told them, bleeding liars, the lot of you.'

Abigail shook her head very slowly. 'I don't need proof. If I came across a boa constrictor, I wouldn't hang about and wait for it to prove its potential. Some things are just bad, and you're one of them. Well, you're on a lot of lists now, London. There's the three of us for a start, then Ellen wouldn't be beyond taking a pot shot if she had a gun. My husband's a clever man, and he's on your tail. Then, when I tell Percy Shaw about how his wife came to die so young, you'll have another reason to look over your shoulder. Theresa's about to be married, and her Tom knows how to use his hands. He's a carpenter, so perhaps he can make your coffin.'

Marie stepped forward. 'And there's Mr Wilkinson,' she said. 'He's after you and all, followed you on Friday, he did.'

His face blanched. 'Followed me where?'

'To the yard at the shop,' said Marie.

He staggered back as if he had been struck. 'I was just having a rest in the lav. That doesn't mean . . .' His voice petered away.

It was then that Theresa pushed herself between the

other two girls. 'I hate you,' she said softly, her tone reminiscent of Ellen's. 'And that's a terrible sin, but I can't help it. I will kill you,' she stated plainly. 'If it means I can save everybody else, then I will find a way to finish you off. And you are so evil, that God will forgive me when I do it.'

Marie knew that her jaw had dropped, and she closed her mouth with an audible snap. Surely this wasn't her twin sister, that poor downtrodden mite who had been scared witless all these years? 'Theresa,' she said hesitantly, tugging at her sister's sleeve. 'Come on, now . . .'

But Theresa was plainly on her own quiet little soap box. 'I'm telling you just this once that I'll do what damage I can to you. If I go to prison, then I go on purpose. If you go, it'll be because you've been caught after being nasty and stupid.'

He raised his hand, but he was too late to protect himself from Theresa's quick reaction to this movement. A clenched fist met the end of his nose with terrific force, and blood spurted down his lower lip and chin. Abigail and Marie pulled hard at Theresa's coat, but her knee had already made contact with London's crotch, and he fell to his knees, eyes wide, bloodied lips rolled back as he fought for air. 'And that,' breathed Theresa, 'is just a taste of things to come.' She wrenched herself free of restraining arms, limping off quickly with the other two girls on her heels.

They reached the edge of the field, Marie and Abigail gasping for breath after running to keep up with Theresa, who was strangely calm and unruffled. 'Theresa,' panted her twin, 'what did you go and do that for?'

Theresa stopped in her tracks and glared at the other two. 'I don't want to talk about it,' she said. 'Except to Father Gorman. Leave me alone.' She walked on, her brain a jumble of memories and guilt about what she had just perpetrated. But she remembered all right, clear as this sky, just as if it had been yesterday, remembered flying through the air, could see him bending over her. It had all happened long ago, when she had been too little to stand up for herself. She straightened her shoulders. Yes, she could stand up now, could defend herself properly. It was a sin, but she could do it if she chose. And she would do it again and again, if necessary. One way or another, the man would be stopped.

CHAPTER SIXTEEN

The Wedding Party

On the first Saturday in July 1943, Theresa and Tom were married at the church of Saints Peter and Paul. As a direct result of the fire, Theresa and her attendants were splendidly clothed, because word had gone out among the customers, and a full set of pre-war bridal wear was lent to them free of charge. So it was a white wedding with the bride in a long dress and veil, while her bridesmaids wore shorter lemon-coloured frocks under little navy velvet jackets. Ellen had rescued her new coat, and Abigail joined the official party because there was a lemon dress for her as well. Ernest and Harold were relatively well-behaved; there was only one small incident involving the baptismal font and half a dozen church candles, so everything went almost according to plan.

The party was to be held at the farm rather than at Abigail's flat, partly because Mrs Carrington had insisted, but mostly because everyone wanted to be out of London's reach. Theresa had never referred to the incident at the shack; since that event, she had been calm and content, as if a great load had been lifted from her shoulders. Only the priests had been informed of her terrible anger, and Ellen had remained unaware of the three girls' visit to London's lair.

Up at Moor Bottom Farm, mothers, babies and expectant mothers joined in the celebrations. Theresa had insisted that they come, and a lavish wedding breakfast was achieved from pooled rations and fresh farm produce.

The living rooms were filled with people, most of the

adults taking advantage of Mrs Carrington's fast-flowing supply of home-brewed wines. Marie did not drink, though. Remembering the last time everyone had imbibed, she stayed near a window for much of the day, one eye on her family, the other keeping watch for her father.

Tishy played to her heart's content on the baby grand, but Ellen could not be persuaded to repeat her performance of 'Burlington Bertie'. Once the buffet meal was over, the table was pushed back and the gramophone poured out dance music from Mrs Carrington's collection of records. In spite of the lack of men, some interesting steps were learned and taught, then the young mothers took their infants off to bed.

Ellen watched her daughters and felt near-contentment. The day had been a happy one, and Theresa would have a good life out here in the countryside. Marie seemed thoughtful, but then that was typical of her these days. She was watchful to the point of nervousness, but this would pass, Ellen told herself stubbornly. There was something going on there – no – she would not think of it today. Tishy looked well and was laughing, while Abigail appeared to be fulfilled at last. Lilian would have been pleased to see her girls so settled.

Cedric, who had received a last-minute invitation at Marie's behest, walked around the farmyard with Percy Shaw. The latter, who had not attended the wedding, was in a state of dire confusion. 'It were young Theresa,' he said. 'She come up last week to mop her floors, brought the kiddies with her on the bus. I went to see her in me dinner hour, and she told me, just come out with it, like. She says Billy London killed our Vera. No proof, nowt worth telling the police, but she's as sure as eggs. And she's a straight lass, that one, never told a lie in her life.'

'I'm afraid that's the top and bottom of it.' Cedric placed a hand on the shorter man's arm. 'He's not right in the head,' he said. 'Set fire to their house a few weeks ago.

I only just missed being a witness to that. Followed him for ages, I did, then I went and got cold, fell asleep across the road. Same as with your missus, there's no proof. He's clever, see. A lot of them are.' He nodded his large head. 'Crazy folk often think faster than what we do. I mean, I know he doesn't act daft, but he's got this fixation with money. He'd do anything to get them shops and houses back. Your Vera likely knew summat about his past, so he had to shut her up.'

Percy shivered convulsively, and Cedric tightened his grip, forcing the man to stop and face him. 'Happen she shouldn't have told you, lad, 'cos there's nowt you can do to mend it, there's no fetching your wife back. But now that you know, keep it under your hat. Don't go tackling him, else you could wake up dead one morning. He's got his horse and cart, so he can get about, and he wouldn't be past setting fire to that cottage Mrs Carrington's given you. Whatever you do, don't lose your rag.'

'I'm getting me kiddies back and all,' moaned Percy. 'She'd no time for children, our Vera, but she might have liked it up here in the fresh air. I've given the Noble Street house up now, and she might have enjoyed living in the country, then she'd not have had chance to . . . go out and meet other men. He wants killing, Cedric.'

They walked on a few paces. 'I loved her,' said Percy quietly. 'She were no oil painting to look at, and she had some funny ways, but I thought a lot of her. She had summat called stigmatisms, I think, in her eyes, and she couldn't see proper, so the house were always a midden. There were all kinds of men coming and going when I was out. She had kiddies that I don't think are mine, and she used to lose her temper with me. That were 'cos I'm a bit on the slow side with me bad heart. Any road, when the war kicked off, we'd had a bit of a row, so I went away to Birmingham with the ambulances. I'm qualified in first-aid, you see. Could have been a doctor if I'd had chance.' Percy nodded. If he'd been a doctor, happen he might have saved her . . . 'But I thought everything would be all right after the war.' He paused for breath. 'He's took that away from me, that chance to make things straight with our Vera. He's took my life away, Cedric.'

'Nay, lad . . .'

'He has. You know what it's like to love a woman, don't you? How would you feel if he killed Ellen?'

'Well, I . . .'

'It's all right, I understand how you feel about her. Suppose you could never see her again 'cos he'd killed her, eh? What would you do if he finished her off?'

Cedric thought for a few moments. 'I don't know. But when he near burned their house down with all of them in it, I felt like . . .'

'Like what?'

The tall man swallowed. 'Like murdering him. Only I didn't murder him, did I? That's what I mean – no matter how annoyed you get, you've got to hold back. No use us all coming down to his level, Percy. He's mad and we're sane, that's the difference.'

'I wouldn't know about that, I've not been this mad in a long while. What am I supposed to say to him next time I see him, eh? Do I buy him a drink and carry on the same road as ever? Because that won't be easy, I can tell you.' He paused, staring down at his shoes. 'Anyway, we'd best get back in to this here party, else they'll all be wondering where we've got to.'

They walked back towards the house in silence, Cedric looking over his shoulder from time to time, as if he half expected to see the horse and cart coming up the lane. 'Does he know about today?' he asked as they reached the path.

Percy shook his head. 'I've not seen him, not lately. He seems to be keeping out of everybody's road. Come to think, he's not been around much since that fire. I've been to the pubs down Deane Road and Derby Street on me days off, but I've never caught sight of him.'

Cedric pushed the kitchen door open. 'Happen he's learned to keep his head down, then. Mind, he always knew how to do that. I hope he's not up to something again . . .'

Theresa was in the kitchen, radiant and beautiful in her wedding dress. She looked so like Ellen, that Cedric felt his breath catching in his throat. Marie, Abigail and Tishy came through from the hallway, all three of them laughing and chatting about the wedding. Then Ellen entered the room, and Cedric smiled down on the whole family. He would protect them. No matter what happened in the future, he would always be there whenever he was needed.

'Have you had enough to eat?' Ellen asked him.

He grinned broadly. 'I've got everything I want, lass. Well, nearly everything.' Someone tapped him on the shoulder, and there was urgency in the touch. He turned his head. 'Oh, Mrs Carrington.'

'Will you step into the hall, please?' Her voice was controlled.

He followed her into wide, oak-panelled silence. 'Phone call,' she said without preamble. 'From a Mrs Duffy.'

'Oh?'

'You seem a sensible chap, and I thought it would be a pity to disturb the family.'

'I see. What's up, then?' This was a rare woman, one who could see past a tendency to stumble over two left feet – it was good to be called sensible. But there was something coming, something unpleasant – he could tell from the look in her eye.

She sniffed, pulling at the collar of a white blouse that didn't feel right any more, damned nuisance, this dressing up. 'Mrs Duffy said to get the wedding over first, then to tell Marie that John is missing. The poor woman is terribly distraught, and she wants Marie to be informed gently. However, she could not, she says, have slept without passing on the message first.'

He leaned against a half-moon table. 'He's not been abroad five minutes. How can he go missing as quick as that?'

She seemed to stare straight through him. 'If I had the

440

answer to that . . . Stupid, foolish waste of life!' She thrust her hands into pockets that weren't there, then smoothed the dark blue linen skirt. 'Just . . . just see to it, please.' She trudged away, her body bent and older.

Cedric set his shoulders and his mouth, taking care not to bump into anything as he walked back to Ellen. He would leave it an hour. He would leave little Marie just one more hour of sweet ignorance.

The weeks moved along in slow motion, three, then four since the wedding, three, then four since John had been listed. Marie grew pale, almost as pale as Tishy, and she staggered on like a robot, no complaints, no tears, no obvious feelings at all. She got up each morning, washed herself, dressed herself, fed herself. She served customers, counted stock, counted money, counted ration points. People in the shop accepted her the way she was, because her young man was missing. As they said to one another frequently, 'everybody takes it different'.

Ellen, who was with Marie during all waking moments, grieved and suffered for her child. It was almost as if Marie had gone away, leaving behind her a shadow, a long and ill-defined silhouette cast by a dying evening sun. Tears might have helped, but the girl remained dry-eyed and virtually silent, dragging herself doggedly through each day, going to bed early in spite of summer nights.

Marie was weighing out sugar when Mrs Duffy walked into the shop. There was a brief flicker of hope in the young eyes, but this faded quickly when the woman placed herself in the upright chair, head bent beneath the weariness of waiting, hands clasped around her basket as if she were using it to squash the pain. Twice a week John's mother came in to see Marie, and Ellen wished with all her heart that the visits would stop, because Betty Duffy had a tendency to 'go on about things', always repeating herself, forever going on about John in a way that was surely no good for Marie.

Yes, she was off again. 'I bet he's lying in some flaming desert,' she said lugubriously.

Ellen dusted the counter briskly. 'Missing's not dead, Betty. As long as they list him missing, then there's hope.'

'In a desert? I know that's where he is, because he was always looking at photos of camels. They fascinated him, did camels, because they spit and they attack their masters once a fortnight. The Arabs have to give them their coats to eat, you know. That settles the animals for another fortnight, because they think they're in charge, think they've eaten their masters. What the hell would he eat in a desert? His bloody coat?'

'He might not be in a desert, Betty.' Ellen's tone was overlaid with careful patience.

But Betty, inattentive as usual, carried on. 'There'll be nowt but sand and camel droppings. I told him to keep tight hold of his mates. "Don't be on your own," I said, "always stop with the others and near food," I said. But did he listen? Did he ever blinking listen? He were the same at school. I kept telling him to stop away from trouble, but he always come home with marks on him where them horrible nuns had beat him halfway to kingdom come. I wonder how they'll feel now, them cruel women? When they hear my boy's likely dead in a desert?'

'Betty, he might not be in a desert,' repeated Ellen with as much conviction as she could muster in the face of such determined negativism.

Marie stacked some soapflake boxes in a small pyramid.

Mrs Duffy, whose mouth seemed to be pouring like a tap without a washer, continued to talk. 'He used to fetch the telegrams, now they're fetching blessed telegrams about him. He didn't like that job, you know. He felt as if everybody were staring at him, blaming him for the news. It's cold in the desert at night, I hope he's got some extra socks. You'd never know it, but he suffers with his feet, gets them chilblains and scratches them till they bleed. If he gets sand in his chilblains, they'll go bad ways. I'm sick of telling him . . .' On and on she went, while Marie stood swaying until a newly-arrived customer noticed and reached out to catch her. The pyramid collapsed, seams of boxes bursting to release a soapflake snow shower.

Ellen rushed round the counter. 'Marie,' she yelled, but her daughter's face was whiter than ever, and there was no response. Two more women entered the shop, and everyone gathered in a circle after the girl had been placed on the floor. 'Marie?' said Ellen again.

Ellen flew to the door, locked it, then displayed the CLOSED sign. 'Go out the back way,' she told the women. 'Come round after and sort the money out, just take what you need and leave the coupons.'

While the purchases were sorted out, Ellen knelt on the floor beside her child. She looked like an infant too, very small and young, completely vulnerable . . . 'Marie?' she whispered. 'Come on, love.'

Mrs Duffy stared at the pair on the flags. 'I never thought she'd take it so bad, Mrs Langden. But I had to talk to her, didn't I? She was close to him, and there was nobody else to talk to except me sister and me daughter. Well, our Shirley – she's me daughter – lives in Leigh now, so I've nobody really . . . John was the only one at home. Is she moving? I'll swear she moved just then.'

As the three customers walked out through the back door, Marie surfaced, her eyes glancing wildly from Ellen to Mrs Duffy. But at least this was some sign of life, some reaction, Ellen thought.

'Never mind, lass,' said Mrs Duffy. 'Happen he's building sand pies.' When this small attempt to lighten the situation brought no response, she picked up her basket and went to the back of the shop. 'I'll come and see you again, love,' she said before going out. 'He'd want that, would our John.'

Ellen helped Marie into a sitting position, placing her spine against the counter for support. 'Don't move,' she ordered. 'I'm putting the blinds up.' When she had covered the windows, she returned to Marie's side. 'How long?' she asked simply.

Marie blinked, her tongue loosening after weeks of near-silence. 'Eh? How long has he been missing? How should I know? He'll be a prisoner, won't he? Don't they have to look after prisoners? As long as they feed him – he needs plenty of food, does John. I think I can stand up now.' The words, delivered staccato and without expression, were, Ellen thought, a sure sign of hysteria.

Ellen used her hands to prevent the girl from standing, pushing gently against the stiff shoulders. 'How long since you had your monthlies? I'm not daft, lass, I can see you're swelling up round the middle. That bridesmaid's frock fitted where it touched. How far gone are you?'

Marie sat in frozen silence, eyes wide and gaping.

'I know you've never been regular, but when did you last have a show?'

'I . . . can't remember.'

Ellen let out a sigh which became a moan. 'And did you and John, I mean . . . did you?'

Marie jerked her head. 'It was my fault, I made him. We—'

'I don't need to be told all your personal business, love. I just want to know how far along you are. We'll have to get things ready, see Clive, have you watched and looked after. I won't say I'm pleased, because I'm not, but I don't want you to think you can't trust me.' She paused. 'Was it just the once? Do you remember . . . I mean how far gone . . . ?'

'I don't know.'

'When did it happen?'

'Winter, the first time. It was cold, it was so cold.' Her speech slowed to a pace that was almost normal. 'Then there were other times. But I thought I was all right. I mean, I go months without periods anyway, and I haven't felt ill. I noticed ages ago a lot of rumbling in here.' She placed a hand on her belly. 'Like indigestion low down. Then I thought I was just getting fat. Till the last few weeks.' She nodded. 'The last few weeks, I've known. But it's difficult when you're not regular.'

Ellen cursed herself inwardly, knowing that she herself had ignored the evidence, had been pushing her suspicions to the back of her mind, leaving them filed away in a safe place, an unreachable niche . . . 'That's your baby moving, Marie.'

'I know that. How big is the baby now?'

'Well, if it's six months since you and John . . . it'll be ready in about twelve, fourteen weeks.' She gabbled on stupidly, senselessly, causing a noise to happen, a noise that would wipe out momentarily this awful, grinding agitation. 'Mind, you're not showing that much yet. It's often the case with the first. We'd best nip up and see Abigail, she's got a lot of sense. Then when Clive gets back from his visits, he'll have a look at you. You'll have to stop at home for a bit, make sure you keep well. Good job Tishy's with Cissie today, she'd never have coped with this without telling everybody about it.' She bit hard on her lower lip, trying to stop this mindless chatter.

Marie took a deep breath. 'But people will have to be told, Mam. If I'm having a baby – and I am – they'll all have to know.' The enormity of the situation seemed to be hitting her. Talking about it, listening to Mam – it was suddenly real. Skulking in the silence was no longer possible . . . 'You can't hide a kiddy, can you?' She paused for several seconds. 'Mam, what are we going to do?' she asked finally. 'How are we going to manage with everybody pointing at me and talking about us? It's going to show you up, is this. I'll be the one who had the baby outside wedlock, I'll be cheap and you'll get called too for being my mother. What'll we do?'

Ellen smiled as encouragingly as she could. 'There's a few things, love. If you don't want anybody to talk, you can clear off now to somewhere like Moor Bottom and have your baby there. There's others like Mrs Carrington, you know, it doesn't have to be her. Then, when it's born, you can have it adopted or give it to our Theresa. She wouldn't mind pretending it was hers. Or, if you like, I'll start shoving a cushion up my skirt, I'll say it's my baby.'

She attempted a broader smile. 'I'm still young enough, you know.'

Marie frowned. 'I'm not giving him or her to anybody,' she said. 'I am going to keep this child, Mam. Babies belong with their mams. If you don't want the disgrace, I'll—'

'Hang on a bit,' said Ellen. 'I'm not bothered.' She gritted her teeth against the taste of these lies. 'It was you I was thinking of, lass. Your whole life could be ruined if you keep this child. But I'll . . . hold my head up whatever you decide.' Could she? Would she really be able to do that? 'You can live with me for as long as you want, you and the kiddy. I was just trying to work a road round things, find some way of you not being known as an unmarried mother. I mean, if you want to get wed, having one child already will hold you back. Unless . . .' She paused momentarily. 'Unless John comes home. Would he marry you? Is that what he wants?'

'Yes. If he ever gets back.' She tugged at her tightening waistband. 'I know this is a daft question, but what does missing mean?'

Ellen shrugged. 'It means they can't find him in his own regiment. See, they get split up, love. Happen he's joined another group of soldiers after he lost his own. It's easy done in war. Last time round, they'd all sorts fighting together, folk who could hardly remember whether they'd kicked off as Lancashire Fusiliers or Irish Guards or what. And he could be a prisoner of war. They get moved about, do prisoners, shipped all over the shop with the other side. If the British and Americans keep gaining ground, the camps will get shifted. He'll likely finish up back in Germany if he's been took. And you're right, they have to look after them, love. Same as we have to look after theirs. It's like an international rule.'

Marie sniffed significantly. 'He'd not be a good prisoner, Mam. He wouldn't behave. John Duffy's never known how to stop out of trouble. His mam was telling the truth, the nuns did beat him up a lot. School with nuns is a

446

bit like prison, and he was always a rebel. He'll be telling the guards to bugger off and calling them Kraut and Nazi and stuff.' Her face crumpled. 'He'll not get home, Mam. There's no way that lad of mine will come home.'

Ellen put her arms round her daughter, grateful to see some tears at last. 'God is good, lass. There's a reason for this baby, a reason for everything. I feel in my bones that John will come home when it's all over.' She forced herself to continue now, finding words to bolster her own confidence. 'The Red Cross might find summat out. It's amazing what the Germans will tell them. We'll just have to wait and see, Marie. Now, dry your eyes and think about yourself and what we're going to do. John wouldn't want you worrying and fretting over him, not with his child inside you. He's a nice lad, I always liked him. Stand up.' She helped Marie to her feet. 'And we'll go home for a good hot cuppa, then it's off to Chorley Old Road.' With grim determination, Ellen closed her mind to her own terrible misgivings. This was a pickle she could have done without, but she must try to stand by this girl, this wounded daughter of hers.

Marie dried her eyes. 'What about the shop?'

Ellen opened the door and looked out. 'They can all go to the Co-op for all I care.' She glanced at Marie. 'You're more important than a few bob and a couple of ration points.'

Marie came to the door. 'I love you, Mam,' she said softly.

They walked home arm in arm.

Clive confirmed the pregnancy that same afternoon. He sounded Marie's chest, listened to the baby's heartbeat, then pronounced that all was well. 'About fourteen weeks to go, I'd say. Should put in an appearance some time in December. Eat all the greens you can get, and don't stint on the liver. Remember, liver is full of iron for both of you.'

Marie stared blankly into the near distance, her eyes glazing and failing completely to focus.

'Marie?' Ellen tugged at her sleeve. 'What are you thinking of at all? Don't be worrying, it'll all get sorted.'

Clive leaned over Marie's chair. 'Are you falling asleep?'

'No. I'm just wondering where people are when you need them. Oh, I don't mean you and Mam and Abigail – I'm talking about John. I waved him off on that station, and I thought to myself that he needn't have gone. Not yet. He could have waited till they'd sent for him instead of volunteering for abroad. Then I could have been married and my baby would have had a proper name. But he went. Just like that, he left me and never a backward glance.'

'If there weren't lads like him, the war would be lost,' said Clive. 'You need the ones who believe, the boys who go out there because the call came from inside themselves. He's a proper soldier, Marie, not a conscript. You should be proud of him.'

Marie looked from one to the other. 'How can I be proud of anything? My child won't be legal and proper. He or she will be . . . like I was. Except Mam got married in a way, without knowing that London was already wed. I wanted my kiddies to have a proper dad, a nice dad, not one like mine. This poor mite won't have a father at all.'

Ellen walked to the window and stared out. It was lovely just here, even in the winter time it looked pretty. Now, it was lush and green, all flowers and trees and singing birds. Perhaps Marie could stay with Abigail and Clive, have her baby in the nursing home. She didn't want to think about how Marie felt, didn't want to realize that the girl was comparing her own experience with Ellen's, as if history had repeated itself. Ellen had been 'married', but Marie couldn't even go through a sham like that . . . She shook the thoughts from her head. John would come back, then Marie would be able to get properly wed to him. And there must be no shame attached to this baby, none at all. Ellen inhaled deeply. The shame was in herself, and she would need to root it out.

Abigail came in with Patricia. 'What's the verdict?' she

448

asked, though she had known the answer for some weeks.

'Very pregnant,' answered Clive. 'And a bit upset about it.'

Abigail pushed the baby girl into Marie's arms. 'Get some practice,' she said. 'Stay with us and help with Patricia. If you don't want your neighbours to be staring and making comments . . .'

Ellen swivelled on her heel. 'Marie will come home with me,' she announced. 'She's robbed nobody, killed nobody, done nothing really wrong. Let them talk all they like.' She breathed slowly and raised her head. 'It's just a baby, not a crime. We'll bring the child up between us, and Marie can live in her usual place. We're not hiding this,' she said determinedly. 'She wants to keep the kiddy, so it's as well if we start off the way we mean to go on. My girls have had enough, Abigail, and so have you and Tishy. I see no reason to cower in corners just because there's a little one on the way.' She picked up her handbag. 'Come on, Marie. We've things to do.'

Marie stared at her mother. 'Are you sure?'

'I've never been more sure of anything in all me life. This baby of yours is going to have the best, do you hear me? The best we can get with a war on. Except for you resting a bit, we carry on as normal.'

Marie returned Patricia to Abigail, then followed her mother to the door. 'Thanks,' she said over her shoulder. 'I'd rather stay with my mam.'

Abigail and Clive watched the pair of them as they walked down the road together. 'Setting off on a journey,' mused Clive aloud. 'There'll be many obstacles for them, not the least of which will be that damned arrogant religion. Poor Marie will be judged by those priests, she'll be put down as a Mary Magdalene.'

Abigail patted her baby's back. 'Marie is sound in mind,' she said. 'She can manage anything, so can Ellen. That won't be the only illegitimate child to come out of this war, not with the Yankees wandering about with nylon stockings and chocolates. And anyway, I've got a strong suspicion that this baby of Marie's is not exactly unwanted. It's a piece of John, you see. Even if he never comes back, he will always be with Marie.'

Clive studied his wife. 'Hey, you,' he grinned.

'What?'

'Where's the no-nonsensical woman I married? What's all this waxing poetical and understanding the feelings of others?'

She smiled broadly. 'Would you like me to revert to type?'

'No. Don't cry on the child, that's all. These cheap bonnets shrink if they get wet.' He ducked as a book flew past his head. 'Is nothing sacred?' he asked as he picked up the medical volume. He went out, leaving her to stand by the window with the child in her arms.

She stared through the glass, watching the figures of Ellen and Marie as they got smaller. 'Love doesn't make any difference,' she whispered to herself. It didn't stop wars, didn't keep people together, didn't solve any problems at all. Close love between two people did not insulate them against the cold world. And it was a pity, a terrible shame to know that love did not alter anything. If love could have brought John back, then it would have been a useful emotion.

She sighed, turned from the window and listened to her husband singing in the bathroom. He wasn't here because she cared about him, wasn't here because of love. It was the job that kept him at home, the Hollywell, the practice, the routine, the fact that his name had stayed in the hat when doctors had been chosen for the war. A tear gathered in the corner of her eye. She thought about Marie and John, about their baby, about Ellen and the effect all this would have on her. For such a strong emotion, love was singularly ineffectual. And it wasn't just the old Abigail who thought that. She nodded, knowing that Marie felt it too.

Towards the end of 1943, Italy declared war on Germany, her erstwhile friend, ally and defender. Marie, large with child, read for weeks about the Allies inching up the boot of Italy 'like a bug up a leg', two steps forward and one step back because the aerial cover couldn't get through the weather. Perhaps John was there, perhaps he was a bug, a little lost thing looking for other bugs and a nest to hide in. Italy was a terrible place to be, it seemed. The Germans were transporting thousands of Italians for slave labour, and many more were being shot and mutilated by booby-trap bombs. No. She decided that John would have a better chance with Betty Duffy's camel.

She turned the few pages that constituted a paper these days, reading about penicillin and how it was saving lives, even the life of a soldier delirious with septic wounds. John might be in a hospital with a broken leg or something of similar simplicity. He could be safe, because records got lost in a war, names got mixed up, wirelesses failed, the post was not reliable.

The next page was not much fun, two archbishops going on about moral laxity in war, venereal disease, illegitimate babies . . . She shook the paper to a different page. Here was Ernest Bevin, large as life, full of sense and enthusiasm, insisting that men should be called up for mining instead of going into the forces. She threw down the newspaper and let out a quiet moan, wishing that John was down a pit. Then her baby could have been official, and the archbishops needn't have worried about her.

The twinges started then, just a little bit of backache, a few grindings in her belly, a tightening, a slackening, a feeling of being dragged down slightly. She glanced at her mother who was shining shoes, her face bright in the firelight, tongue pink as it poked out of the corner of a concentrating mouth. 'Mam?'

'What?'

'Don't worry.'

'I'm not worried. I'd be less worried if this cheap polish had a bit of body to it.' She spat on the rag. 'Me dad always spat on his boots. I can't think why, it only makes them more patchy.'

'It's coming.'

Shoes clattered to the floor while the rag remained clutched in Ellen's hands. 'Are you sure?'

'Yes. It's not like anything. I mean I can't describe it. I just know there's something going on that hasn't happened to me before.'

'I . . . er . . . I'll . . .' She moved about a lot, forward and back, like a child on a rocking horse. 'I'll go and get Polly Shipton.'

'All right.'

Ellen stopped moving, became riveted to the spot. 'Is the layette ready?'

'Yes, Mam.'

'And I've got clean towels, yes, I have, I have.' She nodded with the words, her eyes never leaving Marie's face. 'Does it hurt?'

'No.'

'Then how do you know that—?'

'Get Mrs Shipton, Mam.'

'I will. Yes, I will, I'll just go and get . . . yes.' She flew through the doorway, workday clogs clattering down the hall lino.

The strains of 'Faith of our Fathers', which Tishy had been executing with wild abandon, faded away. She came to the door, a puzzled look on her face. 'Where's Ma—, I mean where's Ellen?'

'Gone for Mrs Shipton. Tishy, call her Mam. Not Mrs Shipton, my mother. I know you call her Mam. It's all right.'

Tishy beamed. 'You are ever such a nice person, Marie. Did you know your chair's all wet?'

'Yes.' The waters had just broken.

'And it's dripping on the floor? Is your baby coming?'

'That's right.'

Tishy sat down importantly. 'Excellent. I am very good with babies. Did Abigail tell you what I did all by myself with no help?'

'She did.'

Tishy leaned forward, the violet-grey eyes apparently trying to see through Marie. 'You know Mrs Banks? The lady with one tooth and a bad smell and a shawl that trails on the floor?'

'I do.' She wanted to shout 'shut up', but she managed not to.

'Well, she says I'm fey. Fey means knowing things. Marie?'

'What?' The sweat was starting now, especially on her back. She could feel it pouring, settling round her waist, all damp and horrible.

'He's alive, you see. There, now that will make you feel better.'

'Oh, Tishy – please don't.'

'Marie!' The voice was suddenly mature, almost aged, certainly commanding. 'You must believe me. It is important that you believe. He is alive.'

Marie stared into the beautiful face, seeing for the first time something like intelligence. No, it wasn't even that, it was more. It was knowledge. Pure, simple, undiluted fact. When Mrs Shipton and Ellen came in, Marie went through an uncomplicated labour, her face turned all the time to Tishy, who simply nodded from time to time, sending across the space between the two girls a silent message of encouragement.

So little Elizabeth Marie was born, on 2 December 1943, into an atmosphere of hope and relative peace. Marie's tranquillity did not last, though. As soon as the post-natal euphoria left her, she shrugged off Tishy's 'feyness', returning to the here and now with that matter-of-factness that was so much a part of her essential self. John was missing. The words 'believed dead' had not yet been appended to his situation, but Marie could find no vestige of hope in her heart.

Her baby was perfect, seven or eight pounds of lusty health and a terrible thirst for milk. The infant-down was strawberry blonde when it dried, but apart from that, she was a tiny replica of her mother, round-faced and dark-eyed, though, of course, all her features might alter with time.

Ellen looked down at her exhausted daughter. 'Well, you were quick,' she said. 'If we'd blinked, we would have missed it.'

'Like Abigail,' said Marie.

Polly Shipton laughed. 'Nay, you'll have no bother rearing that one, love. She near took me finger off looking for food. This is nowt like Abigail's trouble.'

Marie lay back on the pillows. 'No,' she said softly. 'Nothing like Abigail. Abigail's Patricia has a father.'

A heavy silence hung in the room. The two older women busied themselves with the tasks that follow a birth, then Mrs Shipton left to inform John's mother of the new arrival.

'I wish you hadn't sent for Mrs Duffy,' Marie said to her mother. 'You know how she goes on.'

'I'm sorry.' Ellen set the kettle to boil yet again. 'The woman's a grandmother. She's got every right to be told that her John's got a daughter.'

Marie kissed the tiny head in the shawl, fighting the pangs of self-pity. But it hadn't been so easy, not really. The birth had been all right, but the months preceding it had not been a laugh a minute, folk talking behind their hands and pointing at her through windows. It was over now, over and just starting. Now they could all point at Elizabeth too . . .

Mrs Duffy ran in behind Tishy. 'Thanks for sending for me, Ellen,' she gasped breathlessly. 'Ooh, I've run like the wind to get here. Let's have a look at her.' She picked up the baby. 'She's the spit of John,' she declared. 'Specially round the nose. Hey, you'll have to watch her, Marie. If there's any of her dad in her, she'll be a little tinker. Has the doctor seen her?'

'No,' replied Ellen. 'Clive will give her the once over, only it was an easy birth, so we'll get him tomorrow. Shall I make a brew?'

'Aye.' Betty Duffy placed herself in the rocker and

cuddled her grandchild. 'He would have been proud,' she said, her eyes glistening with moisture. 'He'd have been a good dad, our John. He always played with the kids in the street, was forever letting them have a go on his bike. And thanks for calling her after me, it's a good name, is Elizabeth.' She looked at Marie. 'I'm sorry, lass. I didn't mean to upset you, not at a time like this.'

'It's all right.' She had named the child for Princess Elizabeth, but there was no point in advising Mrs Duffy of that particular truth.

'And I shouldn't talk as if he's dead. We've heard nowt, and they say no news is good news.' She returned the child to Marie, all the while smiling her forced reassurance.

Marie turned her face to the window. She should have stayed upstairs instead of letting Mam bring the bed down here. It was too public, and she didn't want to grieve in front of everybody. He wasn't coming home, not ever. All she had of him was this little scrap of humanity, this child who had already been judged by the neighbours, a bastard, a mistake, a burden . . .

'Don't cry,' said Ellen. 'You might spoil your milk.'

'I'm registering John as her father.'

'Course you are. And we'll get her baptized all proper, she can wear the frock you had on for your baptism. She's no different from any other kiddy.'

'She is. She's John's, so she's special. I might . . . go away, Mam. I might live somewhere else so I can pretend to be a widow. That would be the best thing for Elizabeth.'

The two new grandmothers stared at one another. 'Don't make any plans just yet,' said Ellen carefully. 'When you've just had a baby, you don't think straight.'

Marie fixed her eyes on the child. 'Oh, but you do. I've never been clearer in my mind. It's important that she's not picked on. I don't want her left out at school, separated just because her mam was never married. Children are very cruel. Don't forget, it's not that long since I was a child. They'll hear their mothers talking about Elizabeth Langden having no dad, and she'll suffer. Anybody like that stands out in a class. I shall have to move on.'

Silence descended once more, then Tishy stepped towards the bed. 'No,' she said clearly. 'You can't leave Mam.' She touched Marie's cheek with a gloved finger. 'And you can't leave me, because I love you. John will come back. I've always told you that he will come back. He's in a secret place till it's time to come home. It's dark where he is, all black and smelly.'

Marie tried to smile at the lovely face that hovered above the pillow. 'Tishy, I wish I had your faith.'

Ellen brought a cup and placed it in her daughter's hand. 'You do what you think's right for Elizabeth,' she said. 'Only don't go too far away from us all. Mrs Duffy and me will want to see her growing up, so stay as near as you can.'

'I will.' Suddenly tired, she sipped her tea and wished with all her heart that everyone would go away. Yes, even Mam. She wanted time to think, and a chance to be on her own with Elizabeth, some space in which she might get to know her own child.

Ellen took the baby, burying her face in the shawl. She could not bear this, could not stand to see her daughter lying there knowing that her man was dead. Her whole body was rigid with fear for Marie – where would she live, how would she live all alone and . . . ? Tishy arrived to comfort her. 'It's all right,' said Tishy. 'I'm here now.'

Betty Duffy walked to the bed. 'Hey,' she whispered. 'I've lost our John many a time before, but he's never been missing this long. Shall I keep his supper warm?'

Marie reached up and put her arms round Betty's huge neck. 'She'll have a dad after all, won't she? He will be home, say he will. Say it, please.'

'He will that, lass. And a happier dad you'd never find.'

They both turned and looked at Ellen. And in that moment, Marie realized the size of her mother's love. Not just for her, but for everyone and for life itself. 'Thanks,

Mam,' she said, her voice cracking. 'For standing by me these past months. Thanks for being my mam. I shan't leave you. I'll face the wagging tongues some road.'

Much later, when Betty had left, the young mother leaned back on her pillows and stared at Tishy. 'How do you know he's alive?' she asked.

'I just do. I know things. I think Our Lady tells me.' She pointed to the statue on the dresser. 'We have little talks before I go to sleep. The hand doesn't come very often now. I think she's sent it away.'

'What does the hand do when it does come?'

Tishy shivered visibly. 'It waves about and touches its face.'

'It has a face?'

Tishy nodded slowly. 'But it doesn't seem to have another hand all the time.'

Marie thought about this. He'd never worn gloves, hadn't Billy London. And he usually kept one hand in his pocket . . . She pushed the idea to the back of her mind as Ellen passed the baby to her. There was a lot to learn, too much to be spending time worrying about Tishy and her ghostly hands. Elizabeth screwed up her little face and began to wail. It was time to feed her baby again.

He stood in the doorway of the shack, a half-smoked Passing Cloud drooping from his lip. Anyone seeing him would have thought he looked calm enough, just another man standing in another place waiting for a war to end. But inwardly, he was fuming. A dozen times he'd been over it in his mind, wondering why and how he had failed. According to Percy Shaw, it had been Marie who had saved them all, that cheeky young devil with all the bloody answers. And now, he was hearing nothing from Percy, because Percy wasn't talking to him. They'd met in the Albert one night, and Percy had walked out without so much as a greeting, so that particular avenue of information was closed.

He turned his head and stared into the hut, his eyes

watering as they rested on the squalor in which he was condemned to exist. There was an iron cot, a card table, a chair and a paraffin heater. Water was obtained from a tap outside, and he was forced to heat it on a small oil stove. This was his home. This was where a war veteran lived, a man who had given his life for his country. Yes, he had given his life, because it was scarcely worth carrying on with half a stomach and lungs like over-stretched elastic.

Yet he did carry on, driven by a force that was somehow bigger than himself. The object of being alive was to retrieve all his properties, and he had no qualms about what he might have to do to achieve that end. There was no single plan now, no way of collecting the women together and doing away with the lot in one fell swoop. They were spread out all over the place, one up in the country, one down Chorley Old Road, three in Noble Street. So he was having to work on separate ideas, and these took time and energy, the sort of energy he didn't really have any more. His health was suffering; there was no-one to cater to his dietary needs, and his chest grew worse because of the dampness in the hut. But he had not lost sight of his goal.

So many to shift, so many to remove. He tugged at the collarless shirt as jagged fragments of the past entered his mind, unbidden, creeping up on him while he wasn't ready. Fire. He knew all about fire. She shouldn't have burnt his stuff in the street, because he was an expert on burnings. Annie's house. Tipping the oil out of the lamp, striking the match, creeping out of the bedroom. Annie catching him for some different, smaller crime, pushing him into the dark under the stairs, the click of a lock. Screaming. He could hear them screaming, the foster-brothers and sisters. He listened as they died. In his secret place, he waited for Annie to burn . . .

He would have to watch this. His thoughts wandered at times, leaving him behind, putting him in a place where he had no control. Like he'd had no control in the cupboard

458

under the stairs. But he was not insane. He must hang on to the knowledge that he was not mad.

He ground the cigarette into the dust, squashing it with the sole of his shoe. Yes, he would put all their lights out. Once they were gone, bits of paper wouldn't count. He glanced up at the sky and saw that it was red, a sky that promised a good day tomorrow. Seeing this as a sign, he went indoors to work more closely on his plans. This was Tuesday. By Friday, he would have it all worked out. A smile lingered on his thin lips as he filled a whisky bottle with an interesting substance he had found in Dobson's rag sheds. Ellen's days were numbered now. The 'good little body' was on her way to becoming a good little soul.

Ellen took Cedric into the front room. 'She's asleep,' she explained. 'And so's the baby. What have you come for?'

He placed himself in one of the easy chairs and stretched his long legs. 'I got hold of some stout. It's good for expectant mothers, is black beer. I didn't know she'd given over being expectant, did I?'

She sat opposite him and smiled. It was funny how comfortable they were together now, how he had all but stopped being so clumsy and daft, how she had almost forgotten to worry about what the neighbours might think.

'Well, I just hope she pulls round now,' he said. 'I've watched her, and I could tell she wasn't herself. Always reminded me of champagne, did Marie. All giggles and bubbles, she was. Happen she'll start being her old self now.'

'Aye.' Ellen stared into the empty grate. 'When's it going to be over, though? It's gone on a long while. I thought these Americans were supposed to finish it off for us.'

'Give them time, they've only been in it five minutes. Any road, I'm here on business as well.' He stood the two bottles of stout in the hearth, then sat up straight and looked her in the eyes. 'You've a house empty over the road, number twelve. I want it.'

'Eh?' Her face registered shock. 'What? Leave that nice cottage in Barrow Bridge and come down here? Don't talk so stupid, Cedric. You've no wish to live in Noble Street. That's your own house and all, isn't it? What do you want to give that up for?'

He dropped his gaze. 'It would be handier for work,' he said.

Ellen studied him. 'You great soft lad,' she said quietly. 'That job takes you all over the place, so it makes no difference where you live.'

'I'd be nearer the depot here,' he answered. 'And I'll not give me home up, I'll rent it out to some young couple. Marie and John might like it when he gets back.' He sighed. 'If he gets back. Aye, I'll save it for them. It was me mam's house, so I'll hang on to it. Yes, that house was all she had, and she kept it lovely too. No, I just fancy being a bit more central for a while. So, what do you say?'

'I don't know.' And she didn't know. It would be nice to have him near, a good friend, a man she could talk to about the war and about the girls. He was so much like the sort of husband she would have appreciated . . . 'Eeh, Cedric,' she said. 'They'd all start rattling their dentures, this lot round here. I mean, they know how . . . they know we're . . . friends, like. They'd think there was summat going on.'

'Don't talk so wet, Ellen. How could there be anything going on while you've got everybody living here? We'd have no chance for carryings-on. And anyway, I wouldn't dream of—'

'It's the neighbours who'll do the dreaming.'

'Oh, I see. So you're refusing to rent me the house?'

'Well, it doesn't seem right. It would look awful.'

He leaned forward. 'Listen, I'll put the full deck on the table. I'm bothered, if you must know. I'm worried over the crazy feller and what he might have up his sleeve. I can't be falling asleep under cellar steps every night, can I? And if I'm speaking plain, I might as well tell you that

460

there's hearts in these cards, same as there is in every pack. I love you, lass. It's not the sort of love people talk about, because it can't be, not while you're a married woman. But love means I have to look after you the best road I can. If I move in across the street, I'll feel easier in me bones and I'll sleep better. You'll see no more of me than you do now, but at least you'll have somewhere to run.' He stood up. 'Right, I've said me piece, so I'll be off. Think about it.' He nodded, pleased with himself. He was getting quite good at speechifying.

After he had left, she thought well into the night. It had been an eventful day anyway, too eventful for sleep to be easily courted. A baby born, its father showing no signs of turning up in one piece, Marie threatening to leave home. Oh, she wouldn't go now, she'd promised to stop at least for now, but it had all been very disturbing. And to put the tin on everything, Cedric was offering to live on their doorstep, just to keep an eye out for that evil swine who was still wandering about out there, likely up to all sorts of no good.

Poor Cedric, though. He reminded her of a dog, one of those easily pleased types, like a spaniel or a retriever, clumsy and well-meaning and totally lovable because of its predictability and transparency. He was a good man, a man who deserved better than a view from across the street. And she couldn't give him more, she couldn't even give him a bit of hope. London was a sick man, but he was alive and still kicking, alive and trying to get rid of every obstacle in his path.

She sat bolt upright in her chair as the baby started to cry in the next room. Elizabeth. Elizabeth and Patricia were a new generation, another pair of targets for London's sights. Dear God, what if he tried again? And in that split second, Ellen made her decision. As long as Cedric kept his cottage on, she would let him have number twelve. There was something comforting about Cedric – the man's very size made her feel protected. Aye, happen they would talk, all that crowd out there with nothing better to do. But the main thing was to keep this family safe, and Cedric would be a willing shield.

She went through to the kitchen and helped Marie with the baby, showing the new mother how to change a nappy, how to wash the child's crumpled red face, the most comfortable hold for breast feeding. Then she sat and watched the miracle that was life, and she knew that she would have to protect these valued people until London died or moved himself back to the city of his origin. It was not wrong to use Cedric. Cedric wanted to be needed, he would be happy to be their guardian.

Tishy wandered in, her eyes heavy with sleep. 'The hand's outside,' she said.

Ellen tutted her impatience. 'See, you get back to bed this minute. You've a stall to run tomorrow, all that nice stuff you've made. You'll be half asleep come morning. Go on, get up them stairs.'

Tishy hesitated.

'And you're sleeping in gloves again. It's getting beyond a joke, all this about you don't like hands. They're dreams, love, just bad dreams. We all get them.'

Tishy sighed, picked up the skirt of her long nightdress, then went back upstairs.

Marie shifted the child to her other breast. 'Mam? Remember how he never wore gloves? And how he usually stuffed one hand in his pocket?'

'Eh?'

'London. He doesn't wear any gloves, even in winter. Do you think it's him Tishy's seeing in the street? He might be watching us.' She held the baby closer. 'I'm scared, Mam.'

Ellen thought about this. 'Nay, I reckon it's just one of madam's fixations, this. Mind you, after that fire . . . Shall I go and look?'

'No.' Marie shook her head fiercely. 'You've not to go out there on your own, not in the dark. Stay with me, though. Here, put Elizabeth back in her cradle, then get in bed with me. There'll be room if I hunch up to the window. I don't want to be on me own. Tomorrow, we'll move this bed back to its proper place. I want folk round me in the night.'

Ellen settled the baby, then went upstairs for her nightdress. Tishy was by the window, one hand pulling the blackout from the side. 'What are you up to, lass?'

'He's next to the wall, so I can't see him.'

'Who is?'

'The hand.'

Ellen joined the girl, dragging the thick curtain well away from the glass. 'There's nobody there,' she said after a few moments. Then a quick movement caught her eye, just a flash of white in the blackness. It was him. With undeniable certainty, she knew that this was the monster she had married. Not wanting to frighten Tishy any further, she eased the girl back towards the bed. 'Tell me about the first time you saw the hand,' she said gently. 'Tell me what you remember.'

'It pushed,' said Tishy.

'Pushed what?'

'Another shape in the dark.'

Ellen inhaled sharply. So it was true, then. Vera Shaw had been murdered, and poor Tishy had been a witness to the crime. But who would listen now to Tishy and her wild ramblings, who would care with Vera long dead and buried? 'When was that, Tishy?' she asked carefully.

'In the cold, when there was a lot of ice. Then, afterwards, I had a nice time, because we went down the shelter and I learned some songs. But when we came back, I remembered about the pushing hand. Sometimes, I dream about it and that's why I wear gloves. I don't like seeing my own hands, especially at night.'

This, thought Ellen, explained a lot of things. No wonder Tishy was nervous about being alone at night, no wonder the girl liked a night light to burn on the mantel. 'It won't hurt you,' she said now with as much conviction as she could muster. 'Mr Wilkinson's coming to live across the street, and he'll see that hand off for you.'

463

Tishy leapt into bed. 'I like him. He's big and strong and he gives me sweets.' The large, lustrous grey-violet eyes stared at Ellen innocently. 'He likes you, Mam. He likes you ever such a lot.'

'I know.'

'And you like him too.'

'Yes.'

Tishy pulled the sheet up to her chin. 'Will you marry him?'

Ellen smiled sadly as she kissed this beautiful adopted daughter. 'No. Go to sleep.' She stood in the doorway and watched Tishy feigning sleep. How many more times would the girl get out of bed and check for the hand? How many more nights would be disturbed? She closed the door and began to descend the stairs. In her mind, she answered Tishy's question. 'I can't marry him, love. I can't marry anyone, because I am wed to the hand.'

CHAPTER SEVENTEEN

BOLTON EVENING NEWS

Tuesday 4 January 1944

The body of Mr William J Langden was discovered this morning in Back Noble Street, Bolton. Witnesses informed our reporter that what appeared to be a large carving knife was protruding from the deceased's chest.

Police are currently searching the Deane and Daubhill areas for clues, while Mr Langden's family is being comforted by friends and neighbours. According to our sources, Mr Langden had recently left his wife after a disagreement. He was in the employ of Charles Dobson at the time of his death. A Londoner by birth, Mr Langden leaves four daughters. He was a well-known figure, having been a shopkeeper for many years.

CHAPTER EIGHTEEN

Questions

'I can't, Father. I can't and I won't.' She lowered her head and prayed, irrationally, hopelessly, for the burden of knowledge to be removed from her soul. Mankind's original sin had been knowledge, hadn't it? All dressed up by the Bible, serpents and trees and a beautiful garden, but that was just decoration, because Eve's real offence had been finding out the difference between good and evil. Knowledge. Of course, it would have to be a woman who discovered immorality . . .

'Ellen?'

'Don't ask. We've had all that with the police, who was where and what was what and when did we all go to bed. I just came here because I didn't understand where else to go.'

'Unburden yourself. Put it all into my hands, because it will travel no further.'

'No. I'm not saying it. It's not mine to tell, so it can lie with him in the morgue.' She pulled air into her mouth, gulping thirstily, fighting against thought, against awareness. 'It's out of my hands and yours, Father.'

He shifted noisily, pushing his face against the grille. 'The thing sits on your conscience too, just as it plagues the real sinner's mind. You become a party to the murder by holding it to yourself, by shielding—'

'Oh, we've had all that and all. Accessory before the fact, after the fact, during the fact. Don't push me, else I'll fall over, Father. We can all take so much and no more, and I'm not keen on going crackers. Somebody . . .

somebody I know did this, killed him, got to him before he could get to us. I'm grateful. I'm glad he's dead.'

He muttered a brief prayer. 'Murder is a mortal sin,' he said. 'Don't share in that vile act by staying silent now.'

Her hands clutched the rosary beads so tightly that she could feel the bevelled edges cutting into her palms. 'I will share. If keeping quiet is sharing, then I share.' Her voice arrived weak and faint, because her body had been depleted by lack of sleep and food. 'God is my judge, and I choose to carry my part. If this means I'll be excommunicated, then there's nowt I can do. I just came to church because there's nowhere else. Like I said before, there's nowhere at all I can go now.'

He sighed. 'You will not be excommunicated, Ellen.'

'Then why do you need to know? Isn't it up to the person involved? Let him or her do the telling. Or are you just curious like everybody else, like them from the newspapers who're all hanging round our house, a plague of blinking vampire bats?'

'No.'

'I'm sorry.' She lifted her head. 'Will you absolve me, then?'

'Say your Act of Contrition,' he whispered. 'And as many prayers as you've time for. Pray for guidance, ask the Holy Spirit to show you the way to grace. I shall offer a mass for you and yours.'

She watched the black shape making the Sign of the Cross in the air. '*In nomine Patris . . .*' he began. She shouldn't have come here, there was no help for this, not anywhere. Except, perhaps, inside herself. London was dead, finished, cut down by his own malevolence. Ellen's perceptions, all the real answers for police and priests, would have to stay locked away, because she could do no good by allowing their release.

Duly absolved and blessed, but feeling no comfort after the sacrament, she came out of the church and stood on Pilkington Street. It was very cold, so when she began to walk, she moved briskly, trying to get some blood to flow through chilled limbs. Then she found herself running, just as she'd run on that Sunday, the day of the starling, when war had been declared. And her feet took her in the same direction too, down to the centre of Bolton, away from the scene of the so-called crime.

There were things she should be doing, proper things, like looking after Tishy who was ill again, helping Marie with the baby, keeping the pressmen from the door. Or she should be standing in a shop, a shop that was closed down, customers likely queuing from Deane to kingdom come, ration books at the ready, feet frozen to January pavements. They'd have to go up to Cissie. Aye, Cissie would see them right, nobody would starve. But she still felt guilty about sneaking out of the back gate and leaving everybody to get on with it . . .

She slowed down when she reached the market, walked along between rows of stalls, stepping carefully, making an effort to look normal. Yet folk were still staring at her, drawing aside as she approached, jabbering quietly as soon as she'd passed by, a terrible gluttony for gossip showing in a stilled hand, an awkwardly held basket, a gaping jaw. They'd read their papers all right. They'd read about it, feasted on it, torn all the gristle from the bones, sucked out the marrow. How many days since he'd been found? Three? Four? Time enough for them to shape it into a Shakespearian tragedy, for London to become the pitiable, sad victim of his family. After all, hadn't she thrown him out, and wasn't his body found not ten yards from her back gate? Yes, he'd make a grand King Lear, this time with an extra daughter to torment him. Was it King Lear, she wondered. Mad as a hatter, ran around wasteland with a fool. She hadn't read the play, hadn't seen it, but she'd found the gist of it in a magazine article. And had she been acting the part of the fool for all those years? Dear Lord, what a time to be struggling to remember a blessed daft stage play!

She wanted to stop, shout, bellow from the depths of her lungs, tell these people everything; bigamy, theft, murder, arson. Most of all, she wanted to yell aloud about him crippling a child, but she couldn't. No, it all had to stay inside with the other knowledge, the truth she couldn't bear to allow near the front of her mind.

She stumbled into a UCP, grabbed a cup of tea and a biscuit at the counter, found a corner near the window away from all the headscarves and Pasha smoke, a safe distance from whispered confidences. There was a crack in the cup, and this would normally have offended her sense of decency, but she drained the tea in one gulp, then swallowed the biscuit like a starving dog. She had forgotten to eat, couldn't remember remembering to eat.

'Hello there.'

She looked up. Audrey Carrington was easing herself into the opposite chair. She was all dressed for town, muffled up in an ancient fur coat, a twenties style cloche pulled resolutely down to the eyebrows, brown leather gloves and a bag that looked like alligator. 'Shopping,' she announced to the world in general. 'Baby clothes, extra blankets. Like gold, of course.'

'Yes.' Ellen made to stand.

'Don't go.' The gloves were off, hands stretched palms down on the table. 'Talk to me.'

Ellen sank back into the comfortless chair. 'There's nothing to say.'

Mrs Carrington swivelled her head towards the steam-wreathed counter. 'Tea here,' she shouted in a voice that would brook no nonsense. 'Tea for two and anything you've got, toast or some such thing.'

There was a brief stillness in the room. They weren't used to gentry here, and this one was thoroughly weird, wrapped up till she looked like an escaped grizzly, and vocal chords on her that would have been better placed in a parade ground. They nudged and giggled, pointed to the dated hat, bit into their food, lit another cigarette. The hubbub got back to normal in seconds. 'Nine days' wonder, that's all it will be,' smiled the large lady. 'It was the same when I lost the Galloping Major. We'd had our

469

disagreements, some of them fairly spectacular, so a few in the village wondered if I'd arranged his accident by drugging the horse. I didn't, of course. Rather fond of horses. I was fond of the old man too.' She folded her arms. 'Well?'

'Neither did I. Kill my husband, I mean.'

'Quite.' She glanced through the window as if arranging her next words. 'Theresa and Tom have been questioned. Even Percy Shaw's had a grilling because of where he used to live. He cracked, of course, told them about his wife's fall.' She breathed deeply and returned her attention to Ellen. 'Gave himself quite a motive, wouldn't you say?'

Ellen slumped forward, elbows on the table, chin in hands. 'Everybody's got a motive. We're all in trouble. And they've been through our street with a fine-toothed comb, questions and fingerprints, watching and poking about. Not to mention the newspaper reporters trying to get in the house.'

'It will pass.'

'Will it?'

'Of course.' She paused just fractionally. 'Because none of you killed him.'

The tea came, banged on to the table by a woman whose face was living – yet scarcely alive – evidence of practised and perfected surliness. Mrs Carrington gave her a threepenny bit. 'Try to cheer up, old girl,' she whispered, patting the waitress's arm. 'Otherwise you are going to look extremely old very soon. A downturned mouth is so ageing.' She poured the tea as the woman stamped away. 'Eat the toast,' she ordered, not unkindly. 'And stop worrying. It will come out as person or persons unknown, I'm sure it will. Then everyone will be left alone to get on with life.' She sniffed the tea suspiciously. 'If this can be called life.' After a small sip, she replaced the cup quickly. 'Bloody muck,' she cursed.

Ellen chewed on the dry toast, which admitted just a passing acquaintance with margarine, and the result of this brief meeting floated in the middle like an oily yellow pool. But she felt better. She must have been short of food, and the starvation had clouded her judgement. Well, she knew what to do now.

'Can I give you a lift? I've brought the old jalopy.'

'No. No, thank you. I've an errand to do.'

Mrs Carrington stared hard at Ellen. 'Don't,' she said.

'Don't what?'

'I'm not sure. Just . . . don't.'

Ellen grabbed her purse and stood up. 'Ta for the tea. I'd best be off.'

'He was a cruel man.' This was statement rather than question. 'Let him rot, Mrs Langden. Theresa has told me everything – well – as much as she knows. You, as his wife, must have been so much more aware, more conscious than anyone else of the man's disorder. Do not take anything on yourself just to protect others.'

Ellen fled, frightened by her own obvious transparency.

She sat on a bench just off the Town Hall Square, the winter frost biting into her bones. They were all suspects, every last one of them. Even Clive and Tom had been questioned closely, simply because they had married into a family where hatred was the norm.

The old soldier was on the corner as usual, the man without legs. His torso rested on a wooden platform with a wheel at each corner, and he used his arms to get about, pulling himself along on padded knuckles. He was stationary at present, selling the daily papers, and she wondered which page would be dedicated to Billy London in tonight's *Evening News*. He'd lost his front page spot now. There'd been a fair amount of coverage, because London was termed a war veteran, and war veterans deserved a more dignified death. The soldier without legs was twice the man Billy London had been . . . She turned away and fixed her eyes on a group of hopeful feral pigeons.

Every one of the girls had a good reason to kill London. So did Cedric and Percy – even Cissie had her grudge against the man. No doubt they would dig around, these policemen, ferret and sniff until they found an answer. They might as well put all the names in a cap and run a raffle, because everybody stood the same chance of being nominated as the murderer. It was like some blinking gangster film, who's going to take the rap, whose turn is it this time? Yes, happen James Cagney would be along in a minute, hat pulled over one eye, gun in a violin case, lip curled over a cigarette. And after a couple of hours, credits would roll and THE END would come up on the screen with an air raid warning and an advert about where to get your shoes mended.

She pulled in the belt of her coat and hugged herself against the cold. It was stupid, sitting here waiting for pleurisy. The place was only a stride away, and she'd be better if she just went in and got the whole thing over and done with. Then, as Mrs Carrington had said, everybody could get on with a life as near normal as possible.

The Town Hall clock was its usual big and beautiful self when she looked up at it. No change there, still one of her favourite things. They used to come here, she and her dad, when the pigeons were young and training. The birds' first flights had been from these steps. Jack used to come with them to release the pigeons . . . Her heart lurched. What if the bobbies started on her brothers as well? She'd kept away from them for ages, just in case London might decide to prosecute after the bother. What if all that came out some road? If they found out that Jack and Joe and Terry had given him a hiding that Christmas . . .

'Right,' she muttered under her breath. 'That's it, Ellen, go and get it sorted.'

She turned left, followed the Civic Crescent's majestic curve, let herself in under the faint and hooded blue light. The sergeant on the desk was about fifty and running to fat. He had an orange moustache that clashed severely with a red, bulbous nose, and one of his eyes was affected by a tic, so that he seemed to be winking all the time. 'Can I help you?' he asked, his affliction making him friendly.

'Detective Sergeant Miller, please.'

'Nature of your business?' He looked over his shoulder to where a young constable was having trouble with a vagrant. 'Can't you shut him up, Charlie? Tell him he can't stop another night.'

'It's about William Langden. I'm his wife – his widow,' said Ellen, speaking to the desk sergeant's left profile.

'No, he can't have his dinner. Send him out, he'll smash a couple of windows in half an hour, after I've gone off duty, I hope, then we'll see him after court tomorrow.' He looked at Ellen. 'What was it you wanted?'

'It's about the Deane murder. I was married to the dead man.'

He paused, looked her up and down, winked a couple of times. 'Well, I'm very sorry, love. See, sit yourself down over there, Charlie'll get you a cup of tea once he's got shut of Ivan the Terrible.'

She didn't know why, but she asked, 'Is he Russian, the tramp?'

'Nay, missus.' He smiled, tried not to wink, expanded his chest even further. 'It's just that none of us can understand a word he says, so he might as well be a bloody foreigner.'

Ivan was steered to the door. 'Gizzabittadinner. Juzzascrap. Mansgottereat,' he shouted.

'He's Irish,' said Ellen. 'Liverpool-Irish.'

The sergeant scratched his nose with the blunt end of a pencil. 'Is he now? Aye well, we learn summat every day.'

While being ejected, Ivan emitted a stream of curses only too familiar to Ellen. It might have been her dad. Yes, if she closed her eyes, her father was back, kicking and shouting his way through life, damning authority and all who wore its uniform. She slid on to the bench, purse clutched in a hand, eyes fixed now on an IS YOUR JOURNEY REALLY NECESSARY? poster. It was. Her journey was the only answer.

The tea arrived, tepid and saccharined, a few listless leaves floating on its pallid surface. A woman asked, through tears, if they had found her little dog, black with a

473

long tail, and a boy reported a stolen bicycle. Papers were shuffled, a telephone rang, Ivan came back and made another impassioned plea for shelter.

In her mind, she rehearsed her lines. They would ask her how she'd done it, of course, and she'd say that the knife was from her kitchen. They'd want to know why. She could write a book about why if they gave her a ream of paper. The next question would be, no doubt, why, at this particular point in the cosmos, had she pushed a knife into a man's chest?

One of the policemen at the scene had let slip about the bottle of poison found in London's pocket. London was coming, she would say, to put rat killer in their milk. Now, how would she know that? Was the stuff marked, did it protrude from his coat? And how had she guessed when to skulk in wait for him to come and skulk in wait for . . . ? This promised to be complicated. Lying wasn't easy. To be a good liar, a person needed a sharp memory and a vivid imagination. She had, at the moment, about as much imagination as last week's cabbage.

A man was thrown in at the door, folded stockings spilling into the room from a split bag. The desk sergeant winked. 'At it again, Freddie? No licence, no bloody feet in the stockings? Go through, lad, you know the drill.' Freddie cocked his hat and walked jauntily through a half-door and into the back of the station. He would be charged with illegal trading. Ellen would be arrested for murder.

Miller walked towards her, a cardboard file tucked under his arm. 'This way, Mrs Langden.' She followed the other criminal through the little door, heard him pleading from a cubicle, 'But I thought they were kosher, honest.'

In a second small room, she faced the man with the file. He wore an ordinary suit and the air of a man who had not slept for several days. 'Glad you came, Mrs Langden. The report is complete. We're closing the case. Sad business.' He shook his head in a suitably sombre fashion.

She cleared her dry throat. 'Oh,' she managed, though it came out high and squeaky.

He clasped his large hands and leaned towards her, his attitude confidential, almost conspiratorial. 'We know what he was up to, love. One of your neighbours put us in the picture, gave us an idea of his behaviour. Sorry to have troubled you, but it's procedure in these situations.'

Open-mouthed, she swallowed, her throat moving of its own accord. The sound of it seemed to bounce off the walls.

His hands released each other, and he took up the file. 'Post mortem's done,' he said. 'Mr Langden died of what they call an occlusion. That means a heart attack. Now, he was plainly loitering with intent, carrying rat poison and the knife. When his heart stopped, he fell on his knife. There was very little blood, because his heart had given out before . . . Are you all right, love? Look, I know it's a bit gory, but you have to be told. You didn't want to wait till the inquest, did you?'

The life was draining from her head. She pushed back her chair, forced her face down to her knees, fought for breath. From a distance, she heard Miller calling for water. He was a kind man. She was carried through to a little holding cell with a hard bed and a chamber pot in a corner. They laid her flat, placed the water on the floor, then left her to cry a widow's tears in dignified privacy.

She turned on her side and stared at the door. It was an open door, but there were bars in it. They were talking in the narrow corridor. 'Aye, well, he might have been a bad 'un, but he was still her husband and she's bound to be upset.' This from the winking sergeant. His voice raised itself. 'You what? No, he can't come in for a warm. Tell him we'll ship him off to the Russian bloody front if he doesn't pipe down.'

Detective Sergeant Miller crept in, saw her wide eyes, helped her into a sitting position. 'There you are, lass. Take a sip of this water.'

She sipped and coughed. 'There's brandy in it.'

'Aye, well don't tell anybody, else we'll be getting a queue.'

She swung her legs over the edge of the thin, lumpy mattress. 'Will it go in the paper? About it being natural causes?'

'It will. There's no evidence to say otherwise, no sign of a fight. And there's no point arguing with medical facts, love. Your husband dropped dead, and that could have happened any time, given the state of his health. We'll make sure the *Evening News* gets this post mortem report as soon as the big boss releases the OK.' He yawned, displaying teeth stained by tobacco and hurried living.

'You need some sleep,' she said.

The yawn became a grin. 'Yes, move over and I'll catch a few winks. Take care, now. Go home when you're ready. This is Ivan's cell, he'll be back in a minute shouting for room service.'

After he had left, she stood up, studied the size of a prisoner's life, then walked out to freedom, waving a grateful hand at the winking desk sergeant. He raised his pen, then carried on filling in details. The dogless woman was back again.

Cold air bit into her lungs, and she tasted it, dragging it over her tongue, savouring the stench of liberty. Ivan had propped himself against the wall. He wore fingerless gloves and a balaclava so full of holes that it looked like lace. A dirty ear poked through one of the spaces, allowing him a lopsided appearance. She took a ten shilling note from her purse and pushed it into grimy fingers. 'Look after yourself, lad.'

Bloodshot eyes flitted to her, to the money, back to her. 'Yeraluv,' he said. 'Getmeselfacuppa.' He lifted an invisible hat, then staggered off in search of warm air and trouble.

A car door swung open. 'Get in.' Mrs Carrington was at her most imperious. Ellen climbed into the untidy vehicle. It reeked of leather, wet clothes and pig. 'Well?' A cynical eye studied her.

'Natural causes.'

'Interesting.' She sifted through the gears, selected the

one that made least noise, then steered erratically towards Deansgate. 'All over, then?'

'Yes.'

The car rattled past the market, bits of harness and shopping bouncing around in the rear seat. 'How did they account for the weapon?'

Ellen hung on to the dashboard as they careered round a corner at an angle that seemed to defy gravity. 'He had a heart attack, then fell on the knife.'

'Really?'

'That's what they think. It's what they're saying.'

The brake was applied with enthusiasm and arrogant disregard for other road users. The car shuddered, stopped with its left nostril on the kerb, the engine phut-phutting confusedly. Mrs Carrington heaved herself round in the seat, giving Ellen the benefit of a full two-eyed searching stare. 'Whatever, leave it alone.'

'Yes.'

Brown leather hands tapped the steering wheel. 'Had a dog with cancer once. Nice old thing, knew every word I said. The vet wanted to open him up, cut the damned disease out. But it would have liked an airing, old Roley's growth. So I refused. Roley and I lived quite happily for another two years with his cancer. Some things are better without an airing, m'dear.'

'I know, but—'

'Leave the butting to the goats. Let things die naturally. Roley went in his sleep. I've still got the collar and lead. Things have a tendency to fade away if left to their own devices.'

Ellen tucked her chin into her throat. 'I know who. And I know why and how.' There was something so comforting, so absolutely trustworthy about this solid woman. 'And that will fade away? Will it fade for the one who . . . ?'

'That's of no consequence. Just go home, comfort your people, open that shop—'

'Not all the neighbours are on our side,' Ellen gabbled.

'There's some talking about Marie and the baby, others going on about me chucking my husband out to live in a shack. And since this happened, they've had loads to sharpen their teeth on.'

Audrey Carrington rubbed at one of the larger marks on her windscreen. 'It's outside,' she said. 'Bloody pig dirt, it gets everywhere.'

Ellen giggled. 'The only answer is to kill the pig.' After this announcement, she finally allowed the hysterics to overtake her. While the ancient car complained, while Audrey Carrington comforted, Ellen poured it all out. When she had finished, the driver chose a random gear and set off for Deane. The knowledge was shared now. And the old saying was true, because half the sick burden had left Ellen's heart.

There was only one reporter outside the house now, a tenacious type with a bloodhound nose that could sniff out a story whatever the direction of the wind. He had a camera around his neck, and a pronounced limp from infantile paralysis, so Ellen felt sorry for him, but not sorry enough to talk.

She directed a silent look of pleading at her erratic chauffeuse. Mrs Carrington, catching the message, poked her head into the street. 'Young man?' He approached somewhat crabwise, depending heavily on the steadier limb. 'Come with me and I shall feed you,' smiled Mrs C. 'A sojourn in the countryside would do you no harm. I offer good home-cured ham, eggs fresh from the chicken, mushrooms from my own orchard. Have you come far?'

He frowned, reluctant to trust, yet his eyes gleamed with the memory of pre-rationed food. 'London's my home,' he replied. 'But I'm covering all points north of Birmingham, so I tend to move about.'

'I see.' She pulled down the cloche even further, and Ellen wondered whether the woman could really see with her eyes all but obliterated by the hat. 'Which newspaper?'

He shrugged. 'Any that will pay.'

'Sensible chap. I'm a firm believer in free enterprise, Conservative Party and all that. Come with me. Mrs Langden is going into her house now, and there will be no further news for you today. Except for a small titbit which I can impart.' She paused. 'Like cause of death?'

He stood by the car while Ellen climbed out. 'Post mortem done, is it?' he asked, his eyes narrow.

'Yes.' She avoided the penetrating stare. 'Mrs Carrington has the details.'

He had difficulty getting into the passenger seat. Ellen watched him, trying to keep the pity out of her eyes. Folk like him didn't want pity, they wanted to be treated like everybody else. Except he wasn't like everybody else, because he made his money through poor souls' suffering. This was no war correspondent, no historian going about to photograph the devastation. No, he handled the sordid stuff, murders and rapes, gangland killings. She'd seen his name the odd time in the Sunday press, in the sort of paper Catholics weren't supposed to read. But they did read them, because they were human . . .

The car pulled away. Ellen put out a hand to feel for the railings along the stone steps, realizing just in time that they had been taken away years ago for munitions. She must be tired, groping for support that wasn't even there. Doors began to open, number six, number three, number fourteen where the deaf woman lived. Number twelve stayed closed, of course, because that was Cedric's new home and Cedric was at work.

She faced them, dragging the courage from the soles of her shoes, standing as tall as her stature would allow. Mrs Shipton emerged, stood on the pavement, face scrubbed, clogs gleaming, a look in her eye that forbade any other neighbour to move. It would be Mrs Shipton who had told the bobbies what he was like, about the beatings and the drinking and the night of the fire. Aye, and Cedric too, he would have put in his sixpennyworth.

All along the street the doors stood at half-mast, bits of faces peering out at the woman whose husband had been murdered. Ellen climbed to the second step and surveyed the area. She was past pain, past rational behaviour. 'Nobody killed him,' she yelled. 'He did it himself.'

The deaf woman came out and made the 'hello' sign. She was a Polish-Jewish lady, and no-one could pronounce her name, so she was called Mrs Ski, 'ski' being the last of a plethora of unpronounceable syllables. Ellen 'helloed' back with her fingers while Mrs Ski smiled broadly. She hadn't a lot to smile about, thought Ellen. Polish husband serving in the British Air Force, corsetry business gone to the dogs because nobody could afford to be fitted. Yet Ellen could feel the little woman's encouragement reaching across the cobbles like an invisible crutch.

Emboldened, Ellen climbed another step. 'Heart attack,' she shouted, her voice high and strained. 'He was carrying a knife and poison to kill us all. When he collapsed, he fell on the blade. It'll all come out in the paper, you'll see.' The lie hung in the air for several seconds, then doors swung wide and people came into the street, murmuring 'Well, we thought it would be that,' and 'Serves him right when you think about it.'

Ellen listened while the tune changed. Seconds earlier, she had been a woman to be feared, someone who had orchestrated a man's death. Now, she was both heroine and victim, because they immediately chose to remember how she had been treated, how odd and strange London had been. King Lear was dead, just another of Willie's fairy tales. She walked into her house and slammed the door against fickle humanity.

Marie was waiting in the hallway, the infant clutched against a shoulder. 'Where've you been?' Her tone was not far short of accusatory. 'That man was hanging about all the while—'

'Yes. Well, I've been to church, then I went to the police. It's all over. Natural causes.'

Marie's eyes widened. 'Eh? But what about—?'

'What about nothing. Never mind what abouting. That's the verdict, and that's what the coroner wrote on his bits of paper. Your father's heart gave out.'

Marie was completely immobile for a moment, as if she had been rooted to the spot. 'I don't understand,' she said finally. 'I mean if he was—'

'Marie!'

'What? I'm only saying . . .' Her words tailed away as she saw the expression on her mother's face.

'It is written down, Marie. There'll be a certificate issued tomorrow and he can get buried. Cedric will see to all that, there's no need for us to be following a hearse and acting like hypocrites. I shan't even have his body fetched home. Get that kettle on, my stomach thinks my throat's been cut.' She walked past her daughter and into the kitchen.

'Mam . . .'

'I'll do it myself, seeing as you're busy with Elizabeth.' She picked up the kettle and turned to find Marie standing one step behind her. 'I need to get to the scullery for water, love.'

'Mam!' Marie raised her voice, as if volume would produce confidence. 'You told them we'd two of them big knives, and I know we had three.'

'It's a common Sheffield make, could have come from anywhere.'

'It was ours.'

Ellen replaced the kettle on its blackened hob. 'Listen, lady,' she said quietly. 'He was dead before the knife touched him. So whatever you think, or suspect, or want to confess to—'

'I never! It wasn't me!'

'It wasn't anybody. On the death certificate, it will say "cause of death". And under that, it will have heart attack or whatever fancy words they use for such things.' She lowered her tone even further. 'Them knives were passed all over. Sometimes they were in the shops, sometimes they were here. So are you going to have Cissie and Linda Tattersall suspected of attempted murder? Or Cedric? He could have picked one up here in our kitchen. Leave well

alone, Marie. He collapsed, then he fell on his own knife.'
She removed her coat in one swift movement. 'His own
knife, one he carried like he carried rat poison. Have you
got that?'

'Yes, Mam.'

'Where's Tishy?'

Marie shrugged. 'Crayoning somewhere.'

'Is she all right?'

'She won't eat at all and she says her head's funny.'

Ellen finally managed the journey to the scullery for
water. Her legs seemed to have turned to jelly, and she
gripped the short counter that held the twin gas rings. It
would be a case of sticking to the story through thick and
thin, and although there were no direct lies involved, Ellen
was uncomfortable with anything less than complete
truth. But, she thought as she turned the tap, when had
there been honesty in this house? There had always been
something to hide, mostly because of him. Now that he
was dead, perhaps this might be the final deception.

Things settled, rested like a fine layer of dust spread over
deeper disarray. Cissie ran the Derby Street shop with a
capable assistant called Ada Benson, while Ellen continued alone on Deane Road. London was buried after a
brief service at a Church of England chapel, and the sole
attendant was Cedric Wilkinson. There were no flowers,
no mourners, and the shops remained open during the
service.

There was a silence in number nine, a silence that
existed beneath the noise and chatter of day-to-day living.
When various members of the family visited, a certain
subject was never broached, even when the newspaper
published the full story. Marie did not dare to discuss the
matter with her mother, while Tishy seemed to be
blissfully unaware of anything untoward. But when Clive,
Abigail, Tom and Theresa called at the house, the tension
hung in the air like an impenetrable fog. It seemed that
everyone was afraid and, in the ultimate analysis, there

was mistrust in the house. This, thought Ellen, was London's final legacy, his last triumph.

After the inquest, the lame reporter began to haunt the street again. He wasn't there every day, but it was plain that his antennae had picked up some invisible radio wave, and he would accost members of the family whenever he appeared in Bolton. Thus the deceptions continued, each participant unaware of the others' feelings, every member of the group alert and watchful, no-one speaking of encounters with the lame man, no-one voicing an opinion or asking a question about London's death.

A breaking point was coming. Soon, someone would talk to the reporter, would let slip a casual remark, a careless word, then all would be lost. Ellen decided to take the bull by the horns. They gathered in the front room on a cold February Sunday, everyone studiedly casual, each face wearing a sensible, everyday look.

'I've only one thing to say,' began Ellen, 'and that's a warning. Don't talk to him. He'll come and he'll go and we'll never know when to expect him. I don't know where he got this bee from, but it's been stuck in that daft hat of his since . . . since it happened. Just give him a wide berth.'

Clive coughed. 'He's been talking to my patients, standing outside the surgery and asking them what they think of the Langden death, do they wonder about the knife, do they believe it was an accident or natural causes.'

'We could have him stopped,' suggested Abigail. 'Get him done for harassment.'

'That would make it look as if we had something to hide.' Tom stopped speaking when he noticed all the eyes fixed on him. There was something to hide, and someone here was guilty of . . . of what? He cleared his throat. 'Look, if somebody did stick the knife in, they were stabbing a corpse. Isn't that all? Isn't that what the report said?'

Ellen rose to her feet. 'We're not here to talk details, Tom. All I'm asking is that you keep clear of that crippled man. I feel like talking to him meself some days, because he looks so frozen standing out there waiting for heaven knows what. And yes, Clive, he mithers my customers too, so they get it when they're shopping and when they're coming for treatment. If we stick tight, he'll get fed up at the finish.'

Tishy dropped a crayon, bent to retrieve it and swayed slightly in the chair.

Marie raised her shoulders. 'Well, I'm just glad we can sleep without worrying. Bombs are bad enough, but poison and . . . other things are horrible. Whoever did it, we should be—'

'Nobody,' snapped Ellen. 'Nobody did anything.'

Tishy's head dropped to her chest. 'She's asleep again,' commented Theresa. 'Does she do that a lot, Mam?'

'Aye.' This, from Ellen, came out as little more than a deep sigh. 'She's eating next to nowt. I wish you could find out what's missing in her, Clive.'

He jumped up and measured the pulse of the dozing girl. 'I think we'll have her in this time, Ellen.'

Ellen strode towards him. 'In? What do you mean? Hospital? She can't go in there. She'll not know anybody and she'll think we've abandoned her. Look, she'll pull round. We've been through it all before, haven't we? Don't take her away . . .' Her words stopped as she saw Clive's worried expression. 'What?' she asked at last.

'She needs blood,' said Abigail. 'I shall give her some of mine.'

'But . . .' Ellen stood for a moment, looked at the pallor in Tishy's cheeks, then went to fetch her coat. 'I'll go with her,' she said when she returned. 'If she wakes up in a ward, I'll be near. Marie, get a message to Cissie, tell her she'll have to cope some road. Ada Benson'll be able to try her luck on her own.'

So it was Tishy who dragged them all together again. During the days which followed, the sick girl was seldom left alone, and the gathered clan abandoned all differences. Those who sought the truth forgot to ask amongst themselves, while the ones who looked for calmer waters were given the chance to watch a different set of ripples. And the person who knew the full story maintained the usual silence.

After a tiring day during which Tishy had been particularly fractious and anxious to come home, Marie and Cedric sat with Ellen at the kitchen table. 'She'll be all right, lass,' he said to Ellen. 'Her's been like this a long while. Remember, her mam told you there was summat up, then Clive's been doing his best to set her straight. Just try and look on the bright side, eh?'

For Marie, there had been no bright side for a while. The only joy she got was from her baby, and that was tinged with sadness. Now Tishy's illness just served to prove how frail life was, how slender the thread between this world and the next. 'They die with pernicious anaemia,' she said, almost to herself. Yes, and they died in wars, didn't they?

'Don't go thinking and talking that road,' chided Cedric gently. 'The lass is running that ward now, giving out cups of tea and telling everybody about Jesus. In fact, they'll be kicking her out any minute because she's that mithersome.'

Ellen grinned ruefully. 'She had them singing "All Things Bright and Beautiful" in the day room this afternoon. And you've never seen a less bright and beautiful crowd in your life. One old woman said she was going to sue the hospital for straining her vocals. And her with the colostomy bag couldn't move for laughing, said she'd heard nowt like it since the siren went on the blink last year. Remember? Aye, it sounded like a dying cow.' She nodded sadly. 'I reckon they'll let her come home tomorrow, if it's only to save the rest of them from having to sing.'

A loud hammering at the front door caused them to sit bolt upright in their chairs. Ellen, fearing the worst news from the hospital, clutched at the tablecloth, wringing it between tight fingers. Marie put a closed fist to her mouth while Cedric, determined to be a helpful male, pushed back his chair slowly. 'I'll get that,' he said. He walked carefully between table and dresser while the banging continued. 'Holy Mother of God,' breathed Ellen. 'Let this not be the price of my silence.'

Marie, hearing her mother's whispered words, kept her counsel. The wall around Ellen was now a fortress that would not be breached even by the horse of Troy.

Cedric returned with Audrey Carrington. 'Damn fool car,' spat the tweed-enveloped lady. 'I've tried everything except mouth-to-mouth resuscitation, and it just keeps coughing and spluttering. There's no hope for it, I'm afraid. And where shall I get another during a war? Will they listen when I tell them of my need, that I'm caring for so many mothers and children? Not likely.'

Ellen stared blankly at the only living soul who knew her secret. Why was she here, and using precious petrol too?

Marie remembered her manners. 'Cup of tea, Mrs Carrington?'

'No thank you.' The gloves were peeled off and tossed on to the table. 'Tea is a misnomer for the dust we buy these days. Oh, I've brought you some wine, it's in that stupid car, a tonic for the girl. Is she still away?'

Ellen nodded.

'Get some rhubarb into her. I'm a great believer in the cleansing properties of that particular weed.' She placed herself in a chair, seeming to dwarf the room by her presence. Though it was not her physical size that made everything small, mused Marie. No, it was something inside, an innate competence, a sureness of self that gave Audrey Carrington her breadth.

'Was it something special, Mrs Carrington?' ventured Marie.

'Ah well.' Audrey Carrington drew back her shoulders. 'My dear departed was a major, don't you know. Carried a bit of clout, as they say, had many friends too. So I've been pulling a string here and there, bending the odd ear.'

She reached across the table and took Marie's hands in hers. 'My dear girl, he is alive.'

Marie froze, the colour draining from her face. 'Eh?' she asked eventually.

Mrs Carrington nodded briskly. 'Lists, you see. Some get ground underfoot, others go missing with the radio operators who collected them. As far as we can ascertain, Private John Duffy is a prisoner of war. In fact, there is little doubt about it, because some chaps who were with him saw the capture.'

'But—'

'Ah, another butter, eh?' She tapped the side of her nose. 'I've known that for weeks, child, wasn't satisfied to give you half a tale. The Red Cross – God bless them – have been haunted by me for months. And they finally got his name out to me. Some of these Germans aren't bad chaps, you know. He is well.'

Marie's body remained immobile, though her face was working, as if she were trying to understand the words.

Ellen wept noiselessly, while Cedric simply used large hands to cover his emotion.

'He will be coming home,' said Mrs Carrington. 'And it won't be long, believe me. The Russians have blown a hole twenty-five miles wide, and Russia was always Hitler's undoing. Napoleon didn't manage the Russians, and neither will this fool. A bit of mopping up and it will all be over.'

'John,' said Marie, as if savouring the name.

'Yes, John,' smiled the visitor. 'Your baby's father, my dear.'

'Alive. In a prison camp.' She shook herself visibly, as if coming out of a dream. 'I must go now and tell his mother. She thinks he's in a desert with a camel that's eaten all his clothes.'

'Pardon?' A grey eyebrow was raised.

'It doesn't matter,' said Marie. 'Nothing matters now. I can hope, I can plan.' She wasn't going to weep. No, she would save her tears for later, for when she would be alone. 'I don't know what to say to you, Mrs Carrington. You've gone well out of your road for this family.' Her voice shook. 'My sister thinks the world of you, she does, she does.' Her head moved in time with the repeated phrase. 'And so do I.' She fled from the room, leaving her chair to crash to the floor.

Audrey Carrington rubbed at an itching eye. 'One does what one can,' she murmured.

Ellen raised her head. 'Aye, lass, only some try harder than others.'

Cedric stumbled from the room, muttering his intention to fetch the wine from the car.

'The other matter?' asked Mrs Carrington. 'Are things under control?'

Ellen wiped her eyes. 'It's gone under the carpet with Tishy being ill, but that fellow keeps coming back. He must think there's something funny, because he pops up every few days.'

'No.' The grey head shook slowly. 'He's a clever little chap, on the tail of some serious racketeering, stuff being smuggled from the American base near Warrington. Some of it is being sold in Bolton, and he has traced a few of the Burtonwood people to here. I suppose he comes round to your house when the trail gets cold, just somewhere to go, somewhere different.'

'He's like a ferret,' said Ellen. 'He's down the hole, and he'll not give up till he gets what he's after.'

'He'll get nothing.' The tone was determined and decisive. 'There'll be another big case in a day or two, a "human interest" story – as he so delicately terms his particular form of journalism. It will be in a different town, and he'll be off like a greyhound from a trap.'

'Not with his legs, he won't.'

'Quite. But you know what I mean.'

Marie came in with the baby in a shawl. 'I'm going to Mrs Duffy's,' she said. 'Then I'll call in at church. You see, there's more than you to thank, Mrs Carrington. And I've not been going to mass, not since John went missing. I still don't believe he's safe, you know. Can you get it in writing?'

Audrey Carrington grinned. 'It'll be with his mother any day now. But you will have the pleasure of telling her first.'

'Thanks.' Marie walked out, head held high, child clutched to her chest.

Cedric stumbled in with a cardboard carton. He placed it on the dresser, then bent to pick up Marie's fallen chair. 'Have I to open one of these bottles?' he asked.

Ellen shook her head. 'Save it for Tishy,' she said. 'We'll have a little party when she gets home.'

Mrs Carrington removed her hat. 'Get the corkscrew,' she ordered. 'I shall fortify myself against the drive home.'

Ellen reached for some glasses. 'We can drink to John,' she said. 'And all the other lads with him.'

So they toasted the future until the bottle was spent. Ellen stood with Cedric at the front door while the ailing Ford 8 hopped off up the street. Half of Ellen's conscience was in that car, shouldered by a woman who never thought of sin. For Audrey Carrington, a sin was simply an act that hurt another human. If the telling of the truth might damage a fellow traveller, then a lie would be preferable. Mrs Carrington's God was a separate issue, a reason for Sunday worship. But Ellen's God was in her soul, and her soul could not rest easy even with the burden halved.

Cedric looked down at her. 'Are you all right, love?'

'Aye. Go home now. I'll see you tomorrow.'

'Ellen?'

'What?'

He studied the drawn, tight mouth. 'Whatever it is, tell me. You should be jumping through hoops now, what with Marie's John safe and Tishy coming out of hospital. Can't you tell me what's on your mind?'

She climbed the stone steps. 'Ta-ra, Cedric,' was all she said before closing the door.

A figure rose out of the well formed by the cellar steps. 'Mr Wilkinson?'

Cedric turned. 'Listen, you little bag of bones. Leave them alone, do you hear? We've had enough of you hanging about like a bad stink. There's nowt here for you, nowt at all.'

'Isn't there? What is on her mind? Why can't she—?'

'Bugger off!' Cedric was appalled by his own vehemence. 'You might be crippled, but I'll clout you, I'm telling you. Now, take your hook or I'll thump you.' He raised a huge fist, and the little man scuttled off towards Derby Street.

Cedric stood in the middle of the cobbles, terrified by the force of his anger. Nobody round here was acting normal, he decided. And although the thought seemed fanciful, he imagined that London, dead and buried, was behind all the discomfort.

CHAPTER NINETEEN

Permission Granted

The lame reporter continued to hop around, leaving no stone unturned, no sleeping dog prone and undisturbed. Except for him, Ellen thought, things might have settled down, but there was still an atmosphere in the area, a tendency for conversations to change gear and direction whenever a 'Londoner' appeared on the scene.

It was into such a climate that Tishy returned from hospital, though she, at least, was shielded due to being confined for much of the time to the house. There was a heaviness at number nine, a tense depression over which Ellen deliberately poured a covering of levity, though Marie was never fooled. Tishy was dying, and Mam was trying to hide the whole rotten cake with icing. Marie made an effort to concentrate on John, on the fact that he was alive, but Tishy's condition was real and to hand. It was difficult to have positive thoughts while death sat so close.

Ellen immersed herself in everyday problems, wore a cloak of carefree and encouraging competence to hide fear and heartbreak. There was much to do, and she rattled about constantly, dealing with the immediate pressures of daily existence. Tishy was still refusing food, there was a shop to run, washing to hang out, and the grate needed cleaning. She walked through to the kitchen where Tishy sat staring into the fire. 'That's right, you sit up for a bit. Stands to reason you'll get weak if you lie on your back all the while.' Her tone was lightweight, almost nonchalant. She glanced at the bed which had been carried downstairs again, the bed in which Lilian had died, in which

491

Elizabeth had been born. 'Now, you've to take this tonic Clive's made for you.'

'In a minute.' The face was thinner than ever, skin stretched to the point of transparency across finely sculpted bone. Ellen swallowed her own pain, plastering a smile across cheeks that ached from wearing false courage. Tishy's wrists were so fragile now that they might have belonged to a child. In fact, the expanding silver bracelets Ellen had acquired for both babies would have fitted these frail arms.

She stepped across the room and placed a hand on a shoulder blade sharp enough to cut cloth. 'Tishy, will you please eat?'

'Later.' Luminous eyes glanced up. 'I am very well now. I don't see why I can't go and work in the shop, give change like Mrs Tattersall taught me. And I want to make some more jerseys and bags. Will I have to be still for a long time?'

'Till Clive says you can start running round again. We don't want to do anything naughty, do we? No use turning to him for help if we've not done as we were told. You should pick up in a day or two.'

Ellen set the noon meal on the table. Mrs Carrington had sent farm vegetables and liver from a fresh-killed lamb, but Tishy would touch none of this nourishing fare. As usual, she devoured her pudding and any sweets she could find, but she flatly refused any savoury offerings.

Marie, when she came downstairs after putting Elizabeth in her cot, tried her best. 'Eat your liver, Tishy. It'll make you strong again.'

'I don't like it.' The lower lip protruded in an infantile pout.

'Then you won't get well.'

Tishy glanced at the Immaculate Conception and smiled. 'Mary's looking after me.'

Marie ground her teeth noiselessly. 'Mary looks after them that look after themselves. She can't feed you. Only you can do that, only you can try to mend your blood.

Liver's very good for folk with your condition.'

'It tastes awful. I'd rather not eat anything.'

'Then you'll . . . not get better.'

Tishy's smile grew broader. 'I know. Then I'll see Mum and Jesus and Mary. Father Gorman told me.'

Marie tried another tack. 'Wouldn't you miss us? Me and Mam and Abigail? What about Patricia and Elizabeth?'

Tishy shrugged her shoulders. 'I'll still be able to see you, all of you. People in heaven can see anything and go everywhere. And they don't have to eat liver and greens.'

It was hopeless. Marie turned to her mother. 'Well?' she asked shrilly. 'What do we do now? She'll not have any of this food from the farm. All she's eaten is a jam butty and two mint imperials. Who's going to improve on mint imperials?'

Ellen perched on the edge of a dining chair. 'We can't force-feed her, love. What do you expect me to do? Tie her to the bed and shove a tube down her throat? Anyway, it seems to make no difference what she eats. Clive says her blood's not able to absorb the goodness, so what's the use? Might as well let her sit there eating Uncle Joes till the cows come home.' She studied the two girls for a moment. 'Can you look after one another while I go to the shops? Only Cissie's been on her own for long enough, and I need to check on the stock and the points. Will you cope with Tishy and the baby, Marie?' She had to get out, just for a short time. If she didn't escape for half a day or so, she would . . . no, she wouldn't. But perhaps coping might be easier after a break.

'Yes, course I will. But I'm not sitting here all day waiting for madam to eat. By the way, that reporter's been hanging round the shops again, Linda Tattersall told me. He's wanting to write Billy London's life story. They're talking of doing a big piece about him, all the stuff about his bigamy and stealing Lilian's money. I think the neighbours have been chattering. So watch yourself in the shops, Mam. The papers are very interested in . . . well, they're just interested.'

Ellen bridled slightly. 'Listen, I don't want any of you lot talking to the newspapers. If that man with the limp comes knocking here, put a flea in his ear and send him to me at the shop. We'll have the story straight.'

Marie bit down on her tongue as she watched and listened to her mother's bravado. It was plain that Ellen had something to hide, too much to allow anyone else in the house an opinion. 'Go on, Mam,' she said quietly. 'We shall manage. I'll get some of that beef broth down her if I have to use a funnel.'

Ellen left the house by the rear door. She was partway down Back Noble Street when the young man caught up with her. 'Mrs Langden?' he asked breathlessly. 'It's Sam Caldwell again . . .' He struggled along, anxious to keep up with her.

'Go away. There's nowt for you, nowt worth the price of printer's ink.'

He shook his head. 'I don't believe that.'

She stood still and glared at him. 'Why aren't you in the trenches? There's stories there, you know. And a lot more exciting than our little bit of trouble.'

'My legs,' he replied. 'And asthma. In case you haven't noticed, I'm not exactly in one piece . . .'

'You manage,' she said sourly. 'And if you're that bad, you should be at home, not stood here pestering the likes of me. What do you want, anyway? Haven't you had most of it from the neighbours? He was twice wed, a thief, an arsonist and an apprentice murderer. He died in this back street, had a heart attack, fell on the knife he was carrying.' She looked him up and down. 'Well? Do you want a map drawing?'

He hesitated. 'I just want your feelings, Mrs Langden. And any photographs you might have, pictures of his daughters, of his weddings, any letters . . .'

Ellen folded her arms. 'Got a pencil?'

He nodded, pen poised above his pad.

'Write this,' she said. 'If you harass my daughters, I'll set a lawyer on you. There are four girls, two born to me

494

and two adopted by me. I want them left alone. And my name will be O'Hara soon, I'm changing it by deed poll. As for photographs of my . . . of him, there isn't any, I destroyed them. He was a bad man, and we don't want reminding of him. Print what you like, but if you set one foot wrong, if there's the smallest hint of libel and suchlike, I'll see you in court, lad. Fetch your doctor with you, because you'll have more than a bad leg and a funny chest if I get my claws fixed in you. All right?'

'But I only want to make a living.'

'Same here. So get out of my road before I shift you. I might be only little, but there's nowt wrong with my feet, and I kick like a horse.'

He sidestepped to let her walk past him.

'Hey,' he shouted after her. 'What about that knife? Some say it wasn't an accident.'

She swivelled on her heel and squared up to him. 'Go on,' she whispered. 'Let's hear what some say, let's hear the words you're putting in their mouths. Because that's what's happening, lad. It's you that's causing all the bother.'

'Well, I was just stating an opinion.'

'Whose? Your own? One that would suit them rubbishy Sunday papers you write for?'

'A general feeling. He was a hated man, so isn't it possible that one of his family . . . well . . . isn't it?'

'No.' Her teeth were bared now. 'It's not possible, Mr Whoever. Nobody in my household is a murderer. Even the police reckon he fell on the knife. Look, I'm sick unto death of repeating meself, but he was carrying poison, bottles of rat stuff to put in our food. The knife was just a little bit of extra protection for him.' She took a small step in his direction. 'Print any other explanation, and I'll separate you from your breath permanently. You'll need more than steam and a drop of balsam when I've done with you. Do you understand me?'

He swallowed. 'Yes. Right, I'll bid you good day, then.'

'And stay away from my girls,' she shouted. 'I'll talk to

you when I'm ready, happen tomorrow. Don't go bothering the neighbours any more. There's been enough embroidery in the local papers. We don't need it in the *News of the World* as well.' She sucked in her cheeks as he staggered away. London was dead and buried, yet he was still bringing trouble by the minute. And this fellow would have been a good mate for Burke and Hare, because he let nothing rest in peace, did he?

Determinedly, she pulled herself together and walked towards the Deane Road shop. No-one would find out, not from her. The main thing was to carry on as normal, to make it look as if she wasn't bothered. And she would have to warn Abigail and Theresa all over again about this Caldwell chap. After she'd done that, she would sit him down in her front room, give him the story he wanted. It looked as if that was going to be the only way to get shut of him, so she would need to spell out her life with London in order to deflect the man's interest from . . . from the other thing. If he came back yet again, and she had no doubt that he would.

A delighted Cissie Tattersall greeted her at the Deane Road shop. 'Everything's fine, Ellen. That there Ada Benson what we took on is great, learned all about shop keeping from her mam. She's doing a grand job up Derby Street. How's Tishy?'

Ellen shrugged listlessly, grateful to let go of her armour at last. She could confide in Cissie, up to a point. 'Not good. She looks like something off a holy picture, all pale and saintly but without the halo. I shan't be in the shop much, Cissie. I'll have to see her through it whichever way it goes.'

Mrs Banks came in, long black shawl trailing on the flags in her wake. 'Got rid of him, then?' croaked the ancient voice.

Ellen sighed heavily. 'What can we do for you, Mrs Banks?'

The old woman slapped a filthy ration book on the counter. 'I'll have a loaf, me margarine, and them sweepings that pass for tea these days. Did you kill him?' A steely eye peered from the gap in the shawl. 'And if you did, how are you getting away with it? Felt like doing away with my old man many a day, I did. Fifty-six years I put up with him. If I could have done what you did . . .'

'She did nothing,' shouted Cissie.

'I'm not deaf,' yelled the old lady.

'Then mind what you say.' Cissie's tone remained stern.

'It's all right,' whispered Ellen. 'She's not far short of her century, and she's only saying what they all think.' She turned to Mrs Banks. 'It was natural causes.'

'And I'm the Queen of Sheba,' came the swift response. 'I'll have a packet of Rinso and a bar of Fairy soap.' She snatched up her purchases and hobbled through the doorway.

Ellen sank on to the customers' chair. 'Moving wouldn't do any good, there's still the shops, I'd have to come back every day. And it's no use running, because problems always catch up with you in the end. There's the houses too, I have to look after them. And we can't sell up till all the girls are of age. It's getting no easier, Cissie. He's dead and he's still putting me through it. What the heck do I have to do to make folk stop talking? Will I put an advert in the paper, summat about me being innocent?'

Cissie wrung her hands. 'Eeh, I don't know, Ellen. See, it's this knife. Some folk don't want to believe that he fell on it. They seem to think one of you sneaked up and pushed it in just to make sure he wouldn't come round.'

'He was face down! Do they really believe that I turned him over after he'd died, shoved the carver into him, then rolled him back again? Is that what they're wanting to prove?'

'I don't know, do I? I'll tell you this much, though, they're not on London's side. Sneaking about in the night with rat poison – they're all against him even now he's dead. They just want summat to natter about, summat to liven things up. There's nowt much happens round here, so they're using this as their bit of entertainment.'

'At my expense, though. What have I ever done to them?'

Cissie looked away from the stricken face. 'You've a successful business, so happen they're jealous. Take no notice, it'll all blow over in a matter of weeks.'

Ellen took off her coat and donned the working apron. The customers were unusually quiet, conversations stopping in mid-sentence as soon as they walked into the shop. Meaningful looks were passed from one to another and, as the clock reached five, Ellen had had enough. When the tea-time lull arrived, she announced her intention to go home. 'Better off without me,' she muttered. 'I couldn't sell a bucket of water to a man on fire, not if he didn't want to do business with me.'

'See it through,' chided Cissie. 'They're just embarrassed, like. They don't know what to say to you, lass. I mean, when a woman's husband dies, everybody gathers round and says how sorry they are. They're not sorry, and they know you're not either. So what are they expected to do? Tell you how glad they are for you? Whatever gets said or done is wrong. So nobody knows which road to look at you.'

'Like a human being. That's all I ask, that they treat me like a normal person.' She opened the door and stepped into the street, almost colliding with Marie and her pram. 'You've left our Tishy, then?'

'Just for half an hour. Elizabeth needs a bit of air. People have been smiling at me, Mam. Smiling, but saying nowt. I can see they want to talk to me, but it looks like they don't know what to say.'

Ellen nodded quickly. 'Aye. Even the rents from across the street get shoved through the door in bits of newspaper now. I feel like a flaming leper. Come on, stick your head in the air, but don't go flat on your face in one of these pavement cracks. We've got to put on a bit of side, pretend we're a cut above and we don't care.'

As they made their supposedly regal way along Noble Street, a figure emerged from a house, a slight woman wearing a turban, four steel curlers perched on her forehead. Ellen recognized her as one of the few in the six houses who had never needed a reminder about rent. 'Hang on,' she said to Marie out of the corner of her mouth as the neighbour drew nearer. 'I reckon the silence is about to be broke.'

'Hello, Mrs Langden. Marie, what a lovely baby.'

'Yes,' chorused Marie and Ellen.

An awkward silence followed. Nora Hunt fingered her metal curlers and made much of studying Elizabeth's pram. 'Nice blankets,' she commented.

'Yes,' repeated Marie. 'Tishy crocheted them out of old jumpers.'

'Very nice.'

Ellen decided that she would probably scream if the word 'nice' should be used again. 'Did you want us for something, Mrs Hunt?'

'Eh? Oh aye, yes I do. See,' she shuffled her feet and glanced up and down the street, 'we've had a bit of a meeting, a little get together down the air raid shelter.'

'Oh?' Ellen's eyebrows were raised. 'Funny place for a meeting. Hard to see what you're talking about in an air raid shelter.'

'We had candles.'

'Good.'

'And a couple of paraffin lights.'

'Better still.' Ellen fixed her eyes on Nora's face. 'And?'

'I got appointed.'

'Oh, right. Well, I'm very pleased for you. It isn't every day somebody gets appointed, is it, Marie?'

'No. What did you get appointed to, Mrs Hunt?'

Mrs Hunt took a deep breath that only served to further emphasize her total lack of bosom. 'Spokesman.'

'Marvellous.' Ellen nodded slowly. 'That's very, very good. And what are you supposed to do as spokesman?'

Nora floundered. 'Speak,' she said lamely. 'To you.' Her words tumbled out in a flood then, pouring from her lips almost before she had time to organize them. 'We're sorry for you, all of us. The men and all. We know you wouldn't do nothing to hurt nobody. It was all a shock when . . . when he got found like that, with a knife stuck in him. It was like . . . what was that funny big word? Like a retribution.' She smiled at her accomplishment. 'There wasn't one in this street that liked your husband, Mrs L, only we didn't know what to say after he'd popped his clogs. Like, if you'd been a happy couple, if he'd been a half-decent man, we would have come and talked to you. Only none of us could think how to manage, specially with the police hanging round like a bad smell on a hot day. And we want things back to normal. We don't want you to feel as how we don't care, and we don't want you going to live somewhere else. We like you, missus. You and your girls have always been good to us.' She exhaled in a great long sigh of pent-up breath. 'Right, I've said me piece. Happen I should stand for the town council one of these days, eh?'

Ellen gave a brief half-smile. This was all very well, but nothing would get truly sorted until the fellow with the limp had cleared off for good. 'Aye, happen you should, Nora Hunt. And . . . thank you. Tell them all not to worry, things'll blow over. Isn't it funny how it's always us little women that have to come forward at the finish and do the dirty work? They say good things come in small packages.'

'Aye,' said Nora. 'But so does poison.' Her face fell. 'Nay, I didn't mean to put you in mind of . . . I mean, I never meant . . .'

Marie giggled. 'No use watching what you say all the while, Mrs Hunt. Things can't be normal if we have to be careful with words.'

Nora collected her thoughts. 'Oh, and there's been a man at your house while you were out, that youngish man – him with one of them notebooks, same as they use in offices for doing shorthand and stuff. Your Tishy let him in, then she let him out again not ten minutes since. Smiling fit to bust, he was. One of them there reporters, him as walks a bit peculiar. Bloody leeches, they are.'

Ellen released the pram handle. 'In my house? Talking to Tishy? And after what I said to him and all.' She took a step towards home. 'I'll see you later,' she called over her shoulder to Nora.

Marie almost had to run in order to keep up with her mother. 'Mam,' she called. 'I shouldn't have left her. But I never thought, and she's been told not to let anybody in while she's poorly. I'm sorry . . .'

'Can't be helped,' breathed Ellen. 'And she could tell him nowt any road, can't organize her thoughts, specially now while she's bad ways. Happen he'll publish some of them daft poems, all that stuff about Tinkle sleeping in the oven.' She threw open the front door, pausing only to help Marie carry the pram up the steps. 'Tishy?' she called. 'Where are you? And what were you doing letting that man in?' Her voice faded along the hallway while Marie manoeuvred the pram into the front room. Then a loud shriek emerged from the kitchen, and Marie ran with the child in her arms, stopping abruptly in the doorway when she saw her mother leaning over a prostrate form. 'Mam?' Marie's tone was hesitant. 'Is she all right?'

Ellen shook her head sharply. 'No, she's hardly breathing. Put Elizabeth back in her pram, then run up to the surgery, get a doctor. We'd best not move Tishy, I'll cover her up where she is. I don't like her colour, Marie. Hurry up and get gone.'

Tinkle stood guard over his mistress while Ellen piled blankets on top of the unconscious girl. Tishy's breathing was shallow, and the skin of her face, which had always been pale, was a lifeless paper-white. A blue-veined eyelid flickered, then both eyes suddenly opened to reveal a brilliance that was both beautiful and terrifying, so fiercely did the smoky irises glisten. Again Ellen was reminded of the collection of holy pictures she kept in her missal, saints with ashen faces and burning eyes. 'Mam. I do love you.' The girl's lips were a gentle mauvish colour, as if she had just been eating soft fruits.

'You've messed about too much, that's the top and bottom,' said Ellen gently. 'So we need to get you back into bed. You should never have let that man in, worn you out, he has.' Grimly, Ellen clung to her senses. Tishy was an imaginative girl, and she might have told the reporter anything that came into her head. Or she might have remembered something, might have . . . God forbid! Anyway, this was not the time to mither over such things, because Tishy looked so bad . . .

'He was nice, the man. His name's Sam.' She blinked rapidly as if trying to focus. 'He gave me a pencil and a new notebook, no pages written on and none missing.' She frowned, her eyes still glued to Ellen's face. 'Why are you so far away? Come closer, it's hard to see you.'

Ellen shuddered. 'Don't talk so daft. I'm here, knelt on the floor next to you. See, here's Tinkle and there's the fire and the kettle. Our Marie's gone to fetch some help.'

'What for?'

'For you, love. You've gone all weak again, and I can't lift you. Neither can Marie, not after just having a baby. And Cedric's at work, so we're having the doctor.'

Tishy's lips parted in a winning smile. 'I am a terrible nuisance. Abigail used to say that, because I followed her everywhere.' She turned her head and stared into the burning coals. 'I used to like the dark, till the hand came. In the dark, I could pretend and do whatever I liked. But the dark stopped being my friend.' She paused, a frown arriving between the fine, arched eyebrows. 'Now, I can see such a bright light,' she whispered. 'A wonderful warm light.'

Ellen, sensing that Tishy's bright light was not connected with any illumination on earth, blessed herself hurriedly. A dreadful sense of hopelessness was crushing her heart, so she reached for Tishy and drew her close, as if trying to hold on, to deny and defy the inevitable.

'Mam?'

'What?'

'Who was Burlington Bertie?'

Ellen fought the wetness in her eyes. 'He was a Londoner, a poor man who pretended to be rich.'

'He had no shirt.'

'That's right.'

'But he had gloves.'

'Yes.'

Tishy stared directly at the woman she thought of as 'Mam', the one who had helped her ever since Mum went for ever. 'No need for gloves.'

'No need, lass.'

'Not now. No need to be frightened of my own hands.'

Ellen nodded, too choked for speech.

'Can I go in the garden? Can I?'

Ellen gulped noisily. 'I don't know, lass. It's not for me to say. That's your own garden, in your own mind and in your heart. You know where you want to be. There's only you can choose, my little love.'

'Mum's waiting for me.'

'Yes, I suppose she is.'

'And there's a bridge, just like the one on the blue plate.'

Ellen glanced at the willow patterned dish that stood on the dresser. It was such a tiny bridge, the one in the willow story. And Tishy's was a short span too, just a couple of strides between here and eternity. She placed her blonde head against Tishy's auburn curls, allowing her tears to pour quietly into the silky locks. Tishy was asking permission to die, and Ellen knew that she would have to grant the wish. Who would be here in ten, fifteen, twenty years to care for this special young woman? Who would recognize the talent behind the oddness? And what would those fifteen or twenty years be like for Tishy?

'Go where you want to go, pet. Be happy. And understand that I love you. A little ray of sunshine, that's what you are.'

'I always liked playing in the garden. We had a garden in London. Daffodils . . .' She slipped away on a whisper of breath, just a small sigh escaping the parted lips.

Ellen stared out at the blackness, just managing to discern the shapes of chimneys and roofs across the way. She'd have to cover the window in a minute, she thought irrelevantly. The world was completely soundless, as if it too had stopped breathing. Tishy. She was so beautiful, so unbelievably lovely, too pretty to go beneath the ground. No, she wouldn't be getting buried. Abigail would want her to be . . . oh God, it was going to be like burning a Titian, one of those paintings of women with fabulous hair. Abigail believed in cremation, though Lilian's stated preference for burial had been catered for, so happen Tishy could have a proper funeral after all . . . Her thoughts were becoming ragged, she must organize herself.

Ellen's mind tripped back in time, to another night, a knock at the door, three travel-stained women standing there cold, weary and uncertain, bags of clothes piled at their feet. Lilian, near to death, nearer to finding security for her daughters. Abigail, erect and proud, face set against a world she hadn't trusted. Tishy, open-faced, smiling on the unknown because she knew that it would smile back eventually. Oh, Tishy, she thought, I have loved you. I loved your mam and I love your sister for all her brash ways.

She laid the body flat, crossing the arms over the chest, smoothing the luxuriant hair that reflected the dancing flames. Knowing Tishy had been a rare privilege, an experience that would probably be unrepeatable. 'Aye lass,' she whispered. 'You're a hard act to follow.' She stood up, depending heavily on the table, her legs weakened by sorrow.

The door opened. The thin, dark-haired girl took in the scene, her eyes lingering on her sister before flicking briefly to Ellen. 'Are you all right?'

Ellen nodded while Abigail bent over the still form on the rug. Clive hovered in the doorway, his face pale and set.

Abigail sat back on her haunches. To no-one in

particular, she said, 'From today, my daughter will be called Tishy.'

They heard Marie climbing up the stairs, leaden footsteps muffled by sobs. Clive came into the room, helped his wife to stand, then lifted the dead girl in his arms, placing her on the bed. 'Have a drink first, love,' he said to Abigail.

She shook her head. 'Tishy saved my baby. I remember how she washed her, how she knew what to do. She never stopped for a drink, Clive. I have all the rest of my life to have a drink.'

Ellen went through to the scullery and set a big pan on the ring. There was some Pears soap somewhere, she would find it in a minute. A hand touched her shoulder, and she turned into Abigail's arms. 'I'll never know how to thank you,' sobbed the younger woman as she clung to Ellen fiercely.

Ellen managed not to cry. 'Nay, I'm the one that's grateful. If I'd never known her, I would have missed so much in life. She was the best of all of us, Abigail. She was the only really good person I've ever met in all me born days.'

'I loved her, Ellen.'

'I know, I know.' She patted the shaking back.

'Bury her, Ellen. She was a Catholic . . .'

'Yes, yes. Come on, lass. We'll have to get it done. You just wonder why, don't you? When she was so . . . loving.'

Abigail straightened and rubbed her eyes. 'It was leukaemia.'

A small beat of time passed between them. 'Did you think I didn't realize that? I knew you were sheltering behind that other label.' She nodded slowly. 'Aye, I could sense there was no hope at all, love.'

'Oh, Ellen. Where would we have been without your strength?'

Ellen stared at the whitewashed walls, wondering where folk got the idea that she was strong. It was all an act, just like Burlington Bertie, all show and no substance. Her eyes moved along the pan shelf, finally coming to rest on a piece of butcher paper, all brightly crayoned and with THE GARDEN printed at the top in Tishy's hand. On the picture, birds sat in trees, flowers grew abundantly, children with stick-like limbs played. She almost smiled. Tishy had taken so little, had left so much. Most of all, she had bequeathed them her love. Love, Ellen decided, was strength.

Tinkle brushed past her leg, and she bent to pick up this bundle of feline arrogance. He was a warm reminder of Tishy's compassion, and Ellen hugged the creature close to her body. The striped face was impassive, yet Ellen imagined a question behind the yellow-green eyes. 'It's all right, lad,' she whispered. 'You can stay with me.'

There were three of them in the room, a dark-haired young man, a pretty blonde woman of middle years and, between the two of them, the body of a beautiful girl in a silk-lined coffin. Sam Caldwell blew his nose; the asthma had played up something shocking just lately. He searched for words. 'I'm sorry, Mrs Langden.'

'Ellen. I'm not so sure about the other name, not till I get the papers back.'

He placed his trilby on the piano. 'Bubbling with it, she was. Like she'd just pieced it all together. I wrote everything down, had a job to keep up with her.' He fumbled in a pocket. 'She must have had some sort of a brainstorm just before she . . . well . . .'

'Died,' interspersed Ellen.

He bowed his head and gave up his search for papers. 'Isn't she a lovely looking girl? Such a shame, such a rotten stinking waste. When she opened the door to me, I thought she was the best looker I'd ever seen in my whole life. She was the sort you only get in films and magazine photos. Then she started talking and . . .'

'And you realized that she was a couple of pence short of the full shilling.'

His face worked, and for one awful moment, it looked as if this hard-nosed seeker of the so-called truth might be about to weep. 'I could see she was different. Oh, she had the chairs at home all right, only they were arranged in a way of her own choosing.' He reorganized his features until he appeared composed. With both hands resting on the rim of the coffin, he straightened his back and forced himself to look directly at Ellen. 'How long had you known?'

'Ever since she started to live here. We've always been on borrowed time with Tishy. It was that there pernicious anaemia. At least, that's what we were led to believe. If you can get your hands on a certificate, it'll say something like leukaemia.'

He coughed. 'Not about that. I meant how long had you known what really happened the night your husband died?'

She reached into the coffin and turned the crucifix on Tishy's rosary until the figure of Christ was uppermost. Inside her head, she spoke to Lilian and Tishy, asking them to forgive her for what she was about to do. 'Tishy didn't know the difference between what she saw, what she thought she saw, and what she dreamed. She spent a lot of time writing stories and poems. She used to get mixed up.'

'Really? She seemed clear enough to me, an exceptionally accurate witness.' He nodded knowingly. 'Completely credible and very detailed. She didn't miss much, did she?'

Ellen pushed back her shoulders and met his gaze. 'The doctor will confirm that this poor little thing had fixations. She used to wear gloves and she stood at windows during blackouts looking for floating hands. Whatever she told you will be another of her imaginings. She likely stood at the window again, thought she saw something. If she'd lived, she would have made a story of it.'

'But Mrs Langden—'

'Ellen. If you want a surname, stick to O'Hara.'

507

He pushed a hand through his hair, causing it to stick up in Brylcreemed spikes. 'Mrs O'Hara, I am sure that Tishy told me the absolute truth.'

'So am I. She was no liar. Look at her face – go on – look at her. There wasn't a bad bone in her body.'

He gazed into the coffin. 'Well, then . . .'

'Exactly. It was all nonsense, another one of her tales. She's been disturbed with all the ongoings, then shoving her in hospital did no good. She was a child, Mr Caldwell. Just an overgrown baby.' Ellen felt sick, yet she clung desperately to the knowledge that she must protect this family from further scandal. Tishy and Lilian would both want that, wherever they were. 'You have to take no notice of her. We all found that out.'

He shook his head. 'It was a lot for her to make up, Mrs . . . er . . .'

'Leave it be. If you know what's good for you, let well alone. Or do you want a court case? Because it'll come to that if you publish.' She put her head on one side, as if considering. 'Mind, we could sue the papers, get a few bob put by.'

He cleared his throat and pushed a pastille into his mouth. 'Well, I'll think about it. But it was a very interesting story.'

'She was an interesting girl. She could make baking day exciting, could Tishy. Everything was an adventure to her. The fact is, you're up the wrong tree, Mr Caldwell. Climb any further, and I'll cut you down.'

They stared at one another across the coffin for several moments, then he picked up his hat and walked out of the house.

Ellen sank to her knees, her head almost level now with Tishy's. 'What did you tell him, lass? What did you say?' She touched a cold hand and straightened a fold of the pink dress. 'Never mind, we'll sort him. I got permission for you to get buried with your mother, even though she is on the wrong side of the cemetery. Don't worry, it's all gone through the bishop. And I'll look after Tinkle.' She stood up and gazed for the last time at the perfect alabaster face. Tomorrow, she would not come in. Tomorrow, the lid was due to go on. 'Ta-ra, love,' she whispered.

She went upstairs to find her black coat and gloves. There wouldn't be many at the funeral, what with everybody working and busy at their chores. Yes, it would be a quiet day. The first of many quiet days. Oh Tishy. Why did it have to be you . . . ?

The morning was still, silent, charcoal grey. Shaded fingers of reluctant light poked through the clouds, illuminating the world in patches, as if the sun had lost its heart. When Ellen came out of the house, other doors opened, though every window in the street was covered by curtains. They emerged then, the people of Noble Street, gathering in small dark groups that were punctuated here and there by a flash of colour.

Ellen and the rest of the family stared in near-disbelief at the sight before them, dozens of adults in black, brown and navy, several children in their Sunday best, every girl child topped by a bright Tishy bonnet. They had come out for Tishy, and they had dressed their children in Tishy's work. Not a soul moved as the coffin was borne down the steps and placed in the waiting hearse.

When the vehicle pulled away, the children stayed where they were, but most of the adults joined the procession, picking up more along the way. By the time they reached Pilkington Street, it was plain that the church would be packed beyond its moderate capacity. The family clung one to another, each terrified by the weight and size of this noiseless crowd. Ellen bit her lip against a rising sob. Tishy had pulled the street together again, but she had needed to die in order to achieve that feat.

The service was short, tailored to fit the child Tishy had been. Father Gorman spoke of St Bernadette, of her simplicity, of the power of her faith in the Blessed Virgin. The implication was not lost; he felt that he had known a saint, even if she would never be canonized.

There were only a few at the graveside. Abigail tossed earth on to her sister, then Ellen did the same. Just as the committal ended, a watery sun burst forth, spilling its brave light on the cluster of figures in the cemetery. Ellen bowed her head. It was as if Tishy had sent the sun to warm them, to take the grim edge off this day of mourning.

She was the last to leave the grave. She stood alone, saying a silent prayer for Lilian and her lovely daughter, making a final and private farewell. Something fluttered into the hole, and Ellen blinked, wondering what she was seeing. It was paper, little torn scraps floating down to rest on Tishy's coffin.

'I'm only human, Mrs Langden.'

She sniffed. 'O'Hara.'

'And it wasn't libel. If I'd sold it, it would have been cleared.'

'I know that. And you can still sell it, it's in your mind.'

'Not any more.'

She lifted her face and looked at him. He was just a man, a crippled man with a heart. 'Why?' she asked simply.

He shrugged, but the movement was not light. 'Something about her. I suppose I understand what it's like not to be whole. The stories I write – it's just for the money.'

'Yes.'

'I don't need any money at the moment. Not so badly anyway.' He stared at Ellen for a long time, then raised his trilby before hobbling away towards the gate. The sun brightened, casting its smile into the grave where Tishy, and the story she had dictated, lay waiting to be covered by the mound of freshly dug earth that rested to one side. Ellen wiped her nose, straightened her hat, and turned to walk home.

The cellar was dark and damp, but she knew the place by feel. She made her way past the old mangle, the biscuit tins, the pile of cardboard boxes that rotted quietly in the middle of the floor. Using the tips of her fingers, she wandered along the wall until a brick moved. Here he had stored his money and his IOUs, here he had kept the things dearest to his callous heart.

The bricks came out easily, and she placed them on the floor at her feet, pausing fractionally before reaching in again until her fingers touched fabric. As her eyes adjusted to the lack of light, she saw the white article, and she pulled slowly, holding it gently between thumb and first finger.

There was an upturned tea chest nearby, so she used this as a seat, perching on the rim with her toes balanced on the cold, flagged floor. When she turned, the meagre gleam from the small back window lit her hand, and she drew breath sharply as her pulse raced.

Oh, Tishy! Evidence of the girl's bravery sat in her hand, a single white glove with a small brown stain here and there. How much courage had she mustered to go down in total darkness to dispel the hand? And had she ever really understood what she had done? Or what she had not done?

Ellen pictured her creeping down the stairs to save her family. No doubt she would have put the cat in the oven first, just to make sure that he would be out of danger. The knife was probably in the scullery that night, sitting on the wooden drainer or resting on a shelf. In her mind's eye, Ellen watched the girl picking up this piece of defence, holding it out in front of herself, perhaps waving it about in case the hand might come.

And he had fallen on to it. The police had wondered about fingerprints, of course, because Tishy had left none, and her gloves must have erased any earlier marks. London hadn't worn gloves, so the detectives had decided that the coat had wiped his own prints away. Ellen breathed a deep, shuddering sigh that seemed to tear like a knife at her own innards. Tishy had never mentioned any of it; Ellen had found the glove and hidden it, hoping that the girl had forgotten the event. She had been quite capable of eliminating the unsavoury, had Tishy. But what had she told Sam Caldwell?

Ah well, whatever he knew, he would not use it. Tishy could rest in peace now, as could her mother. Even London had escaped from his particular misery, so perhaps he too was finding some tranquillity at last.

The glove should have been burnt; Ellen had no ideas about why she had kept it. Perhaps it signified something, something about bravery and love and self-sacrifice. She came down from her perch on the crate, folded the glove and replaced it in the cache. She had to go now to cook Tinkle's kipper.

CHAPTER TWENTY

Peacetime

From the back, he looked like an old man, spine bent slightly, feet splayed outward as if seeking proper balance, trousers flapping round legs that were thin and wasted. The front view was not a prepossessing one either. Gaudy freckles punctuated a sickly pale skin, and the eyes, set in cavernous hollows, were cold and dead. High, prominent bones jutted from fleshless cheeks, and the whole countenance was made harder by short, unevenly trimmed red hair.

He steadied himself against the fence, his other hand coming up to secure the limp flower in a buttonhole of the demob suit jacket. It was his wedding day. Sid should have been with him, best mate and best man, but Sid wouldn't be going anywhere from now on.

It was early, still half an hour to go before the others would arrive. He pushed open the church door and stared into the dish of holy water. No point in blessing himself, no point in doing much, really. There was just this day to get through, this supposedly special Saturday which would mark his debut as a husband and father.

He was marrying a stranger. The letters had been few and far between, and the photograph had faded and creased in his pocket. They had taken even that away in the end, stripping him of clothes, dignity and his last few meagre possessions.

After that, he had somehow lost his identity and his will to survive, had become an alien to himself, just a number among thousands of numbers. And when the officers had started on again about going over the wall, under the wire, through the bowels of the earth, he had refused to help. Not out of fear or cowardice, but out of nothingness. It seemed that no-one could lift him from this place where he existed, the twilight zone, the dull, flat and emotionless abyss into which he had been plummeted.

He didn't feel sorry for himself, didn't feel anything at all. They had come home from various hospitals a month ago, himself, Sid and several other bags of bones, some fitter than others, many of them jumping straight back into life, taking great gulps of air as if they had been drowning for ages. Sid had been like that, raring to go, running round with little sense of direction, a young mongrel with so many tails that he hadn't known which to wag. John hadn't taken much notice of Sid, had simply been aware of the noise two doors away, the comings, the goings, music, beery laughter, Sid's mother's voice raised in joy.

It had all stopped now, of course. Since last Saturday, since the FA Cup match between Bolton Wanderers and Stoke City. Thirty-three people had perished when the barriers came down, and young Sid Coleman had been one of them. The lad had survived more than two years on very little meat, black bread and potato soup, had outlived the special cruel arrogance of his captors, and had died at a football match on Manchester Road in Bolton, Lancashire. In England.

John Duffy sat in the front pew, eyes fixed blankly on the altar, hands limp and loose on his knees. She'd done her best to cheer him up, had Marie, bringing the little girl round every day, chatting to his mam and to him about the wedding and what she would wear and what everybody would eat afterwards. He'd been vaguely aware that Marie was smiling less of late, laughing infrequently, frowning more. But he couldn't relate to her or to the little stranger who was his own daughter.

He would have to come back from this dark place, leave the heat and the flies and the stink of louse-infected flesh, abandon the cold memory of winters, frozen water for ablutions, broken boots and a thin shirt and the cheery voice of a middle-class gent with a commission and no idea about men.

His collar pricked and he fingered it feverishly. Was this anger, then? Was he feeling something at last? A figure approached him, a man resplendent in colourful robes, a healthy man with pink cheeks and a benevolent, crescented smile. 'Is this you, John? Heavens above, sure I wouldn't have known you but for this being the day of your wedding. Are you all alone?'

John nodded.

'Your mother will be along later, I take it?'

'Aye.'

The priest sat down next to John. 'We'd the funeral yesterday. 'Tis a terrible thing now for a young man like Sidney to survive a war and then to die in a crush at home. Were you together all the while in the camps?'

'Yes.'

Father Sheedy stroked the silk stole that dangled from his neck. 'My daddy was in the last effort, volunteered almost before the first bullet was fired, and him an Irish pacifist if ever I met one. When he got home at the end, he would never speak of it. There was something in his eyes, a terrible pain, as if he'd photographs in his head. For years he sat by the fire, and the farm would have gone to pot except for Mammy. He was a grand man, yet he let those four years spoil the rest of his life. If he'd talked about it and made it real, then he might have come out of his walking nightmare.'

John sighed and his fingers twitched slightly.

'She's a lovely girl, John, and with a baby to you as well. Will you put out the light in Marie's eyes? Are you after becoming an old man before you were ever a boy?'

'I don't know.' The voice was rusty, as if it had scarcely been used before. 'I don't feel anything. I look at her and I remember her on the station that night, but there's been so much since. I've seen . . .'

He gulped noisily, as if he were tasting something unpalatable. 'I've seen blokes beaten and tortured for trying to escape and I've heard grown men crying like babies.' He swallowed painfully again, his throat moving rapidly. 'Worse than that, there was this quiet, this silence after a bit when everybody had given up. Folk died, British soldiers died in the bunks next to us, and all we cared about was who would get their clothes. We even put off reporting them dead till after breakfast if there wasn't a head count. That was so we could eat their rations.' He lifted his haggard face. 'After a while, you stop being human. I don't think I should be getting wed, Father. I'm only a shadow, somebody that's not really here.'

The priest nodded. 'She'll bring you out of it, son. She's talked to me, so has her mother. They know you've burdensome memories, especially now that Sid has died.'

John fiddled with the end of his tie. 'No sense to that, was there? Mind you, I wish I'd been with him.'

'And why would that be? Are you looking for an easy way out? Isn't that some sort of a feeling, wishing you were dead? Not a good thing, but an emotion all the same. Open your heart, John. Look into the face of that child of yours and know there is a future. I shall pray for you.' He left the pew, genuflected, then walked out of the church.

In the altar boys' dressing room, Father Sheedy picked up a catapult, two cigarette ends and a glossy picture of a film star in a skimpy swimsuit. Ah well, boys would be boys. If only the one sitting in the church could get back to normal.

He opened the outer door and stared into a cloud-patterned bright sky. As ever, he spoke to Mary as if she were a member of his family, a relative who turned up occasionally for special functions and at times of stress. 'Listen,' he whispered. 'I'm asking for a miracle, and don't be saying I'm going too far, for I've never asked you before. And I'm not after anything dramatic like weeping statues and hysterical girls with stigmatas. This is just a small thing, and it won't put you to any bother at all. The man in the church – get him right.' He paused for a moment. 'And while you're at it, would you kindly stop my altar boys smoking, or we'll be going up in flames, there's enough danger with all your candles. Amen.'

In the church, John sat as still as a rock while he waited for his bride. A sunbeam broke into the room, stabbing fiercely at stained glass until it settled between two Stations of the Cross. He glared at the coloured light and saw the dust motes dancing around in this single shaft of brightness.

There had been one window in their hut, one pathetic pane of glass to illuminate the lives of forty men. Sid's bunk had been near the window, and Sid had always cursed the morning sun in the summer time. All Sid had wanted to see was Bolton Wanderers lifting the FA Cup at Wembley. The thought of Wembley had kept Sid going all through, had taken the lad's mind off slop buckets and rancid turnips and the sun's unwelcome reveille. And the road to Wembley had stolen his life.

John dropped his head and closed his eyes. He was thinking at last, thinking about Sid and the war, about the hospital and the poor buggers who'd been kept in with TB, about his own mam and the lonely expression on her face whenever she looked at him. Aye, she would sit there night after night in the chair opposite his, turning his shirt collars, darning his socks on a worn wooden mushroom, chattering on about this wedding and the nice house he was going to have on Noble Street, all furnished and decorated by Marie's mother. Still, at least he was thinking again . . .

Marie. Could he push his mind back to that other time, a time of freedom and tandem rides, of Horlicks tablets and liquorice water? Or would Marie become the one in the chair, the one mending and stitching with only a corpse for company? Her face jumped into his head, round, rosy, dimpling with mischief. And his heart opened with a terrible crash that reverberated round the old church, bouncing off the walls and right back at him.

Then he realized that he was standing, and that the noise was coming from his own mouth, just a single word shouted over and over until his throat hurt. 'Why?' he screamed.

Father Sheedy knelt in the blackness of a confessional box, the rosary biting into tightly clenched hands. Why? Oh God, what a question. Why did the birds sing, why did the flowers carry on growing when millions of people had been put under the sod these past years? Why had the Lord let it happen? While the young man screamed his confusion, the priest held on to the wooden beads as if they were his salvation. Faith was an act of will, and Father Sheedy pushed his will to the limits. It had been pushed there before, right to the edge, when a baby had died, when a mother had gone to her grave leaving a large family. And now, with John Duffy's torment, faith was shaken once more. He sniffed away a tear, made the Sign of the Cross, then went back to the altar. A pair of ruffians made their way along the centre aisle. 'Did you see a man here just now?' he asked them.

'Gone out, Father,' answered one. 'He's run off down the street. Will there be a wedding? Only if there's not, me mam says I can go to the Tivoli, there's a good picture on.'

'Get changed,' he snapped. 'And no smoking.' For good measure, he clipped the nearest miscreant around the ear.

When the boys had gone, he turned to the Immaculate Conception. 'Where were you?' he asked. The statue smiled and said nothing.

Tom waited on the corner of Noble Street and Derby Street, not fully sure about why he had come out. Perhaps he was escaping from the gaggle of females in number nine, the scratching about for an unladdered pair of matching stockings, some small squabble about the even distribution of Abigail's last drop of Chanel Number Five.

He lit a cigarette and leaned casually against a wall. John Duffy was in a right state these days, not fit to get wed, really. Ah well, the sky was hopeful, plenty of blue showing through scudding pillows of cloud. Tishy would have written about that sky, or she might have drawn a picture. They were all framed now, Tishy's bits and pieces, framed, glazed and distributed equally between three houses. She had been a grand lass, it was a pity she'd had to go so young.

He glanced across the road, ground the cigarette beneath a foot, then fixed his eyes on the figure that propped itself against the surgery gate. Even from this distance, Tom could make out the shaking limbs, the set of the jaw, a terrible tension in the tightly clenched fists. With studied nonchalance, he crossed the road. 'Hiya, John.'

There was no reply.

'Shall we wander a bit? Just up the road and back?'

They set off at John's shambling pace. 'How are you feeling then, lad?' Tom kept his tone light. 'It's a good day for it, nice weather.'

'Aye.'

They walked in silence until they were opposite the Tivoli cinema, then Tom grabbed a thin arm. 'This is no good, you know. You're not helping anybody in this state. What about your mam? And what about Marie and Elizabeth?'

John raised his head. 'I'm not here,' he said. 'They sent me away, and I never came back. This is somebody else.'

Tom pursed his lips and watched the young man's face working. There was suffering here, the sort of pain Tom knew about. Aye, he'd been a brief expert in mental torment, hadn't he? He placed a hand on each of John's shoulders. 'I've a story on the wireless Monday afternoon.'

'Oh.' The eyes were blank and unreceptive.

'I do that, write for the BBC. Two plays now, a dozen or so short stories. But this one on Monday's about a man who got lost. He hadn't gone anywhere, John. He'd just disappeared inside himself.' He dropped his arms, shoving hands into the pockets of his suit.

John blinked, appeared to be listening.

'Your mind's full of hiding places, see. You can go inside your head, shut yourself away, and you can stay there for as long as you want. Only trouble is, you've just yourself for company. There's room for nobody up there, John. The longer you stop in, the harder it gets to come out.'

The ginger head jerked in agreement.

Encouraged, Tom continued. 'It's a selfish story, this one on Monday. Mind you, most of the best tales are a bit self-centred. I've been where you are, friend.'

'Eh?'

Tom studied his shoes, rubbed a dull toe on the back of a trouser leg. 'When my wife died – my first wife – I did a runner inside myself. There was one lad called Tom Crawford went in the army, and a different man came out. They were both me. Pulling them together again wasn't easy. Without Terry, I'd never have managed.'

'I'm . . . not good enough.'

'There's none of us good enough.'

'I just sat there. In the camps, I just sat and waited like a dog. I wasn't like that, Tom. When the nuns . . . at school . . . all the fights. I was the cock of the class.'

'War's not school, you know.'

John stared at the front of the picture house. They were advertising *A Tree Grows in Brooklyn*. He used to take Marie there, into the back row for a quick kiss and a cuddle, dark nights, black spanish or a packet of liquorice root. A man used to come round selling Vimto lollies and the films kept breaking down. The manager had a fat red face and spats, looked like something from Chicago twenty years ago. 'Is Al Capone still running the pictures?' he asked without knowing why.

'I'm not sure.' This was progress, but time was getting on. 'Could you live without Marie, John?'

'No.'

'How do you know that if you're not yourself?'

A shoulder raised itself fractionally. 'Because I remember who I used to be.'

Tom stared along the road towards the church. They would all be gathering there in ten minutes, and there was no groom. It was too soon for the lad, too quick. Though perhaps this would be the making of him – if Tom could get him there. 'John?'

'What?'

'She might not turn up. I think she's a bit sick and tired of you not trying.' He bit his lip. Was he going too far? Still, it was late enough now to take any gamble, any odds at all would do. 'She's not happy. Happen she'll call it off, John.'

A dim light arrived in the sunken eyes, and Tom caught a brief glimpse of the boy who had returned as a damaged man. 'She'd not do that to me, would she?'

'Well, you know Marie when her dander's up, she could give the devil a run for his ha'penny. She threw four customers out of that shop in one week.'

'What for?' The face showed real interest now.

'They were fighting over a banana. It got squashed in all the pushing and shoving, so Marie played merry hell.' He glanced casually at the sky. 'And it was the last banana. There's a lot of fire in yon madam.'

'Aye. Aye, there is.'

'Good girls, that crowd. I should know, I married one. She's reliable, is Terry. Very dependable. She'd never have changed her mind. Now, Marie is more . . . volatile. If she sets her mind against the way you've been . . . well . . . you know our Marie.'

John hesitated. 'Will I be all right, though?'

'You will. Just hang on to who you are, not who you were when they had you locked up like a bloody animal. I've been there. I've been locked up. Your pride will come back. That's all it is at the bottom, injured pride and a lack of faith in yourself.'

John nodded. 'She'll fetch me back from where I got put. There'll be no peace for me, Tom. Her'll put her foot against my backside and kick me back to life.'

Tom inhaled deeply. 'Right, then. Go and get her.'

'Eh?'

'They should have been on their way by now. I've seen no wedding parties coming out of Noble Street. Have you?'

John pulled at his tie. 'Now as you come to mention it . . . Will you stand for me? Best man, I mean. Sid—'

'I'll do that. Yes, I'll go and wait at Peter and Paul's. Go on. Get on with it, lad.'

Tom stood and watched while the young man ran in a strangely crooked line, arms and legs flailing against unaccustomed freedom. He felt choked, sickened right down to the guts of war and what it did to folk. Next, it would be atom bombs, total devastation, no chance for any living thing. Meanwhile, the show would go on, weddings, christenings, parties and frivolity. The whole world was wounded, and it licked the raw sores with a tongue that was still hungry, greedy for power. And the ordinary people just carried on playing charades, games that helped them forget or ignore the earth's sick leaders.

He marched smartly down the road, wishing, not for the first time, that he could stop being a writer. Writers thought too much, weren't useful, spent a lot of time thinking without participating. A piece of timber and a chisel would put him on the right track, bring his feet back where they belonged, on the ground.

John was lingering on the corner of Noble Street. Tom stood and willed the lad to move, knowing that the answer, or part of the answer sat in a house a hundred yards down. 'Do it,' he whispered to himself. 'Grab hold of her, she needs you.'

He could do no more. With a determined stride, he set off for the church, suddenly anxious about the ring. He was best man, so he should have a ring in his pocket. Perhaps John's mother was holding it. Ah well, not to worry. He would be there, standing up for his brother-in-law. And that had to mean something.

The children had all been farmed out, because Marie hadn't wanted Elizabeth on the wedding snaps. She would

522

tell her daughter the truth in time, but she intended to protect her for the moment. Marie stood now at the front window, a bouquet of bright flowers clutched against the pale green of her suit. Abigail and Theresa were upstairs putting the finishing touches to their finery. Clive and Tom had been laughing in the kitchen, likely cracking jokes about weddings until Tom had gone out. But this was no joke, no fun at all . . .

'Marie?'

She turned her head. 'Hello, Mam.'

'Cedric's nipped up to the pub to make sure the cake's still in one piece. Are you all right, love?'

Marie shrugged, the movement almost listless. 'You know what? I miss Tishy today. She would have enjoyed all this, would Tishy. And she could have played the piano for us afterwards. Sometimes, I really wish she was still here.'

'So do I. And Lilian. Even though I knew her for just a few weeks, I really liked her.' She glanced at the clock on the mantel. 'I hope Cedric hurries up. We'll have to set off in about ten minutes.'

Marie placed the flowers on the piano. 'I'm not going,' she said with the air of one whose decision, though quick, is final. 'I've changed me mind.' A rush of air was suddenly expelled from her lungs, as if she were letting go of all the worry and tension. 'I've thought about it, and I know he doesn't love me. Elizabeth and me have been managing without him up to now – with your help – and I don't see why I should get married just to make things look right. We'd not be happy, Mam. He's changed so much . . .'

'What did you expect, lass? The same chap you waved off from Trinity Street? A boy, a lad with no experience of life? Marie, John has been to hell and back many times over. He's a man now, and he's been forced to grow up all of a rush. It'll take time for him to catch his breath.'

'Then we'll give him time. I don't know why there's all this fuss and rush . . .'

'She's two years old.'

Marie waved her arms in the air. 'You don't have to tell me how old my daughter is, Mam. I know when her birthday is, I was there when she was born. But can't you see what you and Mrs Duffy are pushing us into? There's no way out once you're married. You know that well enough. Remember what it's like to be wed to a man you can't stand? You'd still be married to him if Tishy hadn't . . .' Her voice tailed away.

'Hadn't what?' Was she interfering again, pushing her nose in after she'd sworn not to . . . ?

Marie averted her eyes. 'If she hadn't frightened him to death. That's what happened, and everybody's guessed. Anyway, it's not about the way London died, it's about the way he lived, the way he made us live. Do you want me to have a life like that? And Elizabeth too?'

'No.'

'Then leave me be. Send somebody up to the church and get this explained. The neighbours can go round to the Albert and eat the food. I'm sorry, Mam, but I'm not budging.'

Theresa and Abigail came into the room. 'Are we ready for off?' asked Theresa.

Ellen clicked her tongue. 'She's . . . postponing it.'

Abigail, swollen with her second child, crossed the room as quickly as her girth allowed. 'Nerves?' she asked.

'Common sense,' came Marie's swift reply. 'He's hardly spoke two words to me since he got back home. I've tried, his mam's tried. It's like talking to the fire back. Just sits there, he does.'

'Tom understands that,' said Theresa. 'He had a do with his nerves after Alice died. He says this is nerves and all, this quiet spell that John's having. Marie, everything's ready. People have chipped in with all sorts, and Mam's made you that lovely cake.'

Marie rounded on her twin. 'If there was a hearse out in the street with a coffin my size, would you tell me to climb in and save wasting it? Would you? Because it's the same bloody thing. Just think about it, all of you. I'm not sitting looking at him for the rest of me life. I love him, yes I do. But I love the John I remember, the John from before. This is a different bloke. It's not his fault, I understand that. But it's not my fault either. You can't expect me to take the blame for the whole blinking war and what it's done to everybody. I never started it, but I'm finishing it now.' She flounced out of the room, burnished curls bobbing beneath the brim of her hat.

'Well.' Abigail lowered herself on to the piano stool. 'A pretty kettle of fish this is. Don't be surprised if I go into labour at any minute. Why didn't she say something before?'

Ellén lifted her shoulders. 'A horse never refuses till it gets to the jump. She's feared of the way he is, frightened he'll not get back to normal. I've talked to her, I thought we'd sorted it out. But I was wrong, and not for the first time in me life. I'd best get up to church and see John. Theresa, you can sort the pub out later on.' She went through to the kitchen to tell Clive the disturbing news.

Upstairs, Marie stood in the front bedroom, forehead pressed against the cool glass of the window. She wasn't sorry, and kept telling herself that she had nothing to regret. She had just experienced a narrow escape. For the rest of her life, for the rest of Elizabeth's life, she would have to remember that this had all been for the best. And she was wearing a six guinea suit, a beautiful suit that she would never wear again because it would always remind her of the narrow escape.

She glanced down into the street, and there he stood like a scarecrow, all angled limbs and a head too big for its body. 'Go away,' she mouthed through the pane.

His upper lip twitched. 'Marie Langden?' he yelled. There was faint colour in his cheeks, and an echo of the old John in the almost strident tone.

She stepped back as if she had been struck. What the hell was he up to this time? Quiet as the grave for a month, now yelling like a daft kid out in the middle of the cobbles, showing her up . . .

'I've been sat waiting for you up at Peter and Paul's,' he lied with all the vigour he could muster. 'And me mam's fetching Nan's wedding ring for you, twenty-two carat. Is that not good enough for you? Marie? I know you're in there.'

She marched to the window and threw it open sharply. 'Where do you expect me to be? Yates's Wine Lodge? Get away from here, I've changed me mind.'

'I love you,' he shouted. Several doors opened. Marie banged the window down and sat on the edge of the bed, fingers pushed into her ears.

'I'll stand here and shout till you get up to the church and marry me. I'll stop here till tomorrow, all next week too. If it rains, I'll get pneumonia. I'll get pneumonia on purpose.'

The voice was muffled, but she could still hear it. The bedroom door opened, and Ellen stepped in. 'He's come round,' she said.

'I can see he's come round, Mam. I can hear he's come round.'

'I don't mean that kind of coming round. I mean he's started . . .'

'Yes, I know what you're getting at. What'll I do?'

'I don't know.'

'You always know. Ever since you threw London out, you've known the answers. So tell me what to do.'

The noise outside continued. 'I'll get a tent The neighbours are here, Marie, they'll feed me. And I'll shout all day and all night because I love you. I loved you before I went, and I love you now I've come back. Things got a bit mixed up, that's all.'

Ellen looked at her daughter. 'He lost his best friend at the match last week.'

Marie tossed her head. 'He'd never spoke to Sid for a fortnight. He's been like a tailor's shop dummy.'

'Well, he's not like a dummy now, love.' Ellen looked

through the window. 'His collar stud's gone, the flower looks as if it's been jumped on, and I think his tie must be in his pocket.'

'And he expects me to marry him while he's in that state?'

'Yes, he does. And I can soon clean him up a bit.'

Marie straightened her hat, strode to the window and opened it again. 'Shut up,' she ordered. 'Get in that back kitchen, get cleaned up, then go to church. You are a disgrace. You always were a disgrace, John Duffy. No wonder them nuns got fed up with you. And borrow a collar stud. I'm not having you flapping in the breeze on the photos.' She slammed the window and closed the curtains.

Ellen leaned against the chimney breast. 'Are you going, then?'

'Yes. I'll have to. When we were at school, he always did as he promised, even the most awful things. I reckon he's not beyond squatting in the street. He must be getting back to normal. What am I taking on at all? I should have been grateful while he was quiet.'

'He might go quiet again, love.'

Marie stretched her neck and adjusted the tiny hat. 'I know. I'm ready for it now. He says he loves me, that's what matters. He's come down to tell me he loves me. And he needs me and Elizabeth, that's the main thing. Being needed is important.'

'Aye, you're not wrong there, our Marie. Come on, let's get the show on the road. I'll go down and make sure John's off to church, then we'll all follow on. If you change your mind again, send me a postcard, I'll be somewhere between here and Cairo.'

Marie picked up her missal, and a picture of the Immaculate Conception floated to the floor. 'Remember the day she got you the statue, Mam? Her face all lit up because she'd decided to be a Catholic? And her poems and her stories. Specially that last story, the one about the hand having gone for ever. I used to be jealous of her.'

'Don't, love.'

'She never grew up.'

Ellen nodded. 'That's right. She never worried about pennies for the gas meter or how to feed a family with nowt in the purse. With our Tishy, we saw a world that was nearly magic, something you might look at through coloured glass.' She sniffed significantly. 'You and John have both lost somebody close. Comfort one another.'

'We will.'

'And you know where I am.'

Marie studied her mother. 'I've always known where you were. Thanks, Mam.'

When John had left again for the church, the rest of the wedding party came out into the street. The three girls gathered together outside the door of number nine, Abigail in a navy dress and coat that failed to conceal her bulge, Theresa plump and prettier than ever in dusky pink, Marie radiant in soft green. The neighbours waved and shouted compliments, then everyone turned to walk up the hill. At the top, on the Derby Street corner, Auntie Harrison and Mrs Carrington stood like a pair of over-blown roses, colourful dresses floating in a slight breeze.

Some local women passed by on the other side, nudging and pointing at the well-dressed party. 'Are them Billy London's girls?' asked one.

Ellen reached for her companion, the lovely, solid man she had married six months earlier. He would be giving Marie away in a few minutes, and she hoped he wouldn't stumble over the corner of a pew. He was still given to stumbling at times, was Cedric. She smiled at the gossips, squeezed her husband's hand, then announced in a clear voice, 'Oh no. You've got it wrong, missus.' Her face was radiant as she shouted out for all the world to hear. 'These are Ellen Wilkinson's lasses.'

THE END